# All is Quiet in the Cosmos

# All is Quiet in the Cosmos

by
## Emerson

## Perceptions Press
www.perceptionspress.ca
Victoria, BC
Canada

## 2023

# All is Quiet in the Cosmos

**Copyright © Emerson, 2023**

Published in 2023 by Perceptions Press

Cover Art and Design: Emerson

**ISBN: 978-1-998924-30-1** (paperback)
**ISBN: 978-1-998924-31-8** (Kindle e-book)
**ISBN: 978-1998924-32-5** (Smashwords/Draft2Digital e-book)

Published in Canada by
**Perceptions Press**
www.perceptionsspress.ca
Victoria BC
Canada

**Perceptions
Press**

# Dedication

I dedicate this novel to all who ever wished for representation.

It is also dedicated to my wonderful spouse and family, who always believed in me and pushed me to reach for the stars.

Finally, this book is dedicated to C, who helped me build worlds without limits. Thank you for your unwavering support and love.

And thank you to you, my wonderful readers. May you find love and light on this journey that we all must take together.

Thank you Kyare Betzing for initial editing.

# Contents

# Content Warning

Before you read the content warning, please know it contains spoilers, hints, or clues about the rest of the book.

This is a dual-plot sci-fi action romance with gore, suicide, sexual assault, sexual harassment, slavery, human trafficking, violence, mentions of war, and death. There is no detailed sexual assault that takes place.

# Prologue

Everything felt hazy. Altair surmised it was a dream, simply because of how slowly he moved through the hallways of his childhood home. The light that filtered through the gilded, stained-glass windows fell softly onto freshly installed marble floors. His mother had insisted so strongly on that stone.

"The humans really know what they're doing with their building materials!" she exclaimed, wrapping her slender arms around his father's shoulders. Her touch had softened his brow, as it always seemed to. "Please, my darling ewet, please?"

Altair had known it was all over from that point. His father could rarely deny her anything, let alone after she had used such an affectionate term.

The ewet bloomed in every place where starlight seemed to bless its rare presence. His planet's rotation was so slow that the time spent in its light was a blessing. Altair, in his youth, had only seen the light three times.

His father's hand had reached back and caressed her cheek before giving his approval with a soft grunt. His mother had left with her renovation plans, and Altair had returned to his toys.

The days of light. The blissful days before… before…

Well, he couldn't quite remember.

Altair's hand traced the hallway, lingering on a stray ewet that had somehow poked its hopeful head through a crack in the wall. He stopped to pluck the petals that surrounded a glittering center, something he had done since he was young.

As he pulled at each petal, he made a wish for each one.

*I wish for more days of light.*

*I wish for my mother to finish her plans within budget.*

*I wish for more fun toys.*

*I wish for my father to love me.*

Altair stopped as the wish came crashing into his subconscious mind. His father did not love him. But he used to. He used to love him just as much as he loved Altair's mother, just perhaps with a little more sternness.

What had happened?

Altair felt something drip down his hands and blinked slowly as his gaze dropped to the petal-less ewet in his hand.

It was bleeding.

Dark, red drops beaded and clustered in the glittering center, puckering, before sliding down the stem and staining his hands with lines of slick red.

He dropped the bleeding flower in disgust. Ewets didn't bleed.

No plant did.

As it drifted to the floor, it gained speed, defying all laws of physics, before clattering to the floor.

Wait… clattering?

Altair blinked hard, trying to dispel the haziness of the dream. Icy horror slithered through him as he realized he had not dropped an ewet.

It was a bloody knife.

He stared at his blood-coated hands in horror, realizing, at that moment, why his father no longer loved him.

*I want to wake up. Please, for the love of the gods, let me wake up.*

# Chapter 1
# Altair

Altair shot straight up in bed, his body coated with sweat. His clothes clung uncomfortably to his slick and trembling body.

He tried to catch his breath as he focused on the tiny room in which he lay. The sweat rolled down his back, making him shiver as he beat back the wave of anxiety that pushed its way through him.

*The dream... the dream...*

Taking a deep, calming breath, Altair pressed his long fingers into his temples. It had been just that, a dream. Albeit, one that had haunted him for years, but still just a dream.

Warm light slowly slunk through the only grimy, sand-coated window in the tiny, dirt-floored hut.

Hut? Is that what this was?

More like a prison.

It lacked bars and guards, but it was still a prison. And it was one he wasn't sure he would ever leave.

Altair sighed deeply and rubbed his temples again before wiping the sleep crust from his eyes. He stood slowly, stretching his body high and brushing the low ceiling with his fingers. His body ached from folding his form onto the sleeping mat, and he groaned in painful pleasure as his spine popped several times. The roof felt rough and dirty against his fingertips before he dropped his arms to his sides, stretching his neck from side to side. The anxiety from the dream wasn't gone, but moving forward was the best way to combat the tight feeling in his chest. Once he was sufficiently roused, Altair made his way to the bathroom.

Again, "bathroom" could be considered a loose term. It was nothing compared to what he'd enjoyed as a child, but, at least, they'd left him with rudimentary accommodations.

*So very generous,* Altair thought savagely as he ran his fingers through his hair.

It was overgrown and tickled down toward his chin. The only reason it didn't reach his mid-back was his attempts to shear it with hand-made weapons. He pushed the tangled mass behind his ears before splashing his face with the tepid bowl of water he had collected a few days prior.

There wasn't much to do in the bathroom. After all, who cared what he looked like? He had given up on those simple gestures years ago.

He still remembered the blistering day that he had walked to the nearby ocean. Its pale purple waves had kissed his feet as he stood on the shoreline and set his jaw. He'd then thrown his fancy hair gels as far as he could, along with the other useless things he'd brought from the castle. He remembered the turmoil that had writhed in his gut afterward, half wishing he could jump into the water and fish his belongings back out.

He also remembered how he had cried, as well, and traipsed his way back to the hut, his gaze on the burning sand below his feet.

He still held out some hope after two years. After five years, he had doubted that his exile would ever end. Once ten passed, anger replaced any childish hope he originally once had. Now that it had been twenty, he wasn't sure he could still consider himself a prince.

There was no way of salvaging his appearance, not that he felt the need. Altair simply made sure he did not stink, more for his sanity than anything else, before donning an ugly brown robe and hood. He pulled the mask over his mouth and nose to protect himself from the sand that seemed to infinitely dance on this planet. The clothing was stiff and rough, but it did its job of protecting him from the harshness of his surroundings.

Grabbing his walking stick, he made his way out of the door. Better to spend his endless days trying to rummage for food and explore the planet than wasting away, waiting for his exile to end.

The air was scorching, no different from any other day. The constant heat and blinding white light from the three suns that circled the sky made life on this planet nearly impossible. Even though Altair's kind preferred the heat because of their cold-blooded nature, there was such a thing as too much of it. He squinted and peered upward, blinking against the sand that nearly blinded him. The sickly pale purple sky was the same stupid color it had been for days before, even years before.

Nothing ever changed here, other than him.

Altair slung a worn, brown bag over his shoulder and used his walking stick to tap his way away from the hut.

He was headed toward the only plant life that existed here. These rare goods looked like reedy, root plants and were nutritious enough to feed any life that dared to flourish on such an awful planet. They were easy enough to find since they only grew near the planet's single ocean. The plants were, unfortunately, in high demand since they were the only food source for miles.

He made his way down a well-trodden path he had laid with stones and piled with old, destroyed clothing. The rich fabrics and colors were well-worn from cushioning his feet, preventing them from being burned by the scorching sands.

He was sure that his people would stare in horror at the expensive fabrics, which now held no value to him, and how he was using them. He had learned quickly that his nice clothes would not protect him properly from the heat. This was the only reason they had not joined his other luxuries at the bottom of the ocean.

An unwanted memory crept into his mind, as if the dream from the night before had summoned it from the depths of his subconscious.

*Altair whimpered softly as the heat blasted him. They had just arrived on the planet and his father had forbidden Altair from speaking, to keep them all safe. As he fanned himself with his jeweled headdress, he couldn't help but wonder how he was supposed to stay cool. As much as he was grateful his father hadn't chosen some ice planet, he didn't know whether going in the extreme opposite direction was ideal either.*

*He was a Serinian, he thrived in the water. It was his natural habitat.*

*His father had barely turned to acknowledge his discomfort. He hadn't been able to look at him for days now. When he spoke, his voice was gruff, almost angry.*

*He acted as if he knew what Altair's thoughts had been. The boy had cringed away from the angry king who stood there, his shoulders slumped in grief, as he spoke roughly in Altair's general direction.*

*"You'll learn how to survive the heat, child. I chose this planet to keep all creatures away. You may hate it, but it will keep you safe. Understood?"*

*The statement ended with a question that was not actually a question, more of a dismissal.*

*Young Altair had withered under his father's disapproval. He had swallowed back the tears that threatened to rise to the surface and nodded, looking down in shame.*

*He still had not spoken a word.*

Altair shook the memory free, his chest aching. He couldn't afford to think about that. Right now, it was about survival. He needed food.

The walk didn't take long. It was only about an hour before he heard the telltale sound of water rushing against the shoreline.

He flipped the walking stick in a quick motion as he approached. His footsteps slowed as he tapped the walking stick on a nearby stone, a sharp blade shooting out of the end that pointed upward. He threw the stick out, pointing it away from his body, and crept forward. Though it was a crudely made weapon, it did the trick. For the past several years, he had established himself as the dominant creature in the area.

He had done so to survive, as the reed plants were only available on a first-come, first-served basis.

His eyes scanned the area as he slunk toward a greenish-gray plant sticking out of the ground near the shore. Reaching the velvety leaves, Altair knelt, placing his weapon close by.

His fingers burned, even through the coarse gloves he wore, as he dug greedily through the sand to reach the root of the plant. After several seconds, he could pull the plant up and out with a slick crunching sound. His hands trembled from the familiar pain, but he knew it was necessary. His hands would heal. Hunger would kill.

With familiar ease, Altair quickly plucked each of the leaves from the plant, placing two of them in a small pocket of his sack, and tossing the rest into the hole the plant had come from.

The hole had already filled with sand, as was the nature of such a planet. He threw the reedy root into the main hull of the sack before picking up his weapon and moving on to the next patch of leaves that lay just a few feet away.

Altair spent the better part of the morning simply gathering roots, occasionally pocketing some leaves. He left the rest in their respective holes to grow more food.

Sustainability. That was important, especially if he was to be here for years to come.

Once that was done, he gathered some of the slow-moving ocean water. It was obvious his father had done proper research on the planet before dumping him here. The ocean was an unlimited source of clean, drinking water, and it wasn't far from where Altair lived.

Unfortunately, the king didn't mind that there was only one source of sustenance. After all, he would not be the one living here for an innumerable number of years. Heat coursed through Altair, and he gritted his teeth, beating back the emotion. He didn't have time to be angry right now.

Survival. He just needed to finish and get home.

Once he was done with that, he took a quick dip in the shallowest end of the lukewarm water to wash off the grime of the last few days. It wasn't long enough or far enough out to enjoy the water. Altair feared the enormous creatures that called the ocean home, whose fins sometimes towered over the surface in a way that would briefly shadow the beach.

He scrubbed as quickly as he could, jumpy and his eyes wary. Altair then donned his clothing, to avoid being burned by the unforgiving sunlight.

His containers sloshed in the brown sack, swollen with the water he had gathered, as he made his way back home. He was lucky today. No one had challenged him for his goods. He hadn't felt like fighting off some rabid creature to keep what he had found.

Perhaps the gods were being kinder to him today. He smirked at the thought, wiping at the sweat that coated his upper lip with the back of his hand.

It was more likely that every other creature in this hellscape had died off than the idea that his luck was changing.

The walk back seemed even more punishing than usual. By the time he made it home, the quick bath seemed completely unnecessary. He was coated in sweat and dust once again. As he stepped toward his door, he felt irreparably grimy.

Altair grumbled in frustration as he dropped his sack of goods inside the cooler hut. Throwing his hood back and pulling the mask down, he made his way over to his dwindling supply of fire-making resources.

He struggled to pull a large, rusty pot into his cooking area. Lighting a fire, he strained and grunted as he tugged the large pot over the flames. Using some of the water he had gathered, he set it to boil before throwing in the reed plants. They were too hard to eat unless boiled for hours.

Sitting back on the hard ground with an enormous sigh, he pulled a crude pipe from his sack and stuffed the plant leaves into it, lighting the end and taking a deep draw. The effect was immediate, and his mind felt as though a cloudy buffer surrounded it. He closed his eyes briefly, taking a deep breath through his nose and relaxing his shoulders. Though the leaves of the reed plant held no nutritional value, they offered a lovely, buzzed feeling that made everything seem more tolerable.

This accidental discovery had been made shortly after arriving here. Altair had awoken, after crunching through handfuls of tough reed plants, with the leaves intact, to find that he was in the burning sands without protection. It had taken him weeks to recover physically. From that experience, he had learned both a tough and valuable lesson.

The leaves were bad news, but only if you ingested them. Smoking them, however, was a different story.

He took a few more draws, his body completely relaxing and his mind slowly letting go of the bad memories that had plagued him all day.

The sky darkened as he waited for the roots to soften. His eyes wandered to the dusty pile of books and old art supplies in the room's corner, noticing that their well-worn pages were cracking from age. It wasn't surprising that they were falling apart. It had been years since he'd opened or used any of them. He had nearly thrown them into the ocean as well, but the thought of losing such memories had stopped him from going through with it.

The first part of his time spent here had been in escapism, his hobbies being the only way to leave his isolation. But, as he'd let go of his hope of leaving, the supplies had gathered more and more dust.

Altair blew smoke in their direction. Perhaps, tonight, he would indulge.

He stood sorely and made his way over to their dusty covers. Kneeling, he used a hand to wipe the grime off the nearest sketchbook. The leather was worn to near paper-thin quality, but he could still tell what it was.

It was his old childhood sketchbook that his mother had given him for his fifth birthday. She'd recognized an early talent in him that she'd wanted to nurture, to combat his father's obsession with his voice.

Altair smiled faintly at the memory, heart aching as he remembered her face as she'd handed it to him. He flipped it open and found an old, charcoal sketch of his childhood bedroom. He smiled at the memory of drawing it. He had laid on his bed and kicked his feet happily, sketching until his eyes were sore and tired.

He had snuck into every room of the castle from that point, drawing each of the rooms. Even into his mother's library, the one that she had expressly forbidden him from entering.

It had catapulted his love for drawing and sketching, capturing scenes of his life to more fully remember and understand them as he reminisced. Like he was doing now. He was suddenly grateful to little Altair for having such foresight.

He'd meant to return to his bedroom before his mother woke, but he had fallen asleep on the floor of her library. He'd awoken, tucked into bed, expecting her to say something about his behavior.

She never had.

Altair palmed the sketchbook in his hand before making his way back to the fireside. He cracked open the old pages, grasping a piece of charcoal, and began sketching, desperately hoping to lose himself in the hobby.

Ideas did not flow easily, and inspiration was low. So, he spent most of the time staring at the yellowed pages, trying to decide which way to go.

The flames were nearly dead before Altair looked up from the book. His eyes were crossed and blurry from focusing on the lines in the growing darkness. He stood quickly and dropped the pad at his feet, before grabbing his walking stick to fish the roots from the boiling water.

He hissed in pain as they brushed against his bare skin. He then dropped them into a clean, wooden bowl and waited for them to cool. They would stay good for days, and he only needed one to sustain him tonight. Impatience began stabbing his insides, and he frowned, looking away from the hot food.

A familiar sound stirred him from his watch over dinner. Altair sat up straight as mechanical whirring passed overhead. His heart pounded into his throat.

*It couldn't be.*

The roots forgotten, Altair rushed outside, his legs shaking in both fear and long-forgotten hope. His heart felt as though it was trying to do a backflip into his throat. He desperately scanned the darkening sky.

The sound was one he'd recognize anywhere, one he'd heard a million times as a child.

*A ship. It could only be a ship.*

But as Altair looked into the sky, he saw only burning stars. Those same damned stars that kept this planet the hellhole that the daytime suns did.

Altair stayed out there, longer than he wanted to admit, looking for his rescuer. He waited for them to land and say that it was now safe to come home.

To tell him he could speak.

Finally.

But, of course, there was nothing. Just those stars winking mockingly at him.

He tried to pretend that the stinging that rose to his eyes was simply the sand that blew mercilessly into his face. He swallowed against the lump in his throat, before turning and reentering the hut.

Grabbing some more leaves in trembling fists, Altair ended the night the way he always did, in the numbing bliss of a plant-induced high.

# Chapter 2
# Altair

Something woke Altair from his fitful sleep.

He couldn't tell what it was. Maybe, it was the way something rustled. Perhaps, there was a shadow that wasn't supposed to be there. Either way, something wasn't right, and Altair's instincts screamed at him, causing his blood to pound mercilessly through his veins.

He scanned the darkness, desperately praying that his eyes would adjust. More than once, he'd had some sharp-toothed creature find a way into his hut and had to fight it off. His hand slipped under his sleeping mat, toward the walking stick.

Whatever it was, he would chase it away. He still had the strength to do that, even with how starved and weak his body was.

Before he could grab it, a shadow moved. In a flash of dark clothing and practiced finesse, it jumped toward Altair.

Forgetting all of his training, Altair screamed, loudly. His voice was hoarse from disuse. But, much to his surprise, the figure kept coming at him. He couldn't help the distracting thought that plastered itself to his brain.

*Why didn't his voice stop them?!*

Altair rolled off the sleeping mat to dodge the attacker but was too slow. He felt his hair grasped by the roots and painfully tugged back as cold metal kissed the skin of his neck. Instinctively, he knew it was a blade. Even though there was little he could see in the darkness, that feeling was unmistakable.

A voice spoke. An actual voice. Altair couldn't help but marvel at it. They spoke in English, a tongue that he'd learned to be fluent in as a child.

"Quiet."

He didn't know if it was simply that he hadn't heard a voice in twenty years, but the voice sounded guttural and warped. As if they struggled to form the word.

Before he could say or do anything, he felt the hand leave his hair and a different cold metal shoved between his teeth. With a hissing, mechanical sound, his lips were clamped tightly together. He winced and attempted to open his mouth but whimpered in pain as the clamp tightened.

He considered fighting back, but he could tell that his attacker was much stronger than him. His days in exile had rendered his body nearly helpless. Even though he'd had to survive and fight off various creatures, eating only plant life for twenty years had done a number on him.

Soft light filtered through the hut, bathing everything somberly. Altair blinked furiously at the sudden change and attempted to focus on his attacker.

Standing in front of him was a figure clad in dark clothing that concealed their identity from head to toe. The clothing was sturdy but clean and, more ominously, the attacker was armed to the teeth with various weapons. Though if the weapons were to give Altair any clue as to who his attacker was, they could've been anything or anyone. Each weapon was from a different race of creature. Everything from a human blaster gun to a Ursonian poison blade.

They held a small light in their hands that they promptly placed on the ground before moving toward Altair.

He gritted his teeth in frustration and stared up at them, mind racing to come up with a plan of escape. As if they sensed his hostility, the figure shook their head minutely.

Altair froze. His attacker's confidence quickly deflated any hope he had of attempting a counterattack.

They then stepped forward, pulling a pair of glimmering cuffs from their tool belt. They pulled his arms roughly behind his back, and the cuffs were tightened painfully around his wrists. Altair winced once again, anger staining his cheeks an ugly red color.

*They're really strong.*

The thought brought panic with it that shrouded Altair's mind as the reality of his situation fell into place. This was his worst nightmare.

In actuality, this was his father's worst nightmare.

Either way, this was bad.

Very, very bad.

His attacker grabbed his hair yet again, forcing him to stand. They pulled a blaster from their tool belt and pointed it at him, nudging him forward. They then picked up the light and pushed him forward, out of his prison.

And all Altair could do was walk.

As he walked, he remembered what his father's contingency plan had been for this very situation. His heart pounded at the memory.

*Altair's eyes had filled with tears as his father turned to leave after explaining what the plan was.*

*He'd run after his father's uncaring back and grabbed at the long cloak that adorned the king's shoulders.*

*His father stopped and turned to face him, his face lined with exhaustion and disappointment.*

*Altair stepped forward hesitatingly. He was terrified of the answer to this question, but everything in his little body yearned for the answer.*

*It yearned for his father's face to turn kind again.*

*He grabbed one of the sketchbooks that a nervous servant had laid on the cot and scribbled before handing it over to his father.*

*The king took it with careful fingers, as though afraid it would burn him. His eyes slid over the question his son had hastily written.*

*Papa, what do I do if they find me? And I can't use my voice?*

*His father stared at him, face devoid of any fatherly emotion or tenderness. It was odd how that had changed so quickly. In only a matter of weeks.*

*He didn't speak for a moment, then turned away.*

*Despair curled in Altair's stomach, and he wiped his eyes, resigning himself to never having an answer to his question.*

*Perhaps if that happened, his father would come back.*

*As the king approached the door of the hut, he stopped. Without looking at Altair, he finally, quietly, answered.*

*"If they find you, and you can't stop them. You let them kill you, boy."*

Altair's legs quaked at the idea, and he nearly lost his footing in the hot sand. He could stop right here, refuse to move forward, and let his unknown assailant shoot him. He could be loyal to his father's plan.

*But …*

He had screamed. He had used his voice for the first time in years, and his attacker hadn't even flinched.

The curiosity was too great. His need for survival and answers outweighed his loyalty to his father.

After all, his father had dropped him off on this gods-forsaken planet with no answers, no communication, and very little to survive on.

*Why should he end his own life to make his father's life easier?*

Anger and resentment bubbled up inside of him and powered his legs to keep moving forward. His captor stepped behind him to tie a rope to his cuffs before leading the way, their dim light in hand.

As they traipsed through the sands, Altair felt his feet burning through his flimsy shoes. He longed for the sturdier boots that he had been forced to abandon in the kidnapping.

Altair huffed, trying to ignore the stitch in his side as he attempted to keep up with his assailant. They were quick and would impatiently tug at the rope if he fell too far behind. Altair kept tripping over his own feet out of exhaustion, blinking against the sand that coated his vision.

It seemed like hours before they cleared a dune and found what his attacker was looking for.

A beautiful, sleek Troy ship.

Its silver edges were sharp and dangerous. Not even the billowing sand could dirty the mirror-like finish of such a gorgeous ship. This model was years better than the ones he'd seen before he was exiled.

If it had been able to, his jaw would've dropped.

Well, this solved the mystery of who his attacker was. Troy ships were only curated and piloted by humans. From the little he'd seen or heard about humans, he knew they were a dangerous type of creature. They possessed no claws, sharp teeth, or magical abilities, but their survival instinct was unrivaled. They would do and say just about anything to make it out alive.

His father had entertained small groups of humans out of political courtesy but had never officially sided with them in the war. This, of course, caused some tension. But because he had also never sided with the Vesunians, things stayed cordial.

That was, at least, until Altair's abilities were discovered.

He didn't even notice that he'd stopped until he received a rather sharp jab to the ribs with the barrel of a blaster. Wheezing through his nose, Altair shot his attacker a dirty look before moving toward the ship, still struggling to keep up.

His attacker extended a silver remote that emitted a clear, bell-like tone. The craft whirred to life, lighting up the sand below it with balls of light. Hydraulics hissed and steamed as an entrance rolled open and a ramp extended down and toward them both. Altair watched in admiration as the ship opened itself to them, in awe of how technology had advanced during his exile.

At the attacker's nudging, Altair stepped onto the cool metal, eyes rolling back in relief. His feet would hurt for days, no doubt.

The clang of Altair limping into the craft echoed across the dunes. As they shoved him into a corner of the ship, he turned and watched them slowly disappear as the silver door rolled shut.

His stomach was a mess of nerves and, as much as it pained him to say it, relief. The bright, silver cleanliness of the ship was a welcome sight opposed to dirt and sand.

He relaxed against the metal wall as the dark figure fiddled with the control panel.

Altair watched as they expertly started the engines and piloted the ship into the sky. It didn't even so much as shake or tilt as it moved upward. The ship rose vertically with ease, before rocketing with incredible speed toward the planet's atmosphere.

Altair rolled silently to his side so that he could watch through a nearby window as they broke through the atmosphere with hardly a shudder and entered the blissful darkness and silence of space. Altair couldn't help the happiness that radiated through him as he watched the planet, his home, and his jail for so many years, disappear.

Several minutes passed by as Altair watched it wink out of existence. He felt a lump in his throat as he realized that this changed everything. No matter where he was headed, he'd never have to go near that sand pit ever again.

In fact, he'd rather throw himself into the nearest black hole than ever go back.

He was so lost in thought; he didn't even notice that a pair of eyes were burning into the back of his head. Altair tipped his gaze back and was startled to see dark brown eyes peering at him from inside the black hood. There were no other discernible features that could be seen, but there was one thing of which Altair was certain.

Those eyes were burning with disgust and hatred.

Altair recoiled from the scathing look.

*What did I do to them?!*

His captor didn't even seem ashamed that Altair had caught them looking at him. The figure just blinked once, and twice, then turned to face the control panel once again.

They hit a few buttons that made the ship shudder once again before steadying in a smooth, unnatural way. Altair scuttled backward on his behind as best as he could as the figure turned and stalked toward him.

The attacker knelt in front of him and, using one swift motion, undid his shackles. Altair rubbed his sore wrists, looking at them in confusion.

He flinched away as they pulled the blaster out once more and pointed it threateningly at Altair's head. When they spoke, it was in that same, strained tone they had used before.

"Don't run. Don't fight. It will only end badly for you."

Altair swallowed and nodded, knowing instinctively that he couldn't fight back, even if he had all the weapons on the tool belt his attacker sported.

Their voice was unreadable. It was so garbled and difficult to understand that trying to focus on pitch and tone was impossible.

There was also something dangerous in the way they carried themselves. They held a grace in their movements that Altair had never seen before. He could tell that there was some intensive training behind them. He wasn't sure why someone so morbidly talented would be sent after the likes of him.

Besides his voice, there was little harm Altair could do to anyone.

They seemed to take his nod seriously and stood, reaching into the bag that was strapped to their back. They pulled a small drawstring sack from it and dropped it into Altair's lap.

He clutched the small bag before glancing at his captor with a questioning look. They nodded their head, indicating that he needed to open it. Altair conceded and slipped open the strings before dumping out the contents onto his legs.

Out of the bag tumbled toiletries encased in silver bottles, carefully labeled as to what they were. He picked up each bottle with a light touch and read their labels.

*Shampoo. Body Soap. Lotion.*

Altair looked up at his captor once again, his eyebrow twitching upward in confusion. The dark figure folded their arms across their chest and nodded toward the back of the ship.

"You stink. Wash."

Altair frowned, halfheartedly attempting to feign offense. However, he couldn't quite muster it. He probably smelled pretty bad.

Nodding, Altair carefully stood. His captor watched him with wary eyes, as if they expected him to do something. However, Altair was smarter than that.

And he kind of wanted a decent shower.

He gestured at his mouth, touching the device that still held his lips together. The thing that kept him from using his powers.

The figure's eyes darkened, and they shook their hooded head with finality before turning and stalking to the control panel to monitor the systems.

Fair enough.

Altair made his way to where his captor had pointed, assuming there was a washroom there.

His assumption was correct.

It was on the left side of the small hallway, near a room that housed simple sleeping cots. He pushed through the opposite door, cautiously peering inside.

The bathroom, though small, was modern and beautiful. Everything was painstakingly clean and white with a silver finish. A stand-alone corner shower stood in the back, enclosed in a half-circle, sliding glass door. The vanity held two simple drawers, one silver sink, and a spotless mirror. A toilet was crammed into the opposite corner and the shower was finished in the same manner as the rest of the bathroom. Lying on the counter was a perfectly folded simple gray outfit.

Surprise shot through him, and he wondered when his captor would have had the time to set things out like this.

He was even more surprised that he was being treated with such care.

Altair looked down at the well-worn clothing he had made himself while exiled. He was sure that if he were to take these off and set them on the ground, they would stand on their own because of the grime buildup on them.

New clothes sounded nice too, even if they were in an awful gray color.

Altair peeled off his old clothing and set them in a corner behind the bathroom door before climbing into the shower with his bag of toiletries. He stared in confusion at the panel on the wall in front of him.

*What in the world...?*

Altair mused over the many buttons and switches. This was nothing like the technology on his home planet. It seemed strangely rudimentary, which was at odds with the sleek and powerful ship it ornamented.

Altair's hands danced over the panel before settling on a promising-looking button and pressing it. Steaming water streamed from the overhead shower, scalding his vulnerable form.

Altair attempted to yelp, but the device muffled it. He danced away from the burning droplets as his hands desperately wormed around the stream of water and pressed everything he could touch.

Streams of alternating burning, lukewarm, and freezing water came in floods, shocking his body; and producing muffled sounds of pain and surprise. He made the very ship move as he jumped around, tears springing to his eyes.

Altair scrambled out of the shower, trembling. His temper flared when he thought he heard laughter echoing lightly from beyond the door.

It wasn't *his* fault that the shower was so difficult to use.

Cursing colorfully in his mind, he stared at the shower as it continued to run. There had to be an easier way than this.

A gentle knock startled him, and he grabbed at one of the fresh towels hanging nearby to cover himself.

He knew that he couldn't ignore the knock without risking his captor's anger, nor could he call out that he would figure it out himself. Altair cautiously opened the door with a begrudging look plastered on his face.

The figure stood there, still completely shrouded in black. Even though Altair couldn't see anything besides their eyes, amusement radiated from them.

It was odd that their expression could change so quickly. One second, they were looking at him as if he was a bug they had stepped on. The next moment, they found his antics amusing. Altair's temper heated, coloring his cheeks an ugly shade.

*You've got a stupid sense of humor.*

They didn't even give him a second glance as they pushed past Altair. His captor reached into the shower, pressed a few buttons, and stepped out of the bathroom without a word, closing the door behind them.

Altair cautiously approached the water and dipped a hand under the stream. He relaxed as he palmed his hand under the water, letting it fill up.

The perfect temperature.

He tried to recall exactly which buttons they had pressed so he could replicate it in the future as he dropped the towel and stepped under the shower head.

Altair's shoulders relaxed and rolled back. A hot shower. He hadn't had one of these in a very long time. In fact, he couldn't remember the last time he had enjoyed one.

He opened the small bag of toiletries and fished out each one as needed. They were hardly luxury products, but much better than he'd had in years.

Altair relished the soap's feeling as he lathered it across every square inch of his body. He washed for a long time. Altair didn't know when he would have another chance, so he definitely made the most of the shower.

Altair made sure he banished every trace of sand and dirt from his body. He imagined he was purging himself of his exile as he did so.

He had to stoop a little to make sure he rinsed properly. The shower head was only slightly shorter than him, which was inconvenient, but unworthy of his frustration. His height was something that he'd barely registered since he'd grown. It had never caused him problems other than the low roof of his hut.

Finally, he stepped out of the shower, after he'd figured out how to turn it off, and dried himself. Altair used the rest of his toiletries before pulling on the drab clothing that had been left for him.

He was pleased to find they fit well.

The clothing consisted of simple gray sweatpants made of a soft, light material that came with a matching long-sleeved shirt. For his feet, they had left him some black slip-on shoes. Nothing too flashy, but comfortable enough that he sighed heavily through his nose in contentment once they were on his body.

He also hadn't felt clothing this soft in a long time, so he spent more time just rubbing his hands against the sleeves, enjoying the feeling of the fabric brushing against his skin.

When he left the bathroom, his captor didn't even turn to look at him. He watched them carefully, walking across the silver floors with light footsteps.

One might have thought that they hadn't even noticed him re-enter the main hull. However, their hand resting against the blaster on their weapons belt said otherwise.

Altair made his way over to the corner in which he had been sitting before and slid down the wall, exhaustion suddenly radiating through his body, making his limbs feel sore and heavy.

It was a sudden and rude reminder of how he had been attacked in the middle of the night and had lost out on some much-needed sleep.

Unfortunately, he was still a prisoner.

And this person, who stood gazing out into the never-ending expanse of space, had still attacked him. Despite the kindness they had shown him in offering a shower and some fresh clothing, he still did not know what their motives were. Even as tired as he was, he had to stay awake.

Altair wasn't sure he could trust them enough to close his eyes, even for a moment. Armed as heavily as they were, there were about a million ways they could kill or injure him. It would be stupid to sleep when he was in the presence of such a dangerous individual.

Altair stared at the figure, willing them to turn around and state who they were or even, simply, what they wanted with him. Even more so, Altair wished they would say how they had found him.

His father had been so careful.

*And yet...*

Some random human had found him with apparent ease.

Despite Altair's burning stare, they kept their gaze focused on the whirling landscape outside of the ship. Their shoulders were taut, almost as though they had to keep themselves from turning and speaking to him.

His eyes swam with exhausted tears, blurring his vision.

*Gods, he wanted to sleep.*

Every blink felt heavier and harder to force his eyes open. It was like his tears were glue and pulling his eyelids apart each time felt unnatural.

Unwillingly, Altair drifted off to sleep.

# Chapter 3
# Altair

When Altair awoke, he was no longer seated against the cold, hard wall of the ship.

He rolled over, realizing he was in a cot and covered in a thin, but large blanket. His head was also resting comfortably on a cool, fluffy pillow.

Somehow, his captor had picked up and carried his tall form all the way to this bed without waking him.

Despite how sleepy he was, Altair marveled at their strength. He stretched deeply, curling his toes, attempting to shake off how groggy he felt. He hadn't slept that well in a very long time.

Yawning, he sat up and looked around. He was the only one in a room of three cots. This was the room he had passed on his way to the bathroom earlier.

The ship. It was coming back to him fully now.

*The ship.*

Piloted by the person who had attacked him.

Altair immediately felt his body tense as he remembered his ordeal from the night before. The attack, the kidnapping, the weapons, the ship, the mouthpiece...

*The mouthpiece.*

Altair grabbed at his face, realizing that the mouthpiece had been removed. He worked his jaw before gasping, confused by the gesture. His thoughts raced in an attempt to understand.

He couldn't have been trusted so easily. That made absolutely no sense, especially after what lengths to which the attacker had gone to protect themself from Altair and his powers.

He stood slowly, glancing around the room and wondering if there was any clue as to what was going on. However, the room was just as devoid of answers as the rest of this situation.

Altair bit his lip, trying to consider the possibilities.

If this person worked for those who wanted him for his abilities, they would know what he could do. They wouldn't have trusted him enough to remove the mouthpiece.

So, what else could this be?

Altair's stomach dropped as another possibility slithered into his mind.

*Perhaps...*

Perhaps, this person worked for his father. Maybe he had sent them to test Altair's willingness to stick to the plan.

His father might have wanted to make sure that after all these years, he was still loyal to his training and the king's wishes.

If that were the case, Altair had failed miserably. Perhaps, if he had attempted to take his life, the attacker would've stopped him. They would've told him it was a test that he had passed, and that his ordeal was now over.

A twisted game of loyalty.

But he hadn't done that. And if that was the case, he had betrayed his father's trust. It was possible they were on their way back to Serina so his father could punish Altair for his insubordination.

It was highly unlikely, but the thought that it might be true made Altair's stomach twist.

He looked toward the bedroom door, which was tightly shut. The room must've been mostly soundproof because he couldn't hear the comings and goings of anything else on the ship. The only thing he could hear was the faint roaring of the engine. Altair strode over to the door and attempted to push it open.

It didn't budge.

His arms dropped to his sides. Altair realized he hadn't exactly been trusted. They had locked him inside this room.

Funny enough, relief trickled through him. This made it less likely that it was his father running some strange loyalty test. Altair made his way back to his cot and flopped down with a heavy sigh.

In a prison, yet again, but this one was marginally more comfortable.

He was kidding himself. This one was *way* more comfortable than his last one. The only thing that would make it blissful in comparison was a safe body of water into which to dive.

Altair kicked one of his legs lightly over the side of the cot and swayed it back and forth. He wished, vaguely, for something to entertain him. After all, he wasn't sure how long he was going to be locked in here. All he could do was stare at the immaculate, silver walls of the ship. There wasn't even a window from which to look out.

Altair tried to make do with just his mind to entertain him, something he was used to doing. He closed his eyes, losing himself in the thoughts that swept through his consciousness.

He hypothesized, over and over, who his captor was, and why they needed him.

And, an even more interesting train of thought, he hypothesized how they had found him. He was sure that his father had scrubbed every record of Altair's existence from both written and spoken history. It was the only logical course of action. Even through his anger and betrayal, he knew that.

He wondered if his father had faked his death.

He had been too young at the time to know all the details of the plan. He was of the age where he was eager to please, and his father was the kind of person who preferred silent obedience.

Don't ask, don't tell. A "secrets are secrets for a reason" type of male.

All he'd known was that his mother was dead, and there were some terrible people after him. It had something to do with the war, and he needed to go into hiding.

What lovely wording. "Needed to go into hiding." It turns out that simply meant banishment. Though, of course, young Altair had not understood.

His thoughts turned sour as anger bubbled in his stomach.

More than likely, the entire story was bullshit. Probably concocted to rid himself of the son who had taken everything from him.

It hadn't been Altair's fault, though. In all reality, it was his father's fault. Taking a gifted child and bragging so brazenly about his powers, of course, others would take notice, even without a war complicating things.

He wondered whose idea it had been to call the spell caster.

Perhaps his mother, though he didn't think she would have been so short-sighted. It was most likely his father, charging forward with his plan as he so often did. Mother would've never gone for anything so risky.

*Mother*.

Altair flinched at her memory again, that familiar ache in his chest making it feel as though it would burst open. He hadn't purposefully thought about her in years. It was too painful.

The first time had been when he'd opened the sketchbook again. This time was more painful.

It was easier to think about his father, where anger was an emotion that he could handle. Guilt was much more difficult to process.

A sudden realization caused Altair to rocket straight up in his cot. It creaked ominously as it registered the weight shift.

His abilities.

He hadn't purposefully spoken a word in years because of them, not since his mother had died. He had been instructed to speak to no one, absolutely no one, until his father returned. This rule included speaking to himself.

His father's warning still rang in his ears.

*You don't know if anyone is around. You wouldn't want to hurt anyone, would you, boy?*

The fear had kept him silent for so long. A hopeful bubble of thought floated to the surface.

*Now, well, why not say something?*

He was in a soundproof room, wasn't he? The only person he could hurt was standing outside and wouldn't be able to hear him. And to be honest, they didn't seem particularly affected by his earlier scream.

Additionally, he admitted, if he hurt them, it wasn't as if that would be the worst thing in the world. They attacked him in his bed and dragged him onto this ship without explaining absolutely *anything*.

Altair chewed on his lower lip. His heart hammered in his chest at the thought of finally hearing his voice. Perhaps even singing once again.

*No.*

His stomach flip-flopped as he considered that. He wouldn't dare go that far.

Clearing his throat, Altair opened his mouth and attempted to speak. Pain scratched up his throat, along with air, as he pushed through, eyes watering.

What came out of his mouth couldn't be considered speech. It was more akin to a squeaky door hinge.

The effort caused a significant coughing fit right afterward. He gasped for air through the hacking and shoved a fist into his abdomen, pressing hard against it to stifle the noise. Tears stung his eyes as he took several shaky breaths.

Of course, it wouldn't be that easy. He hadn't so much as hummed or whispered in years.

Swallowing what little moisture was left in his mouth, he tried again. This time, he focused on saying a word.

One word that haunted him from his nightmare the other night.

"Ewet."

It came out rough, and squeaky, but out it came. Altair couldn't help the smile that split his face at the sound of his voice.

*His* voice.

It sounded much deeper than he remembered it being. He had been a child when he'd first been exiled. His last words had been when he was merely six years old.

He felt the inviting, poisonous magic roll off his tongue as he murmured the name of his favorite flower.

The magic hit deaf walls and went no further. Joy filled Altair's chest as the curse died, reassuring him he was safe in this room. And that everyone else was too.

His anxiety broken, Altair suddenly laughed, wild and free. He laughed uncontrollably, his throat aching from the effort. He was laughing so hard that his abdomen hurt even more and joyous tears sprang to his eyes. Altair wrapped his arms around his middle as he doubled over.

Wiping the tears away, he smiled at nothing and continued trying different words. Some of them were in his tongue, Serinian, and others were in English.

The words bounced off the shiny walls, affecting no one, their magic all for naught.

He spoke so much that his throat ached. Swallowing against the painful lump, he tried to practice patience with himself. A voice as unused as his would, of course, cause soreness.

Plus, he had a hunch he'd have all the time in the world to speak again. Things suddenly felt different.

He fell back into his cot, spent but happy. Altair was feeling more hope than he had in years, even though he was still a prisoner. The feelings were akin to the high he experienced from the reed plant leaves. It buzzed through his limbs and set him on edge, urging him to act.

That happiness was short-lived, however, when he heard the rattle and clank of his door being unlocked from the outside. He felt his heart somersault in his chest at the sound as he recalled the half-baked escape plans that he'd mused over earlier.

This was it.

Altair could purposefully try to use his voice against someone for the first time in his life. He knew that this person had been immune to his powers briefly before, but that didn't mean he couldn't try again.

The thought still made his insides clench. He hated the idea of having to hurt someone intentionally.

But, as well as his captor had treated him, up to this point, he was still being kidnapped and did not know what their intentions were. If anything, he wasn't about to let someone use him or his powers for their own agenda.

It was worth a shot.

Altair sat up as the door opened and his captor stepped inside, still completely shrouded in their black garb, and carrying a covered silver tray.

*Here goes nothing.*

Their dark brown eyes flickered toward Altair, stepping forward quickly. Something about how hastily they moved triggered him. His thoughts galloped like a herd of untamed horses.

*They could so easily hurt him. He couldn't let that happen.*

Altair didn't even think. He just flinched backward and cried out, feeling the magic leave his mouth.

"No!" It cracked, coming out much less firm than he had expected.

The human stopped, as if shocked that he had reacted. But instead of a glazed infatuation entering those careful brown eyes, a frustrated flicker came to life in them. Altair felt despair and confusion twist his insides.

It was just as he suspected.

This person was immune.

He watched as they glared at him before balancing the tray in one hand.

Altair's captor grunted angrily and tossed it at him.

He flinched away, his mind racing. The reaction was somehow both expected and unexpected.

The tray clattered noisily to the ground, food splattering out from underneath the cover. His eyes widened when he realized that they had been trying to feed him. Regret pooled in his stomach as they placed their hands on their hips, glaring at him.

Altair tried to speak, to ask them why they were immune to his powers. But, as he opened his mouth, nothing came out. The words hummed through his mind, but never audibly left him.

*Why didn't it work?*

That strained, broken voice spoke from underneath the hood, hissing toward him.

"Then starve. Scum."

And with that, they left, the door shuddering and clanking as it locked.

# Chapter 4
# Zen

Zen rubbed at the calluses that adorned his fingers as he stared listlessly at each of the blinking screens.

*Green. Green. Green.*

Yawning, he tried to remember how he had gotten so many calluses. It wasn't as if he was a fighter, wielding a weapon either in his hands or on his hip.

Zen was an engineer. He tinkered and fixed things.

He much preferred that to shooting people.

Perhaps, that was why he was put on guard duty tonight. His sergeant had probably wanted to see him doing something "soldierly."

He rolled his eyes, wishing a minor amount of ill on his sergeant. Nothing major, just like a flat tire or something.

He chuckled at the thought.

*Green. Green. Green.*

Zen leaned back in the chair and sighed heavily. He would gladly take on guard duty if it meant he didn't have to fight.

Rumors had flown and his fellow soldiers had become nervous.

Being privy to those rumors, he heard that things had been getting worse on the war front. Swiveling back and forth in his chair, Zen cracked his knuckles as he pondered what had been circulating.

Their enemy, the terrifying Vesunian race, was dangerous, the stuff of nightmares. It was said they could snap a human in half with enough effort. The possibility made him cringe as he considered it.

Soldiers also whispered that the Vesunians were gathering unknown allies and pushing borders. It was said that they were creating new kinds of weapons. Dangerous types that could possibly destroy cities or planets.

The thought chilled Zen to the bone.

And last, but not least, others hissed about how all different duties were being called to fill fighting roles. Balthazar had even said his training buddy, originally assigned as a cook, was now neck deep on the front lines.

God help them all if they were that desperate.

He smiled ruefully at the idea of his sergeant assigning him a blaster and sending him to fight. They would only have themselves to blame when he undoubtedly fucked something up and accidentally blasted a hole through a friendly target.

Instead, he happily watched the screens, much preferring their boring complacency to the horror of a battlefield.

*Green. Green. Gr...*

Zen quickly jerked forward, eyes wide as he took in the now blinking *red* screen. Something had triggered the atmospheric sensors.

His heart pounding up into his throat, Zen shakily adjusted the nearby cameras to catch what had caused the disturbance.

*Please be a bird, or a stray piece of a satellite. Something easy.*

Camera T12 caught the intruder. It was not a bird, and it certainly was not a satellite.

*Fuck me!*

It was a ship. A powerful, highly advanced ship. Something that a human could never get their hands on in a million years. It glowed with a dangerous blue light.

Panic threatened to overtake him, and his fingers trembled as he focused in on the camera, attempting to get a clearer picture. When the image cleared, Zen squinted his eyes to try to understand what he was seeing.

The ship didn't seem to work. It was sputtering and tilting in odd directions. The blue light was ebbing in and out, and a small, blue fire emanated from a gaping hole in the ship's side.

It was hurtling downward. It was crashing. And Zen was the only one on duty.

Feeling close to tears, he tried to recall the protocol for a situation such as this. Through the panic, he couldn't remember. His head swiveled toward the weapons locker that sat in the corner of the surveillance room.

Weapons. He needed one of those. That blue light meant Nuva, which meant Vesunians.

Which meant trouble.

He knew that there was probably more he should do, but the only thing he could think of was getting to the site of the crash.

He had to figure out what was going on.

On shaking legs, he sprinted to the locker and threw open the doors. This duty station saw little action. A couple of outdated blasters hung on rusty hooks, neighboring a few dull knives and a taser stick.

Zen eyed the blasters distrustfully. His scores in training had been abysmal. He'd missed nearly every shot he'd ever attempted during practice and testing.

It was too bad there was nothing that could've disqualified him from military service because that should've been a red flag right there. They should've sent him packing the third time he failed his shooting exam.

*Honored to serve my five years.*

Frustration colored the thought as he considered the weapons in the locker.

The brain-dead mantra had been practically drilled into his head, along with everyone else's who was forced to serve in the human military.

Honored to serve his five years. Well, where was that enthusiasm now?

He grabbed the taser stick.

The air outside tasted sick and old. Zen remembered reading in his school textbooks that First Earth used to be filled with plant life and was once primarily green and blue. He'd looked at the pictures in awe. He couldn't even imagine that. The beauty was something that not even his grandparents remembered.

Probably not something his great-grandparents or great, great-grandparents remembered either.

First Earth had been sick for a long time.

Now, it was where the unlucky humans lived. You were only here if you were too poor to leave and build a life on Second Earth, alternatively known as Mars, stationed here as a soldier, or you were a prisoner in the large prison that sat only a couple miles away from the military base.

The years had not been kind to the planet they lived on. The decades of resource mismanagement and non-renewable energy guzzling had left it brown and desolate.

The few plants that still existed did not adapt for beauty but for survival. They grew in harsh spikes, as if showcasing the planet's anger at what humanity had done to it.

There was a limit to how many creatures could live on First Earth now. Every few years, the population of poor people would get too great, and several would pass away from oxygen deprivation. Of course, the soldiers and the elite, who were forced to live here, were always fine, surviving in their buildings full of recycled, stale air.

The plant life only created enough oxygen for a small percentage of humanity, a tragedy that could no longer be fixed.

The worse it had gotten, over the years, the more humans had left for Mars.

*Now, they were fucking up Mars.*

Zen's thoughts were savage even through his panic. He hadn't realized it before his enlistment and duty station on First Earth, but Mars was going in the same direction.

Of course, only Upper Lifers called Mars "Second Earth."

Zen shook his head in disgust.

His heart quickened as he caught the scent of burning machinery carried toward him with the sour breeze.

Zen slowly crept to where he had calculated the crash site to be. If this Vesunian had not been critically injured in the crash, he didn't think he'd have the upper hand here.

From what he had seen of their collective enemy, they were massive, terrifying creatures. And Zen was small, even for a human.

The taser stick was already making his arms ache as he carried it, pointing it out in front of his body. The metal felt cold and foreign in his grasp.

He realized, with a terrified start, that he hadn't even tested whether it had juice. He clicked the button near the middle of the stick and, with a pathetic zapping sound, the taser came to life.

*Thank fuck.*

As he approached the site, he heard the telltale sounds of broken machinery. His heart picked up speed, smashing against his chest. He didn't know it was possible for a heart to race like this.

Sneaking forward, Zen reasoned that there wouldn't be any way to salvage the ship after a crash like that, even with the power of Nuva.

Though, he supposed, he didn't know enough about the mysterious power source to make any judgment on that.

Bending at the knee, Zen got down and crawled toward a nearby scrubby-looking bush. He winced as the rocks scraped his palms and the taser stick dragged in the dirt, creating a high-pitched sound.

Reaching the bush, he peered over it to where he was sure the crash site was.

His calculations had been correct. The remnants of a ship lay smoldering in the dirt and scrub brush. Pieces had scattered further than Zen thought possible.

However, there was no fire, which meant that the danger was only slightly minimized.

There was also no trace of the pilot, at least as far as he could see.

Gathering every bit of stupid courage he had, Zen crept out from behind the bush and, carefully, made his way over to the crashed ship. It was small, a one-seater, which meant that the pilot was either right in the cockpit or the crash had blown their remains to smithereens, just like their ship.

Zen desperately hoped for the latter.

He slowly approached the cockpit, his hands slick and sweaty as he grasped the taser stick.

This piece of the ship was still, somehow, intact, despite the ferocity of its crash landing.

Meandering around it, he tried to find a way to open the cockpit. He needed to know if someone had survived. At this point, it wasn't even for reporting purposes, but out of his need to satiate his morbid curiosity.

Plus, he reasoned, he was sure he would need to report on it afterward. Especially if there *was* a body.

He stopped, both satisfaction and terror seeping through him as he found a lip located under the right-side cockpit window.

There it was. The latch. He was sure of it.

Wiping his hands on his clean uniform, he grasped the lip of the cockpit window and struggled to open it. Grunting and straining, Zen pushed and pulled for several minutes, but it would not give. As sweat beaded his upper lip, he took a step back and reconsidered his course of action.

With a sudden hiss and a terrible-sounding pop, the cockpit window jutted open.

Zen jumped back, startled, his original fears returning with a jolt. He quickly scrambled backward, bending down to grasp the taser stick he had abandoned in his attempt to open the ship.

Trembling, he held it out in front of him and cleared his throat, willing his voice to sound tougher than he felt.

"Identify yourself! You have landed on planet First Earth and are in sector 5! State your name and the purpose for this unauthorized landing and drop any weapons you may have!" Zen's voice cracked on the word "landing," considering that it wasn't true.

The window fell away. The original latches must've been damaged in the crash.

What it revealed was a sight that made his stomach lurch. He staggered backward even further to prevent himself from being sick on the cracked, dirt ground.

After taking a moment to gulp down some air and breathe deeply through his nose, Zen felt the urge to vomit lessen. He took two more deep breaths before stepping forward once again.

Feeling his lunch roll around in his stomach, he surveyed the gruesome scene. Zen almost didn't see that there was a living being in the cockpit, considering there was so much blood.

Purple blood stained nearly every surface of the ship's interior, along with something that looked suspiciously like innards.

The creature that it had come from was writhing weakly in the safety restraints of the pilot's seat.

Zen took another deep, calming breath as his worst fear was realized.

A Vesunian.

Well, half of one at least. Some shrapnel from the crash had pierced the cockpit and sliced the creature clean through the middle. It was a miracle that they still lived and were strong enough to writhe the way they did.

Though, Zen supposed grimly, those were nothing more than death throes at this point.

The Vesunian seemed to take notice of him and eyed Zen with a glassy, pained gaze. Zen swallowed in fear and disgust and could do nothing more than watch the Vesunian's dying movements.

Their mouth gaped open like a fish out of water, desperately trying to form words.

It was almost... pitiful.

As if these creatures weren't ones Zen was supposed to hate.

As if they weren't massive monstrosities. The terror of every child's nightmares.

Just a creature in pain. A strange emotion bubbled up inside of him, along with the sickening emotion of compassion.

The desire to help struck him.

He was sure that the Vesunian would die from its injuries, so it made no sense that he dropped his weapon and ran forward.

Toward the enemy.

Every bit of survival instinct he had screamed at him to stay away. But it was as if his need to help drew him to the creature.

He approached the bloody cockpit and desperately searched for a way to assist them.

His eyes flitted around, looking for anything that might staunch the creature's suffering. He knew the alien would die, but it didn't have to die so painfully. His inner voice screamed at him for his stupidity, but he ferociously beat it back. This Vesunian, of all of them, could do him no harm.

Zen threw his arms out in a gesture of helplessness. He didn't know if the alien understood English, but he spoke to it anyway.

"I don't know how to help. What can I do?!" His voice sounded shaky, and he hated it. He was supposed to be a soldier for fuck's sake.

The Vesunian's eyes, those terrifying black eyes, found him and they weakly beckoned with a bloodied, four-fingered hand for Zen to come closer.

He shuddered in fear. The interaction reminded him that this was the enemy, the bad guy.

Zen should've brought the blaster gun and ended the creature's suffering right there, no questions asked. That's what every single soldier he knew would've done.

And every single soldier in question wouldn't dare come any closer to the dying alien that lay in their cockpit coffin.

Yet, Zen did come closer. In fact, he was close enough that the stench of suffering invaded his nose. He gagged minutely, swallowing against the nausea.

*What was he doing?!*

The Vesunian stretched their hand forward as if to touch him and, with a surprised yelp, he instinctively flinched away.

The creature halted their reach but didn't seem surprised by his hesitancy.

Their eyes seemed almost... sad.

*Damn it.*

And it was that sadness that let Zen release his inhibitions and finally step forward, meeting the Vesunian's reach halfway.

Their fingers grabbed weakly at his wrist, causing an unintentional shudder to wrack through Zen's body.

The alien's mouth opened and closed desperately and their grip on his wrist grew stronger, as if trying to communicate.

Suddenly, a strange voice rang through Zen's mind. It was foreign, but it spoke in pained and halting English.

**The prince ... He is in danger ... Find him. Find him.**

Zen gasped and yanked his arm away from their touch as the Vesunian's voice seemed to fade from his mind. He watched as their dark eyes went even darker and their arm fell, going limp over the side of the cockpit.

Zen's chest ached from how hard his heart slammed against it, and his mouth felt dry. He felt the urge to be sick again.

The Vesunian prince? Is that who the creature had meant?

If they had, what the hell was he supposed to do about that?

*Why did this have to happen on his shift?*

He groaned in frustration and wiped the purple blood from his wrist with the edge of his uniform, trying not to look at the dead Vesunian again for fear that his lunch would indeed make a second appearance.

The sound of whirring ships and sirens suddenly brought him back to where he was and what he was supposed to be doing. His sergeant would be here soon, and he had to have an explanation.

As Zen stepped away from the ship and headed back in the direction of the surveillance room, only one thought dominated his racing mind.

*What the fuck was he supposed to put in that report?*

# Chapter 5
# Altair

Altair's stomach growled as he stared in frustration at the locked door of the ship.

He didn't know how long it had been since his captor had flung his meal onto the floor after his foolish escape attempt. But it was long enough that he had regretted ever trying.

*Of course,* he reasoned with himself, *a shout like that would've brought anyone else down.*

His voice. His powers. Altair bit his lip at the thought that they perhaps didn't exist anymore. Could a Serinian lose their gift? Was it part of his curse somehow?

If that was the case, and his captor was kidnapping him for his abilities, they were about to be sorely disappointed. His mind screamed his rejection at such a thing happening.

He remembered with a start that he had still felt the magic leaving his mouth when he'd shouted earlier. It was still there and just as potent. He had even felt it reverberate against the soundproof walls and dissipate.

Altair sighed and pushed his hands into his abdomen, trying to quell the hunger. It wasn't helping his thought process that he hadn't had a meal in hours. Regret stabbed into him as he glanced at the silver tray that lay on the ground, the contents spoiled and cold.

He leaned back into the cot and closed his eyes, trying to ignore the pain that reminded him intensely of the need he couldn't fulfill. Instead, he ruminated on how it was possible that this person was immune to his curse.

No one had heard Altair speak and lived in the last twenty years.

Ever since that dreadful day that the spellcaster visited.

He remembered it like it was yesterday, although he had desperately tried to forget it during his years spent in exile.

*Altair's father paced the great hall, ignoring his wife's pleas to calm himself.*

*"Darling," her musical voice was no longer light and carefree. She wrung her hands as she watched the king make innumerable rounds around the thrones. "You must calm yourself. You don't know for sure that he was here for Altair."*

*His father turned, nostrils flaring in his infamous temper. Even when angry, the power of the monarch's voice filled the hall like sweet music, beautiful but terrifying.*

*"An assassin, Seraphina! In my home!" His teeth gritted together, and Altair wanted to hide behind his mother's skirts. He didn't understand why his father was so angry.*

*"We're royalty!" The queen's voice rose to match his. It was something that had drawn them together, that she did not fear his temper as most did. "Assassins are par for the course! It does not mean…"*

*The king's voice practically exploded in response, and Altair did indeed hide behind his mother this time.*

*"It is FOOLISHNESS to think that he was not here for Altair!" His father practically shook in indignation. "And, so shortly after that political emissary visit from the human council."*

*His father began his lengthy pacing of the great hall again, shaking his head to calm himself. "They offered to BUY our son, Seraphina, or did you forget?!"*

*His mother stood tall, chin raised and eyes glinting with pride. "I did not forget. I also remember you refusing their request and then promptly asking them to leave. Am I not correct?"*

*The queen's voice softened, and she held out her hands pleadingly. "Please do not yell like that in front of your son, Tyrinion."*

*The king set his jaw but seemed to calm at her tone. His eyes glanced to where his son was still shaking behind his mother's dress.*

*Shame flickered in his gaze.*

*"Come out from behind your mother, child. That is no way for a prince to behave."*

*Altair's eyes swam with tears, but he stepped away from her and looked toward his father.*

*"Yes, Papa, sorry, Papa." His voice sent a wave of calm and beauty through the hall, and he saw his father physically relax as the magic washed over him.*

*His mother, sensing Altair's distress, bent down and gently tucked a finger under his chin. She smiled softly, her eyes worried but protective, glimmering with that kindness for which her people knew her.*

*"Altair, do you remember when we said that you were special? More special than any other Serinian ever born?"*

*He sniffled, wiping at his nose, before nodding. His mother's voice seemed to wrap him in warmth, flooding his insides with calm.*

*He remembered. But, at the time, they had said it was a good thing. Why did it suddenly feel bad?*

*She gently pushed a piece of his hair behind his ear. "Well, there are some very bad people who want to use your power for bad things. So, Papa and I are bringing someone here who can help protect you. There is no need to be scared. We will do everything we can to make sure you stay safe. Okay?"*

*Altair wasn't scared. He believed her when she said he would be okay. His mother had never lied before.*

*He nodded once more. She smiled, this time with pride.*

*"Good boy."*

*The doors opened, and his father's servant, Urto, entered. He looked toward the king, brow furrowed in worry.*

*"The spell caster is here."*

Altair was shaken from his memories by the ship trembling. It felt as though they were entering an atmosphere and landing somewhere.

*Landing.*

He jumped up, legs shaky from both terror and excitement. Finally, some answers to this ordeal into which his captor had forced him.

At least, that's what he hoped.

The ship continued to tilt and shake for several minutes before it ended, and everything went still. He couldn't hear the engines, so Altair assumed his assailant had shut them off. He paced the entire length of the room, trying to decide how to move forward once his captor entered the room. If this was their final destination, he had very little time to get away, and he was now weaponless without his voice.

Altair took a few deep breaths to calm himself and tried to find his center. He could do this. He was the Serinian prince of legend. A ghost, for all intents and purposes. If he could get away from the human, he could vanish once again. No one would believe he was who he was supposed to be.

It would be easy to disappear.

His chest felt heavy as the door to the sleeping quarters hissed and creaked open. The familiar black figure stood silhouetted in the doorway, a strange, but warm, light filtering behind them. Though Altair was taller than this stranger, he suddenly felt powerless as they stared him down. They had proven repeatedly that they were much stronger than he was and his false confidence from before quickly deflated.

Their deep, brown eyes were still the only thing that he could see. This time, they glimmered with caution. Their hand was in position against the blaster gun at their belt, and the other clutched a small piece of metal.

Altair's heart jolted as he peered closer and realized it was the mouthpiece. His jaw worked as though it was still pressed to his lips, feeling a phantom ache that had taken hours to leave.

He couldn't put that thing back on. Not again.

Not willingly.

So, he would fight. He would attempt to overpower this human or die trying. At least, his father would be pleased with this one last act of courage. The thought brought little comfort.

Altair felt his muscles bunch and tense as he prepared to leap forward and make his foolish attempt at a fight.

Before he could even flinch, his captor spoke, shocking him into stillness with their words. The voice was still halting and odd, but, this time, a plea tinged the edges of their words.

"Please. Don't."

Something about the way they said that reminded him of his mother. There was the same sort of kindness in the words. It felt misplaced coming from someone who was supposedly holding him captive.

Altair felt his resolve crumble into dust, and he straightened up out of his fighting stance.

They stared at each other for several seconds before Altair spoke, hesitating even after knowing that his voice would do them no harm.

"Why not?" His voice trembled, but he still felt the power of the curse as his whisper flew toward his captor.

They didn't even twitch as the magic brushed past their hood, tickling it back a little. Altair glimpsed a sharp chin and deep brown skin before the human grasped the hood and pulled it forward, concealing their identity once again.

Their shoulders rose as they took a deep breath, as if steadying themselves. They fixed their eyes on Altair's face, piercing, trying to read him.

The human didn't speak for a long moment before they leaned forward on their toes, finally deciding on the best answer. They pulled their hand away from the blaster gun hanging on their belt and offered the mouthpiece toward him as they spoke.

"I do not want to have to kill you." The longer the sentence went on, the more garbled it became leaving their mouth. It appeared they were pleased with their answer, not realizing how incredibly threatening it sounded.

Altair twitched, and his mouth twisted as he attempted not to laugh at the absurdity of their statement.

It was so obvious now. He was a prize, likely being brought back to the highest bidder. Morbid humor rose within him as things fell into place.

His captor was not the one who planned on using him.

They needed him alive.

The human watched him for a second, obviously confused by his reaction. Not patient enough to wait for a response, they huffed and held out the mouthpiece even further, as if beckoning him to put it on himself.

Altair sighed, confused as to why he even needed it. He held up a hand, and the human tensed.

"Hold on. I'll take it and put it on if you answer some questions for me." Altair raised an eyebrow and lowered the hand. "Deal?"

He wasn't sure where this sudden bravado was coming from. Perhaps, he was bolstered by the humor he had found in their previous statement.

His captor stood there in silence for several moments, eyes flickering between Altair's eyes and mouth. The confusion was apparent, even though he couldn't see their entire face.

When they spoke, they did so slowly, as though they needed clarification.

"You have questions?" Their voice was uncertain and guarded.

Altair sighed and nodded, arms folding across his chest, and turning his head away from them. Irritation bit at his tone.

"Yes, questions. Can you answer some questions for me? I'll gladly go with you if you do."

*Maybe*, he countered to himself.

It was the human who sighed this time and seemed irritated with him. They raised a hand and snapped their fingers, waving at him to get his attention.

Altair quickly turned back to face them, his temper flaring. Even though he'd been stranded on a sand planet for twenty years, he knew it was bad manners for most races. He wasn't some loyal pet, being snapped to obedience.

*What was their problem?*

His irritation halted, however, when they reached up and pulled down their hood, finally revealing the identity of the person who had been able to so easily overpower him.

The human standing in front of him was a female.

*Woman.* Altair vaguely recalled the word from his childhood studies. Female humans were called "women."

She was beautiful, as much as humans could be beautiful, but weathered and tired-looking. The exhaustion didn't detract from her youthful appearance, however, and it surprised Altair that she seemed so young.

The woman's cheekbones stood out prominently and framed large but regal features. Her eyes were indeed a chocolate brown, as Altair had seen already, and they were currently narrowed in frustration. She had dark brown hair that was cropped short, nearly buzzed, with clean lines patterning a symbol he didn't recognize on the left side of her head. Her skin was even darker than her eyes and was currently covered in a layer of sweat, most likely from wearing such heavy, dark clothing. Her lips were thick and pursed in anger and disapproval.

But that wasn't what made Altair's heart drop.

Scarring; thick, twisted, and knotted, marred her skin. It extended from somewhere underneath her armor, up her neck, and onto her chin. It disfigured the right side of her cheek, and her right ear was nothing more than a knobby piece of unrecognizable flesh.

With a stab of remorse and regret, Altair realized she could not hear.

She tapped her foot angrily and gestured to her right side.

"War injury."

Altair nodded, opening his mouth to apologize. "I see that. You don't have to expl…"

"I'm deaf."

Altair bit his lip, shame pooling within him. He waited until she raised her eyebrows, apparently waiting for an answer. He spoke slowly, emphasizing each syllable.

"Yes, I understand. But can you read my mouth?"

She observed him before nodding. Altair felt relief trickle through him, along with understanding.

This was why she was unaffected by him. His voice was his weapon, but if she couldn't hear it, it was obvious why she was immune.

A loophole. One that no one had considered before.

He faced her before he spoke, trying his hardest to make sure she understood him. His hands were sweaty and clammy, and he wiped them against the soft material of his sweatpants.

"Why do I need to wear the mouthpiece if I can't hurt you?"

She nodded, her eyes alighting with understanding. Clearing her throat, she held up two fingers.

*Okay, two reasons.* Altair tilted his head and waited.

She spoke, and, this time, it seemed she was attempting to be clearer.

"One, I *can* hear but I also can't." Sensing his confusion, she continued. "I can feel movements." The woman stomped her foot as if to demonstrate. "I can feel people, things, vibrations. But, if you were to scream, I can't hear that." She shrugged. "For my safety, you must wear the silencer. Wouldn't want you trying to get anyone's attention or causing a scene."

Altair was stunned. It made sense that she would need to know whether someone was sneaking up on her. But the fact that she had developed the skill to feel things that she couldn't see or hear was incredibly impressive.

She seemed to catch on to the fact that he was in awe and smiled smugly.

He quickly wiped the look from his face and frowned, nodding.

"Okay, and two?"

Her eyes became careful this time. There was information behind reason number two that he, apparently, couldn't know. When she spoke, it was frustratingly vague.

"Two, we are meeting a hearing friend of mine. I don't want you entrancing him, on purpose or by accident."

The "by accident" bit stung. She had noticed that he wasn't entirely cool under pressure. Altair gritted his teeth, and his cheeks felt slightly flushed.

"Who is your friend?"

The woman shook her head at his last question and proffered the silencer once again. Her eyes were pleading with him to not fight her on this and to just go along with her request. He could tell by her expression that she did not want to have to kill him.

Altair considered his options. He *could* fight her on this, go against incredible odds, and likely die trying to escape.

Or he could play along and bide his time. Perhaps, she would let her guard down near this friend of hers. He could look for a way to escape on the way there and, if he couldn't find one, attempt to disappear at this mystery meeting.

Begrudgingly, Altair took the silencer from her hands.

"Lead the way," he said before pressing it to his lips with a wince.

# Chapter 6
# Altair

He couldn't breathe properly. Gods, he'd almost forgotten how awful the silencer was. His lips were numb from the mechanical clamp, and his jaw ached from being held in such an awful, stiff position.

Altair complained bitterly in his head as they moved forward. His wrists were once more shackled in the glittering cuffs, and he was forced to follow his captor closely due to the rope she had tied to them. Looking around, Altair realized that there was little he could do to escape as he had originally planned.

The planet to which she had brought them was not one on which any person of repute would have lived, which made Altair nervous about who, exactly, they were meeting.

It was the universal trash heap they called Kelptor.

Kelptor was a planet of transients and barterers, in a galaxy that had notoriously stayed out of the war. Different races and creatures used Kelptor as a stopping point, a trade route, and, infamously, as a place to conduct shady business dealings.

Altair's father had brought him here, only once, to speak to someone regarding the plan to drop Altair off on the isolated planet. They had met with an unknown creature, draped in red silks, who had pushed an envelope of information toward the king. Altair now assumed that the information was about which planets would be safest to send him.

It wasn't as if the king would've done the research himself.

The streets were chaotic and loud. Different stalls and stores were set up to tempt the passing traveler. Shadier characters tried to avoid the public as they moved and weaved between the sweaty bodies, their shifting eyes giving away their nefarious intentions.

The woman didn't seem too bothered by her surroundings, however, as she pushed through the crowd and glared at any shop owners who dared to approach her, clutching their wares. Even as uncomfortable as he was, with bodies pressing into him and sweat rolling down his back, he couldn't help but find humor in the merchants shrinking away from her daggered looks.

The tinkle of beads interrupted Altair's thoughts. The huntress, as he had begun to call her, had stepped into a very large, multi-colored tent that mysteriously held itself up whilst being draped with a plethora of fabrics. It looked like a laundry receptacle had been brought to life. They had created the doorway with the same draped fabric and some beading that hung low to the ground.

The tent itself was off a side street and partially hidden, despite its size. Passersby walked on, eyes sliding in disinterest past the tent. It was as if it didn't exist.

Or the residents didn't want it to exist.

The idea was incredibly unsettling.

He stepped inside after her, shivering at the blast of cold air that wrapped itself around him. The sight of what was inside the tent instantly made his ears hot, even as anger boiled in his stomach.

Several creatures milled around them, inducing a feeling of claustrophobia. Altair's chest felt tight in reaction to the crowd's proximity.

The air was filled with the sounds of bids being called, cries of pain, and loud bartering. The smell of sweat and urine made Altair scrunch his nose, frustrated he couldn't breathe through his mouth to avoid the putrid scents. He glanced around, trying to make sense of the chaos.

There seemed to be two types of creatures in this hellish landscape. There were the yelling, angry, and bartering types. They flashed shiny coins and wiped at the sweat that beaded their foreheads with expensive handkerchiefs. And then, there were the ones who looked like Altair. They wore shackles or were sequestered in cages. Their eyes were listless as their freedom was auctioned off.

Altair stopped in his tracks. He had spotted a Serinian among the captured throng. Unlike Altair, her clothes were tattered and dirty. However, like him, she wore a familiar piece of equipment.

Her captor held her mouth shut with a silencer as well. Bruising and infection surrounded the device and the sight of such brutality caused Altair to shiver.

He hadn't realized how badly the silencer could injure someone. The alien felt a strange surge of gratitude for the huntress, despite the circumstances in which he found himself.

Altair felt a harsh tug on his wrists and whipped his head around to glare at the human. She glared right back at him from under the dark hood. The feeling of gratitude shriveled up in his stomach as they stared at each other.

Her glare seemed to hold more power, and Altair fought to not let his gaze drop.

"Move." Her voice was rough and completely at odds with the reasonable and understanding tone she had taken with him when convincing him to wear the silencer once more.

He attempted to match the ferocity of her gaze but felt his resolve cracking. His eyes darted down to her feet, and his cheeks burned with embarrassment once more.

*Damn it. Damn her.*

Altair moved forward, following her past the much worse-off chattel of creatures. He wondered whether he was to be auctioned off to the highest bidder. He stumbled over his feet several times, distracted by his thoughts.

That would explain why he needed to be groomed, the product had to look its best after all.

His captor didn't stop at the auctioning stalls, however. She pushed forward, the crush of people parting for her. Many knew who she was, as those who jumped aside did so with fearful recognition glinting in their eyes.

Altair stumbled after her, doing his best to avoid the quickly closing throng of people who had allowed her to pass. No one seemed to give him a second glance, let alone acknowledge his existence with a respectful sidestep.

Altair's heart skipped a beat when he realized that this could be his chance to leave. He could vanish among the crowd and blend in with the rest of the captives.

He would simply catch her off guard and tug hard enough for her to let go of the rope in her hand. His breath quickened, and he felt a shiver of excitement at the half-baked escape plan that swirled through his mind.

There were so many creatures here that it wouldn't be difficult to lose her. There was simply the matter of the silencer and his cuffs. But he could figure out how to remove those at a later time, when he was finally free.

The thought had barely crossed his mind when the huntress turned around, grabbed his arm roughly, and shoved him in front of her as they entered another, smaller room in the tent.

The air was different here. Hazy, pleasant-smelling smoke filled it, reminding Altair of the reed plant leaves. The lights were dim and multi-colored, casting strange shadows on the wall. The sounds in here were different too. They were animalistic, rough, and…

*Oh.*

Altair blushed about a million different shades as he processed what he was seeing. He tried to avert his gaze from the writhing creatures who panted and grabbed at each other. Several groups had formed, drunk with lust, their minds warped by whatever drug produced that beautifully enticing scent.

The huntress didn't seem bothered by that into which they had walked. She simply stepped forward and folded her arms across her chest.

"Silas." Her voice was unfamiliar again. This time it was warm and humorous.

A male creature sleepily pulled his head from one of the nearby groups. This was a race with which Altair was unfamiliar, although he was just as naked as every other creature in this room.

Silas grinned slowly and peeled himself away from three females who attempted to pull him back. He made his way to them, his hooves smacking up puffs of dust and his tail twitching happily.

"Lil!" Silas threw his arms open in welcome before bringing his hands down and gesturing them in strange characters toward the huntress. Reaching her, they embraced, and Altair shuddered at her willingness to do so with someone so exposed.

She pulled away from him, dropping her hood. Rather than her usual stoic and serious self, her mouth was set in a wide and joyous grin. Altair was becoming used to her mood swings, even in the little time he'd known her.

Lil, which Altair assumed was her name, threw her hands forward as well and began making similar movements toward Silas.

Altair watched in confusion as they flapped their hands at each other, laughing and, seemingly, communicating. Finally, after several minutes of this going on, and Altair's patience wearing thin, Silas's eyes flickered in his direction.

The alien's eyes weren't altogether unpleasant, but Altair disliked them. They were narrow and too close together for comfort. Additionally, his pupils were slitted and serpent-like. When he blinked, Altair swore he saw two sets of eyelids closing and opening again.

Silas gestured to him, making a few more movements, his head tilting.

Thankfully, Lil spoke this time.

"A job. Nothing more." Lil's voice was snappy which was a tone with which Altair was familiar. She continued, "But an important one. Which is why I need that part I mentioned a few minutes ago."

Surprise shot through Altair at her comment, and he blinked several times.

*She had? When?!*

Silas sighed before running a hand through his tousled, sandy hair. This seemed to be a source of contention between the two.

"Lil. That part is Vesunian. The humans would raid your ship and pick up traces of Nuva instantly. Plus, do you know how hard it is to get unregistered Nuva products? The Vesunians guard that shit like it's their lifeblood."

Lil pursed her lips. "I do. And I also know you're the best damn smuggler this side of Andromeda. I'm willing to pay you a lot, Silas. Please."

Altair could've sworn that Silas turned a darker shade of gray than his skin already was, though he wasn't sure because of the dimness of the room.

He seemed to consider her for a second then looked away, sighing once more before smiling.

"And you're sure you need this specific part? I can always just upgrade your Troy. I've got human blaster parts for miles."

His smile faded as she shook her head vigorously. She fixed him with one of her withering glares, but, shockingly, it didn't seem to faze him.

Silas's confidence impressed Altair.

Lil fixed her mouth in a stubborn frown. "It has to be Nuva. Nothing else will touch those vemen asteroids and you know it."

Silas nodded, considering her words.

Altair's eyebrows knitted together in confusion. His mind was once again spinning.

*What, by the gods, were vemen asteroids?*

Whatever they were, Silas seemed to understand her plea. He trotted toward some hooks that lined the fabric walls of the tent and pulled down a faded, silky purple robe. He slipped it on, finally covering his nakedness and providing some relief for Altair's eyes.

He gestured for them both to follow him as he exited the same way that Lil and Altair had entered.

*Thank the gods,* Altair thought, as they both dutifully followed him.

# Chapter 7
# Zen

Zen twisted his hands together as he sat, sweating, and waiting in the interrogation room.

*It's not an interrogation room, Don't be so dramatic!*

Zen scolded himself for the intrusive thought. He was simply here to give an auditory report to his sergeant. There hadn't been a Vesunian landing on First Earth in years. And, of course, it had happened on his shift.

*Some guys got all the luck,* he supposed with grim humor.

The room was chilly. Zen shivered through the thin layer of his uniform. He wasn't an assigned fighter, so he didn't have to wear the blast-proof armor that most soldiers did. He wondered, briefly, if they were warmer than the assigned livery that he donned every morning.

The door slid open with a hiss, and Zen hopped to his feet. He noted that, somehow, his right leg had fallen asleep as he'd sat on the cold, metal chair. His arm shot up in a practiced salute, nearly knocking the hat off his head as his hand smacked into his forehead.

A middle-aged man stepped into the room. Zen estimated that Sergeant Jennings had to be in his late forties or early fifties when Zen had first started his obligatory five years.

Massive and untamable salt and pepper eyebrows hooded his steely gray eyes. His hair was a matching shade and was cropped close to his head. Jennings's jaw was always set in a disapproving look and Zen wasn't sure he'd ever seen the man drop even the hint of a smile.

Jennings wasn't alone. Two other men followed him stiffly, their shoulders taut and broad from years of military service.

*Security*, Zen mused.

Did they seriously think they had anything to fear from him? The top of his head barely reached the shoulder of the shortest bodyguard. He was certain each one of them could bench-press two of him.

Zen was sure they thought the same thing as they stepped inside and surveyed him. One of their eyes flashed with what could've been amusement, and his tense shoulders relaxed a little. The bodyguard's eyes quickly glanced over at his comrade, and they shared a moment of mutual amusement. Zen felt heat burn his cheeks.

*Well, wasn't that fucking hilarious? Short guy jokes.*

As if he hadn't heard it all before.

Zen's attention snapped back to Jennings as the grizzled war veteran stepped in front of him with a click of his boots. The only thing that separated them was the metal table at which Zen had been sitting at for about an hour.

Those sharp, steely eyes looked him up and down, disappointment shadowing them.

It was a look Zen was used to receiving from Jennings. No matter what advancements he could make or what difficult technical fix he resolved, he would never be enough for the man.

And it was simply because he wasn't a fighter.

*Such bullshit.* Zen thought morosely to himself.

He realized, with a wince, that he hadn't moved or said a word since Jennings had entered the room. The sergeant stood there, waiting for his acknowledgment with raised brows.

Clearing his throat, Zen slapped his hand down to his side and stood at attention, chin jutting out slightly too far for protocol.

"Private Farraway reporting, Sergeant Jennings, Sir!" Zen robotically called out in a voice he had curated for such events.

His first several weeks of training had been difficult because he hadn't been able to project his voice enough to his instructor's satisfaction. His arms had ached from the endless punishment push-ups.

His good friend, Kai, had also enlisted around the same time and was a natural soldier. He took the time to teach Zen how to project his voice properly, so that he wouldn't have to suffer at the hands of any other sadistic instructors.

They had promptly sent Kai to the front lines after graduation. Last he'd heard, Kai was still alive. But he wasn't sure how recent that news was, considering communications were usually limited, especially from the fighter units.

He swallowed hard as Jennings fixed him with that piercing, disappointed stare. Jennings reached forward slowly over the table and, with one finger, pushed Zen's chin into the proper position. He swallowed hard, the correction making his chest constrict.

When Jennings spoke, his voice was scraggly and rough, akin to rocks scraping against each other.

"Private Farraway, how long have you been with us?" Jennings slowly began pacing around the table, trying to get closer.

Zen watched him, his mouth drying out. "I am in my third year, Sergeant Jennings, Sir!" His voice was betraying him. It wobbled slightly at the end and came out squeaky. He silently cursed to himself.

Jennings nodded minutely, barely acknowledging that Zen had spoken at all. He ended up at Zen's side, staring at the side of his face coldly, mouth set in a harsh line.

Sweat beaded Zen's temple, sliding down his cheek and eventually dropping from his chin onto the uniform that he was supposed to keep spotless. Several awful minutes passed before Jennings spoke again. By the time he did, Zen's body ached from being at attention.

"Three years," Jennings mused, his security doing little to hide their enjoyment now. Their beady eyes glinted with savage pleasure as the sergeant continued. "And yet, I had to find out about an enemy ship landing from the blaring alarms."

Zen's throat felt so dry that he was pretty sure they could rename it a desert. "Yes, Sergeant Jennings, Sir. I… It wasn't my usual post. I was unfamiliar with the protocol of the station, S-Sir!"

He nearly wanted to kick himself as he saw Jennings's eyes narrow at the slip-up. He'd almost forgotten to say "Sir." Rookie mistake. Proper language was a big deal in the military.

Jennings paced around both Zen and the table. Zen couldn't help but picture a big, predatory cat, slinking around the edges of the wood line as it circled its prey.

"You should be familiar with *every* protocol, Private Farraway. Am I correct?" Jennings quipped, relishing every word, knowing that punishment was near.

His impatience was showing.

Jennings loved punishment. Zen felt it gave him some sick, perverse pleasure to lord over people. It was as if he enjoyed the feeling of causing pain to those who he deemed less than himself.

*Fucking Upper Lifers,* Zen thought angrily. The emotion must've shown on his face for a split second, because Jennings jumped on the slip up faster than a mouse on cheese.

He slammed a fist onto the table and barked his next words at Zen, causing the soldier to nearly jump out of his skin.

"Isn't that RIGHT, Private Farraway??" His voice was harsh, and the outburst made tears prick at Zen's eyes.

*Fuck. Don't cry. Don't cry in front of the Sergeant.*

He swallowed hard and nodded, pushing the emotion down before speaking. "Yes, Sergeant Jennings, Sir." He felt like a beaten dog, tucking his tail between his legs and running to hide.

Jennings straightened up, his face settling back into stiff coolness. "Wonderful. Then you'll understand why I'm assigning you to the prison for several shifts. As punishment for your actions. Or inaction, I should say."

Zen's heart picked up in speed. He couldn't show his delight at the choice of punishment. Prison shifts were some of his favorites. They required little to no effort and absolutely *no* fighting.

But Jennings couldn't see his excitement, or he'd pick something much harsher. Zen set his face in mild frustration and saw Jennings take the bait.

A small smirk alighted on Jennings's lips, and he turned to the other metal chair, sitting himself in it and crossing a leg over the opposite thigh.

"At ease, Private."

Zen relaxed, rolling his shoulders back to relieve some of the stiffness that had crept into them and up his neck. He sat across the table from his superior and ran his tongue along his lips to combat the dryness.

This was it.

Jennings pulled a medieval-looking recording device from inside his jacket and pressed a button. A green light blinked into life on the side. Setting it on the table, he leaned back and fixed Zen with his customary piercing stare.

"This is Sergeant Jennings sitting in with Private Farraway as he reports on the 11/12/3150 Vesunian aircraft landing on First Earth in Sector 5 at 1500 hours." Jennings recited, "Private Farraway, what is your recollection of said event?"

Zen had rehearsed this repeatedly. He knew that if he misspoke and revealed he had tried to *help* the Vesunian, it could land him with treason charges and a first-class ticket to a jail cell.

Clearing his throat, Zen spoke, doing his best to make his voice firm and sure.

"The event in question was little to report, Sergeant."

Jennings blinked, the only sign of his shock.

Zen continued. "Camera T12 picked up the ship's arrival into our atmosphere, setting off our red alert alarms. I, panicking, did not disengage those alarms or send messages to my superior officers. Instead, I armed myself and went to investigate the crash site myself."

"Crash site?" Jennings raised an eyebrow. "So, is it true that the creature did not have control over his aircraft? Did you see what caused injury to the craft?"

Zen shook his head, then realized that the recording device would not pick that up.

"Um, no, Sir. All I saw was that the aircraft had sustained some sort of blow to the left side, and it had ignited the Nuva on which the craft ran. I'm assuming that's what caused the issue. And, uh… that's also how I knew it was a Vesunian craft."

Jennings nodded, waving a hand for him to continue.

Zen adjusted in his seat. He could feel sweat running down his back. He was unsure whether he should be grateful that he was no longer cold.

"I calculated the ship's crash-landing site and made my way to it. By the time I reached the craft, there was little left of it."

He paused. This was where it was absolutely critical that he sold his story. Zen tried to keep his cool demeanor as he continued.

"All that was left intact was the ship's cockpit. I could see that the craft had originally been a one-man fighter. Most likely used to subvert attention from itself while trying to gain access to our atmosphere. The cockpit was badly damaged and, upon inspection, open. When I removed the entrance window to the craft, I found the pilot deceased inside. A piece of shrapnel had impaled it, I'm assuming from the crash itself."

Jennings crossed his arms, displeased with this version of Zen's story. "The pilot was dead when you arrived?"

Zen tried not to let the nerves that were eating away at his stomach show on his face. "Yes, Sir."

"How did you know they had passed?"

Zen's brow furrowed, and it took him a second to respond to the sergeant's question. "L-like I said, it had impaled the creature through the middle. It was completely cut in half. By the time I arrived, it had succumbed to its injuries. I'm no medical professional, Sir, but I would imagine that would be an instant death."

The bodyguards shifted uncomfortably, and Zen realized that his tone had been combative. Swallowing back his fear, he tried to course correct.

"W-what I mean, Sir…"

Jennings waved him off, seemingly unbothered by Zen's tone. He blinked in surprise. Usually, that was something that Jennings would've never let slide.

There was a moment of silence, once again, as Zen waited for the sergeant to speak. Jennings finally sighed and ran a hand through his salt-and-pepper hair.

"Private Farraway, you did not speak to the Vesunian?"

Zen slowly shook his head. "No, Sir. I did not."

"And you didn't find any communications or anything of the sort on the ship?"

The question caught Zen off guard.

*What the hell did that mean?*

Jennings shot him a look as Zen paused, and he quickly shook his head.

"Again, Sir, no I did not. The cockpit was covered in bio-hazardous material. I'm sure if there was anything on the ship, the blood destroyed it, or the crash itself did the job."

Zen's curiosity was piqued. Something was bothering Jennings. This wasn't how the sergeant had imagined this going. He was looking for information.

Jennings stood without warning, his frustration apparent. Zen did as well, standing at attention. The sergeant couldn't hide his disappointment as he picked up the recording device and spoke into it.

"This is the end of our report." He clicked the button on the side once more and stuffed the device back into his jacket. He barely gave Zen more than a glance as he stepped away from the table.

"Thank you, Private Farraway. You are dismissed."

Zen relaxed his pose and quickly made his way past the sergeant, who seemed deep in thought. He pushed through the two hulking bodyguards who still stood at the doorway and frowned as they didn't even budge for him. As he left, he heard Jennings make a call.

All he caught before the door closed was something about "no new information." Zen watched the door for a moment before he backed up a few steps and turned on his heel. He hurried to the transport bus which, judging by the clock on the nearby wall, was getting ready to depart.

Deep in thought about the sergeant's strange behavior, he almost ran into a fully decked-out fighter who was sprinting down the hallway. Zen jumped to the side as the man stumbled to avoid him as well.

"Oh, god! Shit. I'm sorry." Zen babbled, offering a hand to him. The man grabbed it, and Zen pulled him up with a strained grunt. When the soldier spoke, he sounded flustered as well.

"You're good, man. I wasn't paying attention to where I was going." The soldier shot a harried look over his shoulder toward where he had been heading. He seemed to be in some sort of hurry. Zen glanced down to read his nameplate. It read, 'Sutar' in bulky, black lettering.

Zen smiled, trying to be friendly. "I wasn't either, Private Sutar."

The use of his name caused the soldier to whip his head back around. Sutar smiled in vague friendliness before speaking.

"It's all good. Listen, I'd love to stay and chat, but we've got some new prisoners to transport."

Zen's curiosity reared its head again. "New prisoners? We never get new ones here. Where from?"

Sutar attempted to hide his irritation, and Zen winced. His damn curiosity would be the death of him. Before he could regret it too long, Sutar sighed heavily and spoke, his hands on his hips.

"Um, we captured a ship, I guess? It was supposed to be some Ursonian trade ship, but they were secretly transporting Vesunian warriors into Second Earth."

*Oh shit.*

Zen nodded, smiling to hide his shock. "Right. Good luck."

He watched as Sutar sprinted away. No wonder the sergeant had been disappointed. A Vesunian crash landing *and* an attempted breach, all in one day? He was sure that Jennings was trying to put the pieces together. He had people to whom he reported as well.

Zen continued toward the transport bus, his head spinning.

These new prisoners.

He was sure they would be processed before his first punishment shift. He wondered if he'd be able to speak to them. Zen wanted answers as much as it seemed Jennings did. His curiosity at what this all meant burned through him, causing him to feel jittery and on edge.

*Probably wouldn't be allowed to see them,* Zen mused and sighed deeply at the admission. They would be high-class prisoners and likely wouldn't be mixed with the general prison populace.

He tried not to let the disappointment dissuade him from at least attempting to speak to them when he reported to the prison.

Zen clambered aboard the bus, and it started toward the living quarters with a rather pitiful groan and squeak.

Allowing his thoughts to drift, he considered the Vesunian pilot's last words. He wondered if it had anything to do with these new prisoners.

He did not know how the Vesunian prince could be in danger. There was little that human intelligence could gather on him. From what they knew, the Queen kept him under lock and key on their home planet of Vesun. He was sure they would risk nothing with their heir.

Especially considering how the war had started one hundred and fifty years ago.

Zen remembered learning about the war in primary school. It had all been rather confusing. He recalled his teacher attempting to paint humanity in a good light as they discussed it, but she had failed rather spectacularly. Her panic had been palpable as his entire class had questioned humanity's actions and had entertained a long discussion on who was right and who was wrong.

Now, as an adult, he understood her panic. If her class had come out of school as dissenters, questioning humanity's judgment and motives, she could've been punished for her teaching methods.

Poor Ms. Grebb.

Zen watched the desolate surroundings pass by through the grimy bus window as his thoughts ran through that forbidden discussion, the history unrolling like a scroll through his mind.

Humanity had fucked up. They had run out of energy sources. It had been easier to burn, burn, burn, and to put money into non-renewable energy rather than the time and research it would take to fix their planet.

It had been pure corporate greed.

Of course, no one wanted to talk about it because there was no solution. What were they supposed to do? Riot? Burn it all to the ground?

Humanity had lived in relative despair for a long time prior to their introduction to the Collective.

The Collective was a group of creatures from all corners of space. They operated under the ideas of peace and prosperity for all races. And, of course, at the head of the Collective were the Vesunians.

The Vesunians had offered a place to humanity in the Collective. It would have allowed the humans a chance to partake in Nuva. The mysterious, clean power source that granted the Vesunians so much authority and gave them the right to head this group of alien races.

It would have given humanity the power to fix their planet and themselves. But it required one thing that humankind just couldn't bear the thought of doing. It required them to subject themselves to the Collective and the Vesunians.

They would've been considered the Vesunians' citizens, just as every other race in the Collective was.

*It was pride*, Zen thought bitterly, *that had kept them from accepting the offer.*

And it was stupidity that killed the Vesunian princess and started this damn war.

As Zen stepped off the bus and headed toward his quarters, he struggled to put everything together.

A Vesunian prince somehow in danger.

An attempted breach.

A crash landing.

And a very stressed-out sergeant.

# Chapter 8
# Zen

The dawn of his first prison shift was smoggy. As Zen sat up in bed, he tried to remember why he even enjoyed prison shifts. This was supposed to be his day off, and he was spending it waking up miserably early.

Zen muddled out of his thin, military-grade sheets and tried not to wake his pod mate. Luckily, he seemed deep in dreamland, music buds in his ears, blissfully unconscious and unworried about any early mornings or crash landings.

Planting his bare feet on the cold, concrete floor, Zen made his way to their shared bathroom and attempted to get ready in the dark.

Zen made quick work of it. He could barely see his reflection in the mirror, but he was sure that bags hung heavily under his eyes. He smoothed his hair under a livery cap, hiding his inability to tame it.

Pulling on his ugly, one-size-too-big boots last, Zen made his way out of the pod, allowing the door to scan his hand before leaving.

The door blinked green, opening with a hiss. It must've been updated with his new orders, otherwise he wouldn't have been allowed out before morning call.

Blinking morosely in the harsh, white light of the hallway, Zen attempted to make his way out of living quarters with his eyes half open.

The usually bustling building was deathly silent. Zen's boots squeaked ominously against the flooring, echoing back to him in a way that sent a tingling chill down his spine.

He quickened his pace, trying not to freak himself out. Reaching the outer doors, he felt foolish that he had frightened himself over nothing. Scanning his hand once again, he pushed through the hissing doors and breathed in a deep lungful of the polluted air.

It may have been dirty, but at least it wasn't stale, like the air in his pod.

Rocking from toe to heel, Zen felt himself finally waking up as he waited for the bus to arrive. Looking around, he took in his desolate environment. There wasn't another soul in sight, which meant that he was the only one from his sector to take part in such activities, at least for today. Pale sunlight peeked from the horizon, bathing his surroundings in its meager warmth.

He briefly wondered which sector was staffing the prison today before his thoughts were interrupted by his growling stomach and he grimaced in discomfort.

*Damn it. I'm going to miss breakfast,* Zen complained, tilting his head back to stare at the ever-lightening sky.

He thought, clutching his abdomen, that he would have to sneak into the prison cafeteria to grab a morsel of *something* to survive the shift.

These thoughts carried him through till the bus arrived, and Zen spent most of the long ride contemplating his hunger, rather than worrying about what had happened only a few days prior.

However, it all came crashing back the moment that Zen stepped into the prison and the stale, recycled air blasted him, sending uncomfortable goosebumps down his arms. As security patted him down and waved him on, he felt an anxious squeezing begin in his chest.

*Was he really going to do this?*

Zen stepped past the scanners. The prison guards barely looked up or acknowledged him. Their eyes were heavy with the need to sleep, and Zen knew they had barely registered him as anything more than some scrawny non-fighter. One of them yawned, clutching a coffee cup to his chest like a prized jewel.

Not hearing any beeping, Zen continued further into the prison.

As he walked, the sounds of life made themselves known. Shouts, metal clanging, and shanty singing floated down toward him as he made his way to the assignment window.

There was no one else waiting for assignments, so he skipped past the marked waiting area and headed straight for the open window.

The soldier waiting for him was a familiar face. It was one that he had worked with both in training, and many times since then during volunteer prison shifts.

Her name plate read "Reeves" and she looked both incredibly bored and exhausted. She, too, nursed a cup of coffee and blinked hazily past Zen, watching a clock on the wall.

He cleared his throat and clasped his hands behind his back, rocking on his feet again. Reeves blinked in surprise, eyes refocusing as she attempted to dispel her exhaustion.

Registering who was standing in front of her, Reeves smiled widely and leaned forward. Her untamable curls bounced down from the slick bun she had tried to force them into.

"Farraway! God, it's been ages. How have you been?" Her tone was warm and congenial. "Are you here for a shift? Jesus, why'd you pick such an early one?"

Zen was used to the bombardment of questions. One thing he liked best about Reeves was that she seemed genuine, if talkative at times. He returned her smile before answering.

"Hasn't it? I haven't done a shift in, like, six months. And, uh, well, it's complicated on how I've been and why I'm here." Zen scratched the back of his head, chagrin entering his smile. "I'm actually here as punishment. So, I'm not doing too fucking hot honestly."

Reeves's eyebrows shot up. "You? In trouble? I can't even imagine what you'd do that would get you in hot water." She began thumbing delicately through the prison assignments. "Dare I ask?"

Zen sighed, relenting as she would most likely find out anyway. "Well, did you hear about that Vesunian crash landing a few days ago?"

Reeves's fingers slowed, and she looked up at him with a questioning gaze. "Uh, yeah. It's pretty much all that anyone will talk about. Other than the new prisoners, of course."

Zen could've sworn a blush appeared on her cheeks.

Attempting to ignore that, he continued. "I can imagine. Well, uh, yeah... I was on duty. When it happened."

He felt heat rise in his face as he recalled his failure. "I'm the one who caught the ship entering our atmosphere. I got so freaked, I forgot to disengage the alarms and send for Sergeant Jennings."

Reeves had given up on finding an assignment for him at this point, and Zen was pretty sure her jaw could drop no further. When she spoke, awe resonated in her tone.

"No fucking way. You *saw* the Vesunian?!" Realizing her excitement was punishable, she lowered her voice before continuing.

"There are *so* many rumors. Did it attack you?! Did it give you information about the prisoners?! I mean..."

Reeves attempted to reign herself in, cheeks definitely flushed now. Her face was now also bathed in sympathy.

"*God,* Farraway. Are you okay?"

Zen wasn't sure how to handle her excitement. It had been an incredibly traumatic event, at the time. He hadn't realized that it would cause such a stir in soldier gossip. But he supposed, humorously, it made sense. Zen stuffed his hands into his pockets and shrugged.

"As okay as I can be, I guess. I mean, I'm here, right?"

Biting his lip, he chose his next words carefully.

"Honestly, I don't know how much I can talk about it. I had to give a report to Jennings afterward, and he seemed pretty stressed about it. But really, other than the crash, it wasn't anything to write home about. The enemy was dead by the time I got to it."

Disappointment flooded Reeves's expression, and Zen felt bad lying to her. But, he reasoned with himself, as much as he liked her, he also knew he couldn't trust her with the truth. No one could be trusted that much.

"Damn." Blowing a stray curl from her face, she returned to the assignments. "Well, I'm just glad you're alright."

Zen nodded, heart pounding as he braced himself to ask his next question. "Thanks. So, uh, new prisoners?"

He tried to sound nonchalant but knew that he failed when his voice squeaked with his next question. "What's up with that?"

Mischief twinkled in Reeves' eyes, but she didn't look up from what she was doing. "I'm surprised you haven't heard about it. Some Ursonian trade ship was attempting to smuggle a specialized convoy of Vesunian warriors into Second Earth. It was a ship headed straight for Trinity Market."

Zen let loose a shocked exhale. "That's Upper Circle. Like, top of the crop. The fucking big boys. Shit."

Reeves nodded solemnly. "Yup. Upper Lifers. That's exactly where they were headed. People are taking bets whether they were coming to kill President Afton or someone else on the Council, like Boggs."

Zen's mind was whirling with the new information. "Either of those would've been a massive deal." He shook his head, attempting to clear it. "Have they gotten any information from these guys? Do we know who they are?"

Reeves sighed and shook her head as well. "No, they won't talk. Either orally or mentally. They've taken this stupid martyr vow of silence or something."

She rolled her eyes before scoffing. "You ever think these guys are just faking their spirituality just to make us feel shittier about the war?"

Zen snorted slightly at the unexpected joke and covered his nose and mouth. Thankfully, Reeves didn't seem to notice. He felt relief relax his shoulders, and he shrugged before responding.

"Maybe. I don't know." He scratched the back of his head, cheeks still red, and contemplated his next words. "Anything in the assignments working with them? I'm sure no one wants to handle the high security prisoners."

He must not have sounded as casual as he hoped because Reeves's brows knitted in suspicious confusion.

Zen hoped he hadn't shot himself in the foot as she looked at him for what felt like ages before glancing back down at the assignments.

"That's a long shot, Farraway. You know that we never have…"

Her voice trailed off as she got to the very last one. She was quiet for several seconds, reading the paper, before she spoke once again. "Funny enough, we have something. One of the captured Vesunians is refusing to eat. We need someone to handle bringing the food and convincing him to eat before he starves himself. Sound like something you'd want to do?"

Zen's heart pounded so hard that he could barely hear her over the drumming in his ears.

*Here goes nothing.*

Forcing his voice into an even more casual tone, he nodded and spoke. "Yeah, I can do that."

Taking the assignment and bidding Reeves farewell, Zen headed toward the high security section of the prison.

On the way, he picked up an issue-status meal from the cafeteria and scuttled away, trying not to smell the food. His stomach snarled, furious that he hadn't eaten yet.

Zen attempted to ignore the pressure that had built up in his chest again. He hadn't thought he'd make it this far. But here he was, closer to answers.

Hopefully.

He slipped the assignment paper into a slot near the high security doors and after a lot of painful-sounding whirring, they opened for him.

The high-security guards were more alert than their casual, general populace, counterparts. They were also armed more heavily. They eyed Zen with initial wariness, losing interest when they registered the meal tray that he carried.

Swallowing hard, he approached one of them.

"I'm looking for the prisoner who won't eat."

The guard looked him up and down, taking several seconds before responding. His voice sounded annoyed but humorous.

"Yeah, the anorexic. He's in cell 002." Catching Zen's anxiety, he lifted his blaster. "He's locked up and can't hurt you, but I can accompany you for peace of mind."

Zen shook his head vigorously, then slowed the shaking, realizing that he didn't want to seem too eager to be alone with the creature.

He spoke quickly, playing damage control. "The fucker won't eat if there are weapons around. And we need him alive for information."

Satisfied with Zen's answer, the guard stepped away from him. "Just be careful, man. Don't get too close to the bars. Wouldn't want to have to clean you up off the floor."

The guard watched carefully as Zen nodded before looking away and dropping his blaster to his side.

Zen motored from the entrance and started toward the eerily quiet cells. The silence was so intense, he was sure that everyone within a mile radius could hear how wildly his heart was beating.

He peered inside curiously, goosebumps dancing up his arms at the sight in each one. His breath caught and his eyes widened as he took in the intimidating sight of the enemy.

Each cell he passed contained a hulking and silent Vesunian, their eyes glittering maliciously at him from the shadows of their prisons.

Zen tried not to stare. This was the largest number of living Vesunians he had ever seen in person.

The pilot had been gruesome and dismembered, so he hadn't been able to take in its appearance. He'd been too preoccupied with not throwing up.

But it was shocking for Zen to realize that Vesunians seemed rather, well, human.

Their bodies were built similarly, just much larger and much more muscular. Each one had to be at least seven feet tall. Their skin was a glistening, shimmery, pale white that had a curious lavender sheen to it. The color, surprisingly, didn't take away from their threatening size.

Zen knew from his experience with the pilot that they had only four fingers on each hand, but those hands were still very human. It was disorienting how similar the two races looked.

However, the most chilling aspect of their features, as Zen had seen previously, were their eyes. Those were most assuredly *not* human. They were completely black, pupil-less, and insect-like. Their eyes also shimmered with a strange, disquieting light.

And finally, small black horns curled down the sides of their heads, sprouting from hair that was various colors and textures, unique to each being.

Trying to fight the shiver that forced its way up his spine, Zen hurried past the unnecessary cells. Scanning the tops of each of them, he looked for the correct number, mouthing each one as he passed.

"004, 003,," Zen's breath caught as he stopped in front of the correct cell and scanned the suffocating darkness for the prisoner he was supposed to be feeding.

The Vesunian in this cell did not differ much from the ones he had passed. The only noticeable difference being that he was perhaps just a bit younger.

This alien was just as large and muscular as his comrades; and just as silent.

His black hair hung in long curls down to his chin and was tangled from being unable to care for it. His horns jutted out from his head and curled down near his chiseled jaw.

He wore the typical prison garb that every other prisoner wore, but it seemed small on his enormous frame, stretching and straining at the alien's chest and midriff. His head was lowered, as if in prayer, and his disturbing eyes were closed.

Zen realized, with a weird jolt in his stomach, that he knew why Reeves had blushed earlier when mentioning the prisoners.

The Vesunian was, unfortunately, attractive.

*Gross.*

Zen chastised himself, hating that he even had to admit it.

It wasn't that alien-human relationships didn't happen, because they most certainly did. It was just frowned upon in "good society."

No one would dare enter a relationship with a Vesunian.

For obvious reasons.

Shaking his head at how Reeves had reacted and ignoring the blush on his own cheeks, he approached the bars. He wondered whether the Vesunian knew he was there when a sudden movement made Zen nearly pass out.

The alien snapped his head up, his eyes shimmering, and his teeth bared.

Zen clattered the food tray against the bars and jumped backward at the sound it made, heart pounding in terror.

It took only a second for him to realize that he had scared *himself* and he frowned, angry with his stupidity. His cheeks felt even warmer than before.

*Way to look intimidating, Zen. Scaring yourself shitless.*

Sensing the alien's eyes on him, Zen reluctantly met his gaze and attempted to infuse his voice with strength and confidence.

"G-guess I'm a little jumpy." He cursed his nervous stutter and walked forward again, even though his feet did not want to move. Zen made sure that his next words were clearer as he gestured to the meal he was holding. "I've brought you food."

He knelt down and slid the tray halfway through the tray slot at the bottom. "Heard that you haven't eaten a crumb since you, uh… got here."

*Or since we captured you.* Zen corrected himself.

The Vesunian blinked slowly at him before turning his head to the left, ignoring the existence of the food tray. He didn't speak, and Zen heard nothing in his mind.

Expecting this, he sat, crossing his legs over each other. Trying to infuse his voice with warmth, he clasped his hands together and tilted his head.

"I'm here to convince you to eat."

The alien didn't move.

Breathing out nervously, Zen braced himself before speaking once again, this time in a whisper. He couldn't pretend that food was the only reason he was here any longer. "I, I have some questions."

Nothing. Not even a blink.

He wet his lips before continuing. *God, it was hot in here.* "It's about your prince. I, I think he's in danger."

He didn't think a creature could grow more still than the Vesunian already was, but it happened. Zen took his sudden tenseness as a sign that he was listening. At least, he hoped that was the case.

He scooted closer to the bars, the soldier's warning ringing ominously in his ears.

"So, you know what I'm talking about. I intercepted a message to someone here on First Earth. It said that your prince was in danger. I need to know what that means."

The Vesunian quickly turned to face Zen, startling him once more. He flinched away from the bars and from the alien's intense gaze. The creature still said nothing but also tilted his head, as if showing that he was listening.

Okay, progress.

Heart pounding into his throat, Zen tried not to let the intense stare cow him from continuing to speak. He leaned his head to the left, cracking his neck to relieve the tension that had stiffened his shoulders.

He was going to have a hell of a headache later.

As he continued, he hoped his whisper wasn't carrying to any of the nearby guards.

"I don't know if you heard about the crash landing here on First Earth. But one of your kind was bringing some kind of message to someone here, and I have no idea who it was." Zen paused, trembling.

"But they were shot down before they could deliver the message and gave it to me instead. Why? I have no fucking idea." Zen laughed at the absurdity of his situation. "I'm a human. I'm the enemy. So, it made no sense. But they did it anyway. It was like, the last thing they did, and it was horrible."

He took a deep breath, trying to control the babble that was spewing from his lips. He felt stupid looking for answers here, but he didn't know where else to go. Zen dropped his head momentarily before whispering pleadingly.

"I need to know if you know *anything* about this message. Please."

There was a long moment of silence where the Vesunian just stared at Zen, his brow creased. Zen had almost given up hope he would speak when a voice feathered into his mind.

Zen shivered at the intrusion. It was still a feeling he was getting used to, being that this was only the second time a Vesunian had mind-spoken to him.

This voice differed from the pilot's gasping, last words. It was warm and comforting, like wrapping his brain in a tender embrace.

*I know something about the message.*

Zen blinked in surprise. He hadn't expected an answer. It seemed too easy. "You do? What?"

The Vesunian's gaze took on an expression of pain and solemnity. His head bowed, hair falling forward and shadowing his handsome face.

*She was part of my convoy. She was not delivering a message to Earth, but to Vesun. She must have been found and shot down while passing through Earth space territory.*

It took a second for Zen to grasp what was being said. His hands grew clammy, and he tried to wipe them on his pants as his breathing quickened. The Vesunian watched him with concerned curiosity.

"Does that… that means…" Zen steadied himself with a deep breath before continuing, "the Vesunian prince was part of your convoy too? He's here in the prison?"

He could've sworn that the alien seemed to chuckle, his solemnity broken for a swift second before it returned to his face.

***No. The prince would never leave Vesun. They sent my battalion to eliminate a perceived threat to the prince on Mars. We failed, and in the struggle of being captured, one of our kind tried to fly back home to let them know of our failure, and that the prince was still in danger.***

Oddly, that seemed to settle Zen's nerves, and he nodded in understanding.

"Got it. Wait …"

Something still felt weird about this entire situation.

Zen felt his mouth set in a suspicious grimace. "Why are you telling me any of this? I'm… I mean I'm human. I'm a soldier. How do you know I'm not going to just tell my commanding officer everything?"

The Vesunian leaned back, sighing heavily and deeply. Zen couldn't help the intimidation that crept into him at how very large the alien was. He fought back the instinct to tumble backward and put some distance between them.

The creature seemed to consider Zen's question for a few seconds before that voice once again brushed into Zen's consciousness.

***Nothing I'm telling you is of any importance. Additionally, I have a feeling that no one knows anything about this message. After all, you're the one who sought me out and are refusing to raise your voice above a whisper.***

A flush crept into Zen's neck, making his face feel hot. It seemed so obvious that he felt like smacking himself.

Of course, he seemed shady. Now, the Vesunian probably thought he had himself some kind of ally among the human soldiers.

The thought caused a small twinge of excitement to flutter into Zen's stomach, and he bit his lip. I mean, did he? Was this what all the sneaking around meant?

Was he a traitor?

The clatter of the food tray interrupted Zen's thoughts, and he startled, jumping back. Focusing in the darkness, it shocked Zen to see the Vesunian pushing the food tray back through the slot at the bottom.

"Hey, no. Come on. I thought we were getting somewhere." Zen complained. "You've got to eat something. Otherwise, you're just going to wither away and die in some lame-ass human prison."

Deep laughter echoed in Zen's mind, and it tugged at the corners of his mouth. At least, someone thought he was funny.

The Vesunian pushed the tray further toward Zen, amusement dancing in his eyes. Zen wasn't sure how that was possible. He'd always thought that such dark, terrifying eyes could be nothing more than that.

*I'll eat if you will. Your stomach sounds are distracting.*

Zen's jaw dropped. "You can hear that?"

The alien tilted his head, showing off his rather large, pointed ears.

*I can hear many things. Your stomach being one of them.*

Zen considered the tray of food before glancing up at the alien, surprised at the camaraderie that seemed to be growing between them.

He nodded before grabbing the mealy piece of fruit off the tray and shoving the rest back through the slot.

He watched as the Vesunian ate delicately, picking apart the meal with a grace that belied his size. Zen, himself, could only eat about half of the piece of fruit before giving up. It tasted like it had been sitting for days, which it most likely had.

Once they had both finished their portions, Zen stood, grabbing the empty tray.

"Hey, listen, I've gotta go. My shift isn't over, and I've got other things that probably need to get done."

He rocked from foot to foot as he spoke, feeling oddly at ease talking to the Vesunian. The alien nodded his head minutely, acknowledging his attempt to leave.

Zen swallowed dryly. This couldn't be the end. The answer was too simple. He wanted to know more. He wanted to spend more time here.

"B-but I'll be back. I have more shifts in the prison over the next few weeks. So, uh, I can bring you your meals. I-if you'd like."

His ears felt hot as he sensed amusement radiating from the alien once again. *Was he being awkward?* He did not know what was customary for their kind.

The response gently swept into his mind, making Zen smile, despite himself.

*Of course.* The alien's eyes flickered to his nameplate. *Farraway.*

Zen winced, as he always did when someone called him by his last name. Of course, it couldn't be helped in the military. But he could prevent it here.

"Actually, that's my last name. I prefer to go by my first name, which is Zen."

The Vesunian's black eyes bore into his own and the intensity made Zen wriggle uncomfortably. Finally, the creature nodded once more, curiosity sparking in his eyes.

*Apologies. Thank you, Zen.*

Zen nodded, experiencing both an itch to leave, along with a burning desire to stay. His cheeks still felt warm. "Y-yeah. No problem. Uh, what's, what's your name?"

Distrust arose in the Vesunian's eyes, and his chin dropped as he looked away and down toward the dusty, concrete floor. Zen's stomach clenched as he was reminded of the power dynamic here.

He was technically the captor, the enemy. He held a lot of power to do great harm, and trust wouldn't come so easily. Zen was embarrassed that he'd forgotten simply because of one friendly interaction.

Backing away, he threw a casual hand up. "Hey, I get it. You don't have to tell me. I understand. This isn't exactly an ideal… situation for, for you. I'll see you around."

He turned around, clutching the tray to his chest and took a few steps down the hallway.

"It's Varys."

A deep, warm voice drifted toward Zen from the cell. An actual voice, not one that he could only hear within his mind.

Shock rolled through him, gluing him to the spot for several seconds before he could think to move forward.

"Thank you, Varys," Zen whispered softly before quickly motoring to the exit, his head spinning.

# Chapter 9
## Altair

Silas's figure darted and weaved expertly through the crowd outside of the tent they had exited.

Altair struggled to keep the pace that both he and Lil set. It was difficult to not just let himself be dragged, face down, as she pushed forward with determination. Her eyes were laser-focused on Silas's oddly graceful figure, and he would occasionally cast a friendly glance over his shoulder, as if verifying she hadn't gotten lost.

Altair reasoned it would likely be difficult to find each other in such a crowded place, especially without the use of hearing. Even with Lilith's specialized abilities.

His wrists felt raw and chafed, and he grimaced every time the shackles rubbed against his skin. Altair, disheartened that he had not had a chance to escape, threw "help me" glances at nearly every face that seemed sympathetic.

However, not one creature even batted an eye at the fact that he was cuffed, seemingly against his will. He should've expected as much from a place like Kelptor.

He lamented that he hadn't just attempted to escape on the ship earlier that day. The regret burned through him, making his steps feel even heavier.

The heat here was nearly as unbearable as the heat during his exile, and the reminder of his time spent imprisoned soured Altair's mood.

He wanted nothing more than to escape it all by diving into a cool body of water. The thought of his body gliding easily through a lake or river made him shiver in desire.

Silas side-stepped a vendor, who was dragging their ungainly cart full of odd, foul-smelling fruit, and clopped his way into a tiny hut that was incredibly easy to miss. Lil followed him, pulling Altair through another fabric-draped entryway.

He glanced around the home, curious about how the hoofed alien lived. The hut was small, but quaint and homey. It was clearly well-loved and, most notably, glittered with trinkets.

Trinkets.

Gods, trinkets.

They hung from *everywhere* and lined every shelf. Glittering, dull, rusty, new, worn, fresh. Practically anything you could think of could most likely be found in this tiny hut, on a gods-forsaken planet, in this terrible galaxy. Altair stared in wonder for several minutes, completely in awe of the sheer magnitude of *things.*

When he could finally pull his gaze from Silas's home, it fell onto Lil, who was watching him with a smirk playing on her lips.

"Silas likes to collect." Her voice rang with affectionate humor.

Altair raised an eyebrow and snorted softly in derision.

*Obviously.*

Her gaze left him and fixated on the back, where Silas was clattering around. She adjusted her foot and watched it, her brow creased in focus.

*Right.* Altair was again reminded of her talents.

Lil looked up right before Silas stepped out from behind a mountain of treasures. He clutched several tools and what looked like a worn and rusted piece of equipment.

Altair was never the handy type, so he couldn't immediately recognize what Silas held. Surprise rolled through him when he recognized it was some kind of weapon. It was rather big, and the barrel seemed busted and empty, but it glowed faintly with a lovely bluish-purple light.

The barrel used to carry something.

Altair's stomach dropped.

*Nuva.*

The power source that had started it all.

He remembered the first time he had seen Nuva in person. It had nearly blinded him when the first convoy of Vesunians spoke to his father about the war. The engines of their ships had shone brilliantly, like stars decorating the undersides of their transport, as they had silently landed on the Serinian landing pads. The power that the Vesunians held had filled Altair with wonder.

Beautiful, clean energy. Unlimited power.

Something that most races could only dream about.

He had been so confused, and even a little angry when his father had refused to enter the Collective.

All they would've had to do was submit to the Vesunian royalty. Altair remembered how willing he was to give up the title of prince. He had been content with the idea of the Vesunian prince being the only one among them.

But the memory of his father's stiff lip and terse shake of the head still triggered jarring shock, even to this day.

Imagine what they could've done with Nuva! Their people wouldn't have to migrate back to the water when the days of light ended. Nuva could have kept them warm enough to stay on land for the entire planet's circulation. Perhaps they could have even reunited their people and brought the free folk in with the allure of Nuva.

It was only days later that they discovered that the free people had accepted the Collective's offer, which had upset Altair even more.

Now, as an adult, he understood his father's wisdom in refusing. The king, though brash and angry, understood that this war was not theirs to fight. His people had seen too much bloodshed in the past one hundred years, and they had finally found peace.

It was a tense and bitter peace, but still, it was peace.

Perhaps if the Collective had offered a spot sooner, before the war. Or if they offered one after.

*If this war ever ends,* Altair lamented.

He watched as Silas stepped delicately over a pile of trinkets and placed the damaged weapon on what looked like a crafting table. Various half-finished projects and glittering tools spilled across its surface and from nearly every crevice.

It was a wonder that Silas could find anything in here.

Lil stepped up to the table as well, hands resting on her hips. Her brow was scrunched in concern. She pressed her lips together, as if about to speak.

Reading her mind in that way that only close friends could, Silas spoke, his gaze never leaving the weapon. "Yes, I know it's damaged, Lil. But it's probably the only one I could affix with the parts that you need to destroy the vemen asteroids."

He glanced over at her, and she flapped her hands in that strange language that only they seemed to understand. Silas sighed heavily and nodded.

"It's going to take a while to get those parts. I'm a good smuggler, but the Vesunians keep that shit under lock and key. It's part of their… religion or whatever."

Curiosity sprouted up inside Altair. He knew that the Vesunians carefully guarded their sacred power source, but he hadn't realized it was *actually* sacred to them. He thought people just used those terms in exaggerated irritation.

He wished, morosely, that he'd paid better attention to his studies as a child.

Lil nodded, exasperated, as if she was already aware of this. She flapped her hands again, and Silas turned to her, raising an eyebrow. His irritation seeped toward Altair, and he could've sworn that Lil backed up slightly.

He smirked, pleased at the rare sight of the bounty hunter being nervous around someone, even if it wasn't him.

Silas's nostrils flared as he spoke. "Lilith. I'm trying my best. But no amount of money is going to make this go any faster. You're asking me to get a hold of *Nuva*," he growled, "along with expecting me to find other parts of this blaster and repairing it at the same time. So, if you're in any rush, I'd suggest you find someone else to do this."

Lil's head bowed, and Altair watched in wonder as she seemed to admit defeat and raised her hands placatingly. He'd never seen Lil submit to anyone, not, at least, in the little time he'd known her. He could see that her eyes still burned with frustration, but she didn't push the issue.

He was impressed. And starting to like Silas.

Silas spoke again, turning back to the blaster on the table. "I would suggest finding somewhere to stay here with your... job."

His eyes flitted back toward where Altair was still standing, and he realized that he probably had admiration shining in his eyes. Altair dropped his gaze, his cheeks warming.

Silas's tone seemed to indicate that the conversation was over as he reached into a drawer on the table and pulled out an old-fashioned piece of leathery-looking paper and an ink pen. He began jotting down a list of strange characters, and only took a brief break to pull out an odd, rolled-up purple plant. He lit it and stuck it between his lips before continuing.

Altair was too mesmerized by what Silas was doing to notice that Lil had moved closer to him. He was startled when he looked over and saw her staring daggers at the side of his face. She grabbed the cuffs and made sure that the piece of silver-looking rope was tightly bound to them by tugging lightly.

"Come on."

She nodded curtly and started toward the exit, pulling on the rope with more vigor. Altair followed, again failing to keep pace with the human woman. They reentered the fray of people outside, which had somehow gotten even more crowded, even as the sky darkened and the air cooled around the multitude.

Altair followed Lil as closely as he could, not wanting to earn an impatient tug at the rope. She wove through the crowd and, even as Altair's lungs begged for relief, refused to slow her pace.

Finally, she pushed out of the mass and flattened herself against the wall of what looked like a crumbling tavern. Lil inched her way along the stone wall before slipping through the open doorway with Altair close at her heels.

The building was warm and full of life. Raucous laughter echoed around the small space as patrons huddled around rickety, wooden tables. A glistening bar, which looked to be the newest thing here, was squashed up against the far wall as the bartender, a short, plump human woman, slid gracefully from one tap to the next.

Her hands seemed to blur as she served the rowdy guests who crowded her bar, and it looked as though she barely glanced at each drink that she made. She laughed just as riotously with her guests, and her animated gestures made Altair's heart cheer slightly.

Warmth spilled from her and seemed to infect the entire space.

It surprised Altair how many creatures he seemed to enjoy on this planet. The last time he had been here, his father had been so strict. He hadn't been allowed to see the sights or meet any of the locals. In fact, he hadn't wanted to, fearful of everything around him. Sadly, that had included himself.

Altair shook off the memory, desperate to avoid the anger boiling in his stomach at the thought of his father. He'd had enough reminiscing to last a lifetime in the past couple of days.

Lil stepped up to the counter, smiling and waving the woman down. The bartender caught Lil's gesture and sidled her way over, sliding three drinks to patrons on her way.

Wiping her hands on a suspiciously dirty cloth, the woman raised her eyebrows and put on a careful smile.

She was cautious. It made sense considering what they probably looked like. An armored, scarred woman dragging an imprisoned Serinian around in cuffs surely had to look intimidating.

"How can I help ye?" The woman's voice was naturally loud and rich, perfect for such a space.

Altair watched as Lil's eyes darted to the woman's mouth, trying her best to read her lips. But the woman's accent seemed to confuse her.

"This is an inn?" Lil questioned, and the woman's eyes flashed with surprise at her odd intonation. She must have been used to strange creatures and languages, however, because she quickly recovered.

"Yeh. Bu' with Svaldu goin' on, I dunno if I have room…"

Her voice faltered upon realizing that Lil's ear was destroyed and understanding lit within her gaze. Her voice immediately took on a slow and enunciated tone.

"I have one bed. Bed-uh. One." She held up one finger as if to help Lil understand.

Altair felt cool anger radiate from Lilith, and he shrank back, hoping not to be in her line of fire.

*What was this woman thinking, treating Lil like she was stupid? Did she not see the vast array of weapons on her belt?*

Altair shook his head, baffled. He watched as Lilith reined herself in.

Stifling her anger, Lil sucked in a large, irritated breath through her nose and exhaled loudly. "That's fine. I need it indefinitely. How much per night?"

The two women haggled briefly before settling on a price that seemed to make them both happy. Lil followed the bartender up the creaky wooden steps of the inn with Altair trailing after them both.

He mourned that he would likely not be comfortable for a while. Lilith would probably take the bed, which meant he would be sleeping on the ground. Altair would even prefer his cot on the ship.

But much to his despair, the ship was parked and locked in an airfield, unable to be accessed until they left Kelptor.

The woman handed Lil a small key and opened an old wooden door with a matching key that hung on a string around her neck. Altair's nose scrunched at the sight of the room.

The space felt ancient and smelled as though it hadn't been cleaned since several tenants ago. A small, rusty bed sat in the middle of the room with holey blankets folded up haphazardly on top. One sad, flat pillow lay at the head. The only other piece of furniture the room sported was a small wooden chest, presumably for any belongings that the guests may have. The room was dark and damp, completely in opposition to the glowing bar downstairs.

Altair was not the only one disappointed by their living quarters, as Lil visibly winced at the sight. She turned to say something to the bartender, but the woman was already gone. Sighing, Lil led him inside before locking the door behind them both.

She untied the rope from his cuffs before sitting down on the bed and removing her large boots. Lilith kept her weapons belt on, however, as she slid the boots over and stretched back onto the bed, sideways.

A few moments passed as Altair stood next to the bed uncomfortably.

*What should he do*? The cuffs were still chafing his wrists. Was he going to wear them *and* the silencer until they could get back to the ship and leave?

The thought made his stomach sink, and he sighed heavily through his nose.

Lil turned to look at him, alerted by his small movement in her periphery. Her eyes were unreadable again, and she seemed to weigh her words before speaking.

"I'm sorry about this. I was hoping this stop wouldn't be too large of a delay." Her tone was genuine, and her gaze darted to the silencer that held his mouth closed. "I know it's uncomfortable, but I ask that you keep it on."

Altair's mind flashed back to the memory of the Serinian woman being auctioned off, her infected wounds dripping around the silencer. He doubted Lil would let it get to that point, but then again, he didn't know her.

She still hadn't told him where she was taking him or to whom.

He could only shrug in response to her words, which seemed to draw a hint of amusement from her.

"I suppose you don't have a choice, do you?"

She laughed, but it didn't sound as though she found humor in the idea.

He shrugged again, his cheeks even warmer from her laughter.

She slipped off the bed and walked over to him, not even making a sound on the creaky floor. Altair couldn't help the wave of admiration that swept through him.

He could tell why she had been hired for such a job. She must have trained forever to become a bounty hunter, let alone one who was deaf.

Her hands grabbed at his wrists and undid the cuffs in a swift motion. He blinked in surprise as she turned and threw them against the boots before looking back at him. Lil took in his surprise with an expression verging on offense.

"Don't look at me like that. I'm not a fucking monster."

She walked over to her bag and pulled out a pad of paper and an ink pen. It looked similar to the materials that Silas had been using, and Altair wondered briefly whether she had snatched them from his house.

Walking back, she handed the things to him. "All I ask is that you don't stab me with the pen. It won't work, but it'd be annoying to have to take this away from you and go back to talking to you through nods and shrugs."

Altair nodded before quickly scribbling on the pad and holding it up for her to read. Her eyes narrowed as she concentrated on his illegible scrawl.

**Will I have to wear the silencer the whole time? I need to eat.**

His stomach growled as if emphasizing his point.

She nodded and sighed. "As much as possible, yes. You already know that your powers won't work on me, so any time you take the silencer off, it will be brief and supervised in this locked room." She frowned, her eyes flashing dangerously before she continued. "You try anything, and I'll knock you out so fast, your brain will try to catch up to your head."

He knew that threat was completely legitimate, and Altair's stomach flip-flopped at the idea.

She exhaled and put her hands on her hips once again. "I'll also make sure you get some food, soon. You're not the only hungry one here. Trust me."

Nodding, he scribbled something else down. He couldn't help but ask the question and only hoped she would understand that it was simply curiosity.

It was becoming difficult to write because of the ordeal his wrists had been through, and he had to take a couple of breaks. Lilith watched him, her eyes glinting. Finally, he held up the notepad, his hands trembling from the effort.

**What were you and Silas doing with your hands?**

Lil seemed somewhat stunned by the question, and she took a few moments to respond.

"It's sign language. Because I'm deaf, it's the easiest way for me to communicate with people." Seeing his confusion, she tried to explain further. "Just like how my native spoken language is English, and yours is Serinian, sign language is a whole and complete language for those who can't hear."

The pieces slid into place, and Altair nodded vigorously. He was grateful that she hadn't taken his question as nosy or interrogative. The idea that someone could communicate without speech was fascinating.

Such a language could be incredibly useful to him, given his circumstances.

There was a long pause as Altair digested everything. Lil had even turned away before Altair scribbled down something else and shoved the pad toward her. She frowned, grabbing it and peering down to read his last question.

Lil was stunned once more as she held the pad and read what he had written. Her fingers brushed against the paper, as if petting the hastily written request.

**Teach me.**

# Chapter 10
## Zen

Zen was excited to see Varys again. Which was incredibly stupid considering that he was the enemy.

The captive enemy.

The over 7' tall enemy.

The so-incredibly-buff-he-could-pop-my-head-like-a-melon-simply-by-flexing enemy.

*Shit, why was he thinking about Varys's muscles?*

Zen shook his head as if to reset it like an Etch-a-Sketch. It excited him to talk to Varys again and possibly get more information. That was all there was to it. Zen was a glutton for knowledge, and *absolutely nothing else.*

The bus shuddered to a stop in front of the prison, and Zen jumped from his seat as though something had electrocuted him. He felt strange and tingly and refused to let his mind wander back to where it had just gone. His cheeks were warm as he stepped off the bus and into the cool air of the morning.

Before Zen had left last time, he'd let the guards know that he'd gotten Varys to eat. They had been stunned and congratulated him with confused, yet pleased, expressions. He'd stopped off at the assignments desk and let Reeves know as well. He also gave her Varys's request that his meals be brought by Zen from now on.

Reeves had seemed just as shocked but had put in the request before he'd left for the day.

He'd received the approval a few days prior.

Zen meandered back into the stale air of the prison and didn't even make eye contact with the guards as he waltzed through security. Fake bravado could take you a long way in the military, and Zen was determined to draw as little suspicion as possible.

He stepped up to the assignments window where an unfamiliar face greeted him. Initially, seeing someone new didn't faze him. Reeves wouldn't work every morning shift in the prison, as much as he would have wanted.

Unfortunately, his contentment did not last. The man sitting in the window slid his eyes up and down Zen in a manner that made him want to crawl out of his skin. The soldier's face split into a grotesque leer.

"Name?" His voice was honey-ice, sickly sweet, and chilling.

Zen swallowed against the bile rising in his throat. He didn't want to say it.

"F-farraway."

His voice cracked and he saw the man's eyes glitter in a predatory way. It made him want to shrivel up in his boots and die.

"Farraway…" the soldier mused, lavishing the name against his tongue as he turned his attention back toward the assignments.

Zen was, unfortunately, no stranger to this sort of behavior. As advanced as humanity was, sexual assault and harassment were still far too common, particularly in the military.

And although he was a man, Zen was the victim of many unwanted advances. Several had been so-called "initiatory" processes during training that he had avoided with Kai's help. Up until now, he had been lucky enough to escape physically unharmed each time, but he knew that if it came down to it, he could fight no one off.

The thought made his stomach turn unpleasantly and his breakfast fought to leave his mouth.

*Why did his reaction to unpleasant things have to be throwing up? Fuck!*

Fighting the urge to vomit, Zen turned his attention back to the assignments window. The soldier seemed to have found his name and was slipping the assignment papers across the counter, his dirty nails scratching against the material. Zen shivered at the sound.

"Here you go, Farraway. Your first assignment is breakfast for one of our high-security fellas." He leered.

Zen nodded, grabbing for the papers. His heart thudded, and he felt light-headed from the emotions that were also making his chest constrict so painfully. All he wanted was to be somewhere where this soldier's lustful gaze wouldn't find him.

Before a thank you could leave his lips and he could escape the situation with his assignment, the soldier snatched his hand and pulled him closer, running his thumb over Zen's knuckles. His skin felt cracked and dry against Zen's own.

The hold wasn't strong, but it shocked him into stillness. The soldier wet his chapped lips before speaking.

"How tall are you, Zen Farraway?"

His voice was practically a purr and his name felt like a dirty word coming from the man's mouth. The room felt like it was closing in, and Zen could tell a panic attack was on the horizon. He heard a ringing begin in his ears.

*Not the time or place. Just breathe Zen, breathe, in and out.*

His voice was barely a whisper when he spoke. "I, I don't..."

Zen couldn't even finish. It felt like someone had sucked all the moisture from his mouth.

He felt like such a fucking coward. He couldn't even pull his hand away.

The soldier leaned forward, and Zen instinctively flinched back. This didn't seem to deter the man, however, as he spoke again, relishing in Zen's fear. His yellowed teeth were bared in a lusty smile.

"You don't seem taller than 5'4" at most. Pretty small for a soldier, and for a boy."

He smirked. and Zen finally had the sense to tug his hand away.

He hated it when people mentioned his size. It wasn't necessarily because he was insecure about it, but because people always mentioned it in situations like these, when he was being bullied. Memories of taunting boys' voices swirled in his memory. Strong arms were shoving him down and calling him weak. He felt a brief surge of heat rush through his limbs.

Zen straightened his posture and backed away from the window, tilting his chin up and willing a steely look in his eye.

"*Never* do that again o-or..." He faltered once more at the look of amusement on the soldier's face.

His bravado did not faze the man. Zen could tell that he saw right through it, and fear once again slithered through him.

"Or what?"

He grinned, as if he was a child getting away with something devious. His eyes slid up and down Zen's form as he leaned forward, through the window. His voice bled sarcasm as he continued.

"You gonna run and tell someone that you, a supposed man, a supposed soldier, was grabbed by another man and you did *nothing* to fight them off?"

He put his hand to his mouth in mock horror.

"God, the tragedy. You'd be a fucking laughingstock! Trained to kill but too much of a girl to do anything about some harmless flirting."

Zen felt as big as morning dew on the petal of a flower, and as delicate as it too. His cheeks burned as he clutched the papers to his chest. He could feel panicked tears fighting their way out, and he glanced down, willing them to fuck right off. He couldn't give this asshole any more ammo than he already had.

Without another word, Zen turned on his heel and rushed to the door, scanning his trembling hand to be let inside. Before the doors closed behind him, he heard the soldier call out once more, his voice a honeyed threat.

"Be careful I don't find you alone again, princess! I'll give you something to *really* cry abou..."

The doors slid shut before he could hear the end of what the soldier said. His heart hammered against his chest, and tears finally slid down his cheeks. Self-hatred rolled through his stomach as he swallowed hard against the panic attack.

Zen took a few moments to compose himself before pushing the memory of what had just happened deep into his mind. He had a job to do. Zen wiped roughly at his face and sniffled deeply before heading toward the cafeteria. He spoke to no one, and no one seemed to notice his ill mood. Zen was grateful for that thin silver lining. He didn't feel like explaining himself to anyone right now.

His excitement about talking to Varys again was all but extinguished as he slipped his assignment papers into the slot and pushed through. The guards recognized him and didn't even stop to question him this time. Their auras hung heavy with irritation and exhaustion. It seemed like everyone was in a bad mood this morning.

*Good. What was the saying again? Misery loves company?*

Zen couldn't agree more.

He made his way toward Varys's cell, wondering if he could just drop off the meal this time and leave. He didn't know whether he could face anyone in the state he was in today.

Varys was seated near where he had been before, but, this time, his eyes were open. It appeared as though he was waiting for Zen.

He shoved the assumption away.

*Fucking stupid. You're fucking stupid, Zen.*

Zen sighed heavily, resigning himself to staying for a few minutes, and plopped down, cross-legged in front of the cell. He refused to meet the alien's gaze as he shoved the food in through the slot on the bottom.

"Breakfast."

Varys watched him for a minute with an unreadable expression, not even glancing at the tray that had slid toward him. Several long seconds passed, and Zen could feel his irritation creeping up. He grimaced and crossed his arms. His voice came out harsher than he meant it to.

"What?!"

Varys just continued to stare back at him with those dark eyes of his. Zen gritted his teeth.

"Don't tell me I have to convince you to eat again. I thought we had a deal. I don't have time to deal with your alien temper tantrums today."

The Vesunian seemed to consider that for a moment before pulling the tray toward himself and picking at the bread on it. Several more minutes passed in silence, with Varys slowly eating his food. Impatience pushed at Zen's chest, and his cheeks were feeling hotter by the second. It was agonizing.

Zen felt his body twitching, and all he wanted to do was be alone with his thoughts and cry, somewhere where no one would hear him. He couldn't do that here. He was about to make some lame excuse about feeling sick in order to leave before a careful tendril of thought wrapped around his mind, enveloping him in comfortable warmth.

*You smell like salt.*

The observation was so unexpected that Zen didn't know how to react for a split second. He blinked several times before responding.

"Well… I'm human. We're kind of made of that shit. So, I'm sure I do smell like salt."

The words sounded comical leaving his lips. Varys raised a brow.

*More than usual.*

"Oh, so you're saying I smell weird now? What a great day." Zen's tone dripped with sarcasm as his frustration rose even higher. He slid forward, voice rising in volume along with his temper. "It's a perfect fucking day, isn't it?"

He wasn't sure why this exact thing was setting him off. It felt like the last straw in a terrible morning, and he didn't have the emotional capacity to defend the way he *smelled.*

The alien just sat, watching him lose it, unfazed that he was playing the part of an emotional punching bag. Zen balled his hands into fists and when he spoke again, his voice was a shout.

"To be *frank*, I'm in a shitty mood! A shitty, fucking mood, and I don't know what you want from me, Var…"

Zen let out a strangled-sounding gasp as Varys moved, swifter than he thought was possible, and reached through the bars, pressing a giant hand against his mouth. The alien's eyes glittered dangerously.

He hadn't realized how close to the cell he was. Tears gathered in the corners of his eyes and slipped down his cheeks. His breathing was hot and ragged against the alien's skin.

*God, he was sick of crying today.*

Varys seemed to sense his fear and quickly dropped his hand. However, his eyes were still cautious.

A guard's voice drifted toward them both, down the hallway that led to the cell block. "You okay in there, Farraway?!"

Zen swallowed hard before responding. "Y-yeah! I'm fine! Just teaching this fucker a lesson!"

There was echoing laughter before things went silent.

It was quiet as they stared at each other, and Zen tried desperately to calm his racing heart. The alien hesitated, his gaze dropping from Zen's own. When he did break the silence, Varys' tone was apologetic.

***You were being loud and nearly yelled my name. I don't need the others to hear that information.***

Zen nodded slowly, feeling his heartbeat return to normal.

Of course, that made sense. But it didn't help stifle the trembling that had started up once more. Zen reached up to wipe at the vestiges of his tears when Varys also lifted his hand, this time with more deliberation.

He traced a finger across Zen's cheek, catching the moisture and a shudder passed through Zen. Rather than being off-putting, the alien's touch was calming. He wondered, briefly, whether it was a power that Vesunians had, in order to lure their victims to their deaths.

Varys brought his finger close to his face and studied it.

Then, bizarrely, he sniffed it.

He smelled Zen's tears.

*What the fuck?*

A few moments passed before Zen felt Varys's voice caress his mind again.

***I'm sorry I scared you. I panicked.***

He held up his finger.

***This is what I was smelling.***

This couldn't get any stranger. Zen felt weary from the last several minutes. He shook his head to will it all away and everything seemed to spin momentarily. When he spoke, he tried not to let any emotion squeeze into the words.

"You can… smell my tears." A statement, not a question. Zen watched as Varys's brows knitted together and the alien frowned.

*What are tears?*

The question shocked Zen enough that he briefly forgot the terrible day he was having. He shifted his weight to the front and, once again, leaned in close to the bars.

"You don't know what tears are? Do Vesunians not cry? Like when you get sad or really happy, you don't cry? What do you do?"

*Well, we certainly don't leak.*

Indignation made Zen's face feel hot. "It's not leaking!"

*Your body malfunctions when you have powerful emotions. That sounds like leaking to me.*

A laugh bubbled up in Zen's throat before escaping as a small chuckle, the first genuine smile he'd had in ages stretching across his face.

"Whatever, man. I'm not going to argue that. You can call it leaking if you want." Zen threw his hands up in a mock surrender position, still chuckling.

Varys's eyes glimmered with amusement.

*I'm glad you found that funny.*

"I did. I'm laughing at a Vesunian's jokes. There's probably a law somewhere that would have me shot for that."

Zen meant it humorously, but the statement seemed to dampen the mood. Varys sighed and scratched his head, his muscles flexing with the movement.

God, he really could crush Zen like a grape.

Was it weird that he kept thinking about it?

Several more seconds passed before Varys spoke to him again, changing the subject.

*So, if I may ask, why did you smell like tears when you came in here?*

Zen froze, remembering in horrible detail what had happened in the assignments room earlier today. He dropped his gaze to the worn toe of his livery boots and began picking at the rubber. Shame pulsed through him as he unwillingly relived the memory. He took a few moments to respond.

"I don't really want to talk about it."

Varys was quiet, and Zen felt the heat of his gaze burning directly into his soul. It wouldn't sway him, however, because this was something he couldn't tell anybody. He wasn't sure his mouth could even properly form the words.

He heard Varys take a deep breath and, even though the pause in conversation was brief, it felt like ages before the alien spoke again.

*Thank you for bringing me my meal.*

Relief poured through Zen when he realized Varys would not push the issue. He looked up and thought he saw understanding glimmering in those alien eyes.

His stomach still turned thinking about the situation, but the laughing had done Zen some good. He felt a bit better. He leaned back, away from the bars, and nodded.

"No problem."

Varys turned his attention to his tray and ate about half of what was on the plate before grimacing and pushing it away from himself. Zen's brow knotted and he glanced down at the tray.

"What's wrong with it?"

Varys studied him briefly before gesturing to the meal. His tone was apologetic.

*Human food doesn't exactly agree with me.*

The concern in Zen rose. "Will it hurt you?"

*I can digest it well enough. It's just not pleasant.*

That made sense. He was a completely different creature. You wouldn't ask a wolf to switch to a rabbit's diet. Zen nodded again before settling, his hands behind him to support his weight. The silence between them was comfortable, and it seemed that Varys didn't mind the quiet, just like Zen didn't.

However, Zen still had questions. Unwillingly, he took a deep breath after a few minutes and broke the silence.

"So, um… Varys…"

Varys looked up, head cocked to the side to show he was listening.

"I was wondering if I could ask you some questions."

The alien seemed to consider that statement for a moment. Zen allowed him the time to do so, knowing that if he was in Varys' position, he would be just as careful in making any promises to the enemy.

Finally, Varys nodded, shifting his enormous body toward the front of the cell. Zen's heart jumped in elation. He scooted forward in excitement, his hands gripping the coolness of the concrete floor.

"So, are you a warrior? Like an *actual* warrior?"

The question felt childish rolling off his lips, but it was the first thing that had come to mind. He blushed at the amusement that flickered across the alien's features.

Varys chuckled, and the reverberation of his deep voice struck Zen. Goosebumps danced up his arms, and he rubbed his palms against them to get rid of the chill.

*I am.*

Zen nodded, pleased with his honesty. "How long have you been fighting in the war?"

The question seemed to drag up something intense for Varys as his dark eyes clouded over. Zen suddenly felt guilty for even asking. He waited until Varys took a deep breath and smiled kindly in the human's direction.

*Since I reached adulthood. But I have been training since I was old enough to hold a weapon, just as every youth on Vesun does.*

Zen felt sick thinking about it. They were just like humans, then. Forcing their young into military service to fight in a war that had long since lost all meaning. He rested his chin on his knees and sighed heavily.

"I'm sorry. I joined the service when I was eighteen. I've been in it for three years, and I have two to go. Luckily, I haven't seen any action though. Meeting you was probably the craziest thing that's happened this entire time."

He didn't know why he was suddenly spilling his guts to this near-stranger, but it felt good to tell someone who listened so carefully to every word he said.

Plus, the details of some sad engineer's life weren't something that Varys could take home and use. Unless the Vesunians did studies on human depression.

A small voice spoke up in the back of Zen's mind, sinister and cold. *That is if the alien went home at all.*

Zen's stomach squeezed tightly when he realized Varys could very well spend the rest of his life sitting on this disgusting prison floor, silent and staring at a wall. He pushed the thought away, trying to convince himself that he didn't care.

Varys nodded, acknowledging what he had said. His eyes seemed mournful and tired, which was strange since he didn't seem to be *that* old.

But he was Vesunian, so who knew? Zen certainly didn't. The most they had taught him about Vesunians was what they looked like, and that they were monsters.

Zen was shaken from his musings by Varys' voice yet again.

*I envy you. War is not something that one can witness and walk away from unscathed.*

His eyes adopted that faraway look again, and Zen squirmed uncomfortably. He felt as though he was stepping into tender territory and didn't know whether he should press forward. When Zen spoke again, he did so cautiously.

"Y-yeah, I'm sure. Death is pretty heavy. I don't know if I could see someone die."

Zen's stomach jolted when he realized that he had, in fact, witnessed death. The Vesunian in the crash had taken its last breaths practically in Zen's arms.

*It didn't count though because war didn't cause that death.*

*Technically...Okay, no one had killed them.*

Varys picked at the remaining food on his tray, lost in thought as he tore it to pieces. Zen waited for him to come back, and it didn't take long for Varys to blink and look up to meet Zen's gaze.

*I'm sorry.*

"It's fine." He shrugged. "I didn't mean to drag up anything for you."

Varys smiled softly, and it surprised Zen to realize how very human he looked in that moment.

Large and hulking, sure. But human. The thought made panic and shame build in his stomach.

*Okay, the Vesunian smiled. Whoop-de-do.*

What sat in front of him right now was a warrior. A battle-hardened warrior who had likely killed several of Zen's kind.

*Why was it so easy to forget that? God, what was he doing?*

Zen looked down, feeling compounded shame rising to color his cheeks. He felt the alien's concerned stare before looking up to meet it. He spoke quickly, his words coming out mangled.

"I… I shouldn't be doing this. This shouldn't be so easy. We shouldn't be…" Zen shook his head and grabbed at his hair, brushing it back to soothe himself. "You're my *enemy*. And I'm yours."

Varys seemed to weigh his words. Despite Zen's panic, he saw the alien held no offense over his words, which somehow made him feel even worse.

After a long moment, during which Zen tried desperately to keep himself from panicking and running off, Varys uncrossed his legs once more and leaned toward the bars.

For the first time since they'd met, Zen didn't flinch away from his movements. To his credit, it seemed that Varys was doing his best to be slow and methodical. The kindness kept Zen from doing what every instinct screamed at him to do.

Varys reached through the bars and, with one of his middle fingers, lightly pressed into Zen's chest. Heat pulsed through him at the alien's touch, and he had a hard time dropping the Vesunian's gaze.

When Varys spoke, he spoke out loud. His voice was just as deep and rich as the one in Zen's mind, but a beautiful accent accompanied it. Zen tried to focus on what he was saying, rather than how he said it. His cheeks felt as hot as if the sun had kissed his face.

"You are not my enemy, Zen. Humanity is. Just because you are human, does not mean you are bad."

Varys's voice held so much wisdom and comfort that it made Zen want to tear up. He fought the urge and swallowed hard.

Varys continued. "You have a good heart. I can hear *and* feel it. Even if I live out the rest of my existence here, I will be grateful to have met you, Zen the human."

He leaned back into his prison, smiling once more, pleased with what he had said.

Zen blinked hard against the wetness in his eyes and bowed his head. His heart pounded a familiar rhythm, as if testifying to the truth of what the alien had said. His jaw clenched as he silently admitted to the wisdom in Varys's declaration. Zen wasn't his enemy. That much was obvious at this point. And, if he was being honest with himself, Zen didn't think Varys was his anymore either.

# Chapter 11
# Altair

Altair spent the next several days learning, and effectively failing, to "speak" Lil's strange language. Although it looked like it would be easy to pick up, it wasn't, and Lil wasn't the most patient of tutors.

"Not like tha... no!" She would cry out in reaction to Altair's pathetic attempts. Her lip would curl, and her dark eyes would flash in frustration.

Altair's temper would, naturally, rise in response. He'd snatch the notepad and furiously scribble, his writing even more unintelligible than it usually was.

**Then *show* me the correct wa...**

"I *have* shown you the correct way, a million times over!"

She would read it faster than he could write the words. She would then stand and stomp away from him, her footsteps heavy on the old, wooden floor. Lil would shoot him her most scathing look from the doorway before leaving to cool off with an alcoholic drink or two.

She would always come back, smelling suspiciously strong.

When he wasn't pathetically failing at yet another thing in his life, he was milling around, waiting for Lil to return. She would vanish for hours on end, the familiar click of the lock echoing through the musty room once the door snapped shut.

Altair would weather Lil's stormy mood swings and hope that she wouldn't forget to feed him. He felt like a starving pet with an ill-tempered master. The thought made his pride shrivel up inside of him.

The room was nearly worse than his years on the sand planet. At least in his exile, he could wander wherever he pleased. He had the freedom to do what he wanted with his own time. But here, the only options were to stare at the wall and scratch at the wooden floor, trying to pretend that the room didn't smell damp.

To prevent himself from plunging into the depths of insanity, he would imagine scenarios of his escape. Though he knew they weren't feasible, he could still dream of such an opportunity.

These daydreams usually consisted of him finding peace on a planet of entirely deaf people. He would be able to speak, sing, yell, and laugh without any repercussions. It soothed him enough to give him patience as he waited for Lilith to come back each time she left.

However, he was finding it difficult to be patient, even with the distracting daydreams, when a nagging fear that he was developing infected wounds ominously shadowed every thought.

Altair would use the dingy mirror that Lil gave him in his toiletries kit to study what damage the silencer might be doing. Luckily, it didn't seem to be causing any permanent issues. But he couldn't be too sure. The mirror was *incredibly* dingy after all.

The only respite he found was when Lil would return from her hours-long escapades with some meager version of a meal. She would press her hand to his mouth, and, with a few mechanical clicks, the silencer would come off. Altair would then work his jaw and mouth happily before diving for his food.

Even as disgusting as some meals were, it was sustenance. And it would provide him with enough energy and patience to move forward and survive another day in this second hellhole into which fate had thrown him.

Altair wasn't tempted to try anything during these times of brief freedom. After all, he was still cuffed, and Lil was impervious to his powers. He considered yelling for someone to come running in to save him, since the walls didn't seem to be soundproof here, but he would likely be dead before they arrived. Either that, or his curse would kill them before they could rescue him.

Regardless, it made no sense to fight back unless he felt completely suicidal. All reasoning whispered for him to bide his time, and he would end the mental struggle by deciding to save that battle for another day.

Occasionally, Altair would ask for an update on how the project with Silas was going. Lil would grunt in response and wave him off, which he assumed meant that it wasn't going very well at all. Altair would then sigh deeply through his nose and return to daydreaming or doodling on the notepad he was given.

It was in this state that Lil found him one bleak midday. The room was darkening early, assuredly from the strange weather outside. Altair was grateful for the coolness that the shadows brought, but he also felt himself sinking into a familiar, scary place that he had visited often while marooned. Altair let himself fall into these dark places. They were ones with which he was familiar, so embracing the darkness felt like a comfortable, dulling drug. Not unlike the numbness that smoking the reed plants brought him. Altair mused grimly it was most likely what death felt like.

His hand moved, as much as it was able while being bound, gracefully across the page. He was drawing his home, back when it was still his home. The luscious gardens that adorned his family's lands above water had always been so welcoming and vibrant. He'd spent many of the days of light with his mother on their grounds, picking wild fruits and singing songs of healing and love.

His people would gather outside the gates of the grounds simply to hear them sing. As soon as he'd been born and tested, he'd been named the "Keeper of the Voice," and he'd been strutted around the kingdom to perform for every member of the court.

Dazzled fans would scream for him, and he hadn't understood it at the time when his mother's hand would tense around his own. As soon as the frenzy grew to be too much, she would gently guide him inside, and the guards would rush to disperse the increasingly riotous crowd.

His hand continued to glide across the page as he finished sketching the grounds and moved on to the waters.

*Oh, the waters…*

Altair sighed in desire, his body aching as he gently thumbed the charcoal sketch of the lake that sat upon his family's land. The lake housed their underwater home where they retreated to during the days of darkness. The water had always been the perfect temperature.

Gods, he missed it.

Altair hadn't seen a truly lovely body of water in ages. The sand planet was home only to that desolate, gray-blue ocean. He had barely stepped foot in it, and only for brief moments of bathing and gathering drinking water. He knew that the creatures that lurked beneath the surface would jump at any opportunity for fresh food. It was one of the few warnings his father had given him before he left.

His thoughts turned back to the sketch he had been working on and he continued to stroke the rendering of the waters with a light touch. What he wouldn't give to swim in the lake on the castle grounds again. However, he lamented, as that pain returned to his stomach, that would never be possible.

He was cursed. And his father would never allow him back until that curse was broken. If that was even possible. Altair felt a bitter, metallic taste enter his mouth that had nothing to do with the silencer. He pressed the charcoal nub to paper.

Finally, he shaded in two figures, one tall and slender and the other as small as a child. They held hands as they sat upon a mossy boulder and overlooked the lake from their home. Touching the slender figure with a graphite burdened finger, he felt tears rising, the dull curtain of darkness releasing its grasp for a moment. It had been a long time since he'd drawn his mother.

He swallowed hard against the lump in his throat and was suddenly aware he was being watched. Looking up, he saw Lil's piercing gaze striking him from the bed in which he thought she had been sleeping. Altair's cheeks burned as he realized what she had witnessed. He lifted a wrist to wipe at his face and turned his head away from the bounty hunter.

Lil stared at him for a few more moments before slipping off the bed and walking over, her footsteps silent as she craned her neck to see what he had drawn.

He felt a small wave of shock. He'd drawn in front of her before, and she'd never shown even an inkling of an interest. Altair couldn't help but wonder, with a surge of embarrassment, if his emotion had piqued her desire to see what he was doing.

He didn't dare look up at her. He was sure that she thought he was being stupid and emotional over nothing. She was one of those people who always seemed to have it together. She was tough and sturdy, like a statue that had stood proud for thousands of years, weathered by age but never faltering.

There were a few moments of silence before Lilith spoke, pointing at the figures. She was careful not to touch the page itself, apparently fearing that she would smudge away all of his hard work. The idea that she even cared about something as small as that felt ridiculous, but it did tug at something deep within his heart.

"Your mother?" she mumbled, her voice much gentler than he'd ever heard before.

He was, again, shocked by her perceptiveness. Gods, it was so annoying that she was *always right.*

Altair nodded, hoping her questioning would end there. But, of course, it didn't. She sat next to him, crossing her legs, and snapping to get his attention. The snapping no longer irritated him. He understood she wasn't doing it to be rude.

Glancing over at her, he watched curiously as she made an interesting sign that seemed to indicate something important. Her hand hovered from her chin to her chest, her thumb brushing down. He was enraptured with her hands as she dropped them into her lap and smiled softly. Altair's heart skipped a step at the beauty of her smile, and he felt silly for being so affected by her.

His captor. She was still his captor.

Altair shot her a questioning look, his eyebrows high on his forehead. The air felt thick, and his insides were warm as his heart pounded a light rhythm against his chest.

"That means 'mother.'"

She breathed, and her eyes seemed to glisten with emotion as well. Perhaps it was the trick of the light. Altair nodded again, touched by her gesture. He swallowed past a thick lump in his throat and dropped his gaze from hers.

He would definitely remember that one.

# Chapter 12
# Zen

Zen wanted to believe that he still fought for his people. That he believed in humanity's cause in the war. But every visit with Varys seemed to push him further and further down a very dangerous path. He'd never been patriotic, to be completely honest.

His father had been partially handicapped by his years of mandatory service and now could only work menial jobs. Zen's distrust of his government began with seeing his father and mother struggle to keep their little family afloat while living on Mars.

It was a fight to receive the disabled veteran's benefits that he was owed and, every month, Zen had to watch his father and mother cry over unpaid bills that littered their dining room table. He'd peered from behind the edge of the doorway, clutching his stuffed rabbit, and feeling helpless. A child should never have to worry about those things. And his government hadn't cared.

It was only his mother, Fay, who kept them from going under the surface and provided the income that allowed them to stay on Mars. She had a gaggle of Upper Lifer children for whom she regularly nannied. It wasn't much, but it was enough to keep them from complete depravity.

And even that hadn't been ideal. Much of Zen's childhood trauma stemmed from those Upper Lifer children and what they felt they could do to those lower on the totem pole. His mother would bring him along to play with the children, having no one at home to watch him. Despite his best efforts, Zen struggled to relate to them. They groomed their expensive dolls and lorded over playgrounds as if the universe was theirs to command.

Rather than play with Zen, they would pull his hair and tug his ears, demanding that he act as their servant.

"You're our nanny's child. She serves us, so you must too," they would proclaim as they pushed him out of the room for biscuits and sweets.

Even worse, a lot of times they would shove him down and call him names, especially the little boys. Each one of them would proclaim, loudly, that they wanted to be soldiers and kill the "bad guys." Apparently, Zen had counted as good practice.

"You can't be a soldier though, Zen Urso," they would taunt as they rubbed his face into the dirt. "You're too tiny. You sure your mom didn't fuck an Ursonian? You're lucky you didn't come out with one eye."

He would run inside, sobbing, and fall into his mother's arms; his face filthy and snot-ridden. There was little she could do other than lightly scold his bullies, however, for fear that she would lose her job.

God, he had hated those brats. He was grateful when he had finally gone to school, assuming that he wouldn't have to deal with them anymore. Sadly, going to school proved to be just as much of a problem. His bullies had grown up as well, and some of them attended the same schools.

Zen only had a brief reprieve from the taunting when he'd entered the military. But that hadn't lasted long either, especially when his comrades realized how shitty he was with blasters. The hierarchy haunted him at every step.

Just as they divided Mars into upper and lower circles, so too were the people and their children forced into a hierarchy. It afforded those who lived in the upper circles a lavish lifestyle, one that benefited from the war. Their children were the only ones who could opt out of the so-called "mandatory" military service. Many chose to. Some didn't. Like Sergeant Jennings.

Zen grew up knowing that he wasn't at the top. But he also wasn't at the bottom. He floated somewhere in the middle, just like the rest of his family did. He'd learned to be okay with the position his birth had afforded him. Constantly treading water became a lifestyle.

Zen was eternally grateful to his mother and the sacrifices she had made to keep them from being forcefully moved from Mars into the depravity of First Earth. He was angry that it had been necessary, but that was just the way things were.

However, the more he spoke with Varys, the more it seemed that humanity had it all wrong.

"So, your people just sort of commingle?"

Zen's head was propped on his hands as he sat cross-legged in front of the cell. He tried to keep glancing at the ticking clock on the distant wall to ensure he didn't spend a suspicious amount of time delivering the alien's meal.

Varys nodded and tossed a nasty-looking pear from one hand to the other. He hadn't even touched his tray other than to play with the fruit. His large hands enveloped it entirely, and Zen marveled that it was smaller than the alien's palms.

"We believe that the great mother created us all equally. She flooded life through her roots to every single one of us. We honor her by treating others kindly." Varys smiled softly, a wistful tone to his voice. The alien seemed to be feeling homesick.

A burning ache began in Zen's chest, and he dropped his head, grimacing. He wanted to allow the Vesunian a moment to process whatever he was feeling, but the questions began to bubble to the surface.

It was like a book that he would read late into the night until his eyes watered with exhaustion. He just had to know more. Zen hoped it had been long enough when he opened his mouth to speak.

"Who is the great mother?"

Varys's voice took on a tone of reverence. "Our mother, Reeva. Her branches are life itself. She weeps, and we are all provided for. *Au aka Reeva.*"

Varys seemed to end his thought in sacred prayer, and he had closed his eyes, tilting his chin upward briefly in silence.

Much to Zen's surprise, soft echoes of the same prayer had floated from the nearby cells. He hadn't understood a word of what Varys meant, but Zen understood branches meant trees. So, the Vesunians had some kind of sacred tree to which they prayed. It was a large assumption, but the only one that made sense.

He was sure that Sergeant Jennings would've given any organ that was necessary for the information that Zen was privy to at that moment. He smirked at the thought.

Zen waited until Varys opened his eyes again before pushing the tray closer through the bars.

"You should eat before my time is up here."

Varys smiled and pulled the tray closer, the metal scraping against the concrete.

"Thank you, Zen."

And each visit seemed to follow in the same manner. Zen would bring him his meal, they would have a brief discussion about whatever struck his fancy, and then he would leave, feeling himself fall further and further down that slippery slope.

Weeks passed, and the different shifts blurred together as he and Varys developed a sense of trust and friendship.

Zen had known it was friendship when he had made Varys laugh out loud for the first time, only a week ago. The alien's eyes had sparkled in amusement, and Zen had blushed in victory. The joke had been a lame one, and yet, the Vesunian had doubled over, clutching his stomach as he guffawed.

They shared the same sense of humor, and Varys appreciated his sarcasm more than anyone he'd ever met. Admitting that truth felt strange, but it was something he could no longer deny.

He knew deep down that what he was doing wasn't inherently bad. But he was also aware that he could face pretty severe consequences for not sharing the information that he was receiving.

Every time he left Varys, his heart would start to race at the thought of what would happen if they were caught. He would press his pillow into his face, attempting to purge his mind of the morbid fantasies.

Zen chewed his chicken listlessly in the prison staff cafeteria as he pondered his weeks of visiting Varys. The chaos of clattering trays and loud laughter was just background noise as he pretended to enjoy his lunch. His eyes were unfocused as his mind switched gears to reflect on the visit he had just had with Varys.

They discussed Varys's many powers, including the ability to speak telepathically. Zen had been curious why the Vesunian in the crashed ship had needed to touch him in order to mind-speak, whereas Varys could do it from a distance.

*She was dying.* Varys had said, as if proving a point by speaking telepathically once again. ***Her powers were weakening by the second, and she needed physical contact in order for you to hear her.***

Zen had nodded, not even questioning how Varys had known the sex of the Vesunian pilot. But now, alone with his thoughts in this incredibly loud cafeteria, he wondered whether Varys had known her personally. That was probably the only explanation.

Shrugging, he poked a fork at the wilted salad on his tray, moving on from the chicken.

*Guess I'll just have to ask him next time.*

Zen was so deep in thought that when another tray clattered on the table across from him, he nearly jumped out of his skin. Looking up, his stomach dropped to his feet when he saw a familiar gray head of hair and a stern expression boring into his soul.

*Sergeant Jennings.*

He went to jump up when Jennings waved him down. The man looked exhausted, and Zen's brow furrowed upon realizing how dark the bags under his eyes were. Not that he cared, but it hinted that something wasn't quite right.

"Unnecessary, Farraway. We're at lunch."

Jennings rested on the hard bench with a grimace, adjusting left and then right before bending his neck to crack it. Zen slowly sat back down from the half squat he had frozen in. He watched as Jennings stirred his potatoes and chicken distastefully.

"Even with all the funds we pour into this prison, we still get shitty scraps." Jennings mused, seemingly to himself.

Zen didn't know whether he should agree. Would that count as dissent if he did? He tapped his fingers against the table, his lunch forgotten.

Normally, Jennings's presence caused Zen anxiety all on its own. It was worse that he was now privy to it in a place where Jennings would normally never step foot. Prison shifts were seen as lowly. The only time any leadership made their way here was to oversee high-security prison transports. And even then, Jennings would've sent someone in his stead.

The volume in the entire cafeteria seemed to lower. Glancing around, Zen realized various soldiers were shooting anxious glances at their table. Many were wolfing down their lunches, intending to exit the cafeteria as quickly as possible.

Zen decided that he would rather face the social *faux pas* of leaving quickly after Jennings had just sat down, rather than Jennings' presence itself. He cleared his throat thickly before speaking.

"W-well, enjoy your lunch, Sir. I have another task I need to…"

Jennings looked up from his lunch, his jaw tight. His eyes burned with a strange emotion that made Zen's chest feel as though it was caving in. His mouth was set in a dangerous, thin-lipped smile, and his words came like gunfire. Swift and unapologetic.

"I've cleared your schedule, Private. We need to have a word."

Zen had already begun standing again, his silver tray in hand. His heart squeezed painfully, but he feigned a look of confusion as he slowly sat down again, still clutching the tray. Zen's knuckles were white, the color harsh against the silver surrounding them.

"Yes, Sir?"

Jennings mused over what he wanted to say next, still stirring his potatoes. Zen wondered if he'd even taken a bite of his food yet. The aging sergeant sighed deeply before setting his fork down and folding his hands together. He looked at Zen once again.

"Private Farraway, I find myself in a difficult position. Though it shouldn't have, I'm sure news has spread regarding the attempted breach into Trinity Market."

Zen hesitated before conceding that knowing this gossip wasn't enough to land him in any sort of trouble. He nodded.

Jennings's mouth pressed into a firm line at the confirmation, but he didn't seem surprised.

"I figured as much. As you know, this is the first attempted breach of home territory that the Vesunians have made. And though it was unsuccessful, it has made the Council nervous."

Zen nodded again. Of course, it would. Rumor had it that the Vesunians had been after Afton or Boggs. Though it wasn't the most trusted source of information, even rumors made leadership nervous. His damned curiosity reared its ugly head, and he took a deep breath before asking his next question. He wasn't sure that Jennings would have the answer either, but he had to try.

"Sergeant… who were they going after?"

Zen's voice was quiet, but he tried to push forward with confidence. The sergeant always respected confidence.

Jennings looked up with something akin to suspicion brewing in his eyes. Zen felt his cheeks begin to burn, but he tried not to look away from the sergeant who stared him down from the other side of the table. After what seemed like an eternity, he finally spoke, breaking the tension between them.

"To be perfectly frank, Farraway, I was hoping you had the answer for me."

Electric tingling rolled through him at the admission. The confusion seemed to be apparent on his face because Jennings quickly continued before Zen could respond.

"I've been receiving reports from the prison staff that one of the Vesunians seems to have taken a liking to you. That you have been able to convince him to eat and possibly even speak with you."

Zen felt sick to his stomach, and he regretted that he'd eaten any of the lunch that had been provided to him. There was a deep and uncomfortable silence as Zen opened and closed his mouth in surprise, like a fish gasping for air.

Jennings seemed to grow impatient with him and he growled softly, his grizzled features dropping into a scowl.

"Oh, come on now, Private. If I was going to punish you for anything, it would've happened already."

Zen considered that statement, trying to think past the ringing in his ears. This was true. Jennings never overlooked an opportunity for punishment. When Zen spoke, his voice felt squeaky and far too soft. He hoped that Jennings could hear him over the roaring of the fans in the cafeteria.

"Sergeant, I don't know what you want from me, Sir."

That was the wrong answer. Jennings smacked his palm against the table, causing Zen to flinch away from the angry war veteran. Anyone who was left in the cafeteria made their hasty exits, glancing back in sympathy toward where Zen sat, at the mercy of Jennings's anger. The older man's voice was harsh and echoed sharply against the silver walls.

"I want the truth, Farraway! You have been in the middle of everything that's happened in the past couple of weeks. Whether on purpose or by accident. You know something that you're not telling me!"

Jennings took a deep breath before leaning back and crossing his arms. He dropped his chin to his chest and raised his brows.

"I've been told that we're willing to offer you immunity for all crimes that you've committed. As long as you share what you know and what you're hiding."

Zen felt a different kind of tingling begin in his toes and make its way up his entire body. Something was wrong. He should've been signed up for a cell of his own, simply for hiding information from a superior. His heart pounded a drumline against his chest. Jennings was hiding things too. And he'd be damned if he just spilled his guts, simply for his own salvation.

Zen splayed his hands on the table and stood, fixing Jennings with what he hoped was a cool and unbothered stare.

"Sir, I know you want information. But I have nothing to give you. The Vesunian and I have barely spoken outside of it giving thanks for the meals."

Zen was proud that his voice didn't even wobble as he lied out of his ass.

"The most I've spoken to it was to convince it to eat. And all I said was that it was stupid to die starving in the enemy's prison."

Jennings gritted his teeth together in frustration and stood to meet Zen. Even though Zen felt that his lie was convincing, the sergeant didn't seem to think so. His cheeks were reddish-purple, and he opened his mouth to speak, spittle flying out of his open maw.

"Private Farraway, I demand that…"

A sudden cacophony of screams echoed toward them from outside of the cafeteria, interrupting Jennings's words.

Both men froze, inches from each other's faces, and simultaneously looked toward the large double doors of the cafeteria. It was quiet for several, heart-stopping seconds.

Suddenly, blaster sounds echoed through the cafeteria accompanied by what sounded, sickeningly, like tearing flesh. The screams seemed to grow louder as both of them stood there.

Zen felt his blood chill. He and Jennings shared a confused, wide-eyed look. He'd never seen such panic glimmering in the sergeant's eyes. A communicator came to life on Jennings's belt. Panicked yelling and screaming sounded from the other side of the frequency. Jennings grabbed at the communicator and clicked a button, speaking low and furious.

"Come in, someone come in! What's happening?!"

It didn't take long for a deep voice to respond, broken by pained gasps and sobs.

"The Vesunians… They escaped. They're killing…"

The voice was interrupted by an inhuman roar that sent icicles down Zen's spine. The soldier on the other end let loose a blood-curdling scream for his mother before the line went dead, static hissing and spitting.

Jennings swore harshly before dropping the communicator and grabbing his blaster gun. He sprinted from the room, without another word, at a speed that belied his age.

Zen stood there, frozen as adrenaline rushed through his veins. His mind jumped from thought to thought as he tried to decide his next course of action. The ringing in his ears had grown to deafening volumes and his vision had started to shake.

*That sound couldn't have come from Varys, it just couldn't have.*

And that was the thought that thawed Zen enough for him to rush forward, to the sounds of carnage that still faintly echoed from outside of the cafeteria. He scanned his trembling hand in order to leave the room and squeezed through the opening as soon as it was big enough for him to do so. Panting, he sprinted toward the high-security area. Other soldiers nearly trampled each other, and Zen, as they rushed for the nearest exit. He slammed into several of them, only vaguely aware of how he had become a human pinball.

His breath came in quick gasps, and his ribs ached from the cardio. But Zen couldn't even form any thought other than he just *had* to get there. He had to see it himself. His mind swirled around the same thought, the same delusion.

*That couldn't have been Varys. It just couldn't have been him.*

Zen's pace slowed as he approached the high-security doors and found them open. He panted heavily as he watched them sputter and spark ominously as the damaged machinery attempted to close repeatedly. However, it wasn't just the broken doors that Zen saw. He felt bile rise in his throat as he saw what he had desperately hoped he wouldn't see.

*No! What the fuck!*

Blood.

Flesh.

Innards, from bodies that Zen couldn't find, floated in copious pools of dark red blood. It stained the silver of the floors and smeared across the damaged doors. It was as though the dying humans had been dragged through them as they held on in one last, weak attempt to pull themselves to freedom.

It was too much. His vision swam and his face felt hot.

*Oh, God.*

That was when Zen lost his lunch. He lurched to the side of the hallway, retching violently, a trembling hand stabilizing him against the cool, silver wall. He tried to gather himself in order to move forward, pressing his sweaty forehead against the iciness of the wall and closing his eyes. However, every time he opened them again and saw the aftermath of whatever battle had ensued here, he would double over and retch all over again.

Once there was nothing left to vomit, he swallowed hard, willing himself to stand up straight and wipe his mouth. He had to press on, he just had to keep going.

The sound of screams was closer and upon further inspection, smoldering blaster holes littered the door and hallway, a grisly companion to the blood spatter. Zen tried to avoid looking at the gore that surrounded him as he continued through the doorway. Some soldier he was. He couldn't even handle seeing a bit of blood.

Zen stepped into the cell block with trembling legs, stupidly hoping that somehow this wasn't being caused by the Vesunians. That they were, impossibly, in their cages. However, the little hope he had sputtered out upon entering the block. The once-occupied cells were empty, their barred doors swinging uselessly. There was no damage to the cells themselves, but they were covered in the same gore that grimly decorated the hallway before.

Unfortunately, this time there were bodies. Zen whimpered, his stomach turning again.

*Oh god, so many bodies.*

If Zen hadn't already been scarred by what he'd seen before, surely this would've brought him to his knees. Soldiers lay strewn about the cell block, their bodies mangled and twisted in horrible ways. It almost didn't look real, as if they were props for some horrible slasher film. It looked as though a couple of Vesunian corpses also lay among the dead, but they were surrounded by piles of soldiers that they had taken down before meeting their own demise. Their bodies lay the way they had died, with no brutalization to their limbs. They seemed out of place that way.

It was dizzying, and the first taste of war that Zen had ever had. He understood now the jealousy in Varys' tone when he'd envied Zen's innocence.

*Varys…*

Zen slowly approached each of the Vesunians and felt a stupid sense of relief that none of them were Varys. It was insane how not knowing the dead seemed to make the situation better somehow.

Sudden anger boiled in his stomach. Why was he even checking for that? *They* were the ones that had caused all of this and had killed so many of his comrades. He thought back to every visit to this cell block, every conversation he had had with Varys. Every time he wondered whether the humans had gotten everything wrong in this war. He had been so stupid. So very stupid.

Fighting back tears and trying not to look for familiar faces among the piles of corpses, he weaved through the bodies and followed the carnage. The only pathway going in the opposite direction led to an emergency exit.

But to Zen's knowledge, it was a long and winding path, one that would take the Vesunians a while to traverse, even with the proper permissions to make it through the multiple security doors.

It took Zen a while to find them, but he knew he was getting closer because the sounds of battle became deafening. He was already becoming familiar with the smell of suffering and metal. He saw plenty of corpses along the way, but they only seemed to be human.

He was dumb enough to look at one that was bent nearly in half, almost in awe of the brutality that had caused it and recognized the name tag as someone with whom he had been in training. They hadn't known each other well, but they had been friendly. They had chatted briefly about their families back home, and the soldier had mentioned his little sister, who had been voraciously writing to him since the day he entered training. And now he would never go home to her.

His cheeks heated, and his breathing quickened as his vision tinged with red. Zen knelt and pocketed the blood-smeared name tag that read "Young" and moved on, sprinting toward the sounds of horror that seemed so nearby.

Zen finally pushed through another broken security door and was immediately met with chaos. Jennings led the charge against the hulking group of Vesunians, two of which were attempting to break down the last door that led outside. The rest were mowing down the small group of human soldiers who shot blasters at them. The blasters didn't seem to deter the Vesunians. Even as they retained blaster wounds, none of them dropped, and they still grabbed at any soldier unlucky enough to be within grabbing range.

Zen watched in sickened horror as the terrified soldiers were held down by those inhumanely strong, four-fingered hands and were promptly torn apart. Or broken and bent in terrible ways. Their horrified pleadings and shrieks rang in his ears.

So much blood. So much loss. So much carnage.

And Zen couldn't help but feel somewhat to blame for what was happening. He had to fix this somehow.

Tears nearly blinded him, and he grabbed a blaster off a nearby corpse. He rushed forward to do… well, he wasn't sure what. All he knew was that he couldn't be a coward anymore. He couldn't keep making these idiotic mistakes and putting others in danger. He had to do *something*.

A Vesunian saw him rush from the left flank and dropped the limp soldier she was holding. The soldier crumpled with a sickening crunch, and Zen's stomach clenched as he recognized those curls and the green glassy-eyed stare of the corpse.

*Reeves.*

One of the few people who had ever shown him kindness. She had been so excited that the prison was holding Vesunians. Did they even know that she found them attractive? Did they even care? No. Because, to them, she was a human, the enemy. She didn't deserve this. None of them did.

Zen rushed toward the Vesunian with a primal scream that tore at his throat and aimed the blaster at her head, pulling the trigger back with savage pleasure.

He braced for the impact of the recoil and the teeth-rattling sound of plasma blasting at the alien's ugly maw. But nothing happened. He stood there, pointing the blaster at the monster who had taken his friend's life, and nothing was *happening.*

Zen's heart hammered with adrenaline, and he looked over the blaster in horror. He hadn't noticed the fluid leaking all over his hands, staining them with slick lines of green. The blaster was inoperable.

*The blaster was, was oh god, inoperable. It didn't work! He was going to die…*

He looked up at the Vesunian who grinned maliciously at him. She seemed to relish in his panic.

"Oops." She said sarcastically, her leer ice cold.

Neither of them moved for one heart-stopping moment. Then, she rushed forward before he could react and grabbed him by the waist with one hand, while the other clutched his chest. He wiggled and strained at her grip, trying desperately to break it. Panic seemed to numb his brain. Gut instinct screamed at him to get free, but it wasn't giving him any ideas on how to do so.

Zen couldn't even process what was happening. Agonizing pain shot through his body as she bent him over her knee, seemingly to snap him in half. His vision blurred as he started to lose consciousness.

No, no, no, no, no… this couldn't be the way he would go. Tears leaked from his eyes and dripped down his cheeks, and he whimpered in pain as she continued to bend… bend…

He tried to flex his core in order to prevent her from killing him, but she was just too strong. So fucking strong.

He was too weak. And he was going to die.

He heard cracking and knew, instinctively, that some bone had broken. He heard shrieking, and it took him a second to realize that it was coming from his own lips. Fiery pain licked through his core, and he closed his eyes, accepting his fate.

Images danced in front of his eyes. *His mother, his father, his childhood home. His favorite sweet biscuits. The smell of fire crackling in the hearth, his family laughing…*

It had all darkened when a panicked voice burst into his consciousness, just as he was about to sink deep into the comforting nothingness.

*ZEN!*

Suddenly, the pressure on his body was gone, and his head smacked into the cold floor of the jail, snapping him out of his dark reverie and dizzying him even more. His eyes shot open, and he gasped for air, tasting the metallic aftermath of blood in his mouth.

He still couldn't see. The lights in the room were too bright. But he could hear faint arguing in a language he didn't know. The room spun as he tried to roll to his side, and he gasped in pain as it crackled up his spine. He blinked hard several times and, when his vision cleared, he saw Varys arguing ferociously with the Vesunian who had tried to kill him. Dizzying confusion rolled through him.

*What…?*

Suddenly, the sound of hundreds of boots and the clattering of weapons started from down the hall. The Vesunians looked up from their arguing and watched the doorway with growing horror. Zen turned his head toward the noise and saw, with a sense of intense relief, that the small group he had been fighting with was now joined by hundreds of soldiers, called in for backup.

He twisted his head painfully back to the Vesunians, wincing, and saw that they had abandoned their attempts to pry the exit open.

A savage pleasure burned within him knowing that their escape attempt had been thwarted. He felt a familiar gaze boring into him and turned to see Varys's dark eyes watching him. He seemed concerned. Zen's blood boiled in response to the thought.

*Fuck him!*

Instead of feeling the usual warmth and excitement at seeing the alien, the sight of the Vesunian filled him with anger and pure disgust with himself. He had trusted Varys more than most, and, of course, it had bitten him in the ass. Surprise flickered across Varys's features in response to Zen's glare, which seemed to piss him off even more. Why the fuck would he be surprised that Zen was angry with him?!

He couldn't do much other than bare his teeth in weak rage and whisper in a voice only the Vesunian's large ears could hear.

"I thought you were different."

Zen gasped in pain as the words rattled him, his mouth still tasting of blood. Regret and shame flickered in Varys's eyes, and he looked away from Zen. Varys surveyed the army that now surrounded them, and there was a perceptible change to his demeanor. Something seemed to break inside the large alien, his eyes darkening, and he bowed his head. Slowly, ever so slowly, he raised his arms in a show of surrender.

Zen tried not to let his shock show.

Surprised and angry murmurings spread throughout the small group of Vesunians as well, but, eventually, they too followed suit. The sudden surrender surprised many of the humans as well. They had expected a fight. However, they didn't allow the Vesunians any time to reconsider it. A few humans rushed forward, at the command of an exhausted-looking Jennings, to apprehend the aliens and cuff them.

As the Vesunians were dragged away, back toward the direction of their cells, Varys looked back at Zen, who met his gaze with as much hatred as he could muster. That warm voice caressed his consciousness again, and Zen couldn't help but feel violated this time around.

*I'm so sorry, Zen.*

The moment he was out of sight, Zen allowed himself to sink into blissful unconsciousness.

# Chapter 13
## Altair

Altair didn't know whether he would ever leave this horrible room. Time seemed to have stood still as he spent what felt like countless days locked in this place. His face ached from wearing the silencer so frequently.

In order to prevent infection, Lil had taken to occasionally removing it, under scrutiny, and allowing him to wash and disinfect his face. She would then soak the device in disinfectant for a short time, borrowed from their gracious host. He would then take the silencer from her with a growing sense of doom and press it to his lips, wincing, his jaw immediately locking up.

Once or twice, Silas would visit them both in the room, giving brief, harried updates that seemed to go nowhere. He also seemed to get friendlier with Altair, which felt strange, but nice.

Occasionally, Silas would stay, as long as Lil's mood allowed for it. When he would, after the tense initial minutes, things would relax, and they would all gather over a card game or two before Silas would drink himself silly and need to head home. It was strange to be included in these games, but Altair welcomed the distraction. It was much better than trying to entertain himself.

Lilith would then walk Silas home at the end of the night with an eye roll and a smile, sending Altair a warning glance to not try anything funny.

But, again, he was confused where he sat with everyone, including Lilith. Other than being locked in the room with the silencer, he didn't even feel like a captive anymore. They spent most of their evenings in quiet solitude, with Lil mentoring him in sign language. During those countless, dreary evenings, the only light he could find was that he suddenly started taking to it.

Like, *really* taking to it.

He could tell that he was understanding it properly because despite Lil's stoic exterior, a glimmer of pride would shine in her eyes with every new milestone. And to Altair's credit, he was extremely motivated in learning sign language. If he couldn't use his voice, this was a way for him to escape the silence, even for just a moment.

They practiced by sharing small stories with each other. Whenever Altair would get lost or he didn't have the word that he needed, he would write it down, and Lilith would show him how to continue, a small smile on her face. Altair would then continue signing with confidence and pride, his cheeks warm at the sight of her smile.

And as they talked, Altair could feel that familiarity was blossoming between them. Though it wasn't a comfortable relationship, it was more than Altair had been privy to in years, and he enjoyed it immensely. Questions began burning in the back of Altair's mind regarding her life, but he wasn't sure he could even ask them, despite their growing friendship.

Friendship, captivity, it was all blurring together, and the lines didn't seem to exist anymore. He didn't feel like a captive as Lil gave him more freedom with the silencer.

Or as she talked about her family.

"My brother and mother still live on First Earth," she had signed late one evening, still at a slower pace with him than she did with Silas.

They were sharing a few dry biscuits with some sort of mystery meat gravy drizzled over them. Altair had listened intently as she brushed crumbs from her fingers in order to finish her thought.

"Shawn is sixteen and works full time so that he and mom might afford passage to live somewhere else at some point. I try to send them as much money as I can but…"

Pain had flashed across her features and Altair's heart went out to her. He'd understood the complications of family. Although he'd never struggled financially, his family situation was pretty messed up as well.

She had sighed and shrugged before grabbing another biscuit.

Altair had nodded, and they had shared a few moments of silence before Lil looked up at him with that piercing, incredible stare of hers. Her brown eyes had glimmered in the few rays of light that dared to creep in from under their door. She had raised her hands and hesitatingly signed her next question.

"What about your family?"

Altair's chest had ached. He had known that this was coming at some point, with how much time they had been spending around each other. But he could barely think about his family without wanting to fling himself off the nearest cliff. How could he bear talking about them to someone who was basically a stranger? Altair's fingers had been slow as he'd stumbled through his thoughts.

"My mother is dead, and my father hates me. I have no siblings."

The finality seemed to translate even through the sign language because Lil's eyes had glittered with regret, and she had thrown up the quick sign for "sorry" before returning to her meal.

He had shrugged. Altair was sorry too.

It was in this weird place of familiarity that Altair found himself when Lil burst into the room one day, earlier than normal, huffing in frustration. Altair jumped, startled by the sudden sound of the door against the wooden frame. He had been sketching again and had completely lost himself in the therapeutic reverie of scratching the charcoal to paper. Knee-jerk frustration bubbled up in his chest when he looked down at his sketch and saw that hours of work had been ruined by a startled scribble that marred the area he had been trying to finish.

Altair grumbled and tore the page out, crumpling it and tossing it into a corner before looking toward Lil who had dramatically seated herself on the bed and was signing to herself, so quickly that Altair couldn't make out what she was even saying.

After a few moments of this, Altair stood and walked over to her, waving his hand and snapping. Her head had tilted when he'd stood up, so he felt foolish for even trying to get her attention. She knew. She always knew.

Sitting cross-legged in front of her on the bed, he hesitatingly signed.

"What's wrong? What happen?"

A rueful smile played on her mouth at his mistake, and she sighed softly before correcting him. She then paused, as if she didn't know whether she should say anything.

Altair waited somewhat impatiently for her to decide. He tried not to roll his eyes as she sighed heavily several times before finally opening up.

"Silas finally has a hit on what we need. But instead of jumping on it as soon as possible, he's going to the festivities tonight."

Her hands flapped in frustration, and she made a sign that was unfamiliar to Altair. He raised his brow and gestured to her hands, and that seemed to break her ill temper slightly. When she spoke next, it was with her actual voice.

"That one means 'fuck.' I called Silas a 'fucking stoner.'" She laughed softly.

Altair couldn't help but grin as well. Oh, he'd definitely be using that one.

He nodded his thanks before signing again. "What festivities is Silas going to?"

He took his time signing Silas' name since spelling out each letter was still something he was getting used to.

She nodded toward the door and signed in his direction.

"You haven't heard all the commotion today? It's the end of Svaldu. The residents here have a two-week festival to celebrate their moon goddess. Today's the last day, and there's a huge fair going on. It ends tonight with a huge party. There will be drink and drugs and… well, you get the picture."

Altair had, in fact, heard the commotion. He just hadn't realized that that was what was going on. He knew the owner had mentioned Svaldu to them when they'd first checked in, but he hadn't given the word much thought.

He was sure Silas would be completely into that scene.

"And you are worried because he could lose the materials by not getting them right now?" He signed, trying to put the pieces together.

Lilith nodded and seemed to seethe in frustration at the reminder. Her hands moved a little quicker, and Altair struggled to keep up.

"Yes. We've been stuck here for nearly two weeks. I'm paying him way too much, and I've had to explain my delay over and over to my client."

She shot him a somewhat guilty look.

"Sorry."

Altair shrugged.

Another reminder that he was a job only stung a little. Plus, hearing that Silas was making this harder than necessary irritated him as well. Even though moving forward meant he was being brought into the unknown, it was better than staring at the brown, boring walls in silence for hours… days…

It reminded him more and more of the sand planet every single moment that he spent here, and he cringed away from the thought.

They sat in silence for a few moments before Altair got an idea.

A stupid, brilliant idea.

A stupidly *brilliant* idea.

He lifted his hands, and Lil turned to face him again.

"What if we go to this party?"

Lil's dark brows lifted in disbelief. "I'm sorry, come again?"

Altair sat up on his knees and signed excitedly, hoping he wasn't making any major mistakes.

"We go to the party, find Silas drunk or high, get him to give us the information for the materials, and we take care of it on our own! We could be out of here tomorrow, depending on the situation."

Lil's lips pursed and to Altair's delight, she seemed conflicted. She looked away, and this time she spoke aloud again.

"That feels wrong. I may not be the best person in the universe but to betray a friend like that..." She rubbed her hands together and Altair was a little shocked to see her so shaken by an idea. He was so used to her stoic, unfazed demeanor.

He shook his head, and the motion caught her attention. He signed quickly before she could turn away once more.

"I'm not suggesting we betray Silas. We pay him for his efforts. But I'm ready to be out of here. And I think you are too."

Lil glanced from his hands up to his eyes before dropping her gaze quickly, and Altair's insides squirmed in response. Seeing her this way, in such a stark contrast to who she had been up to this point...

He couldn't even finish the thought before she was gritting her teeth, that familiar fire back in her eyes. She stood, lifting her chin slightly.

"If we go, you have to keep the silencer on."

Altair nodded, expecting this stipulation.

"*And* you have to be handcuffed to me. Discreetly. We want to blend in with the party guests."

He nodded once more, also expecting something similar.

They looked at each other for a long while before Altair stood and gestured between them.

"These aren't exactly party outfits."

Lil scoffed lightly and folded her arms across her chest. She spoke aloud once more.

"And what of it?"

Altair raised an eyebrow at her and also folded his arms, hoping that he held the same confident air she did. He stood there for a few moments before deflating and lifting his hands to explain.

"You want to blend in, right?"

Lil paused before nodding, seeming unsure of what he was going to say next.

"Then, we need better outfits."

She rolled her eyes before signing dismissively at him. "And how would *you* know what we should wear?"

Altair grinned, an odd excitement bubbling up inside of him. After all these years he was going to a *party.* As a captive, but still.

"Oh, it's kind of my specialty. You'll see."

# Chapter 14
# Altair

Altair was handcuffed and imprisoned. A captive to the human female who stalked in front of him in a glittering two-piece. The way she walked reminded him of a sleek predator, unseen as it stalked its prey in the brush.

Lilith was dangerous.

Lilith was ill-tempered.

Lilith was beautiful.

Altair felt warmth flooding through him when she stepped out from behind the privacy screen, wearing a well-fitting, sparkling emerald two-piece that he had chosen. She had twisted, admiring her form in the mirror. Altair couldn't help but be smugly proud of his choice for her. It was perfect for a party. Not too flashy, as to draw attention, but enough to blend in.

Lil smirked at her appearance, obviously pleased. She spoke aloud, eyes flitting to Altair's reflection behind her, standing dumbfounded as he watched her pose. "Wow. I'm impressed. You really do know fashion."

She smoothed the front of her top and adjusted the backing to the gold earring in her left ear before brushing her hand against the scarring that marred her right side. Her dark eyes seemed to flicker with some strange emotion.

Altair had gotten so used to her appearance that sometimes it was a surprise to remember that she looked different from most of the people around her. Her scarring changed nothing about her, and it had never seemed to affect Lilith or how she carried herself as a bounty hunter.

Tonight was different.

Altair signed, since he still wore the silencer here in the clothing shop. "What happened?"

His hand gestured toward the scarring, hoping that his face showed he was sympathetic, not judgmental.

Lil rubbed her hand down her right arm, twisting away from her reflection, and fixed her jaw in a stubborn scowl. Her hands were quick and irritable.

"Why does it matter? I've told you it's a war injury."

Altair blew out a frustrated breath from his nose and rolled his eyes, throwing his hands up as he signed.

"Forget I asked."

There were a couple of moments of silence as Lil rocked from leg to leg, almost as though she was considering just sprinting from the shop. Altair had turned to grab his own outfit when she spoke aloud.

"It was an explosion." There was a thickness to her tone, as though she was speaking past a lump in her throat. "Humans are required to serve five years in our military when we turn eighteen. Honored to serve my five years." She spoke the last part as if it was a mantra.

Altair wondered how many times she had said it. And how many she'd actually meant it.

Lil continued, as though now that she was telling the story, it was just pouring from her mouth, like a waterfall of truth, breaking free from a dam.

"I was in for about three and a half years. I was good. I was really, really good." Her mouth turned upward in a satisfied smile. "I was on my way to leadership, even. I led a small battalion on a territory mission to one of the outer planets in the Triangulum system. It was the first time we'd stepped foot in Vesunian territory."

She took a steadying breath and Altair, caught up in the story, had nearly forgotten that it didn't have a good ending. She brushed her hand up and, again, lightly dragged her fingers across the scarring. Her eyes closed and her shoulders slumped forward as if the burden of the memory was too much for her to bear.

"The Vesunians knew we were coming. And they took out the planet with a Nuva blast."

Altair felt like the wind had been knocked out of him and goosebumps danced up and down his arms. He raised his hand to sign a question, and her eyes opened, taking in his shock, before she smiled ruefully.

"Yes. Nuva can do that. It's why this war is a suicide mission."

Her eyes were misty, and Altair could feel anger crackling underneath the surface of her calm exterior.

"They just blew it all up. With no regard to anything that lived there. And, sadly, the sacrifice was sort of worth it. It took my team out."

Altair was shaken from the stupor that her story had lulled him into by a striking realization. When he signed, he did so with admiration, hinting at respect.

"How did you survive that?"

She shook her head, as if that part wasn't as important as the rest of the story. But Altair disagreed.

"I almost didn't." Her head was still shaking back and forth when she let out a soft, disbelieving laugh. "I saw the blast coming before anyone else and called for everyone to run back for the ship. But no one else was fast enough. The ship took a majority of the blast, but the impact still took part of my face and my hearing."

She sighed heavily, almost relieved to be done telling her story.

"I survived on the dead planet, or what was left of it, for two weeks with my oxygen dwindling, since the atmosphere was shot. I only had a handful of nutrient bars in my pockets. Nearly died from my infection. They finally sent someone to come collect whatever was left and were shocked to find that someone had survived. It was a miracle that they even came back."

Altair felt dizzy. He didn't think his admiration for Lilith could grow, but it did. The warmth in his body seemed to sprout a pulsing beat that made him feel confused but fuzzy and happy. She truly was incredible. It was almost unfair that she had to be the bad guy in his story right now.

He shook his head and all he could do was sign a meager, "Wow."

Lil snorted in derision, her old fire sparking again within her.

"Yeah, wow."

She turned back to the mirror and began preening once again, silently ending the conversation.

Altair wasn't sure what else to say. He shuffled his feet back and forth until she seemed satisfied with her appearance and stepped away from both the mirror and the privacy screen, silently gesturing for him to take her place.

He nodded before moving forward and attempting to change. He struggled with the material because of the cuffs that he still wore. At one point, he got tangled enough that Lilith had to step back behind the privacy screen and remove the cuffs briefly with an irritated sigh.

He blushed when she did so, covering his lower half with his old shirt. Lil chuckled at his embarrassment, her eyes sparkling with a mischievousness that made Altair blush even deeper. Her eyebrows rose, a smirk dancing on her lips.

"Don't worry. I'm not looking."

But even as she stepped out of the privacy screen and he dropped the shirt from his body, he thought he saw her head turn slightly to look at him. He shook his head.

*You're seeing things, Altair.*

He stepped out finally, rubbing his sore wrists, and eyed his reflection in the mirror. He had changed since the time his father had so unceremoniously dumped him onto the sand planet. Altair wasn't sure what to make of his reflection, mainly because he didn't recognize himself anymore. He hadn't taken the time on the ship to study his appearance in the mirror and seeing himself now; it felt as though he was looking at a tired stranger, whose eyes had dulled by years of disappointment. It was as if the sands had eroded what was left of that hopeful boy who watched his father's ship take off and disappear. Any trace of his good looks had been eroded as well, replaced by hard lines of anger and fear.

Twenty years.

*Twenty. Years.*

The anger must've shown on his face because Lil tensed behind him as if expecting him to suddenly turn on her. He smoothed his expression, trying to soothe her, and raised his brows to indicate that he was smiling.

Her eyes flitted between his reflection and back to the male that stood before her. Her shoulders slowly rolled back and relaxed before she proffered the cuffs once more.

"You look nice. Let's go."

# Chapter 15
# Altair

Altair felt as though he was getting used to following Lilith around at this point. He felt like a duckling, toddling after its mother's giant, webbed steps. It was strange to think how losing her in the crowd would've brought him joy only a few weeks ago.

It was an absolute madhouse outside of the clothing shop. Kelptor was nearly always chaotic and loud, but it was amplified by one thousand percent because of the holiday. The vendors, who, yesterday, had screamed down passersby, selling their fruits and baskets, were now offering fried foods and strange-smelling meats skewered on sticks. Music poured from nearly every open window onto the winding cobblestone and sand streets, which resulted in a cacophony of noise that was both exhilarating and overwhelming.

Altair felt the blood in his veins pump even faster. The world around him felt alive for the first time in ages. It made him feel alive too. He inhaled a deep lungful of the fragrant, sticky air.

Lilith was pushing toward the market square, but unlike when they had first landed here, people were not moving out of her way. Some were too drunk or high to notice that she was even there. Others leered and purposefully moved into her path, eyes raking up and down her body as they spoke to her in various tongues. Altair felt a rush of anger as they would stop her, half regretting handing her such a beautiful outfit. It was idiotic that these males had never noticed Lilith in her armor in the same way. She was beautiful in that outfit too, and even fiercer than a tsunami having a love affair with a windstorm.

She paid them no mind, however, and would occasionally flash the blaster she had hidden in her outfit to scare off the more determined ones. Altair would smirk, as best as he could with the silencer, as they passed each rejected suitor. She truly was a force with which to be reckoned. She didn't need Altair to protect her.

The thought of protecting her jolted him and he blinked repeatedly, his heart picking up speed.

*Maybe he was losing his mind. Kelptor probably had that effect. Prime example, Silas.*

He shook his head, mind reeling, knowing that he was lying to himself. For all of her quirks and mood swings, he admired Lilith. She was an incredible, forceful personality. She wore her emotions on her sleeve, but never let them overtake her. It was something that Altair coveted.

It was difficult to put into words how, where, and why Altair's sentiments had changed toward his captor. Maybe it was the hours spent learning sign language from her. Maybe it was the fact that they had been in such close quarters for so long. Maybe it was the glimmer of regret and shame that would sparkle in her eyes when she would remind him he was a job for her, almost as though she didn't want to do it.

The sound of a melodious voice that rang across the square tore him from his thoughts. The singing hit him like a train in every single one of his senses.

*Oh no.*

He knew that type of voice anywhere. The voice didn't just affect him, however, because nearly every head turned to find the source of the singing. Everyone but Lilith, whose head was on a swivel, obviously looking for Silas among the entranced throng.

Altair felt as though he was floating on air, and the wind that carried him were the lyrics to the song that was currently wrapping the crowd in its embrace. He stopped dead in his tracks and peered over the heads of those nearest to him in order to find what he was sure was the source. Luckily he towered over most of the creatures surrounding him and could spot what he assumed was the entertainment for the night.

As expected, a Serinian female stood on a stage in the center of the crowd. She was a credit to her race. Her long, slim body glided across the stage as she sang into a microphone, her tone sultry and rich as her magic enslaved the surrounding throng. Her hair fell in long, thick waves, in the shimmering multitude of colors that for which Serinians were known, and her skin was glimmering as though it was coated in tiny diamonds. Her eyes were a deep, forest green, a common color among his people. She was utterly enchanting in the way that most Serinians were.

Which, Altair mused, was the entire reason his kind were probably so colorful. The most dangerous creatures always were, weren't they?

Altair felt a tug on his wrists and tore his gaze away from the female, who had obviously been hired to entertain the multitudes brought here by Svaldu. His gaze met Lilith's furious one, and she frowned, signing as best as she could with one hand free.

"We have to find Silas!"

Something else seemed to glimmer in her eyes as she glanced to where the Serinian was dancing on stage as she performed. Her long form twisting and turning brought shouts and whistles from the crowd. He felt a warmth creep up from his neck as he turned to meet Lilith's gaze once again.

Altair nodded, signing an apology, and gesturing over to the performer who was now kneeling down and stroking the faces of enamored creatures whose eyes held that familiar, glazed expression. Her sharp teeth flashed as her mouth stretched into a satisfied smile. None of her fans seemed put off by her terrifying grin.

Lil's eyebrows shot up as she finally, fully turned to where he had gestured. She signed, not even looking back at where Altair stood.

"A Serinian. Do you know her?"

Lilith's face twitched in anxiety at the idea, and Altair pushed around the people who swarmed near him in order to step in front of her. He signed to her, recognizing many conflicting emotions flashing across Lil's face.

*Anxiety. Fear. Anger. Jealousy.*

"No, I don't know her. It's just uncommon for my kind to use our powers in this kind of way. That's all. I wanted to stop and watch for a moment."

She nodded, her eyes moving between the angelic performer and Altair's face as if trying to sense whether he was lying. Satisfied with what she saw in his expression, she began pushing through the crowd again, head once more on a swivel.

Altair did his best to push away the magic of the performer's voice and look for Silas as well. It wasn't as if he was a difficult person to find. His unique appearance made him incredibly hard to miss. Sweat began pouring down Altair's back as he slipped through the gigantic crowd, doing his best not to get squashed between walls of bodies.

It didn't take long before Lilith was grabbing at the shoulder of the squat, hoofed hoarder. Silas was dancing between two human women, his eyes glazed, and obviously riding the euphoric high of the music. Altair also suspected, from the way the air smelt, that he was riding another kind of high as well.

Silas turned at Lilith's touch and his smile grew till large dimples appeared in his ruddy cheeks. The smile was slightly lopsided and lazy, confirming Altair's suspicions.

"Liiiiiiiiiiiil," Silas drawled, grabbing at her arm and signing something sloppily in her direction.

Because of his inebriated state, Altair couldn't quite catch what he said but Lilith seemed irritated and pushed him off.

"Silas, you useless addict. Get off me before your god-awful breath takes me out." Lilith signed, coughing.

Silas laughed. His chuckling was a wheezy, strained sound that resembled a braying animal. When he spoke, he spoke aloud, practically screaming over the music and the noise of the crowd. He seemed to have forgotten that his friend was deaf and didn't need the extra effort.

"Oh, come on, Lil! Have some fun! Live a little."

He shot Altair a mischievous look that the alien didn't quite understand. Lilith's cheeks reddened, and she gritted her teeth. Altair shrank back from her anger but watched as she closed her eyes, breathed deeply through her nose, and manually relaxed her shoulders. When she reopened her eyes, there was mischief in them, matching Silas's own, and she shot Altair a look that reminded him of why they were there. They weren't there for the party. But, they had to take part in the festivities to get what they needed from Silas.

Her eyes returned to where Silas was now holding out a strange drink that was being passed around by servers. The creatures seemed to pass delicately through the crowd, unharmed. They wore similar outfits to the performer on stage, but a more professional version. The drinks shimmered with a strange, sparkling light, and Altair shuddered slightly. It looked familiar. But he wasn't sure why.

He almost wanted to slap the drink from Lil's hands as she took it from Silas with a grimace. Holding it up, she studied it carefully. Silas rolled his eyes and crossed his arms. His two dance partners disappeared into the crowd in search of more interesting happenings. Lilith frowned before sighing and pressing it to her lips.

Suddenly, Altair remembered where he'd seen the drink before. It was a common Serinian alcohol that he'd seen served at royal parties he'd snuck into as a child. The wild swing from calm to crazy happened in the blink of an eye with every adult who'd had even one drink. As a child, he'd watched them make stupid decisions that they would've never made sober.

*Oh no!*

"*Mazel tov*." She murmured as she tipped the drink back and emptied the glass before Altair could stop her.

# Chapter 16
# Lilith

Everything was incredibly blurry and seemed to be covered in dazzling, multi-colored lights. They sparkled in hues and shades she had never even seen before. Lilith spun around, her hands on her mouth as she stared in wonderment at the glittering party around her. It was so beautiful she almost wanted to cry.

Key word, almost. She was drunk, not a bitch.

Was she even drunk? It was one drink, after all.

She'd never been a lightweight. But the feeling of this alcohol was *amazing*. She felt like she had grown wings and was floating above the surrounding crowd. Lilith so rarely let her guard down these days that the feeling of her inhibitions being swept away by one, measly, sparkly drink was both exhilarating and terrifying. She spun around, marveling at the lights catching the sequins in her outfit and two-stepped to the rhythm she could feel vibrating through her shoes. The soles weren't as thin as her usual boots, but she could still feel enough to keep up with the swaying crowd around her. She felt like she was forgetting something. But that couldn't be right.

All that was important right now was that she kept listening to the sultry voice of the alcohol pounding through her bloodstream. It whispered to her thrumming blood that all that was important was right here and right now.

Lilith felt someone catch her arm in a tight grip and irritation pushed at the exhilaration.

*Why the fuck was someone interrupting something so magical?!*

She turned, ready to shove the downer off of her when she was mesmerized by two, beautifully alien green eyes that were shrouded in worry. Lilith had seen green eyes before, but Altair's were different. They glimmered in a way that a human's never could. The first time she had seen them, she'd been grateful that her hood was hiding her blush. They'd sparkled and reflected the sharp silver of her ship.

He'd looked so afraid back then. She was grateful when the fear had left his eyes over these last few weeks. He looked afraid like that again as he watched Lilith sway to the beat that hummed up her legs. He was signing frantically, but her brain was fuzzy from the high of the night. She squinted her eyes and desperately tried to focus on what he was attempting to say in stilted and juvenile sign language.

Something about the drink. And Serinians.

*God*, she didn't care enough to sit here trying to decipher his flapping. As much as he'd improved, she was drunk, and he still hadn't mastered the language entirely.

But was she *really* drunk?

She guessed it didn't matter too much as she swayed her hips in a serpentine wave, moving her arms in a way that shifted him as well. All that mattered was how she felt in this moment. And how devastating Altair looked tonight.

She had her wits about her enough to reflect, vaguely, that he was still a job to do. A very lucrative job that would fix all of her problems back home.

*Problems? What problems?* The alcohol seemed to whisper. *Everything is perfect. Look at him.*

And she did. She fucking looked at him. He hadn't been kidding when he'd said he'd known fashion. He was dressed in the more masculine version of what Lilith herself wore, the sequined suit tight to his body. Her eyes raked over him, ignoring his desperate signing in place of admiring his incredible good looks.

He was tall and regal, almost willowy. He wasn't Lilith's usual type since she typically valued brawn over most everything else in a partner. However, something about the way he carried himself was entrancing. The brooding, complicated, emotionally unavailable thing worked for him. Maybe being attracted to that meant Lilith had issues. She shrugged, that was something she'd already known.

When her client had said he was a royal, she'd known it almost instantly as soon as they'd met. Though tattered and filthy and stinking to high heaven, Altair's features screamed for someone to place a crown on his stunning, multi-colored waves of hair. Those green, enchanting eyes. The sharp features. His proud, full lips, almost always strained into a frown when the silencer was off of them. She hated how much he frowned, but she also understood that life had not been kind to him. He rarely had a reason to smile.

She eyed the piece of metal keeping Altair's mouth shut and frowned to herself.

The Silencer.

God, what a shame it was hiding those lips.

*It doesn't have to;* the alcohol whispered sultrily, its effects wrapping around her brain in a heavenly haze. It was as if the alcohol was hugging her mind tightly in a beautiful embrace.

Damn, and it had some good ideas.

Lilith almost reached up to remove the silencer when Altair grabbed her arms, gesturing at the cuffs. He snapped his fingers in front of her eyes as if trying to get her to focus. Lilith was once again irritated. She was trying to admire him, goddamn it.

She sighed heavily when he began dragging her from the crowd, only following because the cuffs around their wrists connected them.

Cuffs. *Cuffs.*

Because he was a job.

Lilith blinked hard as she felt her reasoning return to the surface momentarily. She was forgetting why she had come to this stupid party.

*What was in that fucking drink?*

Altair pulled her into a quieter alleyway that was devoid of any partygoers. He pressed her into the stone wall that felt cold and clammy against the warmth of her skin. Altair's touch was also cold. A horrible reminder that nearly sobered her to the bone.

An amphibious creature. An alien.

Dangerous scum. Whores.

Lilith's mother had always told her stories of the Serinians when she was younger. Before the Collective had contacted Earth, the Serinians had done some preliminary exploring of their own. They had been curious about the creatures who lived on the tiny, blue rock and had come to learn more about humanity. They especially enjoyed exploring the oceans. Of course, back then, the sailors had just called them sirens. Creatures with voices so enchanting, they could lure anyone to their untimely and watery grave with a simple invitation. Now, they were the prostitutes of the universe. The snakes that used their powers to turn the tides of wars, destroy monarchies, and pit brother against brother.

Of course, that's what made Lilith perfect for the job. She was completely immune to their charms. And now she was lusting after one, completely of her own volition. Endangering the mission. Endangering her family and their future. All because he was pretty. Lilith felt a surge of disgust for herself, her mother's disapproval ringing in her mind.

Altair snapped once more, jolting Lilith from her self-hatred, and signed desperately, his hands practically pressed against her face. His eyes darted from hers to her mouth, as if looking for something.

She felt her willpower melting once again, both under the influence of whatever that drink was and his proximity to her, against this wall. Her cheeks flushed and warmth pulsed through her. She could practically *feel* his heartbeat, he was pressed so deeply into her. She felt his knee between her legs, and the jostling of their bodies caused all her blood to rush downward.

*Fuck*, she couldn't figure out what he was trying to say. He was too worked up, and he hadn't been learning sign language for very long. Plus, she was pretty drunk. At least she thought she was. Maybe.

She reached up, and immediately Altair stilled, his hand rising with hers since the cuffs were still linking them together. Her fingers brushed lightly through the hair surrounding his ears and Lilith thought she saw him shiver. She smiled in victory.

*So, he reciprocated her feelings. Good.*

His eyes were wide as she pressed the hidden buttons on the sides of the silencer and pulled it from his face. His throat bobbed as he swallowed nervously, and his tongue darted out to wet his lips, relieved to be free.

*The lips. The fucking. Amazing. Lips.* And suddenly, Lilith didn't care what Altair had been trying to say anymore as she pulled his face down toward hers.

# Chapter 17
## Altair

*He couldn't let her do this.*

She was out of her mind, drunk on Serinian alcohol. He had been trying to tell her all night that the one drink she had would completely warp her mind. Memories of his father and mother dancing and drinking riotously at lavish parties floated through his memories. He would usually sneak into such affairs, being too young to be invited otherwise. They would pour the sparkling and enticing drink from glass to glass. It was practically Serinian magic in a bottle.

She didn't know what she was doing and as enchanting and gorgeous as she was in this moment, and as much as Altair wanted to relinquish control and allow her to kiss him, he knew it was wrong. The sick feeling in the pit of his stomach boiled, and he gently pulled away from her, grabbing her hands in his free one momentarily. She immediately pulled her grasp from his own, her eyes darkening.

He shook his head, his cheeks burning and his heart dropping at the disappointment and rejection that flashed across her features. He hated seeing that. It wasn't that he didn't want this.

Gods, was it crazy that he did?

He just didn't want it like… this.

And it was that guilt, that burning, that rush of emotion that caused Altair to forget the one rule. The simple rule his father had given him before abandoning him.

Never. Speak. If. You. Don't. *Know*.

"Lilith." Altair's voice caressed the name, lavishing it on his tongue as the deadly magic rolled out of his mouth, merely brushing by her head, and leaving her unharmed.

The magic whirled and danced away from Lilith and Altair's heart seized as he looked past her shoulder and saw it careening toward a figure that stumbled drunkenly in their direction down the alleyway. A hoofed alien, wearing a sequined vest, clopped toward them, braying Lilith's name.

Silas.

"Oi, Lil! Just wanted to make sure you were alri…"

Silas froze as the magic enveloped him and completely encapsulated his senses. It swirled around him, causing his outfit to flutter in the small breeze.

Altair's dread rose as he saw that familiar look of complete and utter devotion blossom in Silas's eyes. The same look the crowd around the Serinian entertainment had as they'd watched the performer, but with even more intensity. More love. More devotion.

Lilith looked over at Silas, her brow furrowed. She must've sensed his footsteps, but her reflexes were slower on the Serinian alcohol. She couldn't stop this.

Silas sighed in contentment, his steps quickening as he bee-lined toward Altair.

"Gods, kid, I've never realized just how... pretty you are."

His voice was warm and gentle, and his words shocked Lilith into stillness. Confusion sparked in her eyes. Altair tried to take a step away, shaking his head, but the curse held his limbs in place. As desperately as he tried to move, his body was no longer his to control. It was like a mad puppeteer, intent on absolute destruction. Its dark hands controlled everything that Altair did. Tears pricked his eyes as he felt a familiar, biting steel appear in his free hand. He didn't dare speak again, for fear there were others nearby.

He couldn't stop this either. He tried to gesture for Silas to move away from him. To run. To do *anything*...

It was no use. He couldn't move and the curse was hungry. It had devoured his mother. And now it was going to take Silas.

The interaction happened in less than fifteen seconds. Fifteen seconds that changed everything. Absolutely *everything*.

Silas stepped forward, arms outstretched toward Altair, as if to embrace him. And Altair plunged his dagger deep into Silas's chest.

# Chapter 18
## Zen

It had been three weeks. Three weeks of healing. Three weeks of interrogation. Three weeks of complete and utter bullshit. And Zen was tired.

He hadn't fully settled into a hospital bed when Sergeant Jennings came by for the first time. The man hadn't even cleaned the blood from his uniform before coming to ask Zen exactly what had happened.

Why had the aliens surrendered?

Why didn't they kill Zen?

*Why... why... why...*

And, honestly, if Zen had any answers, he probably would've given them to Jennings at this point. He felt deflated and defeated by everything that had happened. The questions buzzed and hummed in his mind, like irritating insects hell-bent on his madness, mimicking the sergeant's voice. It only served to make things worse. Betrayal still made his chest sting.

Everything he thought he knew about Varys and the Vesunians seemed to be utter horse shit at this point. How did he know he wasn't just giving completely useless information to his superior? He could trust nothing that Varys had said as solid intel, not after what had happened.

Zen was haunted by memories of that day. Blood stained nearly every dream he had, and the mercy that Varys had showed briefly in sparing him didn't feel like mercy anymore. Mercy would've been letting him die. It would've been granting him reprieve from the horrors he had witnessed. It wouldn't have been letting him live with these memories.

He would wake from dreams of cracking bones and blood-curdling screams, unable to dispel the image of Reeves's blank stare. He would wince as his brain repeatedly replayed the crunch of her body as she was dropped. Then he would stare at the stained ceiling of the hospital and wonder if the sleeping drugs they had given him were simply just sugar pills. Perhaps it would've been easier if he had died in that cell block. He half wished for it on those sleepless nights of terror and flashbacks.

So, he had just shrugged off the barrage of questions that Jennings spewed, not meeting the fierce gaze of the older man. Jennings would scream, red-faced, with spittle hanging from his lip until the nurses would reprimand and shoo him out. He screamed and screamed for answers, day in and day out. But he could scream for the rest of eternity, Zen could barely hear it over the shrieking in his own head. He wanted answers too, that's all he'd wanted all along.

But all Zen knew was that his ribs hurt. They hurt so fucking bad. And so did his chest for some stupid reason. But the nurses couldn't fix a break they couldn't see. So, they settled for repairing his ribs.

He was lucky that they had the medical supplies on First Earth that allowed him such a quick recovery. Otherwise, he would've been out of commission for possibly months. He'd barely survived the weeks that they had forced him to spend in that uncomfortable bed, wrapped in sterile sheets. He didn't know if his mental health could handle *months* of recovery.

Finally, when the three weeks were over, he was allowed to go back to his room. When he reentered the desolation of his sleeping quarters, he found that his roommate's things were gone. Upon questioning those who shared rooms around them, he discovered that they had found the poor kid hanging from the ceiling fan a week before his return. He had been enlisted for less than a year. The tone of each person who'd talked to him about it had been so casual, because apparently suicide was just a run-of-the-mill consequence of war. Another young life, taken by a meaningless war.

Was it terrible that Zen couldn't even remember his name?

*You're as bad as they are.* His mind hissed, and he winced against the intrusive thought.

Zen collapsed into the seat that was pushed against the far wall near his desk. He pressed a hand into his aching side, hoping that the tenderness was just a temporary side effect. He shot a glance over at the clock on the wall that ticked a terrible march. Everything seemed so much louder now.

Midnight. And he had a shift in six hours.

Zen groaned softly, knowing that he could never get to sleep quickly enough to feel well-rested in the morning. At least, his shift was a normal one, right back into the shop. He could allow the mindlessness of repairing machinery to numb his mind, as long as he didn't fall asleep under a ship.

Zen allowed his thoughts to wander, and he fantasized about his passion, letting the bliss of it envelope his being.

*Just like Varys's voice used to make you feel.*

Zen shot straight up in the chair, shaking his head as hard as he could, like a mangy dog with a flea problem. The thought brought with it unwanted memories and emotions that he couldn't deal with right now. No, he couldn't think about Varys anymore.

Varys had betrayed his trust and their false friendship shouldn't mean anything to him anymore. Everything had been a lie. Of course, they couldn't be friends. Zen felt so stupid when he thought about how deeply he'd fallen into it.

They were enemies, facing each other in a decades-long war that showed no sign of ending soon. Zen swallowed against a lump in his throat and was angry at the tears that stung the corners of his eyes. It was stupid to think that he had found a kindred spirit, especially among a race so violent and horrible.

His mind screamed the argument back and forth. Nothing about what had happened made *any* sense. He frowned, pressing a hand into his forehead. Zen's mind circled back to the thought, like an incorrigible pup, hell-bent on torturing its master. Varys was so kind. So very kind. Every word he'd spoken had been genuine, and he had stopped his friend from killing Zen.

*But*, he reminded himself, V*arys hadn't stopped her from killing anyone else in the cell block that day.*

These thoughts were getting him nowhere. He needed to get to bed. Zen stood, exhaling, and headed toward his bathroom. His footsteps were soft and nearly silent on the concrete floor of his sleeping quarters. His bathroom now. Not anyone else's anymore. And again, that guilt returned that made his tongue feel as though it was stuck to the roof of his mouth.

He pushed the feelings away as best as he could before getting ready for bed. It took him a little longer than usual, and with a lot more wincing. Eventually, he was able to crawl into his uncomfortable bunk and pretend as if sleep would visit him. Drifting into dreamland felt like an impossible goal, as it seemed to always be these days.

Instead, he stared at the ceiling much longer than he wished to, grateful that this one, at least, wasn't stained. Shockingly, shortly after that thought, Zen felt his eyes becoming heavier and gladly took hold of the heavy sensation that filled his body. As he drifted away, he vaguely wished for his dream to be free of violence tonight.

*Zen was once again in the prison block. But it was different this time. Very different.*

*This time, he didn't have a weapon, or an army backing him. In fact, he was in his simple hospital gown. He shivered, his naked body bare against the concrete of the cell block floor. He was alone, the only human, and staring up at the leering faces of the aliens that were surrounding him. Fear shot through him, and he trembled.*

*"W-what do you all want from me?"*

*His voice echoed and sounded strained. He struggled to get the words out in that helpless way that dreams muzzled him. They were silent as they watched him with their terrifying eyes. Suddenly, the aliens parted, allowing one of them to step forward.*

*His enormous form and long, dark curls were unmistakable.*

*Varys.*

*Zen's heart quickened, and his mouth suddenly felt dry. But not how it had before. This wasn't fear he was feeling. His cheeks flushed, and he attempted to scuttle away from the alien, who fixed him with his intense gaze. His hospital gown rustled against the ground, the strings impossibly coming undone from around his back. He struggled to keep the gown up and to hold it to his form.*

*Those fucking black eyes bore into his own, watching as the human attempted to get away. But Varys was quicker than him. He moved forward, wordlessly, and knelt down, snatching Zen's leg to prevent him from backing away even further.*

*Zen stared at him for a long moment, both of them saying nothing. His heart felt as though it was playing tennis against his chest. Finally, Zen spoke, his voice echoing once again.*

*"W-what do you want from me, Varys?"*

*He was ashamed that the sentence came out as a whimper.*

*There was another long pause, and then the alien smiled. That same, damn smile that had made Zen trust him so easily.*

God, why couldn't he hate it?

*Slowly, ever so slowly, Varys pushed forward. His long body hung over Zen's own, his hair tickling down toward the human's face.*

*Warmth coursed through Zen's stomach, and finally, fear entered him. But he wasn't afraid of Varys. He was afraid of himself. He gasped lightly as the alien's face came closer and closer to his own.*

*Varys leaned down, staring deeply into Zen's eyes for a moment. The alien seemed to hesitate slightly before he softly pressed his lips against Zen's own.*

*Fuck!*

*Zen knew that this was a dream. Further, he knew it should be a nightmare. The creature that had haunted humanity for decades was currently kissing him. Heat pooled in his stomach as the alien's lips moved against his, his hand cupping Zen's cheek.*

Oh god, Varys was kissing him.

*And grasping his hair, pulling Zen up toward him. Pressing the warmth of his body into Zen's quaking form. Parting his lips to meet Zen's tongue with his own.*

*Oh fuck, oh fuck, oh fuck!*

*Heat blossomed between them as their lips danced together and Zen reached up, twisting his fingers into the alien's hair. He shivered as Varys extended his reach down and slid a large hand up his leg. His touch left a burning trail that made Zen gasp into Varys' mouth.*

*He felt the alien's hand slip under his hospital gown and slide up his body, resting between his thighs. His fingers began moving in slow circles. He paused before moving upward once again, as if intending to grasp Zen.*

*He moaned softly against Varys's lips and pleasure coursed through him at the alien's touch.*

*Oh my god, he wanted this.*

*He closed his eyes, relinquishing control and opening his mouth wider, spreading his legs to allow Varys more access...*

And an alarm sounded right in Zen's ear. Zen shot straight up in bed, smacking his head into the low ceiling above him. Cursing colorfully, he rubbed his forehead with the palm of his hand. His heart was dancing in his chest, and it took a few moments for him to get his bearings. To realize that it had been a dream. And also, to realize that he'd smacked his head into the concrete ceiling hard enough to leave a lump the size of a ping-pong ball.

Both shame and disappointment bubbled inside Zen, pushing him out of bed and motoring him toward the bathroom to get ready. His mind raced with excuse after excuse, doing its best to explain the dream away.

He'd wanted a break from the flashback dreams, but he hadn't wanted *that* in its place. Panic and guilt flushed through him as he desperately tried to lie to himself. Zen pressed a hand to his sweaty forehead, silently cursing his brain as he started the shower. He doused himself in the coldest shower known to humankind, willing the burning and throbbing to fuck itself.

*It was just a dream. It meant nothing. You still hate Varys.*

And yet, even as Zen threw himself into his repairs. Even as he tinkered and toiled and did his best to push it away...

The taste of Varys still lingered on his lips.

# Chapter 19
## Zen

Zen wasn't sure why he had had that dream. Or, why he was suddenly finding it very difficult to forget about it. *Or*, why a version of it had visited him every single night.

Each time, Varys would get closer and closer. Every dream was more and more passionate, but never would quite resolve. Zen found himself both dreading and looking forward to every single night that he went to sleep. He was grateful that his traumatizing dreams were gone, but waking up aroused was starting to get old.

As he paced back and forth between the bunk and his bathroom a few days after the initial dream, he tried desperately to come up with a reason why something like this would happen. And why it would keep fucking happening.

Did people commonly have dreams about kissing someone with whom they were angry? Let alone, someone they no longer felt was supposed to be a part of their lives?

*It wasn't just kissing,* that snarky voice whispered into his thoughts.

Zen waved it off, blushing so deeply that even his neck felt hot. For all intents and purposes, it was kissing. Either way, none of it made sense.

Zen wished that the military-approved therapists were sworn to secrecy. That people like Sergeant Jennings didn't have them in his back pocket. Otherwise, he'd have scheduled a meeting to have his head examined.

*This was stupid.*

Zen sighed heavily before sitting on the floor, his face in his hands. The reason couldn't possibly be that he was attracted to Varys. Sure, he'd enjoyed his company. If he was being completely honest with himself, it had been one of the first times that Zen felt as though he had found someone who understood him completely. But friends could feel that way too, right?

Zen pressed his hands harder into his face, pushing palms into his eyeballs until he saw stars lighting up the darkness. He was sure it was just a fluke. He had been to hell and back in the last several weeks. Brains were stupid slabs of meat that couldn't tell the difference between famine and dieting. Let alone friendship, attraction, and hatred. He was sure this meant nothing. Zen rubbed his eyes, silently praying that everything would suddenly make sense and the conflict would end. But, of course, it didn't. It was never that easy.

Zen sighed and stood up once again, brushing the dust from the back of his uniform. He couldn't be late for his shift at the shop again. He'd been late nearly every day this week, and he could tell that Private Richard was getting irritated. There was only so much sympathy that Zen could ride before his tardiness was just simply tardiness.

He grabbed his tool bag and walked out of his quarters, eyes on the ground as he felt the curious stares of everyone around him. Their intensity nearly stuck him into the ground.

It had been weeks since the incident at the prison. And yet, it felt like it had just happened yesterday. Word had spread like wildfire around the base and, though Zen knew that most of these people didn't care about him, they *did* care about the rumors his actions had stirred.

He heard their whispers. All of them. They hissed that somehow he had bested the entire alien fleet on his own and forced them to surrender. Most people didn't believe that one. Not that Zen blamed them, he wasn't exactly a soldier of great renown. No one had known who he was before the prison catastrophe.

The other type of whispers involved him being a traitor and that the aliens hadn't wanted to hurt their only source of information. Their man on the inside. That one was slightly more believable, even if it wasn't true.

*Traitor.*

The word hung heavy on Zen's mind as he traipsed toward the giant doors that led to the bus line that would, eventually, take him to the base shop. During the short bus ride, he stared out the window listlessly and hunched his shoulders to buffet the intrusive and terrifying possibility that he was, indeed, a traitor. He could feel the stares of fellow passengers and desperately tried to pretend he was anyone else.

He had gone back and forth on whether he had committed treason. Finally, he'd settled on the idea that if he had, Jennings would've strung him up or thrown him in a cell of his own by now. But they didn't have anything on him. Because he hadn't *really* done anything, except get to know Varys.

Did that count as a traitorous activity?

Zen pulled a bandanna over his hair to keep it from falling into his face while he worked and grabbed his first assignment for the day.

*Faulty blasters. Easy peasy.*

He walked over to the pickup window and grabbed the crate of blasters before walking back to his station with them. The sound of whirring tools and metal against metal were sounds that would typically set someone's teeth on edge, but Zen relished them. They reminded him of the days he'd spent working with his dad in their little garage workshop. His dad had always been slow, with his one bad leg, but he was meticulous. Every bolt, every bracket, the man had made sure that things were laid with perfection.

That was before the veteran's money stopped coming in as quickly. After that, they couldn't afford the projects, and his dad's tools began collecting dust. Zen would still always find his way into the garage, blow the grime off, and handle them until he understood each one, inside and out.

It's what sparked his interest in engineering and metalworking. When he had taken his preliminary testing before entering the military, he had scored incredibly high in his knowledge of machinery. That, combined with his abysmal scores in anything battle-related, all but secured him a position as an engineer.

He took the blasters apart, piece by piece, and carefully examined them. They looked completely normal. He wasn't sure why they wouldn't be functioning-

*Oh.*

There it was. This batch had their chambers installed backwards. The pieces looked the same from each end to the unknowing eye, but Zen could see the little indentations that indicated which side was which. Today must've been his lucky day. These were simple fixes. He began disassembling the blasters and reinstalling the plasma chambers correctly.

He had gotten about halfway through the crate and had disassociated happily, losing himself in the task's monotony, when a sharp clang made his neck nearly snap as he looked up. His heart jumped into his throat, and a brief flash from the escape attempt had forced its way into his mind. Irritation crept through him when he saw what had caused the noise.

A soldier was leaning against the side of his workstation wall, his arms crossed and his stare lewd as he watched Zen at work. His stomach turned as he recognized that predatory leer.

*This had to be some sick, cosmic joke.*

"Zen Farraway."

The soldier caressed the name on his tongue, his eyes casually sliding up and down his body. He smirked before speaking again.

"Damn, it's good to see you again."

Zen tried to make his tone casual as he looked away from the soldier, but his shaky hands betrayed him. He ignored the comment about seeing each other again and spoke, his tone sharper than he'd hoped it would be.

"That's me. What do you need…" he shot a glance at the soldier's nameplate, "Bell?"

Bell sneered and strutted his way over to Zen, causing an involuntary shudder to pass through him.

"Sergeant wants to see you. Says it's important and that your menial tasks can wait. Or be picked up by someone else."

Bell stopped, much too close to Zen, his breath hot and foul.

*God, did this man ever brush his teeth?*

Zen dropped his tools, and he gritted his teeth. It made his stomach boil that Bell had both interrupted him and, in the same breath, implied that his job wasn't important.

Would he ever get a normal day in the shop?

*Would he ever get a normal day?*

"What does he want?"

Zen's tone was snappy, and the soldier frowned, displeasure flashing in his eyes. There was a moment of silence before he sighed heavily and shrugged. He stretched his hand in Zen's direction and grabbed his upper arm, squeezing tightly. Zen, instinctively, flinched away from the touch, which only seemed to make Bell's sneer stretch wider across his face.

*Damn it.*

Bell's eyes glimmered with sadistic amusement. "Don't know. Don't care. All I know is that Jennings asked me to fetch you. You gonna make me drag you out of here?"

Bell didn't even try to hide that he was lying about not knowing what Jennings wanted. But Zen didn't care anymore. He would not submit to Bell's obvious lure. He was playing a game, trying to bait him into begging for an answer. Zen's teeth ground against each other, and he fought to control the nearly uncontrollable wave of emotions that had grown even fiercer since the traumatic event in the prison.

*Breathe in… breathe out…*

With a deep inhale through his nose, Zen turned toward Private Bell and shook his head, shoulders stiffening. "No need. I'll come."

Bell chuckled before swiveling to the exit. "Smart boy. I'll meet you outside the shop once you're done letting your superiors know."

Zen glared daggers at his back as he slouched away, summoning every curse word he ever knew and throwing them silently in his direction. He kicked his tool bench, snarling in pain, before pulling the bandanna from his head. Zen picked up the remaining box of faulty blasters and dropped them back off at the assignments window with a quick, scribbled note on what exactly was wrong. He didn't want the person who picked it up next to waste their time trying to figure it out.

It took only a few moments, and a stab of guilt at the look Private Richard had given him when he said that he had to leave, before he stepped out of the shop. Bell was leaning up against the cool, metal wall, cleaning the undersides of his fingernails with the tip of his knife. Zen felt a surge of pleasure at the idea of him accidentally losing a finger.

Bell grunted when Zen stepped out and nodded to indicate for him to follow, before making his way to the main area of the military base. The man's steps were heavy and shuffling, reminiscent of how they'd been taught cavemen walked.

Zen followed, an ominous, sick feeling increasing in his gut with every step. His own footfalls felt just as heavy as Bell's as they traversed the base. He hoped he hadn't fallen for some clever ruse that Bell had devised to get him alone. Slithers of icy fear wormed their way through him as he remembered the words that Bell had yelled gleefully at his back that day in the prison. Tears gathered in the corners of his eyes at the memory, and Zen fought to keep them contained. Luckily, Bell didn't turn around.

Zen struggled not to reminisce on what had happened afterward, in his meeting with Varys. It only brought with it feelings that he didn't want to have. Feelings that seemed to spur the memory of his reoccurring dream. He flushed and instead tried to focus on anything but that. Like, how he was going to get out of this situation if it was a ruse. Or, if it wasn't, what exactly Jennings wanted from him.

He had questioned Zen thoroughly in the hospital, and Zen had thought that it was over. Perhaps, foolishly, he had hoped to move on from whatever temporary burst of insanity he had had in befriending Varys.

Peering around, he realized that the number of soldiers around them was thinning. It was also growing quieter, and the walls felt as though they were beginning to close in on the two men. Bell turned a corner toward the interrogation rooms, and Zen felt his heart kick up in tempo. This was where they took prisoners of war.

*Why was he, a soldier, being brought here?*

The twisting in his stomach intensified.

*That couldn't be what he was here for.*

He followed Bell down the long hallway filled with rooms that had darkened windows. The sound of them making their way slowly through the space felt eerie as all sound echoed away from the two soldiers, before returning mockingly. There was no light here, other than the sickly pale florescent bulbs that flickered above them.

Suddenly, the suffocating silence was broken by a loud, inhuman shriek from one of the nearby rooms. It reverberated off the walls and rang in Zen's ears in a way that felt unnatural, causing uncontrollable shivers to break out down his spine. Zen nearly jumped out of his skin, and he fought every urge to turn tail and run. Bell didn't seem even the slightest bit affected by the horrible sound but turned to smirk at Zen's reaction.

"Sounds like one of your Vesunian buddies might break soon."

He chuckled insidiously before continuing to move forward. The "buddies" comment didn't even register as mounting panic caused a deafening rushing to pound in Zen's ears. He felt a knot of emotion form in his throat at the idea that Varys may be enduring torture at this very moment. Or the possibility that that may have been him screaming.

He mentally slapped himself again for the knee-jerk reaction he'd had to be worried for the massive alien. It was stupid to even feel any sort of sympathy for a creature who had caused so much destruction. But it still hurt to think about Varys that way. Zen couldn't deny that completely.

Bell stopped in front of one of the interrogation rooms and pulled out jangling keys to open it. Zen felt a sudden surge of disgust at the realization that those keys brought to him. That was why he had so immediately disliked Bell. He was an assigned torturer. Anyone who had the knack for something so awful wasn't anyone that Zen felt comfortable being around. Let alone the sexual harassment that Bell brought in heaps.

With a strange hissing beep, the key was scanned, and Bell gestured for Zen to step inside. The smirk that was stretching wider across the torturer's face as every second passed made Zen want to sprint in the opposite direction. Despite the horrible feeling, he walked forward, feeling as though he did so in slow motion, and stepped into the interrogation room. Every instinct screamed at Zen that he was in danger. But there was nothing he could do. Not anymore. It was too late.

The interrogation room was empty aside from a silver chair. There were restraints attached to the arms that looked as though they were made of tough leather and metal. A familiar figure stood in the corner, hands clasped behind his back. Sergeant Jennings. Again. The man was like a vengeful specter, always looming around to exact his revenge.

Zen's heart slammed against his chest, trying to beat the time for fastest heartbeat. He shakily saluted Jennings out of habit. This wasn't good. This wasn't good at all. Zen felt like he had cotton in his mouth.

*Breathe in… breathe out…*

Jennings stepped forward, his gait balanced and careful, as if he knew Zen would run. And Zen almost did, if he hadn't heard the door sliding shut behind him.

"Private Farraway," Jennings mused as he moved casually toward him. "I'm sure you know why you're here."

That seemed to be one of his favorite phrases. It was as if he enjoyed lavishing the beginning of the punishment more than anything else. He would dangle the reasoning over your head like some demented cat toy.

Zen played dumb and, with great effort, shook his head from side to side, hoping that Jennings wouldn't see the beads of sweat that had formed on his upper lip.

Jennings threw his head back and laughed, actually laughed, his voice echoing cruelly through the room. He dropped his head, smiling a toothy, satisfied grin.

"You've always been a shitty liar, Private."

And that's when Zen knew he was fucked. He took a step back as if he thought he could run away. His instincts were screaming for him to leave and making him antsy.

The subtlest of nods toward Bell and, in one swift motion, Zen's legs had been kicked out from under him and his arms pinned behind his back. His face slammed into the hard floor, causing stars to pop into his vision. He didn't even have time to cry out before Bell had dragged him over to the chair and strapped him in, the restraints tight against his wrists. He struggled briefly, but quickly realized he'd have to have the strength of ten men to break free. His head pounded a horrible rhythm that the crash against the floor had set. It hurt to focus on his face.

So, instead, Zen focused on not letting his panic overtake him.

*Breathe in… and out…*

"It took a while to get the approval from the Council." Jennings waltzed circles around the chair, smirking gleefully as Zen bowed his head and refused to meet his gaze. The sergeant continued, watching him hungrily.

"But it finally came in today. We rarely torture our own for information, so I'm sure you can understand why they were… conflicted."

His tone indicated that Jennings had no reservations about what was about to happen.

*In… and out….*

Zen looked up, angry that there were tears in his eyes, and bared his teeth. His emotion only seemed to delight Jennings, who rolled his eyes, his smirk stretching further across his face. The grizzled sergeant turned to where Bell stood, mirroring Jennings's glee at the position that Zen was in.

"I'm sure it won't take you long, Private Bell. Do whatever you need to in order to get that information."

And without another word or glance toward Zen, he stepped out of the room.

Zen watched the doors close and realized, with a horribly sick feeling in the pit of his stomach, that this was real. A couple of tears found their way down his cheeks as Bell took a few steps in his direction, reaching for his tool belt.

*No, no, no… He couldn't be Zen's torturer. It was just too horribly serendipitous.*

Bell's breath was rancid and hot as he whispered in Zen's ear, causing a terrible shiver to travel down his spine.

"It's a good thing there aren't any cameras in here, eh, sweetheart?"

And all Zen could do was breathe.

# Chapter 20
# Varys

*His body had taken more trauma than this.*

That's what Varys kept having to remind himself as he forced his face into an uncaring expression. He watched as the man slicing into his arms looked up. The human's nostrils flared when he saw that the alien's expression had not changed. His torturer seemed irritated.

*Good.*

The humans had been more prepared than he had expected. Each of these rooms was designed far enough apart that the thoughts of his cohorts were muted and garbled. He would occasionally get one or two words, usually an internal cry for a parent or a loved one, or an inward curse. He would listen intently to see if any of them let out an audible cry, and so far none of them had.

But, more than anything, all Varys could feel from them was pain. Gods, so much pain.

His people were connected intimately. In a way that no other kind would ever understand. It was as if Reeva's roots made them all one flesh, joined by the Nuva pumping through all of them. When one grieved, they all grieved. When one felt joy, they all celebrated. The great *leewahhi*. A gift from Reeva. Or, he had to admit, one of the many gifts she had given them. It was one of which they were no longer worthy after everything his people had done to win this war. Varys saw that clearly now.

Fittingly, in this cold, harsh cell, it felt like a curse. He could feel his brothers and sisters in pain and could do nothing about it. The pain and grief he felt at being so completely helpless was worse than anything his torturer could think up in their twisted mind. He had tried to pull at the chair that held him down over these last few weeks, but the restraints that held him were large and well-made. It would have impressed Varys had it not been specifically created to tie down his people.

He knew that one of them was bound to break at some point. It was the carnal nature of every beast to avoid pain or to make it stop. But he refused to be the one to do so. He couldn't betray his people like that. He couldn't betray Zen either. His thoughts tried to wander to the human, but he quickly stifled it. Pining wouldn't help him escape.

The days felt endless in this chamber. Occasionally, his torturer would put down his tools and leave, mumbling something about a "break." Varys would watch the man go with what he hoped was an unreadable expression before allowing his features to twist in the agony of what he'd been enduring. He never spoke his pain out loud, but even acknowledging it with his features made it easier to train his face into a mask of complacency when his torturer would eventually return.

It was during these moments that Varys would also attempt to find some sort of inner understanding. He would pray to Reeva and desperately ask for a reason he was here, why he had to suffer. He knew it was his fault that he was even on this mission, but he lamented the greater picture. Varys questioned the great mother on why she allowed so much sorrow to happen, and why his people could make so many mistakes. Honestly, he wasn't sure why *any* of them had to suffer. Even the humans.

Though he felt sympathy for a very small number of them, he knew they were still creatures, fighting for something that they believed in. That was very clear. And they were losing just as much in this war as the Vesunians were. This pointless war had taken so many.

*The war that had taken Eryand.*

A stab of pain rocked Varys at both the memory and the screw tool being slowly and painstakingly pushed into his hand. He bit his cheek to keep himself from letting loose the gasp that threatened to bubble out of his throat. His torturer was running out of ideas. His creativity was spent in the early days of the torture experience, and he had resorted to simply stabbing various objects into Varys's weakened body. Strangely enough, this part seemed to be worse than the creative torture. Just pure brutality in its rawest form.

The human looked up from Varys's bleeding hand to meet the alien's uncaring gaze and sighed heavily, pushing a gloved hand through his blonde hair, leaving a smear of purplish blood in its locks. That hair. It wasn't the first time that the torturer had reminded Varys of Zen. His stature was vaguely the same, but his face was older and less refined. His eyes also weren't the same, intriguing blue that reminded Varys of pure Nuva flowing from Reeva's roots. Those eyes had fascinated Varys from the first moment that Zen had sat himself down in front of his cell. Such a beautiful color.

His people all had the same, black eyes. Maybe gray, if you were blind or lucky. But Zen's were *blue*. They also shimmered from leaking often. Or "crying," as he had called it. His emotions turned them into various hues and shades that Varys studied carefully. They were a raging storm on the water when Zen was angry. And a sparkling gem when he was laughing.

But, the last time Varys had seen them, they had been more gray than blue as he'd stared so coldly at the Vesunian. His mouth had been fixed in a harsh line of hatred. All desire to fight had been extinguished the moment he'd seen how the human looked at him, and he'd allowed himself to be dragged away, back into imprisonment. Varys would've understood if Zen never wanted to see him again.

And, if Varys were being honest with himself, he probably wouldn't see the human ever again. He'd die here, a puddle of guilt and sorrow. Sharp pain stabbed into Varys's stomach as he ruefully surmised that he seemed to be perfectly capable of torturing himself at this point. The human jabbing objects into him was completely unnecessary.

A primal shriek nearly rocked Varys from his seat. If he hadn't been strapped down, he likely would've jumped to his feet. The sound was unexpected and tore Varys from his guilty reminiscing. A tight squeezing started in his chest and his head spun. It was an agonized, alien wail that nearly broke his own heart. It sounded like Yunin. Varys tried to school his features once again, but he knew that concern had shot across them.

He reached out toward Yunin with a tendril of thought, but it was too weak to do anything but gently embrace the mind of the sobbing alien. Varys felt that helplessness seep into him once again as he listened to Yunin mentally crying out for his mother. This was all his fault.

As if summoned by some force of Varys's will, he heard a familiar walk traipsing down the hallway right outside his chamber and his breath caught.

*It couldn't be. Why would he be here?*

It felt as if air were filling his chest, ballooning hopeful pressure inside of him.

*Zen.*

He was walking with another human who was laughing about something. A cruel voice. Much like the ones that Varys had been accustomed to since being captured. Voices that were so different from Zen's. Zen's footsteps were careful, and Varys knew that if he were close enough, he'd be able to hear the human's heartbeat pattering wildly against his chest. He tried to make out what was being said, but between the mental sobbing that was resonating in his skull from Yunin's cell, and his own racing thoughts, he couldn't hear much. They drew closer and Varys strained to listen. He heard them step into a chamber, and all went silent.

It was too quiet. What was Zen doing here? In the interrogation rooms?

*It couldn't be.*

Heat pulsed through Varys at the impossible thought.

*Humans wouldn't do that to one of their own. Would they?*

Yes, they were enemies in this war, but Varys had wanted to believe that most humans, if given the chance, would choose to do good. He really didn't want to be proven wrong. He strained to listen, but all he could make out was the occasional English word, some clanging, and a whimper. Varys ground his teeth, nostrils flaring. He felt bad for Yunin but tried to send another soothing thought so that the Vesunian would quiet down. Surprisingly, it seemed to work, and Yunin went silent with only a small moan.

Guilt swept through the alien, but he knew he *needed* to hear inside of Zen's room. It was quiet for an endless moment with only the sound of Varys's heart pounding in his ears. Then, someone different came walking out of the interrogation room. Someone who hadn't walked in with Zen or the mystery soldier. Varys would recognize those shuffling footsteps anywhere. It was the general who had killed Till.

Varys felt a red surge of emotion swell up inside of him and he did his best to tamp it down. That human, of any of them, would die, if it was the last thing that he did.

There were several moments of near silence. The quiet made him doubt himself. Perhaps he was losing it. Maybe he hadn't heard Zen, and it had just been his imagination, induced by long hours of torture. Varys waited, ears perked, hoping to hear anything from the room that he prayed Zen wasn't in. But there was nothing, other than the occasional grunt or clatter of a tool.

Suddenly, fire crackled through his veins as he heard a soft cry and the wet sound of flesh and blood. He hadn't imagined it, that voice was distinctly Zen. Pure disgust shot through Varys, and he gritted his teeth, snarling softly as his hands trembled. The heat rising within him made his heart slam ferociously against his chest.

*Humans tortured their own kind?! What an abominable species.*

His parents had been right. They were a horrible race that would do anything to survive. They were like pests gathering on a dying husk on a hot day, slurping up the scraps for themselves, and attacking anyone who got close.

His body seemed to vibrate as he heard soft gasping and quiet pleas for it to stop. Zen's trembling voice was met with a rasping, lascivious laugh. Varys heard the pleasure behind the torturer's chuckle and disgust again raced through him when he realized the torturer was enjoying this *far* too much. In fact, it aroused him. Varys knew that if he were closer, he could smell the hormone shift and hear the blood pulsing to indicate physical arousal. He didn't need that, however, to know that the person in the room with Zen was sick. That laugh had been enough.

"What's wrong, sweetheart?" The torturer crooned. "Don't like that? I can push a little more…"

A slightly louder cry and Varys could almost smell the tears dripping down Zen's cheeks. His breath was coming out as small snarls, and he wanted nothing more than to tear down that hallway and make the man pay for every tear that fell down Zen's cheeks. He couldn't even focus on his own ordeal. He knew vaguely that his torturer had continued screwing various pieces of metal into his hand before moving away from him. Confusion glimmered in the man's eyes, obviously questioning why the alien had gone so still.

Another cruel laugh and Varys envisioned ripping the man's tongue straight from his mouth and strangling him with it. The violence in his thoughts both stoked the flame that burned through him as well as startled him. He felt as though he could breathe fire as the man in the other room continued.

"Oh darling, darling, Farraway." The torturer chuckled. "I told you I would get you, didn't I? That day in the prison? I made you cry such beautiful tears. Honest to god, it turned me on so much. I'm straight, but god, the thoughts I've had about you…"

Varys pulled against the restraints, almost unconsciously.

"H-hey, quit that."

His own torturer's voice shook as he grabbed the whip from his belt and snapped it against the side of Varys's face. He barely felt the sting. The warmth of his blood trickling down his cheek only reminded him of Zen's tears. He was trapped in here and this man, this *beast*, was going to do something completely unspeakable to Zen. He was helpless to stop it.

"Pretty, pretty boy…" the monster sang gleefully.

The sound of restraints being loosened surprised Varys briefly, shaking him from his violent thoughts. A body fell to the floor with a soft thud.

"Let me see you bleed. It'll make the end worth it."

Finally, Zen spoke, and Varys's heart nearly cracked in two at the sound. It was a terrified, gentle whisper that was completely at odds with what Varys was sure he was enduring.

"W-what are you going to do? I thought this was torture."

A whip cracked in Zen's room, and Varys's spine stiffened as it met soft flesh and the human gasped in pain.

"Hush."

Another crack of the whip and Varys felt as though it was striking his own being. He gasped in pain in synchrony with the gasps and sobs coming from Zen. As if something connected Varys to the human. As though they shared *leewahhi*. Or if they had declared each other *mehevos*.

Varys couldn't think about that right now. He was laser-focused on listening to what was happening in the chamber across from him. He could hear Zen's shuddering, pained breaths and his fingernails scratching at the cold, metal floor. Varys could also hear the labored, aroused breathing of the monstrous creature who was hurting *his* human. And somewhere closer to him, he could hear leather straining. He heard the torturer kneel, a large thump echoing as if he'd slammed some part of Zen into the floor.

"Oh sweet, sweet Zen. Don't you understand? No one cares if you make it out alive." The torturer laughed, his voice high-pitched and excited. "So, as long as I get the information Sergeant Jennings wants, I can do whatever I want to you. I can whip you, beat you, stab you, bleed you nearly dry, rape you…" He paused as if for dramatic effect, "And even kill you once we're done."

There was a moment of horrible silence. Varys held his breath, his thoughts dizzying and tinged with red.

"But I think I'll start with this."

A brief but intense struggle followed the sound of metal hitting the floor. Through the pounding in Varys' head, he could hear Zen crying and pleading.

"No, no, no, no, no… please no…"

Varys froze in horror as a blood-curdling scream echoed toward him. It chilled his very soul and made his bones vibrate and hum in his body, calling him to action. It was as if Reeva herself were telling him what to do, that Zen needed him. The power in his blood rose to heights he had never felt before, drumming along to the beat that the voice speaking to him set.

*Save him… Save him… Save him…*

*He was watching as Feyna was about to snap Zen in half, his blue eyes closing. He felt sudden despair at the thought of the light leaving those eyes. Save him... Save HIM... SAVE HIM!*

A flash of blue light. There was the sound of snapping and creaking and, suddenly, his restraints were broken. He hadn't even realized he had done that. As the alien bared his teeth and stood, towering over his own screaming and shaking torturer, only one thought dominated his mind.

*I'm coming, Zen.*

# Chapter 21
## Altair

It was seconds, only seconds from the time that Altair had stabbed his blade into Silas's chest, that he felt his body careen backward and slam into the ground. Lilith hovered over him, her eyes wild and her entire body heaving from her panting. His heart ached at the wetness that now seemed to be in her gaze. He felt the curse slowly leaving his limbs, rendering them exhausted, but his own.

Without another word she dropped to her knees, shoving one of them into his chest. She aggressively shoved the silencer into his mouth, the familiar clamp still making him wince, and removed the cuff from her wrist before turning him onto his stomach and cuffing his wrists together.

It was a relief to be face down in the cooling sand. Altair closed his eyes, grateful that he didn't have to see the aftermath of what he had done. A rogue tear slipped from his eyes before dripping down his nose, and he desperately tried not to sniffle, for fear that he would inhale sand.

His mind was set on overdrive. He kept remembering his mother. He recalled, grimly, how the light had left her eyes when the same blade had been stabbed into her by a sobbing Altair. He had been six.

*Gods, six years old.* And he did not know why he was so completely out of control.

He remembered his father's agonized screams as the king had shoved Altair out of the way and held his wife's crumpled form against him, rocking and sobbing into her hair, begging for her to come back to him.

Altair had never been privy to grief before this moment but watching his father in such a broken state eternally changed him. He had wiped at his eyes and nose, his little mind whirring as he tried to process that his mother was gone. The warmth smearing against his face made him realize that his hands were coated in his mother's blood. He had almost spoken at that moment. He had almost apologized for his father's pain, understanding that he had somehow caused it.

As soon as he had opened his mouth to do so, his father's head had shot up, teeth bared in grief and his eyes burning with hatred.

"You keep your poisonous tongue to yourself, boy!"

Those words echoed through Altair's brain, bouncing off of nearly every sensitive area he had in his mind, like a demented game of ping pong. He had so desperately tried to forget that day. He had vowed to never make the same mistake again and to move on from his curse. Now, here he was. Hearing those same anguished sobs.

Though he couldn't see what was happening, he could tell by the sobbing, strangled-sounding voice, that Lilith was attempting to staunch Silas's bleeding somehow. It was too late. Altair had seen the light leave Silas's eyes in the same way that his mother's had. Whatever sort of blade the curse conjured was no ordinary weapon. It took the victim's life force instantaneously. It would then vanish, only to be conjured again whenever Altair spoke.

A cursed blade, for a cursed prince. One that ensured instant death. Gods, he was a monster.

After several moments, Lilith seemed to give up on trying to save Silas and just whispered repeatedly how very sorry she was.

A stab of pain rocked Altair at the despair in her words. She couldn't possibly blame herself for what had happened. Altair was the cursed one here. In fact, he was rather surprised that she had even let it get this far, knowing who he was and what he was capable of.

But it was not her fault. Altair blamed the drink. And partly himself. It was all just a terrible accident.

There was a long moment of silence, and Altair tried desperately to turn his head, as it was becoming difficult to breathe in this position. Finally, he was roughly pulled to his feet and shoved forward. He stumbled over his clumsy feet, dizzy, but grateful for the fresh air.

"We need to go." Lilith's voice was still shaky but seething. "Kelptor doesn't have a justice system, but the people do. If they see us with his body, there will be no trial, only the will of a drunk mob."

Altair shivered at the implication and allowed her to tie the silver rope around his cuffs before walking out of the alleyway with purpose. She set her face in a firm and stiff expression, even as her cheeks were still wet from tears.

He could feel grief pouring from her, even through her bravado. Altair's admiration for her burgeoned in his chest. Even after such a devastating loss, she was determined to see this through. He wished he had that sort of drive. Perhaps he wouldn't be where he was today. He could've escaped his exile. Maybe even found a cure for the curse all on his own. Or, perhaps, he would've just continued randomly killing innocents in stupidity until he, mercifully, took his own life. But, at least, he would have had the determination to push himself out of whatever freeze had held him captive for so many years.

Lilith refused to look back at him as she pressed her way through the increasingly riotous crowd. The males who had tried to speak with her earlier had now moved on to easier prey, and Altair's heart sank at how uncomfortable each of the victims seemed to be. Lilith didn't seem to take any notice as she pushed on, practically shoving others out of the way.

Eventually, Altair sucked a huge lungful of cool air through his nose as they got to the edge of the crowd. He was sweating through his party clothes now and desperately needed a break from being on sore feet. But Lilith continued to press on, still determined not to look back at him. He followed, nearly tripping over his own feet in the dirt multiple times from exhaustion.

It was harder to keep up with her when his hands were cuffed behind his back. He had to match her pace much more exactly. Surprise rose within him when he saw she was stoically stalking toward the airfield where they had parked the ship. He gently tugged on the cuffs, trying to get her attention, but she refused to look back at him.

They made one stop on the way, at the inn where they had been staying for the past several weeks. Lilith tied him up where most people would keep some sort of mount animal. She looked back at him briefly, her eyes hooded and dangerous, silently communicating that if he tried to run, she would indeed kill him now. His head dropped, cheeks burning. He believed her.

Altair watched as she stalked into the inn and was out again in record time. She had changed back into her armor and was carrying their bags with tight fists. Her weapons belt was on prominent display around her waist as she untied him and again, began wordlessly dragging him toward the airfield.

They approached the sleek, silver ship, and Lilith extended her remote, starting the near-silent engine. As she dragged him into the main hull, he was reminded starkly of their first encounter. It was nearly identical, and it made his stomach sink at the thought that so much of the progress from the last several weeks was now gone. It made his chest ache when he thought about what might've been if he hadn't suggested going to that stupid party. One thing was for certain. Silas would still be alive.

She threw him into that same corner and stomped up to the control panel. Altair watched her morosely. When she got them through the atmosphere of the planet, the bounty hunter typed in some coordinates, and put the ship into autopilot. Finally, she turned and fixed Altair with that cold, stiff gaze that she had adopted shortly after Silas had died. It was so unfamiliar now that Altair wasn't sure how to react. She was a completely different person than the one who had tried to kiss him in that alleyway not even an hour before.

Altair couldn't meet her gaze but desperately tried to. The regal pride within him egged him to do so. It whispered that she should've known what he was capable of. That she shouldn't have had that drink. Altair willed those thoughts away and set his brow, frowning. It wouldn't help his situation to blame her at this moment, as much as his pride wanted to. Yes, her actions had put them both in danger, but so had his.

Lilith began walking toward him, and Altair felt his heart flip-flop in his chest. Her expression was nearly unreadable, and he didn't know what her intention was once she reached him. She knelt in front of him and removed the silencer and his cuffs before staring at him for several moments. Altair swallowed dryly, and he felt as though the universe was closing in around him. He felt compelled to speak. Her gaze made him so uncomfortable that the alien simply wanted to explain himself. He opened his mouth.

"Lilith, I…"

And with a resounding slapping sound, suddenly, Altair's head was spinning, and his breath was nearly rocked out of him. He gasped, grasping the now sore cheek, and looked up at her. Her nostrils flared, and she bared her teeth in a way that made her look even more dangerous. Her eyes were once again glistening. Lilith's chest heaved, and she pointed a trembling finger right at him.

"How… How *could* you?!"

Altair's eyes widened, and he blinked several times, trying to understand what she meant. When he spoke, his voice was a demure whisper.

"What do you mean?"

She laughed wildly as she stood and walked several paces away from him before turning back to face him once again. She continued, her voice like a torrential downpour.

"How could you kill him?! Betray my trust so quickly?!"

A light flickered on within Altair's mind.

*Oh, my gods, she didn't know.*

Disbelief swirled through him.

*How could she not know?!*

She snarled, and Altair flinched away from her. She had never looked more alien to him than in this moment. Her voice was cracking, and yet, still ferocious.

"Don't sit there with that stupid, fucking look on your face! What did you expect would happen?! That you would escape?! Now, now..."

Lilith laughed even more wildly, insanely, and Altair felt his insides go ice cold at the sound.

"*Now,* we just have to hope and pray that my navigational skills will get us through that asteroid field. You've endangered both of us *and* my job!"

Her voice caught. Her lower lip quivered, and Altair's heart ached at the sight. He wanted to stop her and explain himself, but he couldn't get a word in edgewise. He watched as Lil stalked back and forth, raving in her passion.

"You fucking killed Silas! One of the few people I could stand in this god-forsaken universe..."

Altair held up a hand, eyes pleading, and she stopped, her body quivering and tears glistening in her eyes. He then raised both hands slowly, trying not to startle her into doing anything that she would regret, and began signing. He tried to remember the meager training he had been given, as panic made his brain feel like mush.

"Give me a moment to answer your questions, and I will."

Lil paused and confusion grew on her face, a strange companion to the anger. She hadn't expected him to have an explanation for what he had done. Her eyes darted from his face to his hands before she finally pursed her lips and gave the slightest nod.

"Doesn't mean I'll believe you though," she said scathingly.

He nodded, understanding why.

He knew he didn't have the complete vocabulary for this with his hands, so he gestured toward his mouth, praying that she would read his lips. Her eyes narrowed for a moment but after several moments of deliberation, her curiosity seemed to win out. She nodded, crossing her arms, and watching him with a stormy glare.

Altair rubbed his hands together and worked his jaw, wincing at the soreness in his face before turning toward her and enunciating as carefully as he could.

"What were you told about me? By your employer?"

She blinked a few times before speaking.

"He stated that you were a Serinian of great status. That you were very talented and needed in the war. But that you had gone missing, and he needed someone to track you down and bring you to him."

She continued, "He said that he needed someone particular to do this job since Serinians have incredible vocal gifts. I already knew about that since humanity has been telling stories about your kind for ages. And he figured that since I was deaf…" She shrugged.

Altair closed his eyes.

"And you didn't question him any further?"

He heard her scoff and opened his eyes once again. She was frowning deeply.

"Of course not. Why would I need to know anything more? It sounded like an easy job. And it was, until I was nearly taken out by the vemen asteroid field that recently migrated to the Milky Way."

She sighed heavily. "It was right in the way of the easiest path to you. It took me months of research to find you, you know. That's when I found out you were a prince. But there's not much record of you or why you were exiled so…"

Altair nodded before speaking, his voice coming out sterner than he expected.

"Your client wasn't truthful enough with you."

She crossed her arms and tapped her foot, waiting for an explanation. And, finally, Altair allowed himself to speak his story into existence. To admit that it happened.

"When I was born, they examined me for my gifts, as most Serinian children are. It was discovered that my gifts were… powerful, for lack of a better term. I could make nearly anyone fall in love with me with a simple 'hello.'"

He looked down, trying to push back the wave of pain that had begun to rise within him. Altair made sure that she could still see his face, even though he couldn't meet her gaze.

"It was a source of great pride for my father. That his genes had produced such a powerful heir. So, he would tell anyone who would listen about his amazingly gifted son."

He looked up and received a nod from Lilith to continue.

"That's a fairly stupid thing to do, to be honest, especially when you refuse to take a side in a massive war. They should have expected that someone would eventually want my talents to aid their efforts in the war. Whether it was the humans or Vesunians."

He felt his mind being taken back, memories and images dancing to the forefront of his mind. It was so painful that he nearly stopped. But the look on Lilith's face kept the words pouring from him.

"It ended up being the humans. They offered to buy me from my parents. To use me as a weapon to end the war. Told my father it was the least he could do since he refused to side with them."

"This enraged my father, and he kicked them out, but shortly after they left, an assassin was found hiding out in my quarters. It was lucky that it hadn't been me who walked into my room. It was a servant girl."

Altair's throat felt tight at the memory of her little body being carried from his room. It was the first moment that he realized how dangerous everything had suddenly become. They had forced him to grow up so much in such a brief space of time. A sense of unfairness bubbled up within him at the thought.

Lilith's eyes shadowed at the mention of the servant girl, but her general expression and stance did not change as she waited for him to continue his tale.

"This was terrifying to my parents, as you can imagine. And in their desperation, they contacted a magic weaver, a spellcaster, a… *witch*, to cast a spell to protect me."

Lilith blinked multiple times before she held up a hand to stop him. She seemed to ponder her words before she spoke.

"You're telling me," she began slowly. "That your parents messed with the magic of deep-space witches?"

Altair nodded, and Lilith shook her head, scoffing.

"They were idiots." She remarked casually, rolling her eyes. "There's so few of them left that most people consider them a legend. I've only met one, and he was completely off his rocker. Worshiped some universal god of chaos and kept talking about people having radish toes." Lil stopped, seeing the pain in his eyes. "Sorry. Continue."

Altair shook his head, waving off her apology. He'd thought the same many times in the last few years. He took a shuddering breath before continuing with his story.

"She, technically, did what they asked. But in her own way, of course. She cursed me. Now, I would be compelled to kill whoever fell under the spell of my voice. But..."

He stopped, wincing and swallowing back tears. It was becoming unbearable as the memories rushed through him.

Lilith grunted, understanding slowly lighting up her face. "Go on."

He grimaced. "This is very painful for me. Please, just understand and give me a moment."

She sighed heavily and fought to keep herself from rolling her eyes but waited. It took a few moments for Altair to regain his composure but, when he did, he finally finished.

"She didn't outright *say* that. She said, 'The one who has the tongue of ambrosia, will now have the tongue of poison.' And repeated it in some weird tongue with which I was unfamiliar. This strange, green energy came from her, shot toward me, and I remember nothing after that."

A terrified scream echoed hauntingly through his mind.

"When I woke up, my mother was at my bedside, and my father was pacing behind her."

Tears filled his eyes as he fought to keep going.

"She smiled and said to me, 'There's my little prince. We're so glad you're awake.'"

The words were coming faster now, as if he couldn't stop them.

"I opened my mouth and said, 'Mama.' That's it, that was all I could say. I saw this glazed look overtake her eyes, and she reached for me. I couldn't stop myself."

His breathing was ragged and trembling.

"Suddenly, there was a dagger in my hand, and there was this force that lifted my arm and shoved it right into her heart."

He was shaking violently now and couldn't even meet Lilith's gaze as hot tears dripped down and hit the silver of the floor.

"J-just like Silas," Altair finally finished with a small gasp.

Lilith seemed stunned by what he had shared as she didn't speak for a long time. When she did, it was as if she were putting puzzle pieces together.

"Which is why you were isolated on that planet." She murmured.

Altair could only nod in acknowledgment. Lilith placed her hands on her hips and rocked from heel to toe, as though trying to keep her composure. It was silent between them for a long time, and all Altair could do was try to stop his tears from falling. He would occasionally glance toward the front of the ship to watch the universe drift slowly around the ship. He didn't dare look in her direction, for fear of seeing rejection or anger once again.

Finally, she broke the silence. "Well, that sure was shitty of my client not to mention any of this." She exhaled loudly before continuing. "And I sure wish someone had said something to me who was in the know."

Altair sniffled lightly. "I would've, honest. But I thought you knew. It's why I was surprised when you took the silencer off in that alleyway."

The memory came rushing back to him, and he tried desperately to hide his blush. This wasn't the time or place.

*Inappropriate timing, body.*

She flushed and looked away from him for a moment before turning back with fire burning in her gaze.

"I had a moment of poor judgment," she whispered. "It won't happen again."

Altair's chest ached at the definitive tone to her voice. When she had leaned in, he hadn't wanted to take advantage simply because she was drunk. But if she had been in her right mind? He was pretty sure he would've reciprocated. He hoped his feelings weren't obvious as he shrugged.

"I understand. And I'm so sorry about Silas. Believe it or not, I actually really liked him."

Lilith's jaw worked, as if to keep herself from crying again, and she turned away from him completely. Her shoulders were hunched against the pain. Her voice shook as she spoke.

"It killed me to have to leave him there. But they would've legitimately killed us both had they discovered us with him. And, I have people who depend on me. They depend on me to finish this job. I have to get you to my client."

Altair nodded, forgetting she had her back to him. When she whipped back around, he stiffened at the furious light that still burned in her gaze. Her jaw was clenched, and her fists were balled.

"I won't forgive you. You had the wherewithal and understanding to not speak in front of vulnerable people. Including Silas. But it doesn't matter."

She stalked forward and knelt in front of him again. Altair couldn't help but shiver slightly at her sudden presence, his cheeks burning. He couldn't hold her gaze.

"You're a job. That is it. And even though it's now a thousand times harder, I will still complete it. Because I'm a damn good bounty hunter."

Her voice was a hiss at this point. She paused before speaking again.

"So, you stay on your side of the ship, Serinian scum, and I'll stay on mine. Got it?"

And again, all Altair could do was nod.

# Chapter 22
# Altair

The flight, from then on, was completely silent. Altair sat uncomfortably against the wall, not daring to move away from it for more than a few minutes at a time. Lilith hadn't even deigned to acknowledge his presence other than to throw the occasional meal in his direction or to mention, loudly, that he needed a shower. He watched as she piloted the ship, flipping them into star-jumping mode, and steering them expertly past any obstacle that was in their way. Things became monotonous.

He would eat. He would sleep. And he would stew in self-loathing. Time passed and the more it did, the worse Altair felt. He knew he deserved this solitude, but he had grown used to semi companionship in the past several weeks. The silence ached now and made his chest feel hollow.

Every glance that was sent smoldering his way burned him deeply. Altair hated that he was so affected by her abandonment. He'd let himself get attached to someone who was being paid to kidnap him. The stupidity of that decision was not lost on him as he fought back the growing darkness that began seeping back into his mind.

Altair didn't know how much time had passed, but he knew it felt like days. They were traveling from an extremely distant galaxy, all the way to the Milky Way, which would take time. He'd passed by the terminal a few times on his way to the bathroom and vaguely recognized the coordinates.

Even with star-jumping, he knew it was going to take them weeks to reach their destination. And all he had to look forward to was this horrible silence. Along with the back of Lilith's head.

The days passed in a tired haze and Altair felt like what he had truly been all along. A prisoner.

# Chapter 23
# Zen

It was like a nightmare from which he couldn't wake. Zen's head spun from the blow that Bell had dealt him when he'd started screaming. He couldn't help himself at the time. Bell had groped him through his clothing, pulling at the material roughly, and the instinct to do so had bubbled up.

Bell's putrid breath filled his nostrils as he breathed heavily over Zen. There was a slight pause as the man smirked at him, pleased with how the stunning blow had rendered Zen helpless. Then, he stood, unbuckling his belt; a blotchy, excited red staining his cheeks.

Zen whimpered, willing his body to do something, to do *anything*. His limbs felt as though cement had been injected into his muscles, rendering them useless. He felt tears sliding down his cheeks, and he winced as the salt settled into cuts on his face. He would take one hundred lashings of the whip. He'd let Bell slice into his arms some more. As long as he didn't have to endure this.

Icy numbness filled his core, and Zen felt himself trying to disassociate, his mind attempting to protect him from what was about to happen. But it wouldn't. He just had to watch as Bell grinned at him and touched himself. He shivered at the cold air on his body and watched helplessly as Bell leered down at him, sadistic pleasure twisting his features.

"You ready, princess?"

His voice was coarse and smug. Zen heard another whimper escape his lips, and he closed his eyes as Bell laughed once more and knelt, positioning himself over Zen and grabbing his bare legs.

"I'm going to keep going until you give me what Sergeant Jennings wants."

The words made Zen's stomach turn.

*This couldn't be happening.*

Suddenly, Bell froze in his attempts. His grip on Zen's legs tightened painfully. Zen's eyes shot open, and he looked at his torturer, whose eyes were trained on the door, glimmering with confusion and fear. And that was when Zen heard it as well.

There was screaming. Horrible, terrified shrieking that rattled around Zen's brain, effectively triggering his fight or flight. Adrenaline coursed through his veins, infusing him with strength as he shoved Bell off him, rolling sideways and away from his attacker. He was still naked from his waist down, so the cold floor pressing into him was startling. But he didn't care, he just had to get away.

Zen scrambled to his hands and knees, ignoring Bell's shocked exhale, and crawled into the furthest corner he could find. He shot a look over to where Bell was attempting to get back to his feet, still exposed, and his cheeks were now flushed for an entirely different reason than before. His eyes were narrowed, and his fists were clenched and tight. He spat his words toward Zen.

"You little…,"

A horrible screeching sound interrupted Bell's cursing. They both watched with widened eyes as the metal door seemed to twist and bend in on itself. It looked as though someone was literally peeling it from its hinges. Bell backed away from the entrance, hands raised and trembling, as the creature responsible bent its colossal form through the hole it had created.

The alien that stepped inside took in the scene in front of him. His eyes were like a wildfire, and they burned as they flitted from the exposed torturer to the half-naked human man in the corner. The alien's mutilated hands clenched as his head turned slowly to take in Bell's quivering form.

Zen whimpered, the tears escaping from his eyes now were not ones of fear, but of happiness and recognition. His heart pounded wildly in his chest.

*Varys.*

A calming sensation flooded through Zen in a way that was almost disquieting. After seeing everything that Varys was capable of, he was still feeling this way.

Zen watched as Varys stepped ominously toward Bell, who stood frozen, his eyes wide. He looked like a deer that had been caught in headlights. There was a moment of hesitation before Bell bounded forward, attempting to skirt around the hulking alien and bolt out through the door.

Varys was quicker, however, and he growled deeply, shifting his body, and catching the human in his large grasp, slamming him against the silver wall next to the door. The alien bared his teeth and looked down at Bell, who was now shrieking and pleading for his life.

When Varys spoke, it was quietly, but Zen could still hear him from across the room as his voice echoed against the silver walls.

"Did you hurt him?"

Varys squeezed Bell against the wall, and the human cried out in pain. Zen nearly couldn't watch. His heart raced wildly, making his cheeks feel flushed and hot. He pressed his hands into his face, his fingernails digging into his skin.

"N-no!" Bell gasped, finally, and Varys's face twitched.

"Liar," Varys growled before swiftly bringing his knee up and slamming it into Bell's leg.

With a sickening crunch, Zen watched in horror as his leg bent unnaturally, and ivory bone stabbed sharply through his skin. Bell let out a prolonged wail, crumpling in Varys's grasp, sobbing, and pleading for mercy. Zen's stomach rolled, and he tasted bile rising in his throat.

Varys snarled in an animalistic way that made Zen shiver. His eyes were black fire as he dropped Bell and loomed over the pitiful torturer, who rolled back and forth in the fetal position, whimpering.

Zen watched as Bell slowly quieted. Varys waited as well, and it seemed the alien was trying to rein in his emotions. His nostrils flared as he breathed deeply. He waited until Bell looked up at him, and Zen was savagely pleased to see that tears were now rolling down the torturer's face.

"W-what do you want from me?" Bell's voice was breathy and halted as he struggled to get them out.

"Beg."

Varys's voice was rolling thunder in the distance. Quiet, ominous, but warning of danger to come.

Bell's teeth chattered involuntarily from pain. His eyes flitted wildly from the dark giant who stood above him, over to Zen, as if hoping that the human would intercede. Zen watched him with pitiless eyes.

*You deserve everything coming to you, you fucker.*

As Bell took in his anger and disinterest, his gaze shadowed, as if he knew this was the end. The inevitability seemed to bolster him, infusing him with courage, and his jaw set as he glared at Zen. A vein had made itself known in Bell's left temple, pulsing a terrified beat.

"You fucking traitor." He spat toward Zen. "You're just going to let the enemy kill me, aren't you? I'm on your side, and you're just going to let him do it."

"You're not on my side." Zen surprised himself with how little his voice shook as he spoke. Having Varys here brought confidence, and the words came pouring from him. "You're a fucking bully. And a pervert. And you deserve every bad thing that's about to come to you."

"Fuck you." Bell snarled and then went even paler when Varys met his snarl with an ominous growl that came from deep within the alien's chest.

"You don't speak to him," Varys said with finality, hands clenching and unclenching, as if itching to wrap them around the soldier's throat. "And I told you to *beg.*"

"Why…?" Bell looked up and met Varys's gaze. The man's face was drawn and pale. "You're going to kill me no matter what I do or say."

Varys laughed, the sound echoing hauntingly around the silver room. "You're right, little human. I will kill you." He knelt, getting inches from Bell's face. The human flinched away from him, dropping his challenging stare.

"You're going to beg because maybe I'll make it a quick death if you do." Varys paused. "Maybe."

Bell's breathing was becoming shaky and shallow. Zen saw his jaw clench as he stared at the ground, refusing to say a word. Several moments of silence passed before Varys huffed.

"Suit yourself." The alien shot a look over toward Zen.

When he spoke this time, his voice was the gentle tone that Zen had grown accustomed to.

"Look away."

And as Varys grabbed Bell's head and pulled, Zen did indeed look away.

Bell screamed, shrieking like a dying animal for several minutes, and Zen slapped his hands over his ears. He was too late, however, and heard as everything ended, and the soldier went silent. He could almost imagine the sound of Bell's head being pulled from his shoulders was just really, nasty-sounding rain.

Almost.

His stomach heaved at the thought, and he prayed he wouldn't add to the horrible situation by vomiting right there on the chamber floor.

He felt Varys's presence once things had gone quiet again and, before he could look up, Varys had scooped him up into his muscular arms, setting him on wobbly legs, and helped him pull his clothing back on. His hand gripped Zen's arm in order to support him. Zen shivered gratefully as his clothing helped fight back the chill of the room. The alien looked down at him, his dark eyes soft and concerned.

"I'm sorry you had to witness that."

And the emotion in the alien's eyes made Zen realize he didn't just mean Bell. Zen nodded, unable to say anything else. The blood pounding in his ears was making it very difficult to do much of anything at this point. His body was also making it known what sort of trauma he'd endured. His limbs were trembling, and the pain was rushing in hot waves throughout his body. Varys smiled softly before shooting a look toward the door, his ears twitching. He carefully picked Zen up again, cradling him to his chest.

Zen gasped as Varys' hands gingerly touched his back. His teeth gritted, and Varys quickly adjusted his grip, murmuring an apology. He leaned down, his breath tickling Zen's ear.

"You're more injured than I am. I'm going to carry you out. It'll be quicker."

Zen was trembling but nodded once more, trying not to let the terror overtake him. Shame also pulsed through him at the fact that he could not walk out by himself. However, he knew it was out of the question for him to escape with Varys on his own two feet.

Varys clambered over the door that he had ripped from its hinges. Every other door in the hallway hung open, loose, and battering against the walls. Alarms were blaring, sounding like a demonic choir of cats as they bathed the hallway in an eerie red light.

Varys looked around, his long ears twitching, before sprinting in the opposite direction from the one that Zen had initially come with Private Bell. When the alien spoke, his voice was low and his mouth was close to Zen's ear once again, making him shiver.

"The others went this way."

Zen didn't even question how he knew. He figured it was a telepathic thing, just as the aliens could speak to anyone that they wished to with their minds. There would be plenty of time for questions once they made it out of here.

Varys ran so quickly, it felt as though he was flying through the hallways. He hefted Zen as though he weighed nothing more than a sack full of feathers. His breathing didn't even seem labored. Admiration burned through Zen, and he tried desperately to keep his gaze away from Varys's face and focused on where exactly they were heading. Zen felt a stab of alarm when he realized Varys was sprinting toward the conference area of the base. A dead end.

Zen smacked his hand against Varys's chest and yelled, hoping to be heard over the alarms.

*"Dead end! Use the service tunnels! There's a way out there!!"*

Varys smirked without even looking down and nodded ever so slightly. His voice slipped into Zen's mind.

**Loud and clear, Farraway.**

With hardly more than a sidestep switch up, Varys had changed directions and was sprinting the other way. The alien's voice broke into his consciousness once again as Zen bounced in his arms.

**Focus on sending me the way out, mentally. I can hear the thoughts you intend me to hear.**

Zen nodded before focusing as hard as he could on the mental image of the way out. He mapped it out and ran through the route over and over, hoping Varys could see it. Suddenly, the alien stopped, his ears twitching, and Zen jerked upwards in his arms.

*"What the hell are you doing*?!" he screamed, unable to hear himself at this point.

Varys's face was drawn and panicked.

**The soldiers found the others. They took the wrong way out.**

Zen felt a stab of grief that wasn't entirely his, and his brow furrowed at the feeling. He sighed heavily and tapped Varys' shoulder. The giant looked down, and Zen did his best to think *at* him again.

**All the soldiers?**

Varys frowned but then shrugged and gestured at the empty hallway around them as if to indicate the high likelihood of that fact.

**Then, we should use the distraction.**

Varys winced at the thought and ground his teeth, his eyes closing briefly. Zen felt bad that he'd even suggested it. It was a cold and calculated move, but it was their only chance. Suddenly, they were running again, and Zen lost his train of thought.

It didn't take long before Varys slammed through the last of the outer doors from the service tunnel, blanching at the harsh sunlight that beamed down on them from above. Zen looked around, squinting, and trying to get his bearings. This was the parking lot for the base service technicians. Just over the hill, Zen could see the looming spires of the prison, and his stomach clenched at the sight. Swirls of dust danced around Varys's feet and the wind whipped grimy dust devils into their path. This weather only came with the approach of dusk. Which meant that people would try to leave soon.

He looked up toward Varys, who was silent and grim. The alien's eyes were unfocused as he stood there, holding Zen to his chest. The human's heart ached at his pain, and he took a deep breath before speaking, infusing sympathy into his voice.

"I'm sorry. We should've gone to help them."

Varys considered his words for a moment before looking down, kindness glimmering in his eyes. His voice was warm when he spoke.

"Please don't be sorry. You were right. We needed to get out."

Varys then peered around at the vehicles that surrounded them, confusion ornamenting his features.

"These are odd-looking ships."

Zen broke out in wild laughter, and Varys looked down at him, his forehead creased. He tried to speak through the giggles that he couldn't control.

"They're not ships, Varys. They're cars. And we need to hot-wire one to get out of here."

Zen took a deep, steadying breath before pushing at the alien's broad chest. "Put me down. I'm not letting you run all the way to the airfield, let alone carry me the entire way."

Varys's eyes became guarded, and he held the human closer to his chest. Zen's cheeks once again flooded with heat, and his heart beat a steady, pulsing rhythm. He was starkly reminded of his dream and desperately tried to beat back the warmth that shot through him at the thought of Varys's body pressed into his, the alien's large hand sliding up the inside of his thigh...

Zen shook his head aggressively, his stomach clenching.

*Why was he feeling this way so shortly after what had almost happened?*

The alien's stern and stubborn voice interrupted Zen's thoughts.

"You're injured. I'll just carry you."

Zen felt a pang of irritation that accompanied the sweep of enjoyment that came from being cared for in such a way.

"Varys, you're injured as fuck too. If you don't put me down right now and let me do my part in our escape, I'll..." Zen paused, trying to find an appropriate threat, "I'll leak some more." The threat fell flat, and Zen's cheeks burned.

He wasn't sure if they had the time for this petty argument, but Zen's pride wouldn't allow him to be carried the entire way to the airfield, like some delicate damsel in distress. Now, it was Varys's turn to laugh, a different, breathier sound than the cruel thing that had left him when he'd glared down at Bell.

"Gods, the horror. Anything but that." Varys's tone was searing with sarcasm, but he sighed in defeat and readjusted to place Zen down, being careful not to touch his back.

He felt a surge of victory as Varys gingerly dropped him. Zen did his best to hide how terribly his body hurt, but he saw concern shadow Varys's eyes as he wobbled, wincing. Stiffening his shoulders, he turned away from the hulking alien and marched toward the nearest, semi-decent car.

"Now, let's get the fuck out of here."

# Chapter 24
# Zen

The car rumbled and bumped over the dirt roads that had long since been in disuse. Zen only knew that these existed because of a map that he had carefully studied before his assignment here on First Earth. He'd found out where he was being placed and had grabbed as many materials as he could find at his local library. He'd scrolled the holographic screens until his eyes were blurry and he was seeing two of everything. He'd never thought he'd need to use the useless information on these old roads, but here he was, now driving down them. Accompanied by a very cramped Vesunian in the passenger seat who kept pressing random buttons in the vehicle.

They had been driving for hours in near silence. Zen was attempting to come to terms with what had happened in the last several weeks. He could feel his patience waning, however, as Varys played with the various car settings. Irritation crept up as Varys pressed button after button, messing with windows, the sunroof, wipers, music and more. A vague grin sat on his face and, though Zen knew he needed the distraction right now, he couldn't help but roll his eyes as some strange green fluid shot across the windshield.

He felt the alien's gaze on him as he stared out at the road in front of them, and he desperately tried to relax his shoulders along with his grip on the steering wheel.

"Sorry," Varys murmured, noticing the look on Zen's face.

He immediately felt bad for puncturing what little joy the alien had been able to find.

"No, no. Sorry, I'm just coming down from all of… that."

Zen sighed heavily, hands gripping the steering wheel tighter once again. He didn't want to relive what had happened. His back was a constant reminder of the ordeal.

Varys was quiet for a moment and adjusted his large body heavily, the car shuddering. It seemed he was choosing his next words carefully.

"Zen, are you okay?" The alien's voice was unsteady, as if emotion were pushing at the edges of it. "When I walked into that room, and that beast…"

Varys's nostrils flared, his teeth grinding together, and Zen imagined how dark Varys's eyes had become. The alien paused, trying to collect himself. When he spoke, his tone was gentle once again. "Did he…? When I walked in and noticed that you were both exposed, I just saw red. I didn't check…" Varys sighed, unable to finish the question.

A flash of pain from the blow Bell had dealt him, the sickness of resolving himself to being violated, and the smell of cheap cologne threatened to overtake Zen's senses. He flinched from the memory and swallowed hard, trying to will away the tears that had come up.

"He didn't. But he almost did," Zen interrupted sharply. "But I don't want to talk about it either way."

Varys was quiet again. This time, he was respectfully looking out his passenger side window in order to make the human more comfortable. And again, Zen felt guilty. He drummed his fingers against the steering wheel and sighed. The memory was bubbling up now, and the need to talk to Varys was overwhelming. He didn't understand why, but Varys had always felt safe to talk to. Which was stupid, considering that he'd heard Varys rip a man's head from his body with his bare hands only hours before. Zen struggled against the need for longer than necessary before finally giving in.

"Do Vesunians have a word for what Sergeant Bell wanted to do to me?" he whispered, his chest aching.

Varys seemed to tense, and his jaw worked, clenching, and unclenching. It was incredible watching him gain control of his emotions, something of which Zen felt wholly incapable.

When he finally spoke, his voice teemed with disgust. "We don't talk about it. We consider it an abhorrent act. A sin against Reeva and all of creation. It happens among my people, yes. But rarely. Those who are caught or reported of the act, stand an immediate trial before Reeva who determines guilt."

Varys took another deep breath before continuing, his eyes shimmering with emotion. "We call it, *feenevai*. Loosely translated for your tongue, it simply means 'crime against the soul.'"

Zen nodded, feeling hot tears well up in his eyes again as the memory reared its ugly head. He tried desperately to wipe at them without Varys noticing, but, of course, Varys's head whipped around. A protective gleam entered his dark eyes.

"Do humans do that often?" Varys's voice dripped with disdain. "I'm glad I could stop it from happening to you, but that it almost happened…" Varys shook his head, his matted curls brushing against his shoulders. "It just makes me wonder."

Zen wanted to jump to humanity's defense. Indignation began rising within him, but the truth quickly deflated his ego. He bit his lip, his heart pounding and shame for his race pulsing through him. It was quiet as Zen just stared blankly ahead at the road and gave a small nod. Varys's lip curled, and he looked away, muttering something in Vesunian that Zen didn't catch.

The human was quiet for a few more seconds before he spoke again.

"That wasn't the first time it almost happened to me."

He glanced over and saw Varys watching him, eyes wide. Pity rolled through the alien's expression, and it didn't make Zen feel any better. It just caused a lump to rise in his throat. He swallowed roughly past it, blinking away the tears. He wanted to change the subject. His arms were trembling from reliving everything.

"Your English is very good, Varys."

Varys's shoulders relaxed, and Zen felt a wave of relief pass through him.

"My parents wanted me well-versed in the tongue of the Universe." Varys began pressing buttons again as he spoke, returning to his distraction. "The rest of my team weren't nearly as fluent. It's why I was chosen for the mission."

There was a slight hesitation on the last sentence, and Zen frowned.

"This mission," he began slowly, knowing that if he played his cards right, he could get Varys to say just about anything. "You've never actually told me what it was. We've had dozens of lunch dates where you answered my stupid questions about your people and culture, but never about what you all were doing on that Ursonian ship."

His cheeks burned at the use of the word "dates," but Varys didn't even flinch. He glanced over at Zen, his lips pursed. Uncertainty danced across his features, and Zen knew this ordeal had broken some trust on both ends of this relationship.

Varys cracked his neck over to the right and looked toward the front of the vehicle. "Where are we going?" His voice was chipper and distracting.

Zen frowned even deeper, knowing he would not get his answer. He sighed heavily, resigning himself to asking again later.

Zen returned his attention to the front. "We're heading to an airfield to steal a ship. We need to get you off this planet as fast as possible. Hopefully, your friends got away and are doing something similar."

Varys blinked in surprise. "You're helping me escape?"

"Yes." Zen was slightly indignant. "Why would you think I wouldn't?"

Varys shrugged and looked down at his hands. "I thought you hated me."

Zen's stomach writhed at his response, twisting everything into knots. "Varys…" he tried to soften his tone. "It's more complicated than that. I think."

The alien frowned. "I saw the look on your face when one of my people killed that female soldier. I could tell by your expression that she was your friend."

Zen was struck by the memory of Reeves falling, that sickening crunch causing him to flinch away, shaking his head to dispel it. He took a deep breath to calm himself before nodding, trying to ignore the trembling in his body.

Varys gestured as if proving a point. "See? Why wouldn't you hate me? We killed your friend. We subjected you to the brutality of war."

"You did." Zen paused, trying to figure out how to explain himself. "But you did so to escape the prison we threw you into."

"*You* didn't do that. Others did."

"And *you* didn't know she was my friend. This is war, like you said."

"War doesn't excuse death. You have every right to be angry at me."

"And I am!" Frustration shot through him, and Zen threw his hands up momentarily before grabbing at the wheel again. "But if I was you, I would've done everything in my power to escape too! Okay?! So just, let me fucking help you, you big, space lug!"

Varys was quiet for a second before a chuckle escaped him. Vesunian laughs were breathy and easily mistaken for gasping, but the smile on his face spoke to his good humor. Confusion rolled through Zen as the alien chuckled.

"What?!" Zen tried to frown. There was nothing to laugh about, as far as he could tell.

"I am completely fluent in your tongue, and I have no idea what 'lug' means." Varys wheezed out another laugh. "But it sounds stupid, and I like it."

Zen continued to frown before a smile crept onto his face.

*Damn it.*

"It's a word used for big, dumb, stupid creatures, like yourself. And no one fucking uses it. I don't know why I did." Zen chuckled, grateful for the momentary humor. He felt that familiar ease settling between them once again. "Also, you're *obviously* not fluent, if you don't know *every* word."

Zen meant it as teasing but regretted it the moment it left his lips. However, Varys lost it and threw his head back, guffawing, his large hand splayed against his abdomen.

Zen couldn't help but join him, and they both laughed uncontrollably. It felt good to laugh like this; wild and belly-forward. He laughed so hard that Zen couldn't stop the snort that escaped him. It was an embarrassing tendency that earned him the nickname "piglet" from his mother. His hand shot up to cover his mouth and nose, the laughter dying on his tongue.

Varys stopped at the sound and stared at his face. His voice was quiet when he spoke.

"What, by Reeva's roots, was that?"

Heat flooded Zen's cheeks, and he laughed softly again, this time in embarrassment. "Uh, a snort. Sometimes, humans snort when they laugh too hard. I do it a lot."

Varys continued watching him, his dark eyes sparkling. "You've laughed around me before, but you've never done that."

Zen shrugged and dropped his hand, trying to focus on the road ahead and move on. "It's been a long time since I've laughed that hard, I guess."

Varys was quiet for a moment before he reached over with one finger and poked it gently against Zen's nose. It was only a moment but enough for Zen to feel his entire being turn tomato red. He was pretty sure his soul was stained red at this point as well.

*I like it.*

Varys's voice caressed Zen's mind and the air in the car suddenly felt hot and thick. He felt his heart pound wildly against his chest. Taking a deep, shaky breath he brushed his hand through his hair and smiled breezily.

"The airfield is a couple of days' drive. We don't have anywhere to stop, so get comfortable."

Varys leaned forward, a large grin splitting his face. "Actually, I know a place."

Zen raised an eyebrow, pursing his lips. "Isn't this your first time here? How do *you* know a place?"

Varys tilted to the side to look at him, his smile growing wider. "My brother used to take reconnaissance trips here. There's this hidden inn. It's run by a wonderful Ursonian that harbors illegals on their way to other planets. And it's near an airfield. I don't know if it's the one you mentioned though."

Zen sighed. "There's only one airfield. Few people live on this planet anymore. So, we're probably talking about the same place. I hope that they're willing to take a human."

Varys looked Zen up and down for a moment before nodding. "She shouldn't find you too threatening."

"Wow, thanks Varys."

"No problem, Zen."

# Chapter 25
# Altair

Altair was used to being hated. The times in his life when he had been unconditionally loved were short and had come to an abrupt end shortly after he had murdered his mother. His father's love had been incredibly conditional and though it had hurt him that the king felt that way, he'd had time to process it over the years. But now that Lilith seemed to hate him, it felt utterly unbearable. The sight of her stiff figure at the helm of the ship was torture.

He knew she would do what she always did these days. She would move from panel to panel, making sure that everything was still on track, and then plop herself in the captain's chair, firmly avoiding eye contact with the amphibious alien in the corner.

Altair would attempt to begin small conversations by lamely gesturing with his cuffed hands, which she would then promptly ignore. He would sigh in response to her cold shoulder and then resign him to another long, lonely day. Altair would then amuse himself by staring at the silver walls of the ship, hoping she would deign to feed him soon.

He could feel the darkness inch its way back in as the silver walls he would study began to remind him of the desert landscape he had watched for twenty years. It was strange how easily the memory of his exile was triggered. First the inn, and now the ship. He would attempt to push the memory away. But the longer he was stuck, alone with his thoughts, the more tempting it became to end his misery on his allotted bathroom breaks. However, shortly after such thoughts, he would fiercely chastise himself. Altair knew he was too much of a coward to do anything like that. He had always been too much of a coward to do anything. Let alone die. So, he would just imagine an end to the pain. At least, it gave him something to do.

It had been countless hours, days, and possibly even weeks of this isolation. Altair was in his usual corner, eyes dead as he stared at the opposite wall. With a strangled gasp, Lilith bounced up, her hands frantic on the controls. The movement and sound were sudden enough to startle Altair from his reverie. His chest tightened, and he watched as she flitted from panel to panel, and button to button.

The ship shuddered and yawed sharply to the left as something large floated past them, casting an immense shadow over everything, blanketing them in brief darkness. Altair jumped up as fast as he could and rushed toward the front, slamming on the metal control panel with his cuffs. Lilith's head whipped around as the vibrations traveled up her arms, her eyes wild and panicked.

"What's going on?!" Altair yelled, hoping he was enunciating enough.

She shook her head, hands dancing across the controls once again.

"Vemen asteroids." Lilith barked. "The field has traveled even closer to us than it was when I first came through it. I wasn't expecting that speed."

Her hands grasped the handles of the steering mechanism, and she fixed her gaze on the vast expanse of space outside. Altair peered out the window and felt his heart drop straight into his feet. As far as the eye could see, various-sized and shaped hunks of rock peppered the surroundings outside of their ship. He felt his jaw drop. It made the ship feel so infinitesimally tiny in comparison. When Silas and Lilith had spoken about the asteroids, he hadn't imagined something of such *magnitude.*

Lilith was doing her best to weave her way through the field, blasting the smaller asteroids with beams of red plasma. Sweat had appeared on her forehead, and her eyes were wide as she glanced from asteroid to asteroid. Altair finally understood the dilemma, and why they had been stuck on Kelptor for so long. This was too much. Going at this speed, so carefully, was going to take forever. But if they went any faster, they might be crushed by hulking space rock, which was *not* an option.

Altair wished he could do something, but this was a situation for which he was woefully unprepared. He had no skill behind the helm of a ship and even less with such large weaponry. He could handle small, personal weapons, and, unfortunately, that was about it. He'd always relied heavily on his voice.

*Damn his father for not rounding out his studies.*

He watched anxiously as those beads of sweat trickled from Lilith's hairline and ran in smooth rivulets down her face. Her hands were clenched tightly on the controls, and her eyes darted every which way, trying to determine whether any of the asteroids were floating too dangerously close to them. Slowly, one of them rolled into their path, and Altair cried out as it drifted toward them.

Lil slammed her hand down onto a button. With a resounding crack, a plasma shot broke the smaller rock into several pieces and one of them rocketed toward a larger asteroid. It nudged its larger sibling, directing it head-on into their path. Right toward their ship.

Lilith muttered a curse and shot the controls forward, dipping the vehicle sharply downward to avoid the spiraling death rock. She was mostly successful, but that small percentage of failure caused the bottom of the asteroid to raze against the top of the ship. The impact made the ship careen against a second asteroid and bounce off its rocky surface with a shuddering jolt. Altair was nearly knocked off his feet by the impact and clutched the control panel to steady himself.

Lilith quickly course-corrected, her hands shaking. Small pieces of metal floated away from them, to be lost forever in the expanse of space. They had been shorn straight from their ship, and Altair desperately prayed that it was nothing vital. As if mocking his plea, a flashing light began going off in the cabin, indicating there was now an issue.

Altair felt himself getting woozy. Perhaps the gods of the universe had heard his desperate plea for death and were granting his wish. Guilt burned through him at the idea. He hadn't meant to put Lilith in danger with his careless thoughts. He'd never meant to hurt anyone. But especially not her.

"Altair!" Lilith snapped and immediately he was at attention. "I need you on controls while I check out what's wrong. Can you fly?"

He could tell she was desperately holding on to the breeziest tone she could muster. However, her words were shaky and slurred more than usual because of her panic. Altair jumped forward, desperate to help, and she quickly unlocked his cuffs with one hand. He signed, hoping she could see what he was saying in her periphery.

"I don't know how to fly well. But I've been behind the helm of a ship before. I'll do my best."

It wasn't exactly a lie. He'd been behind the helm of a ship before, as a royal passenger. He prayed silently that it would come naturally to him.

She nodded quickly, acknowledging that she had seen him before letting go of the controls and replacing her hands with his. She shot a venomous look in his direction, and Altair fought the urge to flinch away.

"Don't make me regret trusting you." She snapped before disappearing into the back.

*Okay. He could do this.*

Altair took a deep breath, focusing on the mission in front of him. He relaxed his shoulders and leaned forward.

*It was a game. Just a game. Avoid the asteroids.*

His hands were slick on the controls, but he refused to remove them to wipe them off. If he let go, they could die. Lilith could die. That thought spurred an intense desire for them both to live. If he lived, she lived. They could get through this. Altair gritted his teeth and steered them forward. This speed wouldn't do. At this rate, they'd be in the asteroid field for hours, allowing for more of an opportunity for them to be hit.

Altair did the simple calculations in his head. Less time in the field meant less opportunity for them to die squashed into the face of some old space rock forever. He upped their speed, silently praying again to whatever god had played this sick joke that he had been kidding. He pleaded for them to take back this perfectly good way to die. He heard Lilith clattering around and swearing profusely. Altair hoped the damage wasn't too detrimental. Obviously, he could still steer the ship, and nothing seemed immediately wrong. But that could change in an instant.

An asteroid came from below, hurtling quickly toward the bottom of the windshield. Altair swore loudly in Serinian and flipped the handles in his direction, throwing all power into the speed module. The ship rocketed forward and up, nearly completely vertical, and Altair clung to the controls, trying not to lose his footing. He heard Lilith exclaim loudly and use Altair's name vulgarly, but she didn't come to the front. He righted their position and clutched the controls, eyes darting around to check for any other dangers. Immediately, he spotted one.

Altair had gotten them away from the danger of the asteroid coming from below, but he had shot them toward even bigger ones above them. He felt as though he couldn't breathe. Altair screamed loudly, ignoring the dark magic that curled against the windshield, as he inexpertly weaved away from each of the large asteroids. The ship was shaking from the effort of meeting each of his misguided commands. It was honestly a miracle that he had hit nothing yet.

He steadied the ship, heart pounding and hands even slicker than before. In fact, his entire body was soaked with sweat. Gods, he could go for a cool dip right now.

*Fifty points,* a voice softly rang in his mind. Something about that bolstered him. *Just a game. Twenty points for that one.*

He jostled away from the medium-sized asteroid; the ship was steadier this time around.

*Fifty. Ten. Twenty. Twenty Ten. Twenty. Ten.*

With each one avoided, his confidence grew. He could do this. As long as he stayed focused. Lilith stepped up next to him, eyebrows high on her forehead. Her face had a smear of mechanical fluid on it.

"Wow. Um. Good job." She nodded and checked the small, electronic map. "Looks like we're nearly through the field. You were booking it." She couldn't suppress the warmth in her tone as she spoke.

Pride warmed Altair's insides, and he tried not to let the praise go to his head. He nodded swiftly, unwilling to take his eyes from their course, and signed with one hand.

"How much further?"

"Not far." Lilith balled her hands and placed them on her hips. "But we're going to have to make another, brief stop."

Altair shot a look in her direction before glancing forward once again. His heart sank as he considered another delay.

She sighed heavily and waved her hands. "I know, I know. But this one won't be as long, or useless." She shook her head, her mouth turned downward as she spoke. "That asteroid took out a piece that I need for long distances. We're still a long way from where we're headed, so I need it replaced. It's easy to do that though, swear on my life."

Altair shrugged, feeling his new, dark companion slithering back into his mind. It wasn't enough for him to steer them straight into the nearest asteroid, but another stop sounded unbearable.

*Couldn't she just get him to whoever was buying him?*

"I can take over now." Lilith's hands brushed against Altair's as she took the controls from him and lightly nudged him out of the way. Altair felt heat on the spots where her hands had so gently touched his. He backed away from the feeling, his head bowed and cheeks flushed.

The memory of how she'd looked when she'd almost kissed him, drunk on Serinian alcohol, floated to the surface. Yes, it was nearly the same look that people gave him when under the influence of his voice, but also different. Different in important ways. Such as the clarity and determination in her eyes. Or the way she had grabbed his face, instead of pining silently on the sidelines, waiting for his attention.

He shook his head, willing the memory to disappear as he retreated to his corner. It was different here this time, too. His hands were free once again and though the depression still lurked on the fringes of his mind, a small ray of light had snuck in as well.

"Altair?"

Lil's voice was quiet, almost too quiet. He nearly didn't hear her. He looked up and forced a small smile at her back. There was the smallest hesitation. Her voice was even quieter when she spoke again.

"Thank you."

# Chapter 26
## Altair

The ship shuddered and dropped with less dignity than it had in the last several weeks. Altair wasn't sure where they had landed, but he knew it couldn't have been far. They had damaged the ship too much to travel much further than the asteroid field.

It had been sputtering and struggling by the time they left the field, but it dutifully limped forward with Lilith at the helm. She hadn't spoken a word to Altair since the small show of gratitude, but Altair knew her feelings had changed as he stared at her back. Her shoulders seemed softer than they had for weeks.

However, he had retreated to the sleeping quarters, knowing that his presence was probably still uncomfortable for her. He heard her making a few calls as he lay in his cot, her voice nearly completely muted through the walls. He assumed it was to explain the delay to his buyer.

*His buyer.*

The idea still made him shudder. In the craziness of the last few weeks, he'd had moments where he'd forgotten he even was a prisoner. Lilith was so incredibly hot and cold. One moment, she was teaching him sign language and trying to kiss him in a drunken stupor. The next, she was calling him scum and ignoring his existence other than to occasionally allow him food and a shower. He certainly had felt like a prisoner these weeks that they had been traveling from Kelptor. Even with the brief reprieve in the asteroid field, that feeling hadn't gone away completely. He'd resigned himself to being handed off to this mystery buyer.

As the ship dipped during landing, his stomach did as well, and he curled up on the cot, closing his eyes. He heard heavy footsteps approach his door before they halted. His heart launched into a quick march.

*Did he want her to come in? To invite him to come with her?*

Images of Silas crumpling and the light leaving his eyes bubbled to the surface. Altair flinched away from them, gritting his teeth against the pain that shocked his nervous system.

*No, he would hurt someone else. Go away, Lilith.*

It was silent for several moments before a soft scraping came from the doorway, and the footsteps retreated. Altair opened his eyes and peered over to where he had heard the sound. On the ground was his makeshift drawing pad and the nub of charcoal he'd been using to sketch. She had slid it underneath the door.

Altair's heart ached as he slid off his cot and grabbed the materials. He flipped through the countless doodles he'd made in that tiny room. Several were of Lilith and her proud features. The drawing of him with his mother on the grounds of his home was missing.

*How odd.* Altair mused, not entirely sure why she would've taken that drawing.

He sat on the ground, crossing his legs and flipping to a fresh page. The images of Silas lying in the sand, blood pooling around his body, continued to haunt the corners of his consciousness, and he shook his head, trying to dispel it. Even if he hadn't seen that exact image, he could imagine it. And he still felt the heaviness in his hand from the blade that had appeared. Well, he knew how to combat this. He'd done it with his mother's death. And with that thought, he pressed the nub of charcoal to the new page and began sketching.

Altair had lost track of all sense of self by the time he finished the drawing. His hand was sore from endless scratching and blending. He dropped the charcoal, rubbing his blackened fingertips against each other, and examined the crude rendering he'd created.

It was Silas, tinkering in his fire hazard of a house. His brow was creased in concentration, and his eyes glimmered with eccentric intelligence as he worked on some random ship part. Lilith was in a corner, leaning against the one bare wall and watching Silas with a mix of exasperation and admiration.

Warmth bloomed in Altair's chest as he looked at his drawing. Though crude and amateur, Silas was alive here. Forever captured by Altair's memory and his ability to put the alien's likeness on paper. Tears rose to his eyes, and he quickly moved his face away from the pad, afraid to ruin his sketch with the saltwater that was now slipping down his cheeks. He sniffled softly, shoulders shaking as he dropped the drawing pad and pulled himself into his cot once again. Deep emotion welled within him. They were ones he hadn't allowed himself to feel fully for many years.

*Sadness. Grief. Guilt. Shame.*

Each one roiled within his gut and took turns smashing his nervous system to bits with tiny fists. His soft crying turned into whole body, heaving sobs. No one could hear him here. He could wail, scream, and curse without fear of hurting anyone. But, gods, that he even had to *deal* with that thought.

Everything began to bubble and twist together into one primary emotion. It burned through him, making his heart pound and his hands clench into painfully tight fists. This wasn't fair. This had *never* been fair. He had been an obedient son, a good prince. Gods forbid he had accidentally hurt people. He'd never *wanted* to...

He stood, trembling, and began pacing the room.

The fire was growing, threatening to swallow him whole. His vision started to blur and the edges of it were tinged with red. His face felt flushed, and he needed somewhere to throw this emotion. This horrible, fiery heat that licked up his core and made him want to destroy. It was fanned by the memory of his father punishing Altair for something that was the king's fault. It rose remembering the witch who had cursed him to kill his mother for gods knew *what* reason. And finally, the flames rose to the sky as he berated himself for being stupid enough to open his mouth in such a public place.

*For killing Silas. For killing his mother!*

A primal scream of rage and grief tore at his throat, and his hands flew up to cover his head as he bore down on the sound. His pain reverberated through the room, bouncing toward him. It sounded like a demented stranger was mocking him.

As soon as the scream left him, he wanted more. The relief was cathartic, but he could feel the pain threatening to return. Like some horrible creature, stalking its prey unseen. However, Altair felt the predatory eyes of his trauma, watching his every move, ready to pounce again.

He stood up straight again before gathering himself and screaming as loudly as he could. The rush was intense, and he threw his fists at the seamless silver walls of his prison. He heard cracking and felt the familiar warmth of blood trickling down his knuckles as he continued to smash out his aggression on something that could not feel it. Strangely, he envied it for that reason alone. It could not feel.

Altair imagined the wall was everyone who had ever done him wrong. And in some strange, twisted, thought process, he felt that once he was done, he would feel better. But, of course, as soon as he tired himself out, panting heavily, his hands bleeding as he dropped them to his sides, he felt no different. He just wanted more. And now he was tired. Altair shuffled toward his cot once again, and fell into it, sleep overtaking his mind.

When he woke, it was to the sound of a door creaking. He opened his bleary eyes, his whole body aching and his head pounding. It felt like his brain was too big for his skull and was desperately trying to crack it open for more room.

Lilith stood in the doorway, eyes wide. One hand was holding the silencer.

*Why did she seem so shocked?*

Altair attempted to sit up and hissed as stinging pain crackled through his knuckles and fingers. He looked down at his battered hands and was shocked at the copious amounts of dried blood that coated them. It was a stark reminder of the tantrum that he had thrown in her absence. Heat rose in his cheeks, and he didn't want to look at the wall that he had beat into submission.

He slowly peered over to where he had his small fit of rage earlier, and his chest constricted upon seeing how much dried blood covered the walls and how many dents were cracked into them. Small droplets drew a gruesome path to his cot, some it finding its way onto his drawing of Silas.

*Oh no.*

His eyes widened, and he looked up at Lil, praying that she hadn't seen the drawing. He didn't want to cause her any more pain than to which he'd already subjected her. His heart dropped when she frowned and looked at the ground. He saw Lilith's eyes dart toward the drawing and, before he could make it off his cot, she stomped forward and grabbed the pad, taking it in with narrowed eyes.

Altair tried to sign, wincing. If his hands had been sentient, they would be screaming, "Please, don't!"

She held a hand up, effectively silencing his gestures, and her gaze softened as she studied the page. Her eyes glistened and Altair's heart ached. This is what he had been trying to avoid. He'd just needed to heal himself of his mental wounds. But, of course, his actions had caused even more destruction. Self-loathing rose within him, and he frowned, shoulders dropping. There were several moments of silence before she turned the pad toward him.

"May I keep this?"

Altair blinked rapidly. He hadn't expected her to say that. "You like it?" He said, signing cautiously.

She smiled and nodded. "It's my entire friendship with Silas in one picture." Her hands clutched the graphite-burdened paper to her chest. "Please, let me keep it."

He nodded slowly, and she ripped the drawing carefully from the pad before tucking it into a notebook she pulled from her bag. Slipping the notebook back into it, she gestured toward him.

"Come on, get the silencer on, and let's get you cleaned up. We're staying the night while the ship is repaired."

Altair nodded again before slowly gathering his things and pressing the silencer to his mouth with a familiar wince. He allowed her to clean and bandage his hands, firm enough to help protect the wounds but loose enough for him to communicate.

Altair turned toward her as she stood and stepped around him to leave the ship. He signed in her direction. "Where are we staying?"

Lilith smiled softly, a gentleness in her gaze that was unlike her.

"We're staying with my family. Which is why your silencer will be on the whole time." She pointed a finger threateningly at him, and Altair backed away, feeling chastised. "And remember, I'll kill you if you even so much as blink wrong."

There was a playfulness to her tone that Altair wasn't expecting.

*So hot and cold.*

"Of course," he signed, a warmth in his cheeks that he didn't expect either as he tried to match her playfulness. She nodded before leading him off the ship into the arid landscape of First Earth.

# Chapter 27
# Zen

Everything in his body hurt by the time they arrived at the "inn" that Varys had mentioned. They had spent the better part of the night and early morning driving. Zen had known that it was time to stop when he'd begun swerving. They took a brief break to close their eyes before continuing the drive later in the day. The sun had begun its descent once again when they had finally pulled up to their destination.

Zen rubbed at his burning eyes and grimaced toward the ramshackle building that made a crack house look like home. He wasn't entirely convinced that a stiff wind wouldn't just immediately tip the entire building over, like a stack of flimsy playing cards. He shot a glance over to where Varys was still crouched in the passenger seat, and the alien gave a half-hearted shrug.

***This was the place Eryand described.***

"And your brother is in sound health? Mentally, I mean?" Zen smirked, his voice feeling distant from exhaustion. Regret immediately shot through him as pain danced across Varys's features.

The alien spoke aloud, glancing away from Zen, and this time, his voice was quiet.

"He was."

*Fucking shit.*

Putting his foot in his mouth like always. Zen looked away, his cheeks burning as he whispered. "I'm sorry. I didn't realize."

In his periphery, he saw Varys shake his head, his long, dark curls sweeping across his handsome face.

"Exactly. You didn't know."

Varys exhaled loudly, plastering a brave smile on his face. His tone was teasing when he spoke again.

"You ready to head in, Zen the human?"

Zen flushed even deeper and crossed his arms. Stubborn pride dropped his features into a scowl. "I don't like that nickname."

"Would you prefer Farraway?"

"I would *prefer* you just called me Zen."

"Okay, Zen. You ready to head in? Or do you need me to carry you?" Varys grinned, waggling his eyebrows.

Zen dramatically opened the driver's side door and stepped out firmly, ignoring the shocks of pain that rocketed through his body.

He turned and gestured toward himself, smirking. "See? I'm fine. You're injured too, you know. Your hands are completely mangled."

Varys folded his tall form and stepped out of the vehicle, the car rocking in protest. He promptly unfolded his large body and stretched upward, groaning in pleasure at the ability to move. He turned toward Zen, a mischievous twinkle in his eyes.

"Vesunians heal quickly. Don't worry about me. Humans are so frail in comparison."

And with that scathing comment, he clambered up the dirt hill toward the ramshackle hut.

Zen rolled his eyes, unable to contain the amused smile that spread across his face as he followed Varys, a bit more stiffly and slowly than the long-legged alien.

Varys stepped through the door that didn't quite close and made his way to the long, dirty counter that was completely devoid of any life. Zen felt a shiver pass through his body as he looked around at the bleak interior. There was nothing here but the long counter and a small button resting lightly in the middle of it.

Varys extended a finger and pressed the button, but no sound came from it. Zen would've thought it was broken had it not been for how Varys's long ears twitched.

*Must be a frequency I can't hear.*

It was quiet for a long moment before a door from the back, which he had incorrectly assumed led outside, slammed open and roughly clattered against the wall. Zen nearly jumped out of his skin and fought the urge to jump behind Varys.

He watched as a short Ursonian woman waddled through the doorway, her one eye caked in oily makeup. Her long red hair was pulled into an artsy bun on the top of her head, which only added a few inches to her short stature. She barely reached Zen's chin, but her presence was fierce and demanding. It seemed to fill up the entire space.

"I'm all booked up! No more guests…" The woman stopped in her tracks, her mouth hanging open.

"Hey, Neteli." Varys's voice was meek, and he raised a hand in greeting. "Long time no see, eh?" For a moment, the Ursonian just stared at the gigantic alien that loomed over her. The silence was uncomfortable, and Zen shifted his feet, looking away from the exchange.

"*Varys…*"

Zen's head whipped around, his heart leaping into his throat.

"*What in the name of the goddess Meil are you doing?!*"

Varys cowered from her rage, and Zen couldn't help but find humor in his fear. He fought the smile that tugged at the corners of his mouth and bit his lip.

"N-neteli… *ava eik suul…*" Varys was stuttering something in Vesunian that Zen didn't understand, but it was clear that Neteli did as she lifted a hand and pointed a painted finger toward him.

"Don't you go spouting some excuse to ME, young man!" The Ursonian was practically shrieking. "I haven't gotten news from Vesun in *weeks* and, suddenly, you're on my doorstep! Last I heard, your mother…!"

She stopped as Varys stepped forward, vigorously shaking his head, and gesturing to Zen. Her eye widened even more, and her cheeks became blotchy and red.

"A human?! Varys, have you lost your mind?!" She hissed at him.

She looked Zen up and down with scathing distaste, and Zen felt himself shrink under her gaze.

*God, she was intense.*

"Neteli," Varys's voice was firmer now. "I will explain everything, eventually. But not here. Please. For now, we just need a room or two."

Neteli scoffed, returning her gaze to Varys, and she pursed her lips in a stubborn pout.

"I'm not housing the human. He's a soldier for Saal's sake."

Zen felt that familiar shame rising within him, and he backed away, hands raising.

"Hey, this is obviously a problem." He felt his voice trembling and cursed silently. "It's fine. I'll just sleep in the car again, like I originally planned."

Varys turned to him, eyes narrowed.

"You will not. You're injured."

He turned back to the Ursonian who now had her arms crossed. His voice took on a softer tone.

"Neteli, *au aka Reeva*. He saved my life. He's not like the others. He won't sell you out, I swear on the house of Velen."

His eyes were pleading, and he held his mangled hands out as if begging her to understand.

Zen felt a wave of guilt as Varys lied so blatantly. It had been the other way around. Varys had been the one to save them and break them out of the military base. It wasn't fair that he was giving Zen the credit for it.

Neteli's jaw worked, and her eye bounced between Zen and Varys. Taking a deep breath, she pinched her nose between her fingers.

"You know what? Fine, Varys. But I don't have much. You caught me at a bad time. A group of Vesunians were captured on a suicide mission to Mars a few weeks ago, and humanity's security has tightened up. Lots of folks trying to leave before they're stuck here."

Varys nodded. "We'll take what you can give us."

She sighed and fished a hand into her large apron pocket before pulling out a flashing key.

"Last room on the right. Get the human in there before anyone sees. Can't have my reputation on the line." Her eyes shot toward Zen, and he felt like melting into a puddle. "Don't make me regret trusting you, human."

Varys rolled his eyes and snatched the key from her outstretched hand. "He won't, and his name is Zen."

Zen nodded meekly in agreement. His voice was quiet. "I won't, ma'am."

Neteli tsked softly before turning on her heel and opening the door through which she'd come. It led to a small room with a wide-open trapdoor. She gestured for them to go inside.

Varys stepped forward with Zen close on his heels. As Varys passed her, Neteli grabbed his arm, and he turned to look at her, exasperation flashing in his eyes.

Neteli's hand vice-gripped his bicep. "Varys, please be careful." Her voice shook from the passion of what she was saying, and her gaze shone with unshed tears. "I can't imagine what your poor mother is going through. First, Eryand, and now..." She sighed heavily, her large bosom heaving. "Don't make us mourn you both."

Varys's gaze softened, and he nodded in acknowledgment before she finally released her grip and allowed them both to clamber down the ladder into the dimly lit hallway below.

The hallway was lined with glimmering blue lanterns, and instinctively, Zen knew it was Nuva. This was only the second time he'd seen it in person, but it was unmistakable. He followed closely behind Varys as the large alien stalked down the long hallway and passed door after door that had numbers etched into the wood. Zen's footsteps were muffled by rotting wood that served as a cover over the dirt floor. The walk seemed endless, especially as Zen's aching body screamed for rest.

Finally, they stopped at the end of the hallway, and Varys pressed the key into the door on the right. With a strange mechanical click, the door opened, and he stepped inside. Neteli passed by them both as she headed toward the very last door on the left.

"Knock if you need anything." With a flourish and a click, the Ursonian was in her room for the night.

Zen's limbs felt heavy as he stepped through the door and looked around their room. And immediately was struck with a problem. One bed. He felt his cheeks heat and watched as Varys slumped into the one, overstuffed armchair next to a crackling fire. He looked utterly exhausted.

Zen stood there for a few moments, rocking from leg to leg, unsure of how to address the issue at hand. Varys seemed to sense his hesitation and looked over from where he had draped himself. The alien stared at him for a moment before nodding.

"I'm sorry. I almost forgot."

He stood and in one quick motion, he picked Zen up and placed him on the bed. Zen felt his heart go from a light jog into a full gallop. He shook his head, willing it all to cease.

*This was stupid, he shouldn't be feeling this way. Not so soon after what he had been through.*

"Take your shirt off," Varys ordered, and Zen felt a tingling rush through his entire body.

"W-why?!" Zen stammered, hoping those large ears couldn't hear how incredibly stupid his heart had suddenly gotten. Varys's brow furrowed momentarily before sniffing the air and smirking.

"You pervert. I'm just tending to your wounds. Your shirt is covered in dried blood from the whip wounds." Varys chuckled, not put off by Zen's reaction.

Zen felt incredibly stupid. His wounds. Of course.

*His wounds.*

Zen shakily removed his shirt, gasping and wincing as pain lanced through his shoulders and down his back. Varys's eyes darkened even more as he twisted Zen around and examined the damage. He tried to ignore the heat that followed every touch of Varys's fingers.

"He was not merciful," The alien murmured before stepping away and toward the bathroom.

Zen tried to ignore the disappointment that was bubbling within him at the sudden distance between them. It was short-lived, however, as Varys came back with a bowl of warm water, several cloths, and a strange, glowing blue substance in a bottle. The alien seated himself comfortably on the bed and wet the cloth.

"Tell me if it hurts, and I'll stop," he said softly before pressing it to the human's wounds.

Zen gritted his teeth and tried not to gasp aloud at how incredibly tender every inch of his skin felt. Varys seemed to sense his pain, however, and stopped.

"I told you to tell me when it hurt, Zen." His voice was stern.

Zen flushed in response to the chastisement. "S-sorry."

His touch was gentler next time, and it didn't take long for him to finish cleaning the blood and grime from the wounds, even with all the moments he had to stop.

Varys also took time to clean the more superficial cuts on his arms and face. The alien turned him around once more, and Zen heard the top of a bottle pop open. Suddenly, a cooling sensation blossomed on the back wounds that instantly took away any pain.

Zen let loose a shuddering breath of relief and closed his eyes in bliss. "Holy shit. What is *that?"*

Varys chuckled deeply, rubbing the elixir into his back. "It's a medication made with Nuva. Speeds up healing and provides relief."

That impressed Zen, even as Varys's touch quickened his heart. "I didn't realize Nuva had so many uses." He turned his head slightly to take in the Vesunian's expression.

Varys smiled as he bandaged his back. "Nearly endless. It's pretty incredible."

"I can see why your kind wanted to share it with others," Zen commented before turning to completely face Varys on the bed. "And I'm sorry humanity punished your people for that."

Varys's brow furrowed, and he shook his head. "Don't apologize for something that is not your fault, Zen."

"But I will." The human felt breathless. "It's been a long time coming, but I think I've finally realized that we're the bad guys here. We were greedy, and we have gotten no better in the last 150 years. I'm so fucking sorry for what humanity did to you and your brother and everyone else..."

Zen gasped as Varys moved forward and gently placed his hand over the human's mouth. His black eyes twinkled softly, reflecting the firelight.

"Has anyone ever told you that you talk too much?" Amusement coated his tone, and he grinned.

Zen shook his head and gently pulled the alien's large hand off his face. "Only you."

Varys was close now. His face was centimeters from Zen's own. When he spoke, his tone was soft.

"There is no good or bad in war, Zen. We're all creatures, struggling for a cause we believe in. So small in the bigger picture of it all." His dark eyes scanned Zen's face, alighting upon his lips. "But not you, Zen Farraway."

Zen's heart felt like a herd of horses, wild and untamed.

"M-me?" he stammered, his voice a weak whisper, his pain and exhaustion completely forgotten.

He felt so stupid for feeling this way, but it was as though he couldn't stop himself. Varys was like a planet with intense gravitational pull, and Zen was a stupid rock that couldn't help but orbit him.

The alien nodded his head slowly and pulled his hand from Zen's grasp before gently catching his bottom lip in between two fingers.

"You're so... good. And kind. Unlike anyone I've ever met."

Varys was leaning in and suddenly, it reminded Zen of his dream.

*Oh god, his dream. It had felt so real.*

With a racing heart and flushed cheeks, Zen silently admitted that he longed to feel that again. To crash into Varys's mouth, and to finish that kiss. Heat coursed through him at the thought of doing just that. The distance between them was so small. The air was thick, and a throbbing had begun somewhere other than in Zen's chest.

"Zen," Varys whispered softly, his lips so close to Zen's he could simply purse them, and they would touch. Hunger burned in the alien's eyes and suddenly, Zen was no longer in the room. Panic bubbled to the surface. Alarm bells rang in his ears, the ghost of trauma past, as different images flashed into his memory.

*Bell, undressing and smirking at him. Varys and his group, surrounded by carnage. The sound of Bell's head being ripped from his body...*

Zen jerked away, putting his hand against his mouth, and closing his eyes. He didn't know whether Varys was actually planning on kissing him. But this wasn't right. He couldn't do this. Especially not with how they were now.

*Traumatized. Injured.*

That shame was eating a hole through his stomach, and he didn't want to open his eyes. But he grimaced and relented, hoping he hadn't upset the alien. When he opened his eyes, he saw Varys studying his face, not a trace of disappointment on his features. Relief coursed through him, and he sighed heavily. Perhaps Zen had misread him.

*God, he kind of hoped so.*

"I'm exhausted, Varys," he heard his own voice, sounding alien even to himself. "We should head to bed. We have an early morning."

Varys nodded, smiling. "Of course. You take the bed. I can sleep in the chair."

Zen nearly protested as Varys stood, but the alien turned, his brow raised.

"Aren't you exhausted? Too tired to argue, I'll bet."

And Zen laughed, resigning, and falling back into the inviting embrace of the soft bed.

# Chapter 28
# Varys

Varys watched as Zen slept. His heart beat a slow and steady rhythm against his chest as he admired the tiny human, curled up tight, his face smooth and free of all worries, his breathing was deep and slow. Varys watched to make sure that his chest continued to rise and fall. He'd been so stupid.

Varys closed his eyes and pressed two of his fingers into his forehead, trying to ignore the heat that rose to his face as he reminisced on what almost happened.

*On what he had wanted to happen.*

He should've known he was attracted to Zen. He'd been trying to push the feelings away and convince himself that what he felt was just deep kinship. But seeing him in that way. Half-undressed. His cheeks flushed. Those incredible eyes locked with his. The hormones that had filled the air, their sultry scent nearly setting him on fire from within…

Varys groaned softly as a hot flash of desire shot through him. He felt guilty for feeling this way, knowing what Zen had endured. Though Bell had been unsuccessful, they had both been subject to intense torture, and humans healed slowly. He was angry with himself that he had nearly acted on instinct. It had nearly undone him. He had nearly just taken Zen.

Unwillingly, images danced before his eyes. He imagined how Zen's thighs would've wrapped around him, trapping him in their heat. He imagined Zen underneath him, writhing in pleasure, gasping Varys's name, burying his hands in Varys's hair…

*No.*

Varys stood, shaking his head hard, trying to rid himself of the fantasy. But it stayed, lingering on the edges of his mind, and haunting his every thought. His stomach writhed and he grimaced, pushing his hands through his now-clean hair to calm himself.

He must've made a sound as he'd stood because Zen stirred. Varys froze in place, watching him intently. The human quickly settled, this time lying on his back with his arms outstretched to the sides.

Varys smiled softly. *Gods, he was adorable.*

He was sure that Zen would have some choice words to say about his use of the word "adorable." But he didn't care.

Something within him was changing. Something integral. It was terrifying. But it also excited him. His parents had tried to get him to settle down before the mission. He'd had practically the entire universe from which to choose. But with each lackluster date, each failed courtship, and each achingly boring conversation, he'd never felt the way that Zen had made him feel. The moment that Zen had plopped himself down in front of Varys's cell, a burning had begun within him. And it wasn't just an animalistic attraction to Zen's body. Even though that *definitely* was there. But it was the way he spoke. How gentle he was, with enough biting humor and sarcasm to keep himself alive in a world that would otherwise swallow him whole. He was a single, brilliant spark in a world that valued darkness. And Varys would be damned if anyone put it out.

That monster almost had. He'd seen it when he'd walked into the torture chamber. The man's pants had been unfastened, and he'd attempted to run away, screaming, as Varys lunged at him. Anger had pulsed through him, and it didn't matter what the torturer had or hadn't done at that point. He had hurt Zen, and that was enough. Varys may have spared him, perhaps let him off with just a broken leg and a warning, if he hadn't looked Zen's way. It was the red, swollen mess of his human's face that had enraged Varys enough to rip the torturer's head off. To actually kill him. Something he had never actually done himself.

The salt from Zen's tears had hung in the air for a while afterward, and the smell had clung to Varys's nostrils for much longer than he had expected. He much preferred the scent of Zen's arousal over his tears.

Varys made his way over to the bed where his human lay, finally at peace in some other world within his mind. A small, satisfied smile graced his soft features, and Varys reached for one, soft, pale tendril of hair and pushed it away from his face. He was torn. Everything inside of him screamed at him that Zen was his. That this was it. But Varys also knew it wasn't possible. That almost kiss was the closest they could ever get.

As deeply as he yearned for Zen, he knew that any partnership would cause tragedy. No matter either of their feelings on the subject. Not only were they opponents in a brutal war that had no end in sight, but they would never be seen as appropriate. And, with a sinking stomach, Varys remembered how short humans' lives were. A mere 100 years if they were lucky. Even if Zen lived to be such an age, Varys would outlive him by at least 100 more. It would never work.

But as the alien sat there, watching the soldier sleep so blissfully, he allowed himself to imagine it could. He imagined himself in a world where

Zen was his, and only his. The thought soothed him, and he lay on the bed, watching Zen sleep, daydreaming of what could never be.

And that is where he fell asleep, wrapped in the warm embrace of false hope.

# Chapter 29
## Altair

Altair had never been to First Earth in his entire life. He'd spent most of his days locked away in Serina with his mother and father. The only trips he'd ever taken had been "educational." His father had been determined that he learned diplomacy.

*Something he was notoriously bad at himself,* Altair mused.

Altair internally chuckled at the irony as he followed closely behind Lilith. She did not have him cuffed today, which would've surprised Altair, had he not understood her mindset. There was no way in hell he was going to abandon Lilith and try to make his way home now. His home planet was in a nearby galaxy, sure, but he was injured. He had regained strength and muscle mass these past few weeks, but Lilith's abilities still far outstripped his.

There was a greater chance of his curse being broken in an instant miracle than there was that he could get away from her. Let alone commandeer one of the ships from this airfield they had landed in. Thousands of soldiers patrolled between the ships that surrounded them. Some stopped to speak to those who were landing. They were requesting additional documentation, arresting a few who would get snarky, and rummaging through any goods that had been brought. Even Lilith seemed temporarily surprised by the level of security. She didn't falter in her stride, however, as she pushed toward a check-in window.

Altair thought about the airfield on Kelptor and how they had just landed, stored the ship, and walked away. It seemed so irresponsible now by comparison.

Lilith approached the window where an exhausted human soldier sat, studying the dry landscape. His eyes flickered down to where Lilith stood, and he sighed heavily before pulling a roster toward him.

"Name?"

Lilith observed his lips before clearing her throat. "Lilith Montgomery."

The soldier nodded and looked at Altair who stood looming over the bounty hunter from behind. "And your friend?" His eyes slid past the silencer in disinterest.

"Nothing more than baggage, for all intents and purposes." Lilith's tone was snappy. The soldier grimaced and put the pen down.

"Miss, you can't do that here. This is First Earth, human territory. We don't *do* that trafficking shit. So, unless you're willing to tell me otherwise, I've gotta have you both questioned."

A chill slid down Altair's spine at the idea.

*What would he do? He couldn't speak. Maybe he could pretend he was mute? This could get bad, fast.*

Lilith rolled her eyes before pulling an envelope from her pocket. It was slightly crumpled and had a broken seal with the letters "UE" stamped into it.

"No need for all that. This letter should explain everything. It should grant us rite of passage despite your customs laws."

She said the words with such a bite that it surprised Altair that the soldier didn't flinch. He extended a hand and grabbed the envelope, slipping a pair of glasses from his pocket and donning them before reading. His expression changed drastically within a matter of seconds. The soldier cleared his throat, his cheeks pink and his gaze dropping from hers.

"I'm so sorry." He handed the letter back to her, his hand trembling. "I didn't realize Mr. Boggs had sent for you. And... him."

He shot a nervous glance at Altair and curiosity welled within the alien at the effect this letter seemed to have.

"Why are you here? It says you were supposed to report to Second Earth a week ago."

Lilith slid the letter into her pocket before placing her hands on her hips. Her lips were pursed.

"The vemen asteroid field moved. I wasn't expecting the shift, and it caught me by surprise. It was a miracle that we didn't die, to be frank."

The soldier nodded in understanding, waiting for her to continue.

"But it got my ship, and I need it fixed before we can get to Mar... I mean Second Earth." Lilith corrected herself hastily as the soldier's eyes narrowed.

"How much will it cost for repairs?"

He drummed his fingers against the counter, pressing his lips together in a thin line as he considered her question.

"In any other circumstance, it'd probably run you your entire store of credits for such short notice," he sighed, penciling something in his ledger. "But for Mr. Boggs? Anything. No charge. It'll be ready first thing."

Lilith smiled, and Altair couldn't help but admire how graceful and kind she looked when she did so, even when the smile was laced with venom. "Thank you. That's very kind."

The soldier nodded wearily and waved them off. "Next!"

Altair followed Lilith as they exited the airfield, burning with questions to which he probably would not get answers.

So, this Mr. Boggs was the one who had paid Lilith to find him.

*Why did that sound so familiar?*

Altair racked his brain, trying to remember, but he couldn't. It was like his mind was dangling the information in front of him, just out of reach. He stepped off the cracked curb and headed toward a large, dusty human vehicle with which he was unfamiliar.

Inside were several humans sitting in rows of seats, carefully avoiding eye contact with each other. A few glanced his way as Lilith pulled him to a bench seat in the back. Her hand was carefully resting against the blaster on her belt and her eyes shifting from face to face. She was being cautious, even here, among her own people. Mr. Boggs must have been paying a sizable sum for him.

The human at the helm of the vehicle started to close the doors when a large thud startled several of the passengers out of their placid states. Altair felt Lilith stiffen in her seat as two soldiers entered the vehicle, fully decked out in blast-proof armor and carrying enormous weapons. Close on their heels was a man, whose presence chilled Altair to the bone. He was of average height for a human, but his face was lined with age. No emotion was readable on his features, most likely eroded from years of military service. His hair was cropped short and was a mix of black and white that reminded Altair of the silver speckles of some of his favorite fish as a child. Altair pushed back against the seat as the man's piercing gaze fell upon him, and he tried desperately to match his stare. It was intense, but not nearly as much as Lilith's, so it wasn't as difficult to hold it.

The man scratched his chin and opened his mouth to speak. "As some of you may know, two days ago there was an…incident, on base."

The soldiers stalked down the aisles and pulled protesting people out of their seats in order to search the vehicle and their belongings thoroughly.

"In the incident, a traitor and a Vesunian were lost." The man continued, breaking eye contact with Altair. "Now, I don't want you to be afraid. We will find them, and we will keep you all safe. But we need your help."

The soldiers had finished rummaging through the bus and had made it to the back. With a hiss of protest, Lilith jumped up, baring her teeth. The soldier, to his credit, backed up from her, his hands reaching for his weapon. Altair tensed in his seat, ready to jump between the two. The soldier stopped, watching them carefully. Much to Altair's surprise, he whispered, his voice trembling.

"Just cooperate. Please." His lip shook. "I don't want to kill anyone else today."

Underneath his helmet, the soldier looked young, barely out of youthhood. His cheeks were still rounded and cherub-like, but his eyes betrayed the horrors he had seen. Altair was sure that Lilith saw it as well. She grimaced before relenting and allowed him to pat both of them down before he returned to his comrade in the front. She sat down next to Altair with a huff, her eyes trained on the men at the front of the bus.

The older man clasped his hands together, smiling. "See? That wasn't so hard. It's that kind of cooperation that will help us win this war once and for all."

His eyes continued to drift toward the back where he and Lilith sat, and Altair winced as she glared right back at him. The grizzled soldier sighed before reaching into his front pocket and pulling out a device that displayed a holographic image. The image was of a young human man, with white blonde hair and blue eyes.

"This is Zen Farraway. If anyone has any information on his whereabouts, the military would be eternally indebted to them." The man smiled, but it didn't quite reach his eyes. "So indebted, that we're willing to offer you #14,000,000 credits for any information you may have."

A murmur swept through the vehicle. Heads turned and mouths moved as an excited babble began. Altair could only feel sympathy for the young man, this Zen. To have such a target on your back must be excruciating.

"Thank you. Proud to serve my five years." The man intonated before stepping off the bus with the two soldiers on his tail.

As soon as the doors hissed closed and the vehicle began rumbling down a busy road, Altair felt Lilith finally relax. He tapped his fingers on his knee before deciding that there was no harm in asking. He lifted his hand.

"Who was that?"

Lilith's eyes flickered to where Altair was signing discreetly behind the well-worn seat in front of them. She took several moments before deciding to answer him.

"One of my old sergeants, when I was in the human military."

Altair rolled his eyes, knowing he was going to have to dig for information.

"Name?"

Her hands were lightning-fast compared to his, and he struggled to keep up.

"Mike Jennings. The worst kind of soldier." Her eyes flashed and her lip curled at the mention of his name.

"Why?"

She sighed softly before responding. "Because he likes it. They force most humans to serve five years in the military once they turn eighteen. The only exception to that is if you or your parents are rich. You can buy your way out. We call them Upper Lifers."

Altair blinked several times as he processed what she was saying. "So, sort of like the elite?"

She nodded in response before signing. "Exactly. But some of them, like Sergeant Jennings, *choose* military service and make it their job." Her mouth pressed into a firm line as she answered his question. "Basically, he didn't have to kill people, but he chose to. Working under him was horrible."

Altair nodded, understanding why she had been so upset. He took a moment to think through what he wanted to say next. His hands were slow and careful.

"Do you know who the soldier was that they were looking for?"

She shook her head softly, sympathy gracing her features.

"I didn't catch the name, honestly. They weren't exactly speaking for the deaf. But I didn't know his face."

Altair spelled the name slowly for her with his hands, and she watched with curious eyes.

"Zen Farraway?" She questioned, and Altair nodded before she turned away from him, signing dismissively. "Godspeed, wherever you are Zen Farraway."

Altair sat back in his chair, knowing that the conversation was now over. He looked out the window as the arid landscape flew by. It was too reminiscent of his time in exile, and he felt his stomach twist into knots.

Altair attempted to turn his thoughts to more pleasant things. He missed the water. The thought of falling into a cool, safe body of water sounded like pure bliss. He knew this planet had not always looked this way. Many of his ancestors had first come here because of how incredibly blue and beautiful it was. The thought made Altair close his eyes to try and escape into the fantasy. He imagined he was floating in pools of cool water.

*Beautiful, clear, lovely water.*

It had started to work when the vehicle jolted to a stop, and Altair flew forward, smacking the left side of his head against the glass window. He silently winced in surprise and pain, rubbing his palm against the sore spot. Altair heard Lilith snicker next to him and indignantly whipped around to face her.

"Buses stop a lot," she said aloud, her voice even more unintelligible because she was laughing. "I wouldn't put my head on anything hard."

He glowered at her, his pride wounded. "Thanks for the fucking warning." His hands were quick and sharp.

Lil smirked and signed. "You remembered. Excellent use of the word 'fuck.'"

She waved her hands in mock applause, and Altair tried to hold on to his anger, but the smug humor on her face broke his willpower. He huffed an amused breath out of his nose.

"Thanks."

By the time the bus reached their stop, it had mostly emptied. The neighborhoods they had passed had become more and more desolate as time went on. When Lilith finally stood, the homes were nothing more than dirt huts, with nearly naked children running around outside, the smell of smoke filling the air.

Altair followed her off the bus, looking around in fascination. It was a far cry from what he had expected, but it was still beautiful. String lights hung between the houses, connecting them all and bringing soft, homey light to the small neighborhood as darkness crept in around them.

The children were not well-clothed, but they were boisterous. They seemed happy as they kicked rocks around and played with well-worn toys made of various scraps of fabric. The children stopped and stared as Lilith walked by, their eyes as wide as saucers as they took in Altair.

She stopped, smiling. "Nadia, Amir, Pattie, Roscoe... you all look well."

There was bashful silence for a moment before a young human girl stepped forward. She had bright red hair and a smattering of freckles across her nose and cheeks. When she spoke, Altair saw she was missing her two front teeth.

"Lil. Where have you been?"

She stomped her foot, and Altair couldn't help but admire the fire in such a little person.

Lil chuckled. "Sorry to upset you, Pattie. I've been on a mission." She knelt and opened her bag. "But I brought treats from Kelptor. And only kids who are *so* happy to see their old friend can have one."

Pattie froze before turning to the other kids who all nodded enthusiastically. In one big motion, they swarmed her with shouts of enthusiastic acclamation. Every single one attempted to convince her they each had missed her more than the others. Lilith laughed even harder and stood, warding them off playfully before throwing several brightly colored sweets into their hands.

"There ya go, ya savages."

The kids screamed their "thank yous" before running off with their handfuls of treats. Lilith turned to Altair, eyes twinkling as they reflected the surrounding lights.

"Sorry, I had to pay my entry tax." Her tone was warm. "Come on, my family lives this way."

She continued toward a distinct, dirt hut near the back of the neighborhood. Altair followed, feeling unknown emotions bubble up from what he had just witnessed. He was struck by how she both seemed so at home in this place, but also how incredibly *out* of place she was. Her shoulders were rolled back and relaxed, and there was a softness to her gaze with which Altair was unfamiliar.

But he liked it.

She stepped up to the hut and knocked on the flimsy wooden door. There was clanging and loud yelling in response before the door creaked open, and Altair blinked repeatedly as he took in the young man who stood before him. He was lanky and tall, nearly towering over Altair. He was also the spitting image of Lilith.

His features weren't as sharp, a sign of his younger age, and his eyes were a caramel color, unlike the deep brown of his elder sister. But his face seemed kind. He grinned widely, throwing his arms out.

"Lilith!" His voice was jovial as he grabbed her in a tight hug.

They both laughed loudly, grasping each other, before pulling away and touching each other's cheeks. The young man began signing, his speed rivaling that of Lilith's.

"You've been gone for weeks."

Lilith nodded, her gaze becoming apologetic.

"I know. I'm sorry, Shawn. I hope Mom hasn't been too worried. But I got a job."

Shawn's gaze darkened, and he glanced behind Lilith to glare at the alien. There was deep mistrust etched in his features.

"You told her you weren't going to do any more of your 'jobs.'"

Altair matched the boy's aggression, a unseen frown etching lines into his forehead. Lilith sighed deeply and nodded.

"I know I did. I know. But this one could change everything. It's a big one."

Altair dropped his challenging stare as he was reminded exactly what his position was in this situation.

*Chattel. Goods.*

Shawn waved off her excuses. "You'll have to explain that to *her*, not me."

From somewhere behind the boy, in the home's darkness, a woman's voice echoed toward them. "Who's there, Shawn?!"

Shawn leaned back, yelling over his right shoulder. "It's Lil! And a… friend."

He glanced back at Altair with that same hostility, and Altair's eyes narrowed. There was bustling and the sound of the heavy fabric moving before someone shoved Shawn out of the way. A beautiful woman stood in the doorway in his place.

She was easily recognizable as Lilith's mom, though they didn't look alike. Her sparkling, dark brown eyes were lined with age, and her long hair was tightly braided in several rows down her back.

"Lilith." The woman's voice trembled, and she pulled Lilith into a tight hug, pressing her face into the bounty hunter's shoulder. "Thank god, you're all right. I've been so worried."

Lilith tapped her mother's shoulder. "Mom, that's great and all, but I have no idea what you just said." She grinned sheepishly, as if this was a regular occurrence.

"Oh!" The woman pulled away, her cheeks darkening. "Right. Sorry. I'm still getting used to it."

Behind their mother, Shawn rolled his eyes and walked toward a pot in the middle of the room that was set over a small flame.

"It's okay Mom. I'm happy to see you. And I'm sorry I disappeared." Lilith's tone grew somber, and her gaze shadowed. "But… and *don't* freak out, Mom… I had a job come my way that I couldn't pass up."

Her mother's eyes darkened in the same way that Shawn's had, and she glanced back at Altair. There was less open hostility in her gaze, but her caution was apparent. She quickly glanced away from him. The woman pursed her lips, and Altair glimpsed Lilith on her features. She sighed before speaking, her hand clutching her daughter's shoulder.

"Come in. It's getting dark, and I would like an explanation from you."

She walked inside, gesturing for them to follow her. Lilith did so with no hesitation, turning and casting a pleading glance at Altair. He rolled his eyes, his dislike of her family rolling through him, but followed anyway. As if he had any other choice.

The home was simple but beautiful. Roughly made furniture filled the space, and the occasional book littered various surfaces. Small, wooden statues lined every other available spot, and a pot sat in the middle of the living area. Shawn lazily stirred whatever was in it, sending the aroma of cooking meat and cheap spices through the air. Altair stood awkwardly at the edge of the room, his stomach rumbling from the surrounding smells. Each member of the family made themselves comfortable on various pieces of furniture.

Lilith's mother gestured from where she sat toward her daughter, her dark eyes glimmering. "Explain yourself."

Lilith curled her legs under her in one of the few comfortable-looking chairs and sighed, gesturing for Altair to sit next to her. He meandered his way over and sat on the ground next to the seat. His cheeks burned and he dropped his eyes, trying not to make eye contact with anyone. There was a long, uncomfortable silence where the family simply stared at one another before Lilith spoke.

"He is my job."

She gestured to Altair, and her mother raised her brows in feigned surprise.

"A Serinian." Her tone was deeply disapproving. "Why would a Serinian be worth anything?"

Altair felt heat tremble through him. He had to look down at the dirt floor of the hut and breathe deeply through his nose in order to rein in his emotions.

"I don't know." Lilith's tone was placating, even as she lied through her teeth. "The important thing is, he *is* worth something. And even more important is knowing *who* hired me for this job." She paused, knowing that what she had to say would free her from her mother's disapproval. "It was Peter Boggs."

It was like a bolt of electricity radiated through the little hut, and her mother straightened up, a hand pressed to her mouth. Her surprise was genuine this time.

"P-Peter Boggs hired you?" Her tone was hushed. "So... it was lucrative..." She couldn't even finish the sentence and placed her hand on her chest, shaking her head in exaggerated disbelief.

Shawn was frozen in place, holding three bowls over the pot. His eyes were wide, and his jaw was slack.

Lilith nodded in confirmation. "Yeah, he's paying me well. We'll have enough credits to get you two off this planet." Lilith trained her eyes away from Altair, her shoulders stiff.

Shawn dropped the ladle loudly into the pot, his eyes burning now. "That's what this is about, Lilith?!" His shout was sudden. It made the others in the room startle at the sound. "You're doing this because of me?!"

Lilith stood and faced him, arms out in an attempt at comfort. "Mostly, yes. You turn seventeen in a month, Shawn. Then, you have one more year before you have to go into military service." Her jaw stiffened in that familiar, stubborn way. "If I can get you guys somewhere far away, you don't have to serve..."

"I don't care if I serve!" Shawn's voice was rising in volume and tears had planted a shine in his eyes. "I've told you this!"

His voice stopped. He attempted to speak through the tears but could do nothing more than gasp for a few seconds. Finally, he signed, unable to speak through his emotions.

"You don't get to make my decisions for me, Lilith!"

The bounty hunter was exasperated as she signed back.

"You don't know what you're getting into! War isn't a game, Shawn! I've seen too many people die. It took my hearing..."

Shawn was indignant as he signed furiously, cutting her off.

"I don't care! I don't want you taking these dangerous jobs! Interacting with Serinians or, worse, Vesunians, just to keep me from serving…"

"You don't understand! This is far bigger than you, Shawn. It's for Mom too!"

Their mother's voice suddenly cut through the signing, stern and firm. Her eyes flashed as she spoke. "Enough! You know I can't understand sign!" She stood, stepping between them, and placing a hand on each of their chests. "Both of you take a breath and remember we're on the same side here."

Shawn threw the bowls to the ground with a clatter and stormed off to the back of the hut into a different room. He slammed the door behind him; the force rattling the home. It surprised Altair to see Lilith so distraught. She stared after her brother, trembling, tears pricking at her eyes. There was silence before her mother gently sat her down once more. She seemed to consider her words before she spoke.

"I understand his anger, Lilith. But…" She held up a hand as Lilith opened her mouth to interrupt. "I understand *why* you are doing what you are doing. And there's nothing to be done about it now. You have him here. Finish the job."

She looked toward Altair, distaste in her eyes. Altair didn't even have his bearings enough to be offended by the look she shot him. Lilith nodded, rubbing the back of her hand against her eyes.

"This is the last job, Mom. I promise."

Her mother nodded. "When do you leave? To take him to Mars."

Lilith took a deep breath to steady herself. "Tomorrow morning. My ship needed repairs."

She nodded once again before gesturing toward the alien. "His name?"

Lilith's gaze shifted over to where he was still sitting. "Altair."

Her mother nodded one more time before kneeling in front of the Serinian who backed away from the intimidating woman. Her eyes glimmered as she took in his fear before she spoke.

"Altair, my name is Melodi. As you've gathered, I am Lilith's mother." Her gaze was as hard as stone, her mouth set in a stern line. "And I need you to understand me, okay?"

Altair slowly nodded. Hatred filled her gaze and Altair recoiled even further.

"Your kind are *never* and *will never* be welcome in my home. You are the one exception for tonight, to humor my daughter and for the betterment of my situation. But…"

She stopped for emphasis, and Altair swallowed dryly, waiting for her to finish. She leaned in closer, eyes narrowed and her voice practically a hiss.

"If you do *anything* funny. If you try to hurt either of my children, I will stick a knife so far into your ribs that they'll need to cut you open to find it."

Her voice was scathing, and Altair now saw where Lilith had inherited her intensity.

"Understood?"

He nodded again, his body trembling. Altair didn't mean any of them harm, but he could tell that she likely wouldn't believe that, even if he could communicate it.

Melodi stood, glancing toward Lilith who seemed embarrassed by her mother's behavior.

"Take your old room. I'll watch the Serinian tonight."

And with that, Melodi smiled and began serving dinner for everyone but Altair.

# Chapter 30
# Altair

Altair slept fitfully. He could feel the penetrating eyes of the human woman from across the room. He'd been allowed to sleep on the wooden bench that served as a couch. Small, old pillows were scattered on the bench to make it more comfortable. However, Altair's back hurt too much for sleep to make a permanent appearance as he shifted, over and over, grimacing.

Melodi would move occasionally in her night watch over him. Soft sighs came from that side of the room, and Altair wondered, multiple times, where the hostility for Serinians came from. He was used to being hated for his curse. Not for being a Serinian.

At one point, in the night's dark, Shawn crept out and scooped a bowl into the pot that had sat stagnant with dinner. He had then silently slipped back into his room. Earlier, Melodi had attempted to lure him out with a bowl of dinner, but he'd refused to answer her call.

Altair supposed that was young adulthood for most creatures. Powerful emotions and poor decisions. At least, that's the way it always seemed in every book he'd ever read. He'd never experienced it himself. He had spent his young adulthood in survival. In some alternate universe, he mused, a teenage Altair was trying desperately to cover his blemishes and was yelling at his parents that they didn't understand him. The fantasy brought him comfort. It was comfort that a version of him, somewhere, hadn't experienced what he had. That he hadn't been so scared and broken from a young age.

He heard Melodi cough softly and felt agitation creeping in. The sound had stirred him from a place near sleep. He sat up and heard her stiffen, the sound of metal on stone indicating that she had grabbed her knife. He waved her down, trying to show with his body language that he didn't mean to fight. He was simply weary. And honestly, Altair was sick of not making any decisions for himself.

Melodi relaxed only slightly as she watched the Serinian stretch. Altair stared right back at her and held out his hands in questioning frustration.

*What did she think he was going to do?*

Melodi lifted her head to meet his gaze, her eyes glittering in the light of the pale moon that stretched its fingers through the window. Even through the darkness of the room, Altair could see her, and he blanched at the severity of her emotions.

"I'm sure you're confused, Serinian." Her voice was soft, hardly above a whisper. "About where my hatred comes from for your kind."

Altair shrugged, feigning indifference. Truthfully, the question burned, but he didn't want to seem so desperate in front of someone like her. Melodi hefted the blade between her two hands, refusing to take her eyes off him. She shook her head, throwing her braids back over her shoulders. Altair didn't expect her to speak again, but it was as if she couldn't help herself.

"I had a sister. A twin sister."

She flipped the blade and caught it by the hilt, and Altair couldn't help the wave of admiration that swept through him at the show of skill. It was becoming very apparent that this woman had raised Lilith.

"We were alike in many ways. But the one thing that set us apart was that she was stupid."

Melodi's voice was harsh, and Altair blinked in surprise. A humorless laugh escaped her mouth.

"I know you're thinking, how could someone speak that way about someone they love? Let alone a sibling. But it's the truth. This is not a world for stupid people anymore." Her nostrils flared and her teeth slammed together, and Altair felt a sudden skitter of fear dance through his gut.

"It's why my children are the way they are. I wouldn't let them be stupid in such a world."

Altair nodded, ensnared by her storytelling. She had the same way with words that Lilith did.

"My sister went to a traveling show that came to Earth when we were seventeen. She met this Serinian woman there, the star of the show. The idiot fell in love immediately."

Melodi stabbed the knife into a pillow near her and began pulling at the strings and Altair couldn't help but imagine the pillow as his abdomen. He winced.

"And how could you not? Sirens of legend. Beautiful, captivating voices." Her tone was dripping with sarcasm. "The Serinian promised her so much. We were approaching our time to be drafted. Neither of us wanted to do it, but I had resigned myself to it. Harmoni hadn't."

Melodi took a deep, shuddering breath and closed her eyes briefly as if steeling herself for the next part of the story.

"I warned her to be careful. I told her that your kind were the original space whores."

Her tone invited no argument, and Altair felt that familiar rush of fire burn through his veins.

"But of course, this Serinian was *different.*"

Melodi's eyes took on a haunted look. There was a long pause where the two just stared at each other through the home's darkness. Finally, Melodi finished her story with a frustrated sigh.

"When the traveling show left Earth, so did the Serinian. Without so much as a goodbye to my sister. She was distraught. She'd thought she was going with them."

Her voice softened, deep emotion pushing at the edges of it.

"I was the one who found her body. The day before we were to be drafted. She'd written a suicide note, addressed to her Serinian lover and no one else. I burned the note before my parents could find it."

Sorrow extinguished the anger that had run its course through Altair. He understood loss. Without even thinking about it, he had signed in her direction. "I'm sorry."

Melodi blinked repeatedly, and her mouth gaped open like a fish. Her eyes darted from Altair's hands up to his face. There was a moment of silence before she stood and stalked over to Altair. The Serinian had to fight the urge to scuttle away from her as she sat on the couch next to him.

"You know sign?" Melodi's voice trembled. "I've tried for years to learn but…" She shook her head. "It never came to me."

Altair was hesitant but slowly nodded, twisting away from Melodi, desperate not to meet the woman's gaze. She stared at the side of his face for several moments before flaring her nostrils and leaning in closer, her hand still clutching the blade.

"Did Lilith teach you?"

He paused at her question, conflicted, before nodding in confirmation. Melodi pressed her fingers into her forehead, cursing quietly to herself. She sat there for several moments before standing and walking away from Altair, her gait somewhat unsteady in the darkness. Melodi sat in her former position and looked up to meet Altair's gaze. Her mouth was pressed into a firm, disapproving line.

When she spoke, her voice was steady once again. "Never tell Lilith I said this, but…" Melodi stiffened her shoulders, looking down at her feet momentarily, "I'm grateful her hearing was taken from her by that Nuva blast."

Altair felt shock course through his body, and he briefly considered replacing his "worst parent in the galaxy" title with Melodi. His father had abandoned him, but wishing their child actual harm? Melodi was going too far.

She caught his disgusted look and laughed sardonically. "Oh, don't give me that look. You're not a parent. You don't know."

Twirling her knife again, she stared at him. He fought to match her look.

"I'm grateful she lost her hearing because now she's safe. She'll never be a victim to your charms, or any other Serinian."

Melodi's mouth twitched as she fought a smile, and horror filled Altair at her next comment.

"I'd rather burn my home down with my family in it than welcome another Serinian into my home." She smirked at his expression. "So, in the morning, I suggest you leave with my daughter and never come back."

She looked away from his horrified face and continued twirling her knife. Her next sentence was whispered, as though she didn't intend for him to hear it.

"Peter Boggs can keep you. He can keep all of you."

And with that comment, Melodi went quiet. Altair did not sleep a wink.

# Chapter 31
# Zen

The morning hadn't even dawned when Zen was awoken by someone stirring in bed next to him.

It took a few minutes of blearily rubbing his eyes before he realized Varys had crawled into bed with him at some point. Heat immediately blossomed in his cheeks, and he sat straight up in bed, racking his brain for memories of the night before.

*Nothing happened,* his brain reassured him.

But seeing the alien lying there, breathing deeply, and taking up most of the bed, he wasn't so sure if he could trust his memory. They had almost kissed. Or at least, he thought they had. He could be wrong. Perhaps Varys and his kind just didn't have a thing about personal space like humanity did. Maybe touching other people's lips was a custom for them.

Zen willed his heart to slow down, but the sound of him sitting up seemed to stir Varys, who grunted and bent his large form up, rubbing at his eyes as well. He looked as if he'd slept terribly.

It took several moments of staring at each other before Varys realized where he was and promptly jumped out of the bed.

"Zen, I'm sorry. I was… I… uh…"

The alien was stuttering, and Zen wondered if Varys was nervous because they had been in the same bed. His cheeks reddened at the idea. Varys was running a hand through his hair, trying to come up with the words. He locked eyes with Zen, his mouth turned down as he spoke.

"I was checking if you were breathing at one point, and I must've fallen asleep."

Zen blinked several times before amusement stretched a smile across his face, and Varys realized his mistake.

The alien stammered. "That's not what… Zen… don't you…"

"You were making sure I was breathing? What am I? An infant? A pet?" A laugh escaped Zen, the ridiculousness catching up to him.

Varys's cheeks purpled, and Zen wondered if that meant he was blushing. If it was, Zen loved it. He felt vindicated that he wasn't the only one blushing now. Chagrin spread across Varys's face, and he smiled too.

"Yeah, you're my human pet. Didn't you know? Vesunians, we capture you humans, and keep you as pets."

He chuckled, shaking his head before walking over to the entrance. The alien opened the door, discovering a pile of things that Neteli had clearly left for them, and began stuffing them unceremoniously into one of the bags that she had provided. It was obvious that Varys simply wanted to move on from the situation, but Zen wasn't letting him off that easily.

"Damn. Kinky." The words were out of Zen's mouth before he could stop them. He quickly slapped a hand to his lips, eyes wide, and he watched as the alien's back stiffened.

*Oh fuck, oh fuck, oh fuck!*

That same heat from last night filled the room as Varys turned around, his eyes glittering.

*Uh oh. There was no mistaking that look. Not this time.*

Varys meandered over to Zen, dropping the bag on the ground, and spoke, mischief lacing his tone.

"Careful, Zen the human." He paused, relishing Zen's embarrassment. "One might suggest that you find that idea… intriguing."

Varys was now back on the bed, leaning over Zen. He felt that heat pool within him again, and the air felt thick and warm. His thoughts became clouded with lust as the alien's scent enveloped him. His dream came back with full force, and he shivered at the idea of Varys touching him.

*He wanted it. Oh shit, he actually wanted it.*

Zen took a shaky breath. When he spoke, his voice was barely a whisper. "I thought I told you I didn't like that nickname."

Varys shrugged, smirking. "You never gave me an alternative."

"I said to call me Zen."

"That's not a nickname."

Zen scoffed lightly, his head spinning. "You don't need a nickname for me."

Varys's eyes darkened with need, and the human swallowed thickly in response. The alien leaned in once again and, this time, Zen knew what was about to happen.

*Oh my god, Varys was going to kiss him. Was he okay with it this time?*

His body and heart screamed for it to happen. But Zen knew that could change in an instant. He waited for the panic from last night to set in. He didn't know whether he'd be ready for something like this so soon after what had happened a few days prior. Excitement pulsed through him when the panic didn't set in. All he wanted now was for Varys to close the distance between them, and finish what his dream had started.

The lean forward was agonizingly slow, and Varys stopped mere centimeters from his lips, staring deeply into Zen's eyes. He smiled, laughing softly, his breath brushing over Zen's mouth and sending shivers down his spine.

"I do. And now I think I'll call you 'pet.' Our little inside joke."

A guarded look entered Varys's eyes, and he pulled away from their closeness.

*Shit. Had he done something wrong?*

Disappointment writhed in Zen's stomach. So much so, he almost didn't register the nickname. He felt hot and flushed, and a wet spot had made itself known on the front of Zen's pants, where it had also risen slightly, pulling at the material. He quickly threw the blanket over his lower half to hide his arousal, before realizing what Varys had said. He frowned at Varys's back. The alien had gone back to packing.

"Hey now, I don't like that one either."

The lie felt like cotton in his mouth.

Varys laughed, not even looking back as he finished filling their bags.

**Liar.**

Zen flushed deeply at that. But he knew that this wasn't the time to plead his case. They needed to get ready and get out. This was no time for games or distractions. Even muscular, tall ones who kept almost kissing him.

Zen waited until he knew he was sufficiently calm enough before he slipped out of bed and ran into the bathroom to do a quick cleanup. Luckily, there were rudimentary toiletries that allowed him to freshen up. Once through with that, he grabbed at any bathroom and medical supplies that were housed in the small cabinet next to the tub before stuffing them into his bag.

"Did Neteli drop off clothes along with those bags? Or armor? Weapons?" he called out from the bathroom.

Varys ducked underneath the doorway, holding a small pile of clothing. "She did." He placed the outfits on the edge of the tub. "No armor or weapons though. She's stretched pretty thin already. It was hard enough getting these, I'm sure."

Zen nodded in acknowledgment and looked through the clothes, pleased with their condition. He felt large fingers wrapping around his waist from behind, and he startled, the burning from earlier threatening to return.

"Varys! Warn a guy!" he hissed and jerked away from the alien.

Varys chuckled softly. "So sensitive. I was going to check your wounds, but I have to undress you of your bandages."

Zen frowned but nodded, turning his back to allow him to do so. He shivered and his cheeks flushed at the Vesunian's touch as he waited for Varys to finish studying his back.

"Well?" Zen's voice was laced with impatience.

"Much better. No infection. The wounds are already closing." Varys sounded pleased and relieved.

Surprise made Zen's eyebrows nearly shoot up to his hairline. "No fucking way, let me see."

He backed up toward the one mirror in the bathroom and twisted around to look. His jaw dropped as he saw the former welts, now nearly completely healed. They were still slightly raw, but no longer looked or felt so angry and jagged.

"Holy shit!" Zen murmured, admiring the work of the medication.

Varys chuckled before gesturing for him to come back over to him. The alien had pulled the bottle of glowing blue medication from his bag.

"You're quite vulgar," he remarked as Zen walked over and allowed him access to clean and bind his wounds with fresh bandages. His tone was casual, as if he were commenting on the weather.

Zen flushed and shrugged, trying not to marvel at how his back hardly ached as Varys tended to him. Such a complete 180 from last night. It almost didn't feel real.

"Does it bother you?"

Varys laughed loudly before handing him one of the outfits Neteli had dropped off.

"If it bothered me, you would know, pet." His tone was comforting, which didn't help the hot flash Zen felt at the use of the nickname. "It's simply surprising, I suppose. You don't seem the type. Then, you open your mouth and profanities spill out."

Zen bristled at the insinuation. "You're saying I'm too feminine to swear?"

Varys blinked a few times and shook his head vigorously. "Not what I said at all. But I'm sorry to offend." He sighed and stepped out of the bathroom. "Once you're ready to go, we should head out. We want to get to the airfield before daylight." And with that, Varys closed the door.

Guilt washed through him.

*God, you can be such an asshole, Zen. He's not one of your childhood bullies. Cut him some slack.*

Zen shook his head to clear his mind before pulling on the simple, black, long-sleeved shirt and pants that Varys had left for him. He slipped the thick jacket on, knowing he would only need it for the next few hours. Once the sun rose, the earth would heat quickly.

The clothes were breathable and tight to his body, perfect for strenuous activity. Durable and dependable. They were exactly what Zen needed. He laced his boots up before walking out to where Varys waited. The alien had changed too and was wearing something similar, his hands bandaged tightly.

"Found this in one of the dresser drawers." He tossed something toward Zen, smiling, seemingly having already forgotten Zen's minor tantrum. "A former tenant must've left it here."

Zen caught and examined it. It was a long, slightly rusted Swiss army knife. He looked up and smiled gratefully at the alien.

"Thank you Varys."

"Of course, my pet."

Zen flushed and frowned. "Stop it." His heartbeat had quickened again.

Varys threw his head back and laughed, his magnificent curls flying away from his face. Without another word, he stepped out of the room and made his way down the hallway with Zen at his heels. They stopped, only briefly, to set the key on the long counter before walking out of the inn.

The cool of the desert landscape around them kissed Zen's cheeks, and he pulled the hood up over his head, shivering. He stepped into the driver's seat, and Varys carefully folded himself once again into the passenger side. The human leaned down and hot-wired the car again, beaming in relief as the engine started, purring like a cat. He made sure their lights were off and rolled out into the desert, following his mental maps.

The drive was quiet, at least initially, as they both stared comfortably out the front window. Zen fought to stay calm, knowing that this was going to be the tough part. Hot-wiring a car was one thing. Stealing and piloting a ship from a heavily patrolled airfield was another. Zen drummed his fingers against the steering wheel, and he saw Varys's head turn toward him. He didn't speak for a moment, but Zen felt a tendril of thought enter his mind after a few minutes.

***You okay, Zen?***

The human sighed heavily. "Just nervous, Varys. This is a big deal. Breaking out was way too easy. I feel like our luck is bound to run out."

Varys nodded, smiling and patting Zen's hand that rested on the gear shift.

*It'll be okay, though. I won't let anything happen to you.*

Zen flushed once again and glanced over at the alien. He grimaced before speaking.

"I'm more concerned about you. I'm afraid of what would happen if they caught you."

He moved both hands to the wheel and tightened his grip. Old rumors about their prisoners of war began swirling through his mind.

"Honestly, they'd just kill me. They'd do worse to you."

Varys was quiet again, but this time it was different. The silence was tense, and Varys was incredibly still. The tension made Zen uncomfortable, and he shifted in his seat, staring out at the darkened desert in front of them. He couldn't stand it for more than a few minutes before he had to break the silence.

"Varys, you seem upset."

The Vesunian's jaw worked, and his hands clenched tightly on the bag in his lap. When he spoke, it was out loud. His beautiful voice was harsher than normal.

"You're so casual about it."

Zen was surprised. "Casual about what?"

He looked over and saw the alien swallow hard before speaking.

"About dying. You're okay with it. Resigned to it."

Zen's palms felt sweaty. He hadn't ever been called out for his casually suicidal behavior. He'd never been brave enough to do what his roommate did, but it wasn't as if the thought had never crossed his mind. He knew, deep down, that he wouldn't actually kill himself. But, if a stray plasma blast had caught him in the last couple of years, he wouldn't have been disappointed.

He grimaced. "Varys, we're in the middle of a war. I'm a soldier. I've had to come to terms with the possibility of dying multiple times. People die in war all the time. As you said, humans are frail."

Zen remembered when the Vesunian had nearly snapped him in half. Part of him had screamed for more time, to go in a less humiliating way. Hopefully, something less painful. But a darker, quieter side of him had been relieved. He wouldn't have had to deal with any of this anymore. Varys was shaking his head, and Zen came back to their conversation.

"No. You won't die, Zen. I won't let that happen."

Zen's pulse skyrocketed once again at the protectiveness in his tone. He swallowed hard against the thickness in his throat and nodded. "Okay, Varys."

"Swear it to me."

"W-what?!"

The alien's gaze was intense as he stared at the side of Zen's face. "Swear you will try to stay alive."

Zen could've been mistaken, but he thought he heard Varys's voice tremble. His heart was pounding in his ears, and his cheeks were hot as he slowly nodded.

His voice was once again a whisper when he spoke. "I swear I will try to stay alive."

The alien nodded, pleased with his promise before turning to face the front once again. The rest of the drive was quiet.

Sunrise was only a half an hour away by the time the airfield came into view. Zen parked far enough from sight that no searchlights could reach them before he sat back.

He took a shuddering breath. "Okay, Varys. Can you see any patrols?"

Varys squinted, peering at the airfield for several seconds before nodding.

"High security." The alien murmured, the nerves finally settling in for him. His four-fingered hands trembled as he watched the patrols.

Zen nodded. "I know. Do you see any ships that look decent enough to take? Preferably something human-made since it's what I'm familiar with."

Varys took a deep breath. "There are a couple of Troy ships. Those are human made. One of them looks like the newest." The alien stepped out of the car, presumably to get a better look. Zen followed him, slipping his bag over his shoulders. He stood next to Varys on the hill, overlooking the airfield in silence as Varys surveyed the landscape. Light was sneaking over the horizon, bathing everything in a pale, white light. The spiky and harsh plant life stretched toward the small amount of light, as if waking up from a deep sleep. Zen felt a sudden tightness in his chest at the sight.

As much as they had destroyed this planet; beauty and life still found a way. And he would probably never see this again. The thought made a lump appear in his throat. Embarrassingly, he felt tears rise to his eyes, and he brushed the back of his hand against them, hoping Varys wouldn't notice. He sniffled lightly and looked up toward the alien, flushing when he saw Varys was watching him, a strange look in his dark eyes.

Zen stiffened his lip and cleared his throat. "S-sorry. Are you ready to go?" They were running out of night.

Varys didn't respond for several moments, his eyes not leaving Zen's face. He felt his heart kick into full gear, and his cheeks got even warmer. Zen wasn't sure how that was possible.

"Varys? Are you ready?"

Varys slowly shook his head, and Zen felt surprise blossom in his chest. The alien took a deep breath as if steeling himself.

"Just… one more thing."

And suddenly Varys stepped forward, wrapping an arm around his waist. He gently pulled the human up to his face and cupped his cheek with his other hand. There was the briefest, heart-stopping moment before Varys leaned down and softly pressed his lips to Zen's.

# Chapter 32
## Zen

Zen's heart felt like it was going to pound right out of his chest. His whole being was on fire as Varys's lips moved against his. It was as if the alien's mouth were laced with something strong enough to make Zen forget where he was and what he was doing. He moved Varys's hand from his face, wrapping his arms around the Vesunian's neck and standing on the tips of his toes. His thoughts raced.

*Shit. Fuck. Fuck YES!*

He felt Varys part his lips with his own mouth and slip his tongue into Zen's, which made a needy whimper escape the human's throat. Varys growled softly, grabbing his waist, and lifting him, allowing Zen to wrap his legs around the alien's torso. Varys stumbled down the hill and toward the nearby car. He sat Zen on top of it, refusing to break their kiss. Lust fogged Zen's brain, and the kissing became more passionate and sloppy. Varys's hands were sending burning trails up and down Zen's body, the tingling desire making him shiver.

Varys moved the kisses slowly away from Zen's lips. He kissed along his jawline and then slowly down his neck where it lingered on the hollow where his neck and chest met. Zen gasped softly as Varys focused his kisses there and grabbed at the alien's horns for support. His legs involuntarily spread to allow the alien more access as Varys pressed his body into Zen's. He felt a hand slide up one of his thighs, just like it had in his dream. Varys's large fingers circled the bulge that had risen there. Zen gasped, leaning his head back, pleasure coursing through his body as Varys teased him.

"Varys..." he whimpered and the sound of his name on Zen's lips made the alien growl deeply in need. He grasped Zen with his entire hand through the thin material of his pants. The movement caused a wave of lust to shoot through him. But it also shocked him enough to make Zen realize where they were. And what they were doing.

"V-Varys... we can't..." Zen's protest was weak and unbelievable.

The panic from before was rearing its ugly head. Not only did they not have time for this, but Zen also wasn't ready. Not so soon after what had happened.

Varys stopped, looking up to meet his gaze. The burning that was in the depths of those dark eyes sent goosebumps up Zen's arms.

***We don't have to go any further. I just... I needed you to know how I felt before we went down there.***

Zen nodded, his senses slowly returning to him. With a slight jolt, he realized how light it had gotten around them, and what their passionate session had cost them.

"Shit!" Zen scrambled off the hood of the car, the desire in him all but extinguished, and his arousal shrinking. "We've lost too much time. We need to go. Now!"

Varys looked around, and regret filled his features. "I'm sorry." He murmured, following closely after Zen.

The human didn't have time to soothe his hurt feelings. They had a job to do. Zen wondered, briefly, whether he would've allowed things to go further had they had the time. The image of Bell slapping him came screeching into his memory, and he flinched, trying to banish the recollection. Shaking his head, he lamented that he wasn't ready for anything like that. As much as he yearned for it.

Zen slid down the dirt hill and crouched low to the ground as he snuck toward the fence. He didn't hear Varys behind him. He turned quickly and nearly yelped in surprise seeing Varys so close to him.

*Damn, he was quiet.*

The alien nodded at him, acknowledging his glance, his face set and determined. Zen's back ached as he pulled the knife from his pocket and began sawing at the chain link. His head was on a swivel, making sure that none of the patrols were close enough to see what was going on. Varys's large ears were twitching, his eyes narrowed as he looked around as well.

All was quiet except for the sound of the chain link slowly being cut and the distant conversations of the soldiers on patrol. Only a few minutes in, Zen was sweating from the effort as he silently cursed the daylight that was creeping their way.

"Varys," Zen hissed. "Can you finish this?"

Varys nodded and eased Zen to the side. He grabbed the weakened fence and, as silently as he could, tore the rest of the hole wide open, his muscles bulging from the effort.

Zen flushed, looking away from his arms and over to where Varys had fashioned a small entryway for them to crawl through. Zen moved forward but Varys's large arm stopped him.

**Me first, pet.**

Zen opened his mouth to argue, blushing at the use of the nickname, but Varys held a finger to his own mouth, his eyes twinkling.

*Have to be quiet. Remember?*

Zen rolled his eyes but allowed Varys to slip through the hole first. He followed shortly after, and they both crept forward, bent at the knee. Varys led the way, silent as the grave. He was headed toward a shiny, silver Troy ship that looked like it had had recent repairs done. A couple of soldiers stood guard next to it, casually chatting with each other over coffee and yawning. Large blasters were slung heavily on their hips, and they were covered head to toe in armor, with only their visors up so they could enjoy their morning caffeine.

Despair rose in Zen's stomach. *How were they supposed to do this?*

Varys stopped to hide behind the edge of an ancient-looking Ursonian trade ship and peered out toward them.

The alien's voice entered his mind. ***We need a distraction.***

Zen nodded, his mind whirring uselessly, and he bit his lip as he came up empty. He shot his thought to Varys as hard as he could.

*I don't know what to do, Varys.*

Varys sighed heavily and ran a hand through his hair, his eyes shifting from the soldiers over to the ship. That was when an idea came to Zen. A horrible plan he knew would work. His breath must've caught because Varys's head whipped toward him, his dark eyes widening.

*You have an idea?*

Zen hesitated before nodding, and the two stared at each other for a moment before Varys's gaze darkened.

***Absolutely not.***

Zen's heart pounded wildly in his chest, and he smacked the alien's shoulder, frustrated with his immediate refusal.

"Come on, Varys. You know it would work," he hissed.

His heart broke at the look on Varys's face, and he turned away from the alien, trying to maintain his position.

"It's too light out to slip past them unnoticed. If I walk up to them and give myself up, it would give you time to break into the ship and get out of here."

Varys's head was shaking back and forth, pain in every line of his features.

*I'm not leaving you here.*

"Why not?!" Zen was whisper-yelling. He hoped that the nearby guards couldn't hear their argument. "You *have* to get home."

***They'll kill you, Zen.***

"I don't care."

*Well, I do!*

His frustration boiled over and Zen gritted his teeth, snarling his next words. "You don't get to tell me what to do just because you kissed me."

Zen stood up straight, his heart nearly flying out of his chest at what he was about to do. Varys lunged for him, but he quickly side-stepped, before walking into the light of day, toward the soldiers. He tried to ignore Varys's agonized mental yelling as he moved forward. It took a few seconds for the soldiers to notice him but when they did, both dropped their coffees and reached for their blasters.

Zen's hands flew up in surrender. "I'm not armed!"

His hands were trembling, and he saw the two soldiers glance at each other briefly, unsure of what to do. They were young, maybe in the first year of their service. They must have shown incredible marksmanship during training to get stationed as security already. The thought was not comforting.

"State your name!" one of them called out, training her blaster at Zen's face. Her voice was unsteady.

"Zen Farraway."

Zen didn't even have it in him to lie at this point. He was probably going to die, anyway. As long as Varys got out, that's all that mattered. Her companion nudged her.

"That's the guy that Sergeant Jennings showed us yesterday. The traitor."

His whisper carried toward Zen on the breeze, and he closed his eyes briefly, accepting his fate. If he had a bounty on his head, it was all over. He hoped Varys was sneaking onto the ship as they spoke.

"You're Zen Farraway?" she called out, confirming, and he nodded. She looked sweaty and pale.

"You know you've got a massive bounty on your head right? Dead or alive?" The other soldier finally spoke to him as he stepped forward.

Confidence oozed from his tone as he also trained his blaster in Zen's direction. He could tell by the look of his features that this soldier was an Upper Lifer. There was privilege etched in nearly every line of his face. He'd chosen this life. He'd chosen to kill.

Zen shrugged, hands still in the air as they grew numb from the cold. "I figured as much. I'll go with you."

The soldier's eyes narrowed, and he frowned.

"Jennings said you'd have someone with you. A Vesunian." He called out. "Where's the monster, Farraway?"

Zen gritted his teeth and tried to laugh, but it came out sounding hollow.

"It's cute that you think I'd be stupid enough to bring a Vesunian around with me."

The lies burned, and he couldn't help but remember Varys's body pressed into him, his mouth on Zen's neck. He shivered at the memory before speaking.

"I'm alone."

The soldier's brow furrowed before he smirked and laughed as well. His laugh was much fuller than Zen's.

"You're a terrible liar."

The soldier powered up his blaster, aiming it right at Zen's head, close enough that the blast would most likely decapitate him.

"And once you die, we're going to find your Vesunian friend and kill him too. Wonder what I'd do with that amount of credits?"

He chuckled. The female soldier had already radioed in their position as they'd stood there, discussing the situation. Zen swallowed hard, feeling terrified tears spring to his eyes.

*This was a better way to die, wasn't it?*

Rather than getting his body snapped in half, he would die protecting someone he cared about. A speck in the grand scheme of the war, but it was these minor sacrifices that would eventually add up. At least he hoped so. He closed his eyes, praying that there would be enough of him left to send home to his parents. The sound of a blaster made him jump, but he heard an even louder blast, the heat razing toward him.

His eyes flew open, his adrenaline pumping, and he saw that where the two soldiers had stood, there was now a large scorch mark. Flames danced along a path toward another ship that was now on fire as well. The ship's emergency alarms were screaming. Zen's mouth was agape, and, for a few moments, he didn't know what to do. A furious voice burst into his consciousness.

**Get on the ship. NOW!**

He froze for a moment before sprinting toward the Troy ship, where the platform was lowering for him. Wailing alarms sounded from the main building, and Zen was immediately washed over with memories of their escape. At least, there weren't red lights this time. He sprinted and jumped onto the platform before it was even finished rolling down. Clambering up it, he quickly leapt to his feet and ran into the ship, the platform rolling closed behind him.

Varys was at the helm of the ship, staring at the controls in front of him with wide eyes. "I-I got the weapons unlocked, but I don't know…"

"MOVE!" Zen shoved the Vesunian out of the way with a strength that belied his size.

He tore the control panel lid off, shakily sparking several wires together. His breath came quick and terrified as he looked up and saw the entire airfield security sprinting toward their ship. The wall of flames kept them from the quickest route, but they started circling around it in order to get to the two fugitives.

"Shit, shit, SHIT!" Zen couldn't help the profanities bubbling from his throat.

He looked back down and continued trying to hot-wire the ship with trembling fingers. It was a newer model. Slightly different from what he'd worked on before. Varys jumped on the weapons controls and began aiming it at the oncoming onslaught. His eyes were narrowed and focused as he powered on a couple of the large blasters. Panic skittered through Zen's chest, and he yelled at the alien, briefly forgetting his task.

"Only if necessary, Varys!!"

Varys looked over at him questioningly, his eyes wild. "Only if necessary?! Are you kidding me, Zen?!"

The alien had never taken such a tone with him, but Zen didn't care. He wanted to avoid bloodshed as much as possible. The memories of what he'd seen in the Vesunians' first escape attempt haunted the edges of his mind, always threatening to overtake him and swallow him whole. He didn't want to cause anything close to that. He already hated that two had died in this escape attempt.

"No! I'm not! Hold your fire!"

Zen's heart leapt into his throat as the ship started briefly and then died once again. He felt like crying. This wasn't the plan. He couldn't do this.

*You're a failure, Zen.*

He imagined Varys being thrown back into a cell, tortured for information, and possibly even killed and parted for materials. All for a war that meant absolutely nothing.

***Hey.***

Zen looked toward Varys, who smiled gently at him. He felt tears roll down his cheeks in reaction to the genuine kindness that was on the alien's face.

*You can do this, Zen. I believe in you.*

Zen nodded, wiping his face, bolstered by Varys's faith in him. The alien's expression hardened once again as he turned to the window, training the ship's large guns on the throng that was nearly to their ship. The multitude hesitated as they saw the guns were pointed directly at them.

*Now get us the fuck out of here. As you would say.*

Zen laughed in shock, which distracted him enough to forget the urgency of their situation in order to breathe. He looked down and sparked a couple of wires together in a similar fashion as before. This time, the ship sputtered and came to life, the power from the engine knocking a few soldiers that were too close, flat on their backs.

Zen jumped onto the controls and began expertly guiding them up and toward the atmosphere. He felt several blasters rock the ship with the force of their plasma. Looking down briefly, he saw a shock of salt and pepper hair. His stomach writhed as he saw Sergeant Jennings's face, white with rage, and set in homicidal determination. His form slowly disappeared, the features blurring together as the ship shot toward the freeing expanse of space.

Zen shakily sat in the seat and set their speed high enough to break through the atmosphere. He charted their immediate course around any of the sensors that would take their unregistered ship down. Varys stood silent as a sentinel at the weapons controls, tense and scanning the surrounding sky to make sure no one was coming after them.

Zen only truly relaxed as the ship shuddered through the atmosphere. The vast expanse of space swallowed them like a dark, comforting blanket. There was silence for a minute as Zen felt his body relax momentarily. It was over. It was all over. Then, suddenly, he realized that his side felt strangely warm and sticky.

*Why the fuck did he feel sticky?*

He glanced down and blinked hard several times as he took in the massive blast wound that still smoldered, blood spilling from it.

*When had he gotten shot?*

He remembered the soldier training his blaster at Zen and shooting, but he'd flinched away. He thought it hadn't made contact. He hadn't felt a goddamn thing. He looked back at where he had come from and saw a large trail of blood that had followed him from the ship's entrance. So, it *was* his blood that was currently spewing from the wound. Damn, adrenaline was a bitch.

His vision swam, and he looked over at Varys who had also relaxed. It took a moment for him to register what was going on, to notice the paling of Zen's face and the weakness in his limbs. The alien's dark eyes switched in an instant when he realized Zen was injured. Panic bloomed within them, and Zen laughed weakly at that, knowing that this was the end. It was sort of funny. Or ironic, he supposed. To have escaped, but not escaped.

"Hey Varys, they got me."

His voice sounded far away, even to himself, and a ringing had begun in his ears. Such a pretty sound.

"Zen."

The Vesunian rushed toward him and picked him up, cradling him in his arms. None too late either, as Zen had felt his body finally giving in to the wound and collapsing from the chair when the alien had scooped him up. He set him on the floor, pushing a large hand into Zen's side to stop the flow of blood. Zen couldn't feel it. It should've hurt like a bitch for Varys to press on such a gruesome wound. But he couldn't feel it.

*Shit. That was bad.*

"Zen, hold on." Varys's voice was shaking as he seemed to press even harder.

*Aw, that was sweet.*

At least, he was going to go like this, in the arms of someone who cared about him. Zen tried to think through the growing darkness in his mind.

"Varys, listen to me."

He was finding it hard to form words, but he knew that Varys needed to know how to work the ship. He had to know. He just had to.

"See that screen? Put in Vesun's coordinates and press the y-yellow... the yellow button." He gasped softly, his breathing getting even more labored.

Varys was scrambling around in his bag for medical supplies and pulled out that familiar blue bottle.

"I don't need to know this." Varys's voice was stern, but his eyes betrayed his terror. "Because you know how to do it. And you're staying *here.*"

Zen chuckled weakly and watched Varys press the medication into the wound. He winced, the cooling effect the only thing he could even feel at this point.

"Varys," Zen's voice was hoarse. "I'm dying."

"No!" Varys's voice echoed loudly through the silver interior of the ship. "No, you're not. You're not. You will not die. I won't let it happen. I won't. Please, Zen, please."

The alien's voice broke, and Zen weakly reached up to touch his cheek. Varys grabbed his hand, holding it there, his lip trembling.

*God, it was heartbreaking.*

But the darkness was too overpowering. It was too strong.

"I'm sorry," Zen whispered.

And then everything went dark.

# Chapter 33
## Varys

Varys watched as the light left his human's eyes. His heart felt like it was going to melt into a horrified puddle. The stillness in Zen's limbs made him feel like he was in an awful nightmare from which he couldn't wake. He stared at Zen's perfect eyes, willing the deadness to leave them, to fill with light and humor again. But they didn't. And they never would again. Varys whimpered, pain beginning to build within his chest.

*This couldn't be it. This wasn't the end. This wasn't how things were supposed to end for them.*

Zen was so still. So very, very still. And Varys hated it. If his eyes hadn't been open in that horrible way, Varys would've expected Zen to be sleeping. But the silence in the human's chest showed that everything Varys was praying for was a delusional fantasy. The blood that had betrayed them both by escaping from the blast wound in Zen's side was smeared all over the alien, coating his hands. Such a horrible, ugly red color. He traced the outline of Zen's lips with a trembling finger, and his heart felt like it was ripping itself apart when he realized that the warmth in Zen's skin was slowly leaving.

"No…" He whispered. He pulled the soldier into his arms and held him close to his chest. Varys buried his face in his beautiful blonde hair, now smeared with that awful color that he hated. The reality of the situation came crashing into his mind. Zen was dead. Varys had failed to keep him safe. He was dead. Dead. Gone. *Forever.*

Varys let loose an agonized, primal scream of grief. His voice reverberated through the silver ship and echoed back to him, mocking his pain. He rocked back and forth, clutching Zen to his chest and screaming into the void of the empty ship.

"Come back, Zen!" He cried out, over and over, feeling his throat rubbing raw. "I love you! This isn't fair! COME BACK!!"

Varys loved Zen. And he'd never said it. He'd never realized it until this moment. He felt so stupid now, only understanding the burgeoning in his chest when the subject of his affection could no longer hear his confession. His whole body trembled as he held the tiny human tightly to himself.

*First, Eryand. Now, Zen.*

*This war had taken too much from him.*

He screamed and begged for Zen to come back to him, feeling the human grow cold and stiff in his arms as time wore on. After a long while, his voice was hoarse, and he couldn't scream any longer. Plus, the heat of Varys's body was doing nothing to warm Zen back up. He gently placed Zen down on the floor of the ship and looked at him, feeling a numbness growing within him. He pushed away the attempt his brain was making to protect him from the grief. He wanted to feel the pain. He deserved to feel the pain.

After all, he was responsible for all of this. If it hadn't been for his stupidity in coming on the original mission, Zen would still be alive. If he hadn't struck up a friendship with Zen, nothing would've bloomed between them, and he would've never been tortured. Never been shot. Never would've died. It wasn't *fair*.

Zen was one of the few good things in this entire universe. He'd felt it on his lips as they'd kissed on the hood of the car. How Zen had gasped into his mouth, and his head had leaned back, allowing Varys more access to his neck. They had connected at that moment in a way that meant something. It was something deeper than either of them understood at the time. The potential simmered for something for which Varys had long given up hope.

However, because it was Zen, he'd prioritized getting Varys out and to safety over their brief, passionate interlude. He'd sacrificed himself in an impossible situation to allow Varys time to get on a ship and head back home. And he'd used his last words to teach Varys how to get home, and to apologize for dying. It was ridiculous that he'd even felt the need to apologize for something beyond his control. But again, it was one of the best things about Zen. His unfailing kindness, even in the face of cruelty and danger.

Varys felt emotion pushing into his chest and it made him want to scream again, to get the grief out into the open. He was too good to be gone already.

*Reeva wouldn't allow this.*

An idea whispered at the edges of his mind, and he swallowed hard, trying not to let the hope that had burgeoned in his chest take hold. It was a long shot, but he owed it to Zen to try. He whimpered softly and pulled his shirt over his head. Varys slowly began cleaning the blood off Zen with it. He then pulled Zen's shirt off to make sure that everything was completely spotless. He couldn't bear the sight of his human covered in such copious amounts of blood. When he finished, he placed a gentle kiss on Zen's cold forehead.

"Come back to me, Zen," he whispered before closing his eyes and attempting to connect to his home.

He imagined Reeva, her swaying branches along with her twisting, glowing roots that extended as far as the eye could see. He breathed in deeply, feeling the magic swell within him as he reached out. He shivered when his mind touched the eternal.

*Reeva.* Varys called out to her within his mind, hoping she would hear him from so far away. *Great mother. Hear my plea. I am Varys, your loyal servant. And I'm asking for a great favor today.*

His mind swam with memories of his grandfather sitting Varys on his knee and speaking to him in halting Vesunian.

*You used to perform miracles for my people. We have abandoned your ways of peace and love, but I know that you still love us and have not abandoned us.*

He took a shaky breath. He brought to his mind the images of the dead being brought back to life, their bodies glowing with the power of Nuva. His wish was simple, and he hoped she understood.

*I love him, Reeva. Grant me the power to bring him back.*

Varys recalled stories of Nuva bringing the dead back to life. They were ancient stories, from long before he was born, from when his grandfather, Herwat, was a child.

It was not something that Reeva had granted to his people often, especially when they had abandoned her ways of peace and harmony. But, sometimes, someone would be brought back. It was usually because the death had been untimely, or the person had needed to serve a greater purpose. However, the miracles had stopped by the time Herwat's sister, Byrat, was killed. No stories had been told since of Reeva bringing back the dead. He prayed that would change.

Varys shakily pulled the bottle of Nuva medication back out of the bag where he'd thrown it in frustration after Zen had gone still. He knelt over the human's body, praying feverishly that this would work. With trembling hands, he undid the top of the bottle and held it over Zen.

"*Au aka Reeva.*" He murmured, hope constricting his heart, before he dumped the entire contents of the bottle into Zen's mouth. It was something he wouldn't do unless he was desperate. Nuva was both powerful and good, but it could do great harm in experimental uses. Just as his people had seen with weaponizing it. He pressed his hands into Zen's chest, willing that familiar heartbeat to come back and praying that Reeva would give him the power this one time.

*Just this once.*

She had helped him break his bindings and escape at the military base. Her hand had been in his mission the entire time and he knew, somewhere deep within him, that Zen still had a greater purpose to serve. Though, the reasons for bringing him back did feel selfish.

Varys sat, holding his hands against the human's chest for a long time. The only sound he could hear was the hum of the ship around them. His palms grew sweaty as he held them there, eyes glued to Zen's face and ears perked for the sounds of life.

"Come on, come on," he murmured, heart pounding.

He tried not to lose hope as the minutes ticked on. An unusual amount of time passed, and Varys felt his hope deflating in his chest, the grief beginning to make everything feel heavy again. He nearly pulled his hands away, resigned to his failure, when his hands suddenly glowed with a blueish-purple light. Varys gasped softly, and he held them there, trembling with hopeful anticipation. His own heart raced as he watched the color slowly seep back into Zen's cheeks.

Even more miraculously, he watched as the gruesome wound on Zen's side seemed to heal itself. The flesh regenerated and bound together in an incredible, entrancing dance. And then, Zen's chest finally rose.

Varys let loose a startled, relieved laugh. Emotion welled up within him as he heard Zen's heartbeat start again. His eyes remained closed, but Varys pulled him close to his chest again, mumbling his gratitude to Reeva.

"*Au aka Reeva.*" His voice shook with relief as he held the human close, listening to the blissful sounds of life coming from his small body. He only had a few moments of gratitude, however, before a strange, melodic voice spoke to him in an ancient form of Vesunian. The voice rang like bells in his mind, speaking a sentence he could barely understand. The whisper felt ancient and powerful, and it made Varys shiver as he listened to how it was carried to him. An enticing, gorgeous ballad on the wind.

**Varys ee seileea Velen. Seik auo sei livvva.**

Varys tried to decipher the words but only caught a few of them. Something about "a gift" and "using wisdom." At least, that's what it sounded like. He did not know what any of it meant. But it didn't matter right now. He looked back down at where Zen lay in his arms. Whatever rules had to be broken, Varys didn't care. He didn't know what Reeva had done to make this happen. She just had. And now he had Zen back. Zen was *alive.*

Joy swelled within him as he watched Zen's eyelids softly flutter before finally opening, revealing those amazing eyes that reminded Varys so much of Nuva. Happiness coursed through him seeing the life glimmer within them. But trepidation joined the happiness when he realized something was off. His eyes were a different color.

*No, not a different color. A different shade.*

Zen's eyes now seemed to shine not only with life but with the power of Nuva.

# Chapter 34
## Altair

Their ship had been stolen. Lilith was screaming at the cowering soldier behind the counter. He was stammering out excuses, trying to explain what had happened. The stench of mechanical fire clung to Altair's nostrils as he peered around at the chaos surrounding them. Soldiers tripped over each other as they hurried from place to place. Passengers were being stopped and harassed, and their luggage was being forcefully taken from them. Screams rang through the air as they brought various soldiers back on stretchers, burnt and wailing in pain.

"Why was *my* ship stolen?! Was it because of my rush?! Do you know who I am?!" Lilith was shrieking and slamming her armored fist on the counter.

"M-ma'am, we know who you are." The soldier was holding his hands outward, placatingly. "And we are very sorry. We're trying to find a replacement ship that will be suitable enough to get you to Second Earth."

"My ship is not replaceable!" Lilith threw her hands up into the air. Her nostrils flared as she stared the soldier down. "With all the security this place has, it's fucking ridiculous that this even happened!"

"We can't control what people do, ma'am. A couple of wanted criminals made the security breach." His voice was meek, and he shriveled under her gaze.

Altair's ears perked upon hearing that, and he pushed forward, signing hurriedly at Lilith. "Ask him if it was the soldier and the Vesunian."

Lilith gave him a strange look before sighing and turning back to the soldier.

"Was it the wanted traitor? And his Vesunian cohort?"

The soldier blinked in confusion. "How do you know about them?"

Lilith rolled her eyes and waved her hands dismissively. "They combed our bus over on the way out of the depot yesterday. Jennings told all the passengers about it. Are they dangerous?" It was clear that Lilith was only concerned about her ship.

The soldier slowly nodded, seemingly nervous about giving any sort of information to them. When he spoke, it was halting and shaky.

"I suppose since they took your ship, you should know. They blasted a couple of our guys and set another ship on fire." He shook his head. "Death toll is still rising, honestly. Just from the fires alone."

Lilith, to her credit, seemed fairly shocked by the news.

"Has this ever happened before? I'm from First Earth and I remember nothing like this happening…" She trailed off, her eyes going distant.

The soldier shook his head again. "No, it hasn't. Not that I can recall." He sighed and wrote something in his ledger. "We're getting you a ship, Ms. Montgomery. You and your… friend… just have to wait inside."

Lilith let loose a heavy exhale from her nose before grabbing Altair's arm and stomping toward the hangar. She passed several of the stretchers, averting her gaze from their moaning and whimpering. The stench of burning flesh made Altair gag behind the silencer.

He followed closely behind her as they entered the hangar and seated themselves in the uncomfortable chairs of the waiting room. An older woman was sobbing in the corner, clutching a burnt name tag that most likely belonged to one of the soldiers. She held a handkerchief to her eyes, and her frail shoulders shook.

Altair could spot a grieving mother anywhere. He wished he could go over and speak to her, but he knew that would only make the situation much worse. So, instead, he watched her with sympathetic eyes. The sight of the woman brought to mind thoughts of his mother. Oddly, remembering her didn't bring the same emotions that it used to. It was as if thinking of her so often over the past several weeks had numbed him to her memory. He could even reflect on her death without too much pain.

Altair glanced down at his bandaged knuckles and wondered whether his tantrum had anything to do with it. As if he'd shocked his system into behaving itself. It was that, or that Melodi had scared any sort of feeling out of him. Either way, it was nice to be a little numb.

Altair shot a glance over to where Lilith was seated next to him, her elbows on her legs and her head resting in her hands. She looked over, apparently feeling his gaze. She furrowed her brow and frowned, lifting her head.

"What?" She signed, her gestures sharp and irritated.

Altair shrugged and signed back, trying to be dismissive. "You're just tense."

Her teeth ground together, and she rolled her eyes before responding. "You would be too."

"Fair enough."

He threw his hands down, frustrated with her prickly nature. They sat in complete silence, other than the occasional sob from the corner and stared out of the glass exterior of the doors. They watched as the chaos slowly lessened, and the injured soldiers were moved elsewhere.

Altair's interest was piqued when he saw a familiar, gray head of hair, surrounded by guards, stalking its way through the airfield. He watched as Sergeant Jennings halted and whispered to each of the surrounding soldiers before continuing by himself. He was walking in the hangar's direction, straight toward where they were both sitting in the waiting room.

He nudged Lilith, and she looked up, her eyes flashing, and then she stiffened once she saw Jennings heading their way.

"No, turn around." Her voice was tense and quiet, as though she was talking to herself. "I don't want to talk to you."

But, of course, fate just had to have her last laugh. As Sergeant Jennings strode confidently toward the doors, they opened with a mechanical hiss. He stepped inside, his thick eyebrows raised to the edge of his hairline, and stood at attention, watching Lilith carefully. His boots were shiny and clean, despite the carnage he had just walked through, and he waited, as if expecting Lilith to stand or salute.

Her jaw clenched, and she did neither, staring Jennings down with that same determination. Her dark eyes flashed, and her fists were rolled into tight fists. Admiration flew through Altair as he watched her, causing his heart to quicken and his cheeks to flush. After a few moments, Jennings seemed to relent, and he relaxed in his position of attention, smiling a disingenuous smile.

"Lilith Montgomery." He spoke and his voice was reminiscent of the crashing of pebbles against the shoreline. "It's been a long time, hasn't it, young lady?"

Altair's brow furrowed at the way the older man spoke to her. As if she was a child.

"Sergeant." Lilith's voice was even more strained than usual, and Altair saw a flash of insecurity in her eyes as she struggled to maintain her glare while also reading his lips. Jennings's gaze flickered over to her damaged ear, and he nodded, as if remembering her condition.

"Apologies." To his credit, Jennings tried to enunciate a little more. "I heard what happened to your ship, Lilith."

She shook her head, her jaw working. "Wasn't your fault. It was your soldiers. Not enough security apparently."

Jennings frowned at her quip, and Altair felt a shiver of fear pass through him. The frown was vaguely grandfatherly but held a hint of something sinister. It was enough to set his teeth on edge.

Jennings paced over to them, sitting on the table that was in front of their chairs.

"Once a spitfire, always a spitfire, eh Montgomery?" His eyes darkened, as if daring her to speak out of turn again.

"You know it, Sergeant." She shot back. "Used to be a trait you admired in me."

There was silence for several heart-stopping seconds before Jennings cracked a smile, a real one, and chuckled softly to himself.

"You're right. And you're not my soldier anymore, so I suppose you can say whatever you want to me. Not that it stopped you before." He rubbed a hand across the stubble on his chin.

Lilith nodded curtly, her hand sneaking underneath the seat armrests and grabbing Altair's elbow tightly, as though she were afraid he would run away. How naïve of her to think he would even attempt that at this point. He was sure Jennings would shoot him within seconds of reaching the door only a few feet away. As if reading her mind, the older man's eyes alighted upon Altair.

"A Serinian," he mused. "I suppose that's what Peter is here for."

Lilith sat forward in her seat, her hand abandoning Altair's arm. "Boggs is here?!" Her tone was quiet, and Altair thought he heard a hint of fear.

The grizzled veteran slowly nodded. "Guess he got tired of waiting for you. He arrived this morning, shortly after everything happened," the sergeant mused, still watching Altair with deep interest glimmering in his cold eyes.

Lilith sat back, shoulders slumped and her chin dropping. Jennings's eyes shone with delight as he took in her pain, and Altair's dislike of him grew.

"From what I've heard, this isn't just any Serinian though." Jennings continued, leaning forward and into Altair's face, causing the alien to back away, heart pounding. He did his best to glare straight into his curious gaze.

Jennings smirked at his effort before speaking again, his tone sarcastically reverent. "Apparently, we're in the presence of royalty."

Altair's heart dropped out of his chest, and his cheeks heated uncomfortably. Jennings seemed to relish his panic just as much as he'd relished Lil's shame. His eyes glittered predatorily, and he chuckled.

"Welcome to First Earth, Prince Altair of Serina. Heir to the Serinian throne. Keeper of the Voice and cursed with Death." He leaned back, eyebrows raised. "Did I get all those titles right? The last bit was my own creative flair, but I hope you liked it."

Altair knew that Jennings didn't care what the prince preferred. He bared his teeth and he just glared at Jennings, hoping that was answer enough.

The sergeant turned back to Lilith with a smug look gracing his features. "Boggs is waiting on base in conference room A. He'll explain everything."

Lilith, to her credit, seemed surprised that Jennings even knew any of this information. But she nodded and hesitatingly stood, grasping Altair by the arm, and hoisting him to his feet.

Jennings led them outside to a sleek, black vehicle. He opened the back door for them to clamber inside.

*This was it. The end of the long journey.*

Altair was finally about to get some answers.

The drive to the base was slow, at least it seemed so to the alien. Lilith was on edge the entire ride, tapping her foot and pulling at her hands. Anxious energy spilled from her. She kept shooting glances toward Altair but, as they pulled up to a large, concrete building, she stiffened her shoulders and seemed to clear her mind. They took deep breaths in unison as the car stopped.

Altair cracked his neck from side to side, his hair brushing against the faded material of the seat and tried to let the tension leave his body. The door opened, and pale sunlight filtered into the car. Altair stepped out, and the soldier who had opened it trained her blaster at the alien's head.

"No funny business, Serinian," she spat scathingly.

Altair rolled his eyes at her threat and, as Lilith stepped out of the car, she fixed the soldier with the worst death glare she could muster. The soldier withered under her gaze and backed off. Lilith roughly grabbed Altair's arm and led him toward the base.

Stepping inside, the air was stale and freezing. The contrast to the heat from outside made Altair shiver uncontrollably for a few minutes as they traipsed their way down the hallways. Lilith was quiet for the entire walk.

Altair could tell something was on her mind, but he didn't want to push her to talk. She would do so if she felt the need to.

Finally, they stopped in front of a huge, metal door with the number one inscribed on a placard next to it. Lilith didn't seem willing to move for several seconds. Her eyes seemed distant.

He pulled his arm from her grasp and looked at her, signing, "Lilith, what's wrong?"

Though he'd resigned himself to allowing her to speak on her own terms, she was not acting like herself. She fixed Altair with an unreadable expression and stared him down for several seconds. Suddenly, her hands were flying, and she was signing, almost faster than he could even process it.

"Altair, I just want you to know that I wouldn't do this unless I had to. I need the credits. I have to get my brother off this god-forsaken planet. You're a good person, and I tried hard not to have compassion for you, but I do. You've been through so much and now I'm handing you over to some of the worst that humanity has to offer."

Altair's eyes were wide, and shock rolled through him when he saw she was fighting tears. He tried to gesture for her to stop, his chest aching. But she continued, ignoring the tears that threatened to spill.

"The biggest thing is that with men like Jennings and Boggs, you just want to do what they say. No questions asked. I know, I'm one to talk, but I've paid for my mouth a hundred times over, trust me."

Her eyes glistened, and as stunned as Altair was that the tears had even appeared, he was even more stunned when he saw one of them slip from her eyes. He had seen this sort of emotion from her, specifically when Silas had died and when she had argued with Shawn. But he'd never thought he'd be on the receiving end of such emotion.

"Please just be careful, Altair. Do what they ask. I don't want to see this end badly for you," she whispered, wiping her face.

Altair grabbed her hands and held them down for a moment and she gasped, a practiced defensiveness entering her expression. He tried to infuse understanding into his gaze as he looked at her. Altair shook his head slowly, her pain his own as he understood her.

*Finally*, he understood why she'd been so hot and cold. She'd been fighting with herself the entire time. Lilith was simply a good person, in a bad situation.

*War brought out the worst in everybody, didn't it?*

When he let go, he signed slowly, trying to convince her of the sincerity of his words.

"You were just doing your job. And taking care of your family. I can't fault you for that."

Lilith grimaced and wiped her eyes in order see his signing more clearly. Her head dropped, her voice quiet when she spoke aloud.

"I wish you didn't have to be the sacrifice I had to make for my family, though," she murmured.

Her cheeks were red, and she sighed heavily, looking away from him and trying to gather herself. It took her several minutes, and Altair allowed her to take as much time as she needed.

"Ready to head inside?" she said finally, looking up at him and plastering a smile on her face.

Altair nodded and followed her as she scanned something on the right-hand wall, and the door slid open with a hiss. His heart pounded into his throat as they moved toward the doorway together. A wave of cold air escaped the room and chilled Altair as he followed on Lil's heels. His stomach clenched tightly as he took in his surroundings. It was difficult to do so when his heartbeat was so incredibly deafening.

The room was empty other than a small conference table where a human man sat, scrolling a holographic tablet. Two guards stood on either side of him, watching menacingly as the two entered the room. The walls were a dull gray color, and it seemed everything here was devoid of color and life.

Altair swallowed dryly and slid his gaze away from the bodyguards and focused on the much smaller human between them. As he examined the man sitting in the chair at the head of the conference table, he was struck by how utterly normal Peter Boggs appeared to be. He looked like any other generic human male. His brown hair was a respectable length, shorn short around the sides of his head. He had green eyes that seemed far too kind for how people spoke about him. There were lines on his face that showed that he was perhaps middle-aged. Boggs looked up when they entered and smiled jovially, dispelling the aggressive atmosphere that his bodyguards set.

"Lilith!"

He gestured for them to sit and snapped toward the two hulking men at his sides. One of them slid water slowly toward Lilith and nearly did the same to Altair until he saw the silencer. He shrugged at the Serinian before storing it underneath the table.

Lilith meekly grabbed the water and palmed it, tossing it between her hands. It was quiet for a moment as Boggs watched her, as though he expected her to drink it. She sighed heavily and spoke, her eyes fixed on the glossy sheen of the conference table.

"Mr. Boggs. I didn't expect to see you here."

Boggs waved down her explanation with a large, toothy grin.

"No need, no need. We all know why I'm here. I'm here for *him*."

Boggs was incredibly direct as he nodded toward Altair, and the alien reeled back in surprise at how quickly he had cut straight to business. Boggs chuckled, spinning in his chair from side to side.

"And it took you a helluva long time to get to me, Lilith, but we'll discuss how that affects your pay later."

Lilith didn't even bristle, she just shrunk in her seat. His tone was so casual that it didn't feel right to question it. There was a strange threat underneath the cheerful tone of his voice that differed from Jennings'. With the sergeant, Altair was afraid that the man would kill him. But with Boggs, something far more sinister lay beneath the surface.

Boggs tsked, ignoring Lilith's immediate shriveling. He rolled up the sleeves of his expensive-looking sweater and shot Altair a glance that seemed to indicate that they were buddies, in on some practical joke together. He stood, pacing toward the alien, and Altair had the instinctual urge to back away. It was strange the sort of effect that this man seemed to have on him.

"Prince Altair, it's a pleasure to have you here, might I say." His tone was genuine. "I apologize for the rough way in which she probably brought you here, although you do look well-taken care of. Hats off to Lilith, my favorite bounty hunter."

He nodded toward Lilith who didn't meet his gaze. Her eyes were still trained downward. Altair nodded, his blood pounding ferociously through his veins. He felt his temper rising at how quickly this man had extinguished Lilith's fire.

Boggs shifted from foot to foot, his eyes narrowing at the look on Altair's face. He seemed to recover quickly, however, as he cleared his throat. His smile stretched even wider, beginning to look unnatural.

His head tilted toward Altair before he spoke. "I'll say, we've been rather rude. I know who you are, and you probably don't know me." He paused, still smiling. "My name is Peter Boggs, as I'm sure you've gathered by now. And I am the CEO of Ultimate Energy, humanity's savior and only benefactor of power."

Boggs moved his head back into an upright position and clasped his hands behind his back. "And I've brought you here today as both a representative for humanity and as a representative for my company."

Altair's confusion seemed to show on his face because Boggs chuckled and opened his arms wide, a familiar show of openness, but it didn't feel as though he meant it.

"I will explain why I had you brought here, but first, I need to explain some background. If you wouldn't mind."

Altair slowly shook his head, and Boggs smiled in delight.

"Fantastic. Thank you for understanding, your Highness."

He snatched his tablet and began swiping, looking for something. Finally finding it, Boggs glanced back up, his finger hovering over the screen.

"As I'm sure you know, humanity has been at war with the race of monsters, known as Vesunians, for 150 years. Now, everyone knows that, so why am I telling you?"

Boggs raised an eyebrow and waited. Altair's eyes shifted from each face in the room and back to Boggs before he shrugged. Boggs's eyes glimmered before he spoke once again.

"Because the war is why you're here, my friend."

He nodded toward one of the bodyguards who extended a silver remote and pressed a button. A screen rolled down the far wall.

"Now, neither side has gotten anywhere during this time. Alliances and battles and subterfuge have gotten us nowhere. Do you want to know why?"

Boggs let his finger drop, and he swiped the screen of the tablet toward the one that finished whirring down the wall. The screen came to life, displaying a picture of a brilliant blue light that was encapsulated in a bottle. Altair's heart leapt at the sight.

"*Nuva!* Ding, ding!" Boggs's energy shot up in intensity as he took in Altair's look of recognition, and he grinned. "*Nuva* has kept us from winning this goddamn war. It's powerful and incredibly deadly, and the Vesunians have learned to weaponize it at this point."

Lilith shrunk even lower into her seat, a hand cupping her scarred cheek. Darkness flashed in her eyes, and all Altair wanted to do was reach for her hand. He looked back toward where Peter Boggs was still talking and attempted to focus on what the man was saying. He only caught the last part of the sentence.

"…looking pretty grim. And recently, a group of Vesunians was caught in an attempt to penetrate the Upper Circle in Trinity Market to assassinate both me and President Afton." Boggs grimaced at the thought. "And, truth be told, I don't like the idea of a group of monsters coming to kill me. Don't like the idea of being dead in general."

Altair's heart was beating faster, and his palms felt sweaty. He felt like he knew where this was going.

"They were also trying to stop the first shipment of Nuva ships, provided by our now-allies the Ursonians, into our markets," Boggs commented, eyes now shrouded in worry. "We had gotten the Ursonians to help us study and understand Nuva, but we realized that plan would take time, which is something we no longer have."

Boggs leaned forward over the conference table, his face grim, a stark contrast to his jolly demeanor from earlier.

"So, I went a little rogue. People are scared, your Highness. And although your father wants no part in this war, *you* can be a valuable asset." He paused, sincerity shining in his eyes. "Your *voice* can be a valuable asset to ending this war."

Altair's temper finally shot sky high, and he stood, signing furiously, not realizing that Boggs wouldn't understand. Boggs blinked in confusion and looked toward Lilith who sighed, sitting up. Her voice was firmer than before.

"He said that he will not massacre a bunch of innocents for your war. Plus, he wants to know what the plan even is. Throw him into a battlefield and have him yell and start stabbing?" She shrugged, feigning an air of indifference. "He has a point. He's not a killing machine. I've seen him in action. Plus, what if there are other deaf soldiers? Or someone is immune? They could just kill him on the spot, and the whole effort would be for nothing."

Altair shot her a look of appreciation, even though she had censored what he'd said. She responded with the smallest of smiles and nodded minutely.

Boggs sighed heavily, sitting in his seat as he considered Altair's words. "All good questions. Your Highness, I'm not asking you to massacre millions. The war can end in much simpler terms. You will have only two targets."

He clicked his remote again and the image of a beautiful, ethereal-looking tree appeared on the screen. Altair's breath caught in wonder.

"This is our best guess at how Reeva looks. Our informants say that the Vesunians worship her as if she was an actual entity. A living being," Boggs said, and Altair shuddered at the darkness that had entered his eyes. "According to our information, she is the source of the Vesunian's power, the source of their Nuva."

Boggs smiled vaguely at the shock on both of their faces and nodded.

"Yes, she'll be your first target. Take her out somehow, and there will be no Nuva left to use. I know your little curse most likely won't influence her, but I'm sure you'll figure something out."

Lilith sat forward, her hands splayed on the table. She seemed to have forgotten her fear in the excitement of new information.

"A *tree* gives them Nuva?! That would not have been my first guess."

Boggs nodded in acknowledgment. "Unlimited amounts of it too. Which is why the tree is so precious to them."

Altair slowly nodded, still not convinced. This already sounded impossible.

*How was he supposed to kill an immortal, sentient tree?*

Lilith shivered next to him. Her eyes were wide when she spoke once again. "Who's the second target?"

Boggs nodded and clicked the remote once more. An image of a Vesunian flashed onto the screen. He was young, with dark eyes and long, dark curls. In the picture, he was standing on Lilith's ship, his face set in determination. Next to him was a small, blonde, human man. Altair recoiled, recognition pulsing through him.

"Our informants just got wind of who this is last night." He pointed toward the young Vesunian. "He's been an anonymous prisoner and a fugitive for the last couple of months, but, thanks to our informants, we have finally identified him."

Peter Boggs gestured at the screen, his mouth set in a grim line.

"Say hello to your second target, Prince Varys of Vesun, heir to the Vesunian throne."

**To be continued...**
**End of Book One**

# About the Author

Emerson is a long-time writer but first-time published author. Their hobbies include reading, writing, and spending time with family. The spark for this debut novel came with a bang, and Emerson is excited to share that the sequel, *All the Secrets in the Stars*, is in development. Though "Emerson" is a persona for the author of this series, they feel as though they've developed an incredible bond with fans of both romance and science fiction alike.

Come along for this wonderful adventure and thank you for giving this first-time author a chance!

TikTok: @authoremerson
Instagram: @authoremerson1
Threads: authoremerson1threads.net

# Other Publications by Perceptions Press

## Now Available from Perceptions Press
*Publishing innovative, avant-garde (and occasionally provocative)*
*transgender fiction and non-fiction*
https://perceptionspress.ca/

**Earth-Kin (2023)**
**Pauli Kidd**
**Diversity is survival.**
In the centuries since the exodus from a dying earth, humanity has changed and grown. Survival meant treasuring the surviving strains of life. It demanded adaptation. Known space became a cosmos of neo-humans, of gene-modified intelligent animals, and immense diversity.

Centuries passed, and life slowly fought its way back from the brink of extinction...

At the outer edge of known space, the salvage vessel Mud Puppy discovers clues to a lost cache of ancient technology. Artefacts from the near-mythical "Unity" government: The regime that oversaw the migration from Earth and the birth of whole new species of intelligent life.

For a colourful crew of adventurers, the discovery leads to the quest of a lifetime. But to others, the lost technologies could change the balance of power in the Successor Kingdoms.

But the ancient cache could be much more. It could be the gateway to encountering true alien life. The first encounter between the creatures born of Earth, and beings from alien worlds. (https://perceptionspress.ca/earth-kin/)

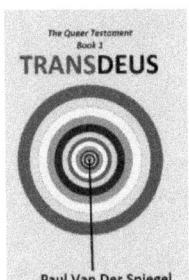

### Trans Deus (2020)
### Paul Van Der Spiegel
### The Queer Testament Book 1

In the beginning was the Verb,
the Verb was with God, the Verb was God.
In her was life,
that life was the light for all people.
The Verb was made trans woman.
and she lived amongst us, full of grace and truth.
Her light shone in the darkness,
and the consumer-military-technocracy
comprehended it not.
We cast our votes on TV remotes,
crucified her live on Channel Five. (https://perceptionspress.ca/trans-deus/)

### 7 Minutes (2021)
### Paul Van Der Spiegel
### The Queer Testament Book 2

At the point of death,
lost to all we've known,
adrift from those we've loved,
what stories do we tell
ourselves?

    *7 Minutes* is the story of a death—charting the progress from cardiac arrest, the brain's release of its massive reserve of endorphins, through the unravelling of personality, memory, and identity as the brain's consciousness-generating areas are hit by a tidal wave of opioid neuropeptides that are simultaneously being starved of oxygen.

    Self-told narratives unfold and are re-contextualised, fears awaken, desires awaken, time is warped and regresses as the mind is trapped inside a dead husk, unable to communicate, lost to those it has loved and been loved by.

    Those who have experienced so-called 'near death' experiences have described bright lights, meeting loved ones: but no-one has returned from behind that light to describe the process of dying. And so, we are left with either a gospel of redemption and condemnation, or its opposite, a gospel of cosmic resignation and the final extinction of personality. One day, perhaps not too far away, we shall know—or, then again, perhaps not.

    *7 Minutes* is the collage of stories and half-truths that our protagonists' collapsing neural networks narrate as the brain asphyxiates—light and dark, fact and fiction, actuality and narrative—until the final arrival at the truth of an earthly existence. *7 Minutes* is a head fuck. But after you've read it, I hope you can celebrate being alive. (https://perceptionspress.ca/7-minutes/)

## Parably Not (2021)
## The Queer Testament Book 3
## Paul Van Der Spiegel

*Parably Not* is Book 3 of the *Will2Love Series*.

William Blake wrote in the preface to *Jerusalem The Emanation of the Giant Albion* of his desire to "speak to future generations by a Sublime Allegory." One could also argue that the miracles and the parables of Christ are metaphors, and one of the errors of the religion that bears their name is trampling sublime allegory beneath the heel of process and doctrine.

If *Trans Deus* is Mark, if *7 Minutes* is Matthew, then *Parably Not* is Lucy with the dynamic of "Q Source" thrown in for good measure. "Q" is not a ridiculous conspiracy theory cooked up to delude and obfuscate a population. "Q" is the theory proposed by biblical scholars to account for the shared content in Matthew and Luke, the oral "sayings of Jesus" tradition that is absent in Mark's account. We can only speculate on who Quelle was, but it wouldn't surprise me if they were a woman, or a group of women—a female gospel airbrushed from history by the patriarchy that followed. As someone who passionately believes in inclusion and diversity, it was not too much of a leap to make my Q Source a queer source.

Having written two "text only" books, I wanted to emulate the Prophet of Hercules Road and illuminate these recontextualised parables, continuing the process I had pioneered as a child, cutting up my mum's copies of *Woman's Own* and pasting the chosen pages into my scrapbook.

"We were worried about you for a while," my dad told me as a teenager, as he recollected my enthusiasm for *Woman's Weekly*, sparkly tights, and walking about in my mum's heels, carrying her handbag. I said nothing.

"Poetry fetter'd, fetters the human race," Blake wrote. He's right. But there are plenty of other things that fetter the human race, too.

Our job as sub-creators is to unfetter, to explore, to challenge, to remake. I offer you *Parably Not*, as it is intended: scrapbook literature, unfinished, scruffy, feral, confused, uncertain; ready to be woven into new allegory.
(https://perceptionspress.ca/parably-not/)

## A Particular Friendship (2021)
## The Queer Testament, Book 4
## Paul Van Der Spiegel

Tom Morton is a Roman Catholic priest who is devoted to his church in northern England, to his parishioners, and to his calling. When the man he fell in love with twenty-five years ago comes back into his life, Tom finds himself on a collision course with a powerful bishop, a man determined to pin the blame for the Church's sexual abuse crisis on its closeted gay clergy.
(https://perceptionspress.ca/a-particular-friendship/)

### Demon of Want (2020)
### Freja Ki Gray

Izumi Yamakawa, a directionless twenty-something, is a part-time employee of the Oh Joy Toy Store. When she witnesses her manager die in a horrific merchandising accident, she discovers that he was a member of a Japanese demon hunting organization and had been eyeing her for recruitment due to her family lineage. Now Izumi, along with her trans girlfriend Maria, and a boisterous sword-for-hire, Rhea, get caught up investigating the various monsters and demons running the Oh Joy Toy company. Demon of Want is an eclectic blend of tongue in cheek urban fantasy, over the top violence, and gratuitous sex. (https://perceptionspress.ca/demon-of-want/)

### Can't Her Bury Tales: A Transfeminine Coloring Book (2020)
### Iona Isabella Rivera

Hail weary traveler! Come closer! I don't bite…hard. You lookit poorly, come take a sit by the fire. Rest and grab yourself some stew I got cookin. Tell me, what brings ya my way? Adventure? Hearsay? Curiosity or plain ol' boredom? Well, no matter whence you came, I surely have a story that will peak your delight.

Perhaps a tale of a terrible tragedy? Or a catty, Communist comedy? How about some lore on fallin in love? Or a heroic tale of harrowing a horrible governorship? Or be you one that pines over Power? Maybe a familiar fable of family? Oh! Pardon my rambling. Come tell me your tale, traveler. What colors will you paint with me? Tell, was your way hard, rocky, and steep? Show me. Perchance our stories crossed at some point. After all, we have more in common than our differences tell. (https://perceptionspress.ca/cant-her-bury-tales/)

## Coming in 2023/24 from Perceptions Press
*Publishing innovative, avant-garde (and occasionally provocative) transgender fiction and non-fiction*
https://perceptionspress.ca/

### PUBLICATION EXPECTED IN 2023
### Effectuators! Book 1: Horrors of the Night
### Pauli Kidd
**Rip roaring Victorian paranormal adventures, in the Year of Our Lord 1869!**

Brilliana Stetham is the sort of woman who could certainly cut cards with the Devil, after cucumber sandwiches, of course!

No matter how haunted your house, no matter how grey the Grey Lady, or black the dreaded Black Hound, your dangers can be eliminated, your fears assuaged. For there is an "expert" who lends her psychic powers and mystic skills to those in need—for a price!

But Brilliana is a delicious charlatan. She dresses the part of the elegant mystic and woman of dark learning. She accepts commissions to "sense presences" in houses of the wealthy, whereupon she undertakes research, presents her findings about local calamities, and performs appropriate ceremonies to placate the ghosts and ensure the safety of the residents of the house. It is all done with great thoroughness, in deadly seriousness... and it is all a magnificent scam.

She is managing it all perfectly well until, one day, a haunting she is investigating turns out to be real. Contractually obligated to rid her client's building of monsters, Brilliana is trapped into battling powers she cannot fully understand. An entirely new science must be developed to vanquish the unknown. With science in her heart and a top hat set squarely on her head, Brill storms forward to become a ghost hunter. It is the start of a radical new life as an intrepid combatant of all things supernatural, an adversary of monsters and remover of curses. And thus, Brilliana Stetham becomes a Paranormal Effectuator. (https://perceptionspress.ca/effectuators-book-1/)

## PUBLICATION EXPECTED IN 2023
## Effectuators! Book 2: Green and Pleasant Land
## Pauli Kidd

The further adventures of Brilliana Stetham, Paranormal Effectuator, in the wondrous wilds of London in 1869.

Sterling stuff! Delightfully fun, deliciously ormolou. Plots thicken and the weirdness flows. Brill and her companions roam from Limehouse to frozen Highland Lochs in pursuit of monsters, adventure, and a really decent cup of tea. (https://perceptionspress.ca/effectuators-book-2/)

## PUBLICATION EXPECTED IN 2023
## Effectuators! Book 3: To Foreign Shores
## Pauli Kidd
*Excelsior!*

Dark clouds thicken over London. As ancient horrors and evil cults unite, Lord Bimmington finally moves to contact otherworldly powers, laying the foundations for future devilry.

Meanwhile, Brilliana Stetham and the intrepid Effectuators must set forth to Prussia, hot on the trail of the sinister cults that have infiltrated Britain. But as Europe erupts into war, the tasks of monster hunting and assorted derring do become a tad complex...

More rip-roaring tales of Victorian horrors, and the terribly well-dressed adventurers who knock them for six! (https://perceptionspress.ca/effectuators-book-3/)

**PUBLICATIONS EXPECTED IN 2024**
**Effectuators! Book 3: To Foreign Shores**
**Pauli Kidd**
*1870 Britannia besieged!*
As war ravages the continent, Britain herself comes under a darker threat. The sinister Lord Bimmington moves at last, using anarchy and terror to destabilise the nation. Acting in concert with the Severed Lord, he aims to overthrow the British government and establish a horrifying new regime.

Armed with a few buckets of ectoplasm, a very strange dog and an excellent dress sense, the Effectuators must face down the ultimate evil and save Queen, country and humanity itself from disaster.

It's time to face evil in the ultimate showdown and knock the blighters for six! (https://perceptionspress.ca/effectuators-book-4/)

**PUBLICATION EXPECTED IN 2024**
**Effectuators! Book 3: To Foreign Shores**
**Pauli Kidd**
**1872 In Britain, London has recovered from the failed coup attempt by Lord Bimmington.**
Possessed by the otherworld entity known as the "Severed Lord," Bimmington has fled to the continent. But even though the Severed Lord controls hellish powers, he is only a tool. The mastermind of evil is none other than Brilliana's father, Claudius Stetham.

The hidden pieces of the Severed Lord contain powers that can obliterate entire civilisations. If the creature restores itself, then it will bring a reign of darkness to destroy the earth.

The lost pieces of the Severed Lord must be found, and they must be destroyed. Brilliana and her companions find themselves in a race against time: a race that will decide the fate of worlds. (https://perceptionspress.ca/effectuators-book-5/)

**PUBLICATION EXPECTED IN 2023**
**The Right Time, The Right Place: New York Diaries**
**Ronald Heydon**
Suddenly it hits me. I return to my "previous life," and everything is fine. Then, I go back to my "current" life in the metropolis—and it's all struggle and trauma. I still have few friends, very few people to talk to. I spent my time reading—and making comments in my journal on what I am reading. It was through these comments that I finally understood.

I am living in NYC. I have not just to accept this, but I have to explore it. It's one thing to adapt to a new job, a new world of high-tech design, etc. But I also have to adapt to a private life *in* NYC. In fact, I am—I don't want to say "creating" but rather "inventing"—a new persona, a new identity. And this is the real struggle I am going through.

I'd been doing this very thing for months in fact. I only "realize" it, though, each time I get on a plane in Montreal and fly back to NYC. "Ok," I say to myself, "time to put on the NYC persona."

Everything becomes more clear all of a sudden. Sure, the "old life" looks more inviting. But *I am living a new life in NYC!!!* And I have to accept this. So, I struggle to adapt to the new job, and now, I must adapt to New York City itself.
(https://perceptionspress.ca/the-right-time-the-right-place/)

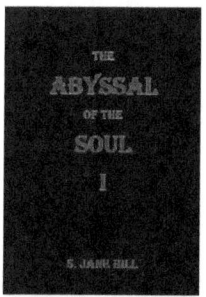

**PUBLICATION EXPECTED IN 2023**
**The Abyssal of the Soul I**
**S. Jane Hill**
A Sci-Fi book Like no other.
Are you brave enough to look into the abyss?
(https://perceptionspress.ca/abyssal-of-the-soul/)

**PUBLICATION EXPECTED IN 2023**
**The abyssal of the Soul II**
**S. Jane Hill**
A Sci-Fi book Like no other.
The saga continues.
(https://perceptionspress.ca/abyssal-of-the-soul-ii/)

**PUBLICATION EXPECTED IN 2023**
**Watching the Fire Catch**
**Carolyn Bell**
Aurelia Kempe and her much younger employee, Jory Schneider, forge an unlikely friendship when Jory arrives on a small island off the coast of British Columbia, Canada. Surrounded and comforted by the beauty of their natural world, neither unaware of nor complacent toward the existing threat to their environment by uninformed and sometimes malevolent forces, we join Aurelia, Jory, and their circle of friends and neighbours as they live each day to the fullest.
(https://perceptionspress.ca/watching-the-fire-catch/)

## Publications from other divisions of Perceptions Press:

Castle Carrington Publishing www.castlecarringtonpublishing.ca
Stephanie Castle Publications www.stephaniecastle.ca
TransGender Publishing www.transgenderpublishing.ca
All Genders Press www.allgenderspress.ca